THE
MOONLIGHT
BLADE

THE
MOONLIGHT
BLADE

TESSA BARBOSA

Entangled Publishing, LLC
644 Shrewsbury Commons Ave., STE 181
Shrewsbury, PA 17361
rights@entangledpublishing.com

Entangled Teen is an imprint of Entangled Publishing, LLC.

Visit our website at www.entangledpublishing.com.

Edited by Alexander Te Pohe and Molly Majumder
Cover design by Bree Archer
Cover images bysharpner/Shutterstock,
roverto007/Depositphotos
Interior design by Toni Kerr

ISBN 978-1-64937-336-6
Ebook ISBN 978-1-64937-337-3

Manufactured in the United States of America

First Edition March 2023

10 9 8 7 6 5 4 3 2 1

entangled teen
an imprint of Entangled Publishing LLC

At Entangled, we want our readers to be well-informed. If you would like to know if this book contains any elements that might be of concern for you, please check the back of the book for details.

For Selene and Evander.

✳ ☽ ✳ ☾ ✳

PROLOGUE

The day our mother left us, we fought. The sky was a dark boiling gray that flooded the roads with rain. Manay Halna and my sister, Kuran, were holed up in an inn to wait out the weather, but I raced after my mother, kicking up mud that splashed up to my knees. The storm drenched me to the bone, but I didn't care.

"Go back, Narra," Inay commanded from atop a borrowed pony. "I'll return from Bato-Ko in a week. I'm only settling some matters with the bank."

"I just want to have a look, Inay," I called as I wiped rain from my eyes. "I'll keep my winter coat on and my scarf wrapped tight so that no one can see my skin. Please! Who will pay attention? Do you truly hate your mother so much that you won't even let us see the place we were born?" I was prepared to walk all the way to the city of Bato-Ko with nothing but the clothes I wore.

"Enough!" she snapped. "Maybe I've been a terrible mother, because I've never stopped you from forming your own opinions or talking back to me. That is my fault, but I am still your mother, and you will listen to me now. Everything I have done is so that you could have a better life than you would in the city. Don't throw it away."

I still feel the sting of her words and the mud in my toes.

"Swear to me that you and your sister will never go back to

Bato-Ko," she demanded. "Promise me!"

She stared at me until I could no longer hold her gaze.

"Fine!" I shouted as she trotted away. "But only if you come back soon."

"I promise," Inay yelled without looking back. Even then, her promise felt as brittle as a thin shard of ice.

It's been eight months since we saw her last, and one since we received word that she was arrested.

I didn't speak for days because anger curdled my tongue. My sister forbade me from going after her. I'd only make a bigger mess of things, she said.

But here we are now, because even Manay Halna could not resist the chance to visit Bato-Ko during the Sundo, when, once a decade, people from all over our country gather to select a new ruler.

I stare down at the city from the ridge where our caravan is camped. This is not the home we Tigangi invoke when the weather turns to ice and we curse the rocky bit of land we made a country. Not the home thick with rustling palm fronds that we glimpse in dreams of past lives. This is Tigang's capital city, Bato-Ko, the place that I was born.

This green gem tucked between a rocky plateau, the wild-dark ocean, and a ridge of snowcapped mountains seems an impossible thing. It is beautiful like the sharp edge of a well-balanced blade, and I wonder if it might cut me apart.

*) * (*

CHAPTER ONE

In a little over two weeks, the country of Tigang will crown its new ruler. This means in three days' time, people will start dying.

Young people not much older than I am already mass outside the gates of the glass fortress. I pass these bright-eyed, confident soon-to-be bodies. I dare not linger, because I am here for a different reason. They are simply in my way.

I stick my hands in my pockets and make myself small. I beg pardon and squeeze past jostling elbows, careful not to touch anyone with my bare skin. There are more volunteers than I expected. To enter the competition might once have been an honor, but my mother always scoffed at the idea.

"Leave it to the desperate and the foolish," she often said. "You are neither of those things."

But the last time I saw my mother, I promised her I would never come to Bato-Ko, and yet here I am.

The months since my mother disappeared melt into a lifetime of dusty roads and secrets.

I'm afraid I will forget my mother completely. It's already getting harder to recall her face. I see nothing of her in my features but my dark brown eyes. My black hair is long and straight, while hers is a short wavy bob that she keeps away from her face with colorful cloth wraps. She is tall, like Kuran, and her skin is a darker shade of brown than mine. But while my sister has something to say to everyone, my mother and I would often sit together for hours in silence.

I don't need silence now. Our aunt, Manay Halna, tells me nothing about my mother because she doesn't care about me, but Kuran tells me nothing because she cares too much.

I need answers as much as I need my mother.

A massive fortress looms above the westernmost tip of the city. It was carved out of a natural stone hill, but you can't tell by looking at it. Rippling glass walls built into the stone remind me of a frozen waterfall, and it gleams too brightly in the sunlight to stare at for long. Pretty would be the wrong word for it. It is blunt. It is unrefined power. No matter where I go in the city, the weight of its presence feels like it's following me, and my skin crawls the closer I get to it.

But the archives are an addition built against one side of the fortress. The two buildings share one wall, but unlike the heavy stone and rippling glass of the fortress proper, it is a dome-shaped building fronted by large, clear glass panes that stretch from the ground to its rounded ceiling. It's almost delicate. A thick green turf grows over the vast expanse of its roof, held up by a forest of wooden poles carved into the shape of branching trees.

I cross my arms and try not to appear impressed. Our family has crossed the continent twice, and I have never seen anything like this before. Through the glass, I spy more books than any one person could read in dozens of lifetimes. Archivists scramble to and fro, carrying books down the narrow corridors like ants busy at their work.

Breathe, Narra. I stop myself from fidgeting and steel my resolve. If I were any other person, I might have spent all day wandering those narrow aisles lined with towering shelves. But I am not. I shouldn't even be here.

I walk through the towering glass doors, thrown open so that anyone may enter. Knowledge is meant to be shared, decreed the first Astar, a Diwata who became human and founded this country. Ever since, a supposed reincarnation of the Astar has lived in the glass fortress and occupied a ceremonial position in the government—an advisor to our Rajas and Reynas. Though there are unflattering stories about the first Astar, I can't imagine anyone who built this library could be all bad. I only wish I had time to explore it.

I pace down long aisles of books and take a furtive glance around. All the shelves are arranged in neat rows and alphabetical order. Not a book looks out of place. And while the towering shelves are tightly packed, the sunlight that filters through the glass walls makes it feel less crowded. Up above, the ceiling is decorated with gilded constellations.

"Move!"

I flatten myself against a wall as an Archivist wheels a cart past me with a scowl. Archivists occupy one branch of our government. Their sect specializes in recording history, running our schools, and accounting our tithes. But they are still holy Baylan, trained in magic far beyond anything I could purchase in a market stall.

Manay Halna calls Archivists "Glorified pencil pushers!" behind their backs, but she's all smiles and bows in person, because one simple spell could reveal she hasn't paid her taxes in years.

I scurry along and look for a friendlier face.

My mother always warned me that the Baylan are not to be trusted, but I'm out of options now. I gather up my resolve to speak to someone and circle back toward a skinny old man seated at a wooden desk. He wears a gaudy-looking tapis skirt in orange and yellow over blue silk trousers, and an embroidered bato jacket trimmed with gold. It looks as though he picked his clothes for no other reason than because they were expensive, because everything clashes. But his skin is as dark brown as my own, and he sits dwarfed by the books stacked atop his workspace. Red streaks edge his eyes, and beads of sweat cling to his receding hairline.

I've encountered Archivists from time to time, recording taxes in city centers and delivering books to libraries, but I have never spoken to one. This Archivist looks too unwell to be dangerous, but a Baylan's word is law, and I must not misspeak.

I roll back my shoulders, tighten the knot of the malong on my waist, and stand tall.

"Yes?" he asks. His fingers twitch as he holds them out. He waits for me to press his hand to my forehead and ask for his blessing, but I keep my hands clasped close to my threadbare tunic, too aware that this is an insult to an elder. It can't be helped, but the guilt gnaws at me.

He drops his hand, and his eyes narrow at my rudeness.

"Do you have a list of everyone arrested this year and where they are being kept?" I bow my head to hide the redness of my cheeks.

"For whom are you looking, child?" he says and stares intently at my face as if trying to place me. "Only those who have committed the most heinous crimes and are awaiting trial in the fortress are listed here."

"Shora Jal." I bristle. I'm *not* a child.

"It sounds familiar…" His eyes widen a moment at my mother's name. He points down an aisle of books. "Five rows down, then three rows left." He jumps to his feet and wanders off into the endless stacks, muttering as if he's lost his train of thought. I hurry off and find a chalkboard built into the rear wall of the archives. Endless curving script decorates its surface, broken only where names have been erased. If my mother is not listed here, I will go to every library in Bato-Ko to find out where she is being held.

The chalkboard is too dark to read by natural light, so I draw a simple orasyon for illumination in the chalk dust with the moist tip of my finger. As I blow upon the spell, my mother's name illuminates. It confirms that she is still alive. She's so close! Just beyond the wall that separates the archives from the fortress. But my stomach drops, because it means something has gone terribly wrong. All I know is that she's been arrested, but not why.

I walk back past the sickly Archivist's empty desk and jump as he suddenly appears in front of me. He thrusts a fat book toward me. A curious expression lights his eyes, and my skin crawls at his scrutiny. This close, I can see a red rash peeking out from beneath his tunic. I take a small step backward.

"What must I do to ensure her release? May I advocate on her behalf? How can I find out what she was arrested for?" I sputter.

"So many questions, child." He slaps the great tome onto the desk and tears fragile pages as he thumbs carelessly through it. "First, tell Manong Alen who your grandmother is."

It's one of the genealogies. I am tempted to peek in it, because my mother never speaks about her family, but I worry he will take too much of my time and Kuran will be suspicious of my absence. My sister warned me against meddling in our mother's affairs, but I can't sit back and do nothing. Not now.

I've sworn to the Heavens that I will fix this, because even if my mother would never accuse me of it, I know that her arrest is my fault.

"Yirin Jal," I say, because I cannot lie to him. He could compel the truth from me with a spell if he wished. He slams the book shut before I can read it and tucks it under an arm.

"I knew it! Which of Shora's daughters are you?" He leans so close that I smell his rancid breath. It's sweet, as if he's rotting from the inside out. I glance left and right for an escape, but before I can stop him, he grabs my arm and yanks me toward him.

His eyes widen, and he springs away from me as if I am on fire. My silk scarf has come undone. He's glimpsed the birthmarks upon my neck: flat black splotches that mark me as a cursed girl.

The whole world seems to pause, and all I feel is my heart hammering in my chest. The Archivist doesn't need to say a word, but I know exactly what he is thinking. Cursed. Dirty. Unlucky girl. And there's no one here to save me.

I run away and wrap the scarf around my neck as I go, scattering people left and right, not stopping to apologize as I careen through the streets.

I'm numb and sweaty by the time I reach the port where Kuran should be waiting, but my heart skips when I turn around. A gaunt shape darts behind a street stall.

I am being followed.

✴ ☽ ✴ ☾ ✴

CHAPTER TWO

The smoke and noise of the market hits me like a wall. A mass of bodies swarms around covered stalls, and I dive into it. I weave between the packed lanes in a frantic nonsense pattern, hoping to lose the Archivist in the swell. I scan every direction for my sister and ignore the grumblings of my stomach.

These all feel like fool's tasks. The air is fragrant with food sizzling in street stalls: sweet meat grilled on sticks, fresh fish served with wedges of precious lemons from the south, and imported bananas fried with liberal sprinklings of sugar. I dodge past merchants unloading their wares. I duck under outstretched arms as shoppers haggle over the price of rice. I dance out of the way as children weave past, chasing after rattan balls. I want to run, but instead, I wait until the way is clear, even though the Archivist might catch up to me, and squeeze through every small opening, afraid to touch anyone and spread my curse.

I don't know how I'll find my sister in this crowd, but I need to get to her. I don't know what else to do. I burst into a small break in the crowd and run straight into a gaggle of street preachers. Each one wears a small golden sun disk that marks them as a cultist. I step back on instinct as they reach out to thrust pamphlets in my face.

"Omu is coming! Bow to Her great vision, and she shall bless you! Refuse and burn!"

Once, when I was young and not so wary, I was torn from my family and caned when a cultist spied my marks. They called me a plague as they kicked me and pulled at my hair. My mother saved me from Omu's worshipers then, but there's no one to save me now. I don't know what they do to cursed girls in Bato-Ko, and I don't plan on finding out. If there's anyone I fear more than the Baylan, it is the cultists—they respect no law but Omu's strict dictations.

They believe that Omu should be made first above all the Diwata, but the Diwata are not gods. They are forces of nature and of places. They are spirits that cannot be controlled or relied upon, either meant to be appeased or avoided. We may bargain with them in exchange for small magics, but we do not worship them. To grant one too much power might threaten the alignment of the cosmos.

The cultists say that Omu will descend from the heavens, but I pray it never comes true. Her aspect is control, perfection, and command. I am neither patient, perfect, nor obedient—if I was, I wouldn't be in here right now.

I dodge their arms and quickly choose another avenue. I finally stop to catch my breath and peer over my shoulder for the thirtieth time. I do not glimpse Manong Alen behind me, but the trees that line the streets have branches twisted into wards of power. They seem to whisper as I pass. Pebbles twist into spirals when I scatter them with my sandals, as if aligning with a magnet buried deep underground. The stories say that even the rocks and the trees in Bato-Ko speak, and when they do, the Baylan listen. So, I keep my face tilted toward my dusty brown toes and worn-out slippers and hope that there is no truth to those tales.

"Clear the way! The Ivy Reyna comes!" Black-clad Guardians bark commands, and I'm pushed aside as the crowd contracts.

I hunch my shoulders to make myself small, but elbows ram into my sides and people yell insults when I try to squeeze past them. I find myself cornered between a wooden fence and a garbage bin that reeks of piss and garlic peanuts gone rancid.

I hold my nose and look for an opening, but people press tight to the buildings that line the narrow road, blocking any escape. Twelve children cast chrysanthemums into the road behind the Guardians, dawdling here and there, so that the procession moves at a crawl. I grit my teeth. I do not see any familiar faces around me. Instead, I glimpse a flash of white and silver through the gap between jostling shoulders.

Silence descends upon the crowd. I forget my stalker and stare.

Our Reyna sits upon a lacquered palanquin carried by four women in white. Her snow-white hair drips with so many jeweled pins and beads that her head dips low from the weight. She wears a gold silk tunic tucked into a wrapped gold silk skirt, all fringed with gold embroidery so delicate it looks like lace. She could not be past her mid-thirties after a decade of service to our country, but her cheeks sag as if there is no muscle left between skull and skin.

Our eyes meet, and I feel the weight of them like a boulder upon my shoulders. Her gaze lingers so long that a Guardian turns from her task to look my way. I hunch into the piss-stained wall, but I glimpse a wry smile upon the Reyna's lips as she looks away.

"What happened to her?" A sticky child gorging on a skewer of sweet pork stares at her, too.

"What happens if you use too much magic," someone replies. "It's why we must choose another."

Two centuries ago, the Ash Raja destroyed an entire conquering army sent to subdue Tigang, but he died doing so. No other country has dared invade Tigang since. I don't know what I would do if I were faced with the same choice. I wonder what hard choices this Reyna made and if they were worth it. Somehow the sight of her only makes me sad.

I shudder as the procession snakes toward the port and the crowd turns to follow her. I'm swept along toward a large ship—painted white, the color of death—even though I struggle against the press of people.

As our Reyna steps down from her throne, someone nearby shouts a blessing. A hail of blessings thunders through the crowd as the feeling catches like a spark.

Then, from everywhere and nowhere, Baylan from all seven sects appear. They slip through the crowd like water through splayed fingers as they follow the procession.

They are here for our Reyna and not for me, but each one can wield magic like a knife. I freeze, a mouse surrounded by cats.

Their skin is patterned with painted orasyon that peek out from beneath colorful clothing. They move as if they do not feel the cold air from the spiny mountains to the north, which sends my skin shuddering even at the end of June. Foreigners call them sorcerers or clerics, but neither word is quite accurate. The Baylan meddle in every part of our lives, and their seven holy sects make up our government: Archivists, Guardians, Makers, Cultivators, Seekers, Interpreters, and Healers.

I have never seen so many in my life. Larger towns might have one or two, but I count nearly a thousand on this street alone. The air fills with the smell of the magic they command: of musk, flowers, sweat, and iron.

The Baylan coalesce around our Reyna. Each one bears a candle lit with a flame that does not waver in the breeze. They snuff out their lights as the Reyna boards her ship in silence for the symbolic funeral, as a sendoff to the next part of her life.

I shudder. How sad that even should you rise so far, only

pain awaits.

The white ship drifts out until it slowly fades into a dot upon the horizon. Our people once crossed this sea as they fled our homeland, Arawan. The crowd loosens its grip and disperses.

Some say the Sundo, the competition we use to select a new ruler every ten years, is cruel. I have always defended our customs as necessary, but now I wonder if they are right.

I slip into a side street to regain my bearings. Tall fences surround family compounds. I can't see anyone in the darkened windows, but my skin prickles as if I'm being watched.

The tree-lined street is quiet. The sound of hawkers pushing food and excited conversation still echoes around me, but there is a softer sound beneath it all, almost like music.

At first, I wonder if the trees are speaking, but the Archivist staggers around a corner.

Alen grasps a paper in one hand and reveals an orasyon. The magical spell is so fresh that the blood he used to paint the symbols drips down the page. My jaws clamp together so suddenly that my teeth crack as magic takes hold. I try to twist and turn, but my feet are glued in place.

The balding old man walks toward me in a zigzag drunken kind of dance, mouth moving in conversation as if he's speaking with someone or something that I cannot see. I struggle to tear myself away, but he grasps the collar of my tunic with his two hands, and though his words are no dialect of Tigangi I have ever heard, I understand him perfectly.

"Impostor," he hisses into my ear in that strange language, as if I am a coconspirator in a terrible crime.

"Please, I don't understand what you're saying." The lie scrapes out of my mouth like a whisper. I flinch back and search for anyone who might help me, but the gates of nearby houses stay closed.

His teeth gleam bright white between peeled-back lips. "I know Shora's secret. I know what she did!"

I snap to attention. "What?"

He dances away from me, laughing, and I reach out to grab him. My fingers meet his clammy flesh, but I draw back when I realize my error.

With such a simple gesture, I might have cursed him, but he doesn't seem to care. He jumps up and down, teeth chittering together like an excited insect.

He stops abruptly and shoves me behind a hedge. I tumble to the ground, still bound by his spell, but before I can utter a single word, a woman's voice fills the space as clearly as a ringing bell. "My little spiders have been looking all over the city for you, Manong Alen."

I peer between the leaves, frozen in place with fear. The air cools by several degrees, and the Archivist shudders like a shaken doll as a tall, young Tigangi woman comes into view. She wears a golden comb emblazoned with the sun tucked into her thick hair like a crown. She clasps her hands in front of a silken sky-blue tunic, and she wears a matching woven wrap skirt embroidered all over with delicate silver thread. It's clothing fit for a Reyna. She wears no paint to mark her as a Baylan, but the air is thick with the smell of her magic.

Magic smells of life, and hers reminds me of peonies grown past their prime: sweet and rotting. I barely stop myself from retching. She stares at the cowering Archivist in front of me and cocks her head like a crow testing whether a scrap on the dirt is edible.

The woman grabs his wrist and clicks her tongue. She slides a fine-boned finger over the bumps of his rash.

"I've heard you've been meddling in politics, Manong."

"Omu curse you, Arisa." He spits, and Arisa digs her thumb into his wrist. He wails so loudly it does not sound human. I cannot look away.

"I rather doubt that." She laughs, and a warm puff of breath escapes my lips in a small cloud. Her magic surrounds us both, and it's as if I've been plunged into a freezing river still crusted with ice. Alen's lips turn blue.

Tremors rack my body unbidden, and I cannot turn away even when Alen's magic releases its grip. Arisa is all that I see. There are marks upon the woman's neck, hot and red, as if a burning hand once picked her up by the throat. Her marks look violent. New. And so much like mine.

Who is this woman? Whoever she is, she has power beyond anything I have seen before.

"Sleep now, Manong," Arisa says in a soft tone. "What I have made, I unmake." The words ring in my ears like an echo from a past life, and they jostle something in me awake. Something turns over in the hollow of my chest, reminding me of its presence. The sensation frightens me more than the Archivist or the strange woman.

Alen drops into a crumpled heap, as if no more than an empty meat puppet, and I bow low to hide my terror. My body aches as if cold, prying fingers have dug into my flesh and squeezed.

I choke on my tongue, but Arisa does not glance in my direction.

When she walks away, a Guardian melts out of the shadows and fills the space with a different kind of danger: all lean muscles and sharp blades.

Without a word, he hefts Alen's unconscious body over his shoulder. I do not see his face, only the back of his head and unruly black curls spilling from a short tail held back with a scrap of cloth. But Alen's eyes remain open and loll toward me, unseeing. Accusing.

My mother's secret fills the silence, and I crouch there trembling. Alen knew the truth just by looking at me. Why am I the only one who does not know what she's been hiding all these years? Why am I the only one looking for answers and trying to save her?

The Guardian stops and turns back toward the bush. I go deathly still as the whole world seems to pause. In one eye, I see him standing there on the street before me: a tall black flame against the street. In the other eye, I see him pressed close enough to kiss. Somehow, I know how the stubble of his chin feels in my hands: a rough contrast to the softness of his cheeks. Somehow, I know that he has a dimple behind each shoulder. Somehow, I know the soft press of his lips against my skin.

My heart aches as if there is a monster inside, and it is starving.

"You," he says.

CHAPTER THREE

I bolt from my hiding spot without a backward glance and hurtle toward the most raucous street I can find. The Guardian's haunted expression keeps replaying in my mind. It feels as though I know him, but surely, I'd remember those high cheekbones, those wide lips, and those unusually dark eyes— almost black, as though they swallowed the light. It feels as though he imprinted himself upon my soul with a spell. I don't even know if that's possible, but this *is* Bato-Ko. Anything is possible. Whatever this means, I am not ready to face it.

"Watch out, you clumsy fool!"

I topple a pyramid of apples laid out on a blanket and squash a tray of strawberries as I spin, dizzied by the lingering effects of Alen's magic.

"Sorry, I…" I toss my last coins at the fruit merchant and grimace back the threatening tears. I slow to a walk, though my every muscle screams for speed. There's no other way through the crowd.

I spot my sister an eternity later, and a little nervous tension finally leaves my body. Kuran and Tanu huddle together on a small patch of grass, busy catching up after a month apart. Her smile for the traveling musician is so bright that it hurts. I'm relieved to see him, too.

"Did you know that the Baylan were once only women and

asog? That changed when we founded Tigang. Now, anyone can become one if they pass initiation," Tanu says.

"Mmm, how romantic." Kuran sighs and leans in close to distract him with a kiss. I know she'd rather talk about anything else at all, but Tanu is a repository of odd facts that spill out when he's nervous. He pulls away from her when he sees my frantic expression.

"There you are, Ate Kuran! Kuya Tanu!" I clasp my hands together and smile so widely that my cheeks hurt. "I've been looking everywhere for you!"

My sister clears her throat, and I glare at her. "What's going on, Narra?"

Two solid-looking Guardians pick their way around the edge of the crowd, questioning merchants.

"Inay is going to be upset if we're late for dinner!" I squeak. Inay is what we call our mother, and Kuran catches on immediately. She hops to her feet because she knows I'm up to no good.

"You better explain yourself when we get back to camp," Kuran growls, but she manages to smile convincingly as she drags me down the street by my sleeve. The bells on her favorite anklets chime happily. Tanu presses a sweet bun into my hand in greeting before slipping casually behind us to block me from view. When I'm wedged between the two of them, no one even bothers to glance my way.

The bun feels like an apology, though I'm the one spoiling their fun. Kuran's mouth is already covered in crumbs, and I catch her licking her fingers even as we hurry.

My sister is all soft curves where I am angles and flat planes. Even her hair waves, while mine remains so straight that no hot implement can tease curls out of it. But our dark brown eyes are the same. They never miss much. She keeps at least three bodies between us and every Guardian in the street. When they get too close, she stops to admire baubles we can't afford and smiles all the while.

Tanu is attractive by most standards. His foreign Brelish-blue eyes are immediately striking against his dark Tigangi skin, but he doesn't smile often, and he talks even less, because he is more interested in books than people. I don't know how he communicates with Kuran, unless swapping spit counts.

They are as different as earth and air, but Kuran still loves him, the way she loves me: with everything.

Tanu checks behind us as we reach the edge of the city. "They're gone."

"Okay, spill." Kuran's tone is so much like my mother's that I flinch.

"Inay is awaiting trial in the fortress. It has to be a mistake, and I want to speak on her behalf. Kuya Tanu, do you know of any way to get her back?" Kuran's silence is dangerous, but I continue. "Bribery?"

"Of course not." He shakes his head.

Not that it would matter. Between the two of us and our carts full of fabric, we would have trouble replacing a broken wheel. How could we afford to bribe the jeweled Baylan?

"The trials are conducted in private," Tanu says. He doesn't sound worried, but he rarely shows what he feels. "The council of first families will decide her fate. Sometimes it takes years for a trial because the sentences are only passed once a year."

My heart refuses to slow down. My world feels like it's spinning too fast, and I don't know where I'll land.

Kuran sighs. "Just drop it, Narra. Inay chose to leave us. She knew this might happen, and she told us not to interfere in her affairs. I promised her that I would look out for you, and you go sneaking off—"

"You knew this might happen to her this whole time?" I sputter. A seed of anger blooms hot in my belly, and I grab onto it. "And you still let her go?!"

Kuran doesn't reply, but I know her well enough to read the answer on her face. She was trying to protect me again, even though I didn't ask for it. I swallow down the growing heat of my temper. It still feels like a betrayal. She should have told me. She should have stopped our mother.

"Leave it, Narra," she says quietly. "Please. Don't be so selfish."

Selfish? I'm the one always busy managing our inventory, our money, and planning how to feed us with scraps. As if things aren't bleeding hard without our mother. As if she doesn't also miss her.

Kuran tries to fill in for our mother, but she is full of ideas, not practicalities, and she's only a little older than I am. The truth is, I need our mother more than she does. Kuran finds friends wherever she goes, and she has the imagination to do anything or be anything at all. I'm the one that's cursed with a life hidden away. I miss my mother's calm and the way she always seems to know what to do. I feel so lost and alone without her.

"Kuya Tanu, how often are prisoners pardoned?" I can't bear to look at Kuran. I rip my arm from hers. There are futures she could pluck if she wanted, and I am only in the way.

He squirms. "It must happen sometimes, or why bother to have a trial?"

I grunt. Not often, then. And why would the council of elders give a care about my mother when her own mother disowned her? A trial would be nothing more than a formal death sentence.

I chew the sweet bun but taste nothing. All my life I've been told "Stay out of sight, Narra" or "Don't ask questions, Narra." This is no different.

But if no one will help me, I will help myself.

I tug on my scarf and wind it tight. My mother saved for a

month to buy the painted blue silk for my sixteenth birthday. It was one of the last things she ever gave me, and I've worn it every day since. It makes me feel as though she's still keeping me safe, even though she is not with me now, even though I am terrified I'll never see her again.

Inay once told me that bravery only exists when you fear. I've hidden my whole life, and it's time for me to be brave.

The gold and gems are not prizes that appeal to me, but if I entered the Sundo, I could find my mother in the fortress and break her out.

I stride into our hillside campsite and ignore my sister's glares. From here, I can see all of Bato-Ko, and the glass fortress gleams like a lighthouse at the edge of the city, guiding me to my fate.

There are three days until the competition begins, and I will be there for it.

CHAPTER FOUR

I grasp a swathe of slippery silk as it plunges toward the cobbled street seeking stains. It would be easier to work without gloves, but Halna would scream if I ever touched the smooth cloth with my bare hands, because the silk is more valuable than a cursed girl. I toss it onto the table in a heap.

"You're in a fine mood today." Kuran snorts.

I turn my back to her and scowl. Of all days for our aunt to fall ill, it's this one. I can't find any excuse to leave the market stall, and of course Kuran hasn't forgotten last night. She won't let me out of her sight for even a moment, so I bristle in silence.

I return to mending the rip in my scarf and go over my plan. It's as full of holes as a sieve, but it's the best I can come up with. The hardest part will be slipping away. No, the hardest part will be leaving my sister, because if I fail—

"Do you have any pineapple cloth?" An old lady with a short cloud of curly hair appears at the table we set up in the market. Though her tunic and trousers look simple at a glance, I can tell by the tight weave of the fabric and the fine stitching of its lines that she is someone with money.

I point out a length of pale off-white fabric hanging from the canvas roof. It's beautifully embroidered with delicate flowers along its scalloped edges. The cloth is stiff to the touch and half transparent. I've only dared touch it once, for it is more expensive than silk—not because the materials are hard to come by, but because few people make it anymore.

"How much?" she asks, and I shrug. I'm only here to guard our wares, not to sell it.

"Narra," Kuran hisses at me and walks up to the woman with an instant smile.

"I'm going to get some water," I mumble and hop to my feet. I hastily grab a water jug as I slink away behind her back.

I check for Guardians, but they must be busy elsewhere. There are so many things to prepare, and I don't have much time. I jog down a few wide streets and stop at an address I dug out of my mother's old notebook. It's not far from the market where we've set up our stall.

I stare at a tall wooden gate with the Jal crest emblazoned on its double doors. I have daydreamed what it looks like, but I have no memory of the place I was born, and it bothers me the way Bato-Ko does. Like I should know it but I do not. Like it is something that has been taken from me.

I raise my hand to knock at the gate and notice an orasyon for protection carved into the old wood. I pass my hands over the posts, and the magic brushes against my open palm like a feather, tickling slightly. *Only the invited may enter*, it reads above a carved symbol. I check the sun. I've made good time, so curiosity gets the better of me.

"My blood allows me entrance," I declare and push the gates open. I do not sense even a ripple to indicate I've crossed the threshold, and it pleases me that not even my grandmother could deny that I belong here.

Beyond the gate, four buildings are arranged around a central square where the sunlight pools. Once it must have been grand. The buildings are two stories, with curving roof beams and wide windows.

This all would have been Kuran's, if our mother had not

taken us from Bato-Ko when we were children. This home should have been mine, too. There are enough rooms for generations of Jals to live together, but only one woman occupies it now. No laughter echoes here, and the patch of grass where children should play grows thick with weeds. It is a mausoleum. For my sister's sake, I fight the urge to run.

I pull a folded letter from my pocket and head to the largest building. The letter contains my meager hopes for reconciliation — that Yirin Jal might have pity on her granddaughter Kuran and take her in.

Before I can wedge the paper under the door, an old woman pulls it open. She grips a cane with gnarled hands. From its carved shaft, the eyes of the seven supreme Diwata peer at me with glittering shell eyes, weighing my worth with grooved lines that suggest laughter.

Yirin is a pious woman, my mother always said, too righteous to see past the tip of her nose. When I raise my eyes to meet my grandmother's, I see my mother in the stiffness of her back, the iron of her gaze, and the sadness that creases the edges of her lips. But she is short, as I am short. We have the same flat nose, straight hair, and wide mouth. She could be an older version of myself.

Yirin's cane clatters to the floorboards. I look like the woman that my mother hated most in the world, and not my father, as she always told me. Another of her lies.

"Narra?" Yirin's voice cracks.

My cheeks burn hot. Freezing Hells, how could she not know who I am when we look so much alike?

This could ruin everything. I toss the letter in her face and flee.

I return to the market without stopping and only remember my empty jug when I spot Kuran. Three black-uniformed Guardians glare at her from across the counter of our stall, and though Kuran laughs and flashes smiles at them, they don't return even a flicker of emotion.

My hands tremble as I go straight to my sister's side and press myself against her as if I'm glued there. I won't let them take her without taking me, too.

"Where did you go?" Kuran asks. She doesn't even notice me toss the empty jug under the table. "These most honorable Guardians were warning me about a rash of thefts lately."

One of the Guardians looks me up and down, and I flinch from the coolness of her gaze, but none of the three is a curly-haired Guardian with unusually dark eyes. I praise the Heavens for that small mercy. The not-quite memory flares into life once again, and as I follow the curve of his smile, the air seems to warm. I sputter at the intrusive thought. "Water." I gasp and reach for the empty jug. This time I curse that I didn't fill it on the way back.

"Please call us if you see anything strange." The Guardian ignores my antics.

"Of course, po." Kuran bows, and I remember myself a moment later. I bow stiffly, and the Guardians move on.

"What really happened yesterday?" Kuran turns me around to face her, but I can't look her in the eyes. "Tell me that you are in trouble, and we leave this instant."

Everything threatens to spill out, and I choke on my words. "I thought someone saw my marks, but I must have been mistaken." I offer the feeblest of smiles. "And if they're looking for a thief, it's not me."

She lets out a long breath. "Good, because I've been invited to sing at a party and you're coming with me."

When she has a free night, sometimes Kuran joins Tanu to perform for extra coin, but it seems odd that she would be invited to someone's home in Bato-Ko so soon. I fight my unease. "There's no way Manay Halna will allow it."

"She will." Kuran grins. "You'll see."

...

I hide my face in my hands. The shouting is so loud that I swear the entire hillside can hear it.

"You will not take Narra," Manay Halna repeats. "I will not allow it. Think of the scandal!"

Like most people we call auntie or uncle, Halna is not really blood. She was our mother's friend and business partner. She inherited two Jals when Inay disappeared and would be happier with only one, but I don't hate her. Some days I think she's right to be afraid of me, because even I am afraid.

"Even if it were a scandal, and it's not, no one cares who we are!"

The thin canvas of Halna's tent muffles nothing. I jam my hands into my pockets, unsure where to run or hide, when I spot Tanu headed toward me. I make desperate signals for help, but his ears are already as red as mine feel.

"You insolent girl! You think you know better than me? I have given you shelter for months and only ask your help in return."

Help? More like every bit of money we manage to scrounge up for ourselves. There's always some unexpected expense that she needs help with: a new dress because we can't look shabby in front of our customers, a new coat of paint on the wagons even though we just repainted this year, money for sweets to entice shoppers to our stall that we never get to taste even when some are left over. She takes everything and gives nothing in return.

"You are not our mother!" Kuran shouts.

"How dare you talk back to your elder! Someone needs to teach you terrible girls some respect!"

I rush into the tent and throw myself in front of Kuran. The flat of Halna's outstretched hand pauses two fingers from my ear, and she shrieks with frustration. She curls back as though singed, even though she doesn't touch a hair on my head. I almost wish she would try it, but she wouldn't dare. She already wears red to counter any ill luck I might bring, even though it makes her skin look sallow.

"Please, Manay Halna. It's been hard being back in Bato-Ko." I lower my chin deferentially and try to make myself small, even though I want to scream back instead. We don't need more trouble.

"What do you know about hard?" Halna caws. "What's hard is taking care of two ungrateful brats—"

I grab Kuran's sleeve and drag her out of the tent before she can say any more, because for now we still need Halna. Seeing Tanu waiting for her doesn't cool the flush of anger in her cheeks. She rips her arm from my grip and strides up to him.

"Tanu, marry me and take us away from here," she commands. No one can deny her anything. It is her power, and she knows how to wield it.

"Kuran, no." Tanu blinks his blue eyes like an owl.

I wait for the other half of the sentence: "not today" but "next year" or "in a few years," because they are both too young.

"I may only be nineteen, but I've been working since I was old enough to talk, and I can sing with you. You know I wouldn't be a burden."

"I've come to tell you that I am joining the Baylan. I can't—we can't…"

I stand there motionless and pray that this is a joke. I would have bet my life savings on Tanu and Kuran getting married one day. It's always been the three of us together on the road, and I never imagined anything different, because I know in my bones that they love each other. I feel my heart cracking, and I can only imagine what Kuran might be feeling.

Kuran asks him to repeat his words twice and goes so still

that I worry she might never blink again. I writhe where I stand, unable to look away from the wreckage sure to follow. She rarely shows what she feels, but I know she feels even more than I do.

"I'm sorry, Kuran." His cheeks are ruddy with shame as he turns around and walks away at a clip, no doubt unsure he could deny her twice.

Freezing Hells, what just happened? I gasp for air. I brace for our pot to go flying toward him, but Kuran sinks to the ground. I slide down beside her, careful to leave a hand's width of space between us. For all the world, I wish I could throw my arms around her or offer my shoulder to lean on, but our lives are so upside down that I don't know if I'm making things better or worse by being here. All I know is I want the hurt to stop. First our mother, and now Tanu. Our world keeps getting smaller.

"I can't keep living like this. This isn't a life," she says.

Tanu has been with us longer than anyone. Our families traveled the same festival circuits for years. So many nights, the three of us sat around the fire swapping tales. We would challenge one another to see who could tell the funniest thing that happened all day. He always lost, because humor was never his gift, but he never complained. I can't imagine a future on the road without him. Kuran is not the only one who is losing him. I will miss him, too.

Kuran takes my bare hand, and I snatch it away from her, though I want desperately to hold on.

Her jaw clamps tight at the unspoken rebuke. I know what she will say next, even though I disagree.

"The curse is an ignorant superstition, just like whistling to call the wind." She whistles boldly, and I cringe. "Or not sweeping the floor at night. Or eating round fruit on New Year's Day. Tanu never found any mention of birthmarks in those boring books of his." Her voice cracks, but her expression remains fierce. "Whatever happened in your past life to earn those marks, they mean you have been given another chance in this one. I know you, Narra. You're not a monster. You are my sister. Manay Halna is just too superstitious."

But I'm the one who wakes screaming in the early hours of dawn, choking for air; the one who hears voices in dead languages—not Kuran. I know this curse is real, just not what it means, just as I don't understand the strange vision I had when that curly-haired Guardian looked my way. Perhaps the curse is all just my imagination, but I do not move closer to her.

"I'm going to the party. Please come with me." Her shoulders quiver as if she's a bee about to take flight, and I might have flown with her if shame and guilt did not weigh me down. "Let's do something daring. Let's be young and foolish. We have the rest of our lives to be sensible."

I fight the urge to smooth her pain away. I know she can't speak about Tanu yet. Her eyes fill with water, and I crack. For all her fiery words, Tanu was her first love. And he was my friend. She's not the only one he walked away from.

But we are in Bato-Ko during the Sundo, I remind myself. The streets echo with music. The air is thick with promise and the heady scent of scattered flowers. Here, I could believe that humans might grow wings and fly or that curses might be broken.

I smile for her, even though she can see through it. My plans slip a little further from my grasp and threaten to come undone, but she's my sister, and I would do anything to make her smile.

"We'll need to find something better to wear," I say.

"I love you," she says. She only tells me this when she's trying to get her way.

"You're a pain in my side," I grumble as she hugs me in plain sight of Halna, utterly unafraid of my curse and whatever it might bring. Sometimes I wish Kuran hated me like everyone else, because leaving her will feel like a knife to my heart.

But there is one more day before the competition begins, so

I can give one night to her. I search for the glass fortress in the distance. Its transparent walls reflect the red light of the setting sun, and beyond it snakes a dark smudge. I wonder if those are storm clouds gathering, called forth by Kuran's whistling, and I shiver in the cold breeze.

✳ ☽ ✳ ☾ ✳

CHAPTER FIVE

The evening streets of Bato-Ko teem with brightly clothed people. Bead-draped locals parade beside us while Eastern visitors thump down the street in polished black shoes. I hear Rythian accents and speakers from the southern country of Malago. Street vendors hawk food from everywhere imaginable and some unimaginable. I smell pandan leaves steaming, curried fish balls, and fried potatoes spiced with paprika. It feels like we are at the center of the world instead of a lonely crack at its corners.

A hawker shoves a bowl of squid near my face, and a little black sauce splatters onto my tunic. Kuran dances away unscathed. She wears her long malong knotted at her chest like a dress, with her shoulders bare and her hair loose. Her ankles jingle with small bells. Even I can't tell that she was crying only a little while ago.

"We should be careful." I grimace and attempt to wipe away the stain, but it only widens into a greasy blob.

"You act like you're my grandmother, not seventeen," she says.

"Hah. You're the one that should be setting a proper example for me, Ate Kuran."

"I am! I'm showing you how to be young!" Kuran's false sigh tugs into the widest of smiles, and it lightens my mood when I should be the one trying to cheer her.

Nothing can ever deflate her. That's Kuran. I love her for it, and I envy her for it.

Unlike Kuran, I wear a malong on my hips, pleated over a simple tunic. The cloth is the finest thing I own, a gift from my father's family when I was born, woven with stripes of gold and emerald. My mother slung me in it as a baby, and perhaps someone will wrap me in it when I die. My blue silk scarf doesn't match, but I refused to go without it, no matter how much Kuran pouted.

I frown when the Toso compound comes into view. Making pleasantries sounds as appealing as sticking needles into my eyeballs. Kuran says I should not be so shy, but I cannot help that my tongue trips up and suddenly my feet do not work right. I worry I'll knock over glasses and break plates. I hate parties, but this is for my sister's happiness, not mine.

We walk through the gates into a space bathed with soft lantern light. Buildings of lacquered wood and generous windows cluster around a large central square open to the sky. It's not unlike our grandmother's home, but here, children peer down from balconies and the outdoor kitchen teems with cooks. Chickens cluck somewhere out of sight, and colorful paper lanterns are strung between the buildings overhead. Soft cushions are strewn in clusters on the wooden walkways that circle the space. It all looks so comfortable and inviting.

Kuran takes me straight to our host, Oshar Toso. It is the woman who asked for pineapple cloth, and she wears it as a stiff shawl over her shoulders as she stands near a table laden with food set up in a corner of the square. A cloud of soft white curls frames a kind brown face wrinkled with smile lines. Oshar is stocky and a little bit short, and she is everything I dreamed my grandmother might look like before I met her.

"Call me Nanay Oshar, my darlings." She does not extend a

hand to give a blessing but squeezes my shoulders as if we are family. "Have you eaten? Come, come, don't be shy."

She introduces us to her wife, Sayarala, a tall Turinese woman with deep russet skin. I paste on another smile and hope it looks pleasant instead of fearsome. Some old ladies come to chat with us at our market stall because they are lonely. I don't mind them, but Bato-Ko has left me cautious, and from the din of voices in her house even at this early hour, Oshar is surely not lonely.

On the road, sometimes we eat thin soup for days, made of bones boiled until there is no flavor left. Here the sweets are piled up on one table: sweet sticky rice wrapped in banana leaves, sponge cakes colored with purple yams, flan dripping with syrup. Much of it is Tigangi fare, made with ingredients hard to come by this far north. My mouth waters at the smells, but Oshar's warm welcome feels too good to be true.

"I thought there would be three of you?" Oshar asks, eyes bright with curiosity.

But before I can answer, Kuran smiles. "Unfortunately, our last performer has decided that religion suits him better than music. He's off to join the Baylan, po." If she's affected by the admission, it doesn't show on her face, but I feel another strike to my heart.

"Heavens bless him, then. I'm sure you will do just fine without him." An odd look that might be sympathy passes across Oshar's face.

"What songs would you like us to perform, Nanay Oshar?" Kuran asks, all smiles and fluttering lashes for our host.

"Let us begin with the destruction of our homeland and the founding of Tigang," Oshar says.

"'The defeat of Chaos by Astar the Builder'?" Kuran raises her brows. It is a song for funerals, not parties. My skin prickles as if awakened. Oshar nods.

"I will sing first and then eat later, Nanay Oshar," she says.

Oshar nods, pleased, but settles down on a cushion and looks askance at us as if confirming some secret suspicion. Could she know our family? I gaze at the grass and hope any resemblance to my grandmother is not as keen as I think.

I busy myself clearing a space for Kuran's performance. She kneels on a cushion under the cozy overhang of a porch and arranges her malong around her feet. She must be missing her musician, and I am only a mediocre performer, but her smile remains convincing.

She opens her mouth to quiet the crowd, but the gate swings open before she can begin. Guests rise to their feet, and Kuran is forgotten. My heart beats wildly, and I am frozen as if magic binds me again.

Arisa enters the house, dressed in scarlet silk. Today her hair is done in an intricate braid topped with the same golden comb from before. Glittering earrings dangle to her shoulders. She looks like someone born to rule others. She locks eyes with every guest who dares to challenge her. "I heard that the Toso family was having a party tonight. I've come to give you my blessing."

I quickly bow my head, worried she might recognize me. I suck air in and out to calm my nerves, but my heart beats so loudly that I am afraid she can hear it.

"You are always welcome, Arisa, our beloved Astar." Oshar bows and presses Arisa's hand to her brow with a grimace she barely deigns to conceal.

I can't breathe. The revelation of who she is brings no relief. What did that Archivist Alen do to incur her wrath? I feel in my gut that it has something to do with my mother, but I don't know why, and I squirm as I stand there.

"May Omu's light shine on you." Arisa finishes the ritual, and amusement curls at the edges of her lips.

Arisa is the Astar reborn, picked by Baylan in her infancy to fulfill the role once taken by the founder of our country—appointed by the Diwata themselves. She is more than dangerous. She is important.

"The entertainment is about to begin, po," Oshar says. Her tone betrays nothing but flawless politeness. Oshar's age should demand respect, but the Astar is above us all, and Arisa seems to revel in it.

When I dare raise my eyes, I spy Arisa's curly-haired guard out of the corner of my eye. I catch only the side of his head as he slips into the compound without notice, but I am certain it is him. His fingers twitch as if it's difficult to keep them still. His movements remind me of a bird, as though his footsteps barely touch the ground. His presence brushes against something deep within me. My breath catches in my chest, and I force it back out.

"Perhaps we should choose another song." My voice quavers, but it carries across the quiet.

Arisa remains focused on Oshar, but Oshar lifts her chin and squares her shoulders. "I have requested 'The defeat of Chaos.' Let us hear it."

With a nod from Kuran, I lift my tumpong to my lips and blow a soft melody through the bamboo flute. Kuran tilts her head to sing, and her voice soothes the tension like a balm.

"In the time before..." Our stories always begin. I imagine the archipelago of Arawan as though I was there. A city perches upon the slopes of a great volcano, and the roads gleam black, cobbled with volcanic rocks. Everything around us is green and dark, and the air is thick with moisture. Always, in the song, it is sunset. The sapphire waters gleam as if on fire. The chirping of lizards and frogs welcomes the end of day as I gaze upon all seven of the islands that make up Arawan. They are so beautiful that Astar never longed for the heavens where she was born.

A country that even the immortal Diwata were jealous of.

My eyes drift over the crowd lulled by the spell of Kuran's song. No one notices that I skip notes and fumble with my flute. Kuran has the attention of Arisa's guard now, too. For a little while, I watch him, even though I should be wary.

His curly black hair is tied back in a short tail. He wears the uniform of the Guardians: a plain black tunic, loose trousers tucked into boots, and a red sash at his waist. I have no idea if the color indicates rank.

He stills as though he is waiting for something. Then he very slowly turns to look at me.

The unfathomable darkness of his eyes draws me in, and I am caught.

There is no way he could recognize me, I tell myself, but his eyes linger too long to be polite. His expression reminds me of a coiled spring. I fear my pounding heart will escape my chest, and I blow several off-pitch notes. Would he give me away to Arisa?

He looks away, and my breathing steadies as the song ends. The people in the room burst into applause while Kuran bows elegantly before them. I nod my head with a grimace and ball my hands tightly.

It feels as though an invisible hand released its grip on my heart, and I slump into myself. I wrap my arms around my chest and wish the night were over.

Oshar incants a prayer to honor the memory of Arawan, then requests a silly rhyme. Kuran cheerfully obliges. This time the children get involved, and the performance devolves into a pandemonium of banging brass gongs that outmatch the delicate sound of my flute. I wish I could share in the hooting laughter and the applause, but I am afraid to meet the guard's unsettling gaze. I'm not needed, so I walk into a corner padded with cushions and try to melt into them.

I mumble polite answers meant to drive away polite guests. I keep my false smile painted on, but it fades every time my eyes drift back to Arisa's Guardian. He leans against a shadowed wall with his arms crossed, and a sliver of warm lamplight caresses his cheek. I wish he would step into the light so I could see him better, but he seems more friendly with the shadows.

I sneak another look. The long sleeves of his tunic hide any paint on his arms, but I would be surprised if he had no ink on his body. He wears no weapon but a ceremonial kris tucked into his sash. Its ironwood sheath is engraved with a serpent design. The handle is a serpent's head banded with gold. Guests walk hurriedly past him as if he is a snake sunning himself on the riverbank.

He does not act like a bodyguard, which is unusual. There is no deference in his posture, even toward Arisa. He gazes at his charge with mild disinterest, and if Arisa finds his attentions lacking, she does not chide him for it. I wonder again what it means, and I fear that he is someone not to be trifled with.

Kuran bumps into my shoulder, and I jump to my feet.

"His name is Teloh, by the way." My cheeks are hot and not red, I hope. I despise that I have been so obvious.

"I can appreciate a fine pair of eyes." My voice sticks in my throat. She doesn't know what happened in the street, and she can't ever know.

"Is that all?"

"I'm not a child anymore." I turn to her, and she skewers me with a skeptical lift of the eyebrows. "Besides, it doesn't matter. I'm not…" I couldn't explain it to her even if I wanted to. To look at him feels like watching an approaching avalanche when there is no time to get out of the way.

Kuran rolls her eyes. "You are my sister, and you need to start acting like it." She has a gleam in her eye that I do not like.

"Let's talk to him."

"No!" I protest so loudly that guests eye us, but Kuran guides me through the throng, and they part for her, smile at her, and she smiles back. She doesn't understand that this isn't some silly girl's infatuation. I curse that there's no escape.

"Excuse me." She puts on her brightest smile and doesn't let me squirm away. "I'm Kuran. This is my sister, Narra." His expression slams shut at the sound of my name. His eyes burn into my neck as though he can see through the scarf I always wear. My skin prickles this close to him, as if there is lightning in the air. But he doesn't see Kuran. He gazes only at me. Kuran slaps my back with too much force, and I stumble toward him. I catch the silk of his tunic to stop from tumbling, and the world falls away.

The vision is like a wave crashing over me, holding me under. In it, we are slipping silently through the darkened streets of Bato-Ko.

"Are you sure no one saw us leave?" I ask. My voice sounds different, and when I glance at my reflection in a passing window, I don't recognize myself, but Teloh remains the same. He's not wearing the black of the Guardians, but a tunic one size too small paired with a red tapis over ill-fitting trousers. I match, only my clothes are too long, as if we've stolen clothes from someone else's closet.

He flashes a grin at me. "And who's going to stop us? In all this time, I've never been to the Lantern Festival!"

Tonight, all the houses have turned out their lights or pulled the drapes, and so for once, nothing lights our way except the moon and the stars.

I glimpse a glow up ahead and catch a little of Teloh's enthusiasm. Soon we'll be discovered, so I sear the memory of his smile into my soul and hoard it like a precious gemstone. I am not fond of touching people, but his hand in mine feels right.

I pull him on, racing faster than him now, toward a lantern made of colored rice paper. It's shaped into a star and dangles from a tree. The candle within it flickers dimly, almost burned out.

"Another one!" I laugh, pointing down the street. This one is a child's contribution, a blobby-looking ball painted with a face. A few other late strollers walk toward the city's most central square, and we follow them. As we approach, the street turns awash in light. A thousand lanterns hang on wires above and several hundred more sit on the ground. It's as though we are trapped within a cloud of color.

Teloh sucks in a breath, and I am secretly pleased, for no matter how long I have known him, some things still manage to surprise him. When I am with him like this, the terrible past loosens its grip, and I revel in the freedom. For a moment, nothing matters except that he is here with me. Teloh's dark eyes drink it all in, as though he's ravenous for color, and when he turns to me, they lose not one bit of that hunger.

I take a step backward and stagger into Kuran as Oshar's house comes back into focus. My head spins as if I've downed a jug of wine. What just happened? Could it be a memory from another life? I've heard such things are possible, but nothing close to it has ever happened to me before. I search Teloh's face for an answer, but I cannot read it in his expression. I hate that I'm disappointed.

Before Kuran can speak, the Guardian raises a finger and points it at me. "Get her out of here, *now.*" His words are like a slap in the face.

Her. Not Kuran but me.

The next instant, we are pushed out the gate and left staring at it like two hungry rats chased with a broom. Kuran doesn't know what to say when Oshar comes running out to apologize. She slips far too much money and plates of food into our hands, despite our protests. But Oshar does not invite us back in, and for once I think that luck is on my side.

I can't get ahold of my heart. It races too fast, and a *boom boom boom* rattles against my chest like a warning. *Run*, my heart warns. *Run away. You should never have come here.*

CHAPTER SIX

I creep along the ground as the farmers paw through our campsite, hunting for me as though I'm a mouse in a granary. My heart pounds. What can a six-year-old girl do against a gang of farmers armed with rakes and shovels? I have no weapons except my dirty hands. I crawl on my knees and head for the bushes nearby.

"Got you!" Someone drags me back by the neck of my tunic, and I fall to the dirt. I kick and scream, but the farmer doesn't care. He drags me in front of the others. A solid shape sprints toward us. It's my mother.

"Inay!" I scream for her, and my vision blurs as tears spill down my cheeks. I may be cursed and considered worthless in this country, but I've never once doubted she loved me. I wish I could be half as fierce and brave, but I am not. I kneel there cowering and crying.

The farmer shrieks as she whips a rattan cane into his knees. I fall flat to the ground as he loses his grip.

"How dare you touch my child." Her voice is as cold as iron. "What authority do you have over my family?"

A farmer strikes the ground with his shovel and leers. A cultist's sun disk swings at his neck—he will have no mercy on me. Mother tightens her bright red headwrap and brushes a speck of dust from her sleeve. She is a Reyna amongst them, no matter how faded her trousers. I've never wished so hard to be more like her.

"Ever since you got into town, the animals have sickened, and our grain has spoiled! You brought this plague here!"

Me. A plague. I scramble behind my mother's skirts and entreat to Omu. I offer her everything she might want so that my heart might be ice or stone, instead of something that bruises so easily.

"The weather is changing. If you stored your grain more carefully, you would not have this problem. My daughter has not stepped foot in your village." She stares at each one in turn. In the flickering light, her eyes lose their color and become like obsidian. "It is not our problem."

"We've seen her marks, woman."

She kicks their fallen companion in the ribs, and he rolls over in the dirt with a wasted scream. "Where are your elders? Let me speak with them."

This will cost us something dear. What this time? Silk? Silver? We hardly manage to hang on to what little we have, and it's all my fault.

They move away, and I pick myself up, shaking. All their faces are a blur.

"Narra, get in your bed and stay there." My mother parts the canvas doors of our tent, and I trudge inside.

"Inay…" I whimper. "You should have given me up when I was born. Why do you keep me?" I swallow my tears to seem as strong as she is, but I am not. I want my mother to hug me, to hold me close, and to tell me everything will be fine, but of course she doesn't. She sits down beside me for a moment, looking tired. I've never seen her cry. Sometimes I think she cried them all out when my father died and there are no more left for me.

"You are my daughter. I loved you from your first moment in the world, no matter what anyone else thinks." She tucks me under the bedcovers, and the waves of her dark hair tickle my *face.* "*Stay,*" *she commands and turns without a glance at my tears.*

"*Inay!*" *I reach for her hands, but she's too far away.* "*Don't leave me!*"

"Narra!"

I crash into my sister's arms as I wake. Kuran is still wearing her party clothes, and her eyes are both wide and sleepy. The canvas of our tent is still dim with pale early morning light. "You were having a nightmare."

"I…" I roll away from her and start tossing clothes out of my trunk. I grab my tunic and a faded batik malong I use for work. I try to hold on to my mother's face and her voice, but the image turns into a faded silhouette.

"What are you doing?" There's fear in her eyes that mirrors mine. "Where are you going?"

I overturn a wooden box and find a yellowing paper tucked in the bottom. I'd been saving the knockout spell I bought last year for an escape from Manay Halna. I never expected it to come to this. It won't last long, but it might buy me enough time to get away.

"I'm so sorry, Kuran." I spit on the paper and press the orasyon to her forehead.

"NA—" Before she can finish calling my name, Kuran slumps to the floor unconscious. I lift her gently back into her cot, careful not to touch her skin.

"I love you, but I need to do this." I quietly memorize her features, and it nearly brings me to tears. I will miss her more than anyone. Leaving her means I will be on my own for the first time in my life, but it's the only way to save our mother.

I need one last thing before I go. My sister is old enough to enter the Sundo, and I am still a month shy of eighteen, so I prick the tip of her finger with my sharpest needle. I squeeze blood into a vial that I tuck into my sleeves.

I reach the edge of our campsite and look back. Almost

everyone in the caravan is still asleep, except for our designated night guard (we all take turns). My family owns two red carts, not so different from the others, and we put up two lopsided canvas tents beside a smoldering cookfire. I know the contents of our trunks by heart: one iron pot, five plates, two knives, three cups. Kuran and I have only two tunics and malongs each, one fine and one rough. Her fine tunic is torn at the side seam, and it needs mending. I turn away from everything I've ever known, and my soul sings a tempting song of freedom. Of escape.

Every step I must take from here is a gamble, and my chances of winning are as slim as threading a needle in the dark, but a slim chance is still a chance. A chance to pay back every sacrifice my mother made for me. A chance to prove I am more than nothing.

I will get into the glass fortress. I will save my mother, or I will die trying.

*) * (*

CHAPTER SEVEN

The glass fortress's walls gleam blinding white in the morning light. Half of the building is built of thick rippled glass, but the rest of the fortress displays the solid rock of the hill that the fortress was built into. It looks as though the whole fortress grew out of the ground like a stalagmite at the Heavens' command. I fight back the knot of queasiness in my stomach and look behind me. There is no sign of Kuran—yet—and I hope that my clumsy spell holds.

A table awaits candidates for the Sundo in the shadow of the gates. A middle-aged man with hollow eyes sits behind the table flanked by a Guardian that stares blankly ahead.

"Name and papers," the man at the table says without looking up. He must be a Baylan, but he wears nothing to indicate his sect. His loosely belted robe reveals a snakeskin tattoo beneath his collarbones and a wiry brown body that looks underfed.

My heart sinks at his bored expression.

"Kuran Jal," I stutter. "I have no papers."

"You are Tigangi, are you not?" He dunks a piece of sweet bread into a mug of black coffee. "If your family is listed in the official records, you may request a copy from the archives. Only those from registered families may enter the Sundo."

I was. Manong Alen had opened our family book and shown me the very page I needed now. If only I'd known!

"But applying for papers could take weeks," I say. "I'll miss the Sundo."

He shrugs and pops the bread into his mouth.

"There must be another way." I place my hands on the table, and he finally looks up, then down the faded blue linen of my tunic.

"One gold bead." He taps the table with a finger, and I force myself to tamp down a sudden burst of anger. The Guardian at his side says nothing when I appeal to her open-mouthed. Tanu left Kuran for *this*? For bureaucracy and corruption?

"I don't have gold." I left everything I had with Kuran, and none of those things were gold.

"I am doing you a favor, child. Go back to your farm or whatever mudhole you came from. This is not for you."

The man leans over his papers, a sign that I've been dismissed. Everyone here seems to think I am a helpless child, but they do not know me.

"I will prove who I am the traditional way," I say.

I take a sharp needle I use for mending clothes and make pretense of pricking my arm. I spill the vial from my sleeve so that Kuran's blood drips all over his table. "I am Kuran Jal, heir to house Jal. It is my right to give up my life for my country, as it is the right of every other Tigangi who is of age."

None past twenty-five, and none younger than eighteen. I try not to shake as I dip a cloth inked with a naming orasyon into the blood.

This is my only chance. I will not be able to perform this trick twice. The Baylan scrutinizes the naming spell. I know it is valid, but the blood isn't mine, and I can't get any more of it. The blood slowly spells out Kuran's name.

"Let her in. We both know that blood cannot lie." The familiar voice fixes me in place.

Teloh appears at the gate, and I cannot read his expression.

The way he does not meet my eyes feels deliberate, and it stings as much as a rebuke.

"You will be punished for requesting bribes, Reshar," Teloh says.

He displays no deference, though Reshar's age alone should demand it. Again, I don't understand where he sits on the hierarchy of Baylan. First Arisa, now Reshar. He's not old enough to demand respect for his age, and that means he must have a special status. Who is he really? Certainly not a simple Guardian.

I slink through the entrance before that rotten Baylan Reshar can protest, but my small hopes flicker, because the corners of Teloh's lips curl up as I pass. I'm not sure if this is amusement or scorn, but I am certain that he knows exactly who I am.

I pass through the iron teeth into the waiting maw of the fortress, grateful that he doesn't follow.

The cobbled courtyard swarms with people. I count just under three hundred candidates cramped into a small space between the iron gates and the glass wall of the fortress. It's a boggling number of people to weed through in eight days. It seems too little time to determine the fate of a country, yet we have done this for centuries.

I don't know exactly what will happen, but I have heard rumors. The candidates are tested by each sect of Baylan and ranked according to a secret scoring system. Some tests are physical, while others test mental toughness, and every Sundo, the tests are said to be different. Many of the tests are a matter of life and death because the ruler of Tigang must make hard choices, and sometimes impossible ones.

While no one wants candidates to die, there are always casualties.

Every year, following the Sundo, a parade of caskets leaves the fortress draped in flowers. Some years, there are fewer than a handful, but sometimes there are dozens. And those that survive never come out the same as they were when they went in. Their memories are erased, and they are taken to a palace outside the city, where they are cared for and waited on by doctors and nurses for a year. Most are plagued by nightmares. Some are trapped in their minds and cannot escape. Others never choose to leave the palace and return to their families. All of them are magically bound to never speak of the Sundo.

I once met a woman who survived, and the moment anyone ever asked her about the competition, she would start screaming and wouldn't stop until her voice had gone hoarse.

Even so, there are fewer desperate-looking Tigangi here than I expect. Several groups of young people greet one another. They are locals from the city of Bato-Ko, by the style of their clothing; by the size of the bags they carry, it looks as if they are ready to holiday, not die.

I am acutely aware that I am the youngest person here, I know almost nothing about the competition, and I have brought nothing except the clothes I wear. I have never been so ill-prepared for anything in my life, and that terrifies me, because I cannot afford to fail.

I chew my lip and head toward the nearest group of candidates, but my voice is caught in my throat, already sticky. A weak "Hello" escapes my lips, but they turn their backs to me like a wall, so I keep going as if I meant to greet someone else. They laugh behind me, and I curl into myself. I wish I could disappear.

I'm already failing. The real Kuran would have been sitting in a circle, talking to everyone as if she'd known them forever.

I shrink back against the cold glass wall and sit on the ground, just a poor imitation.

"I do not know what game you are playing, Narra Jal, but it's a dangerous one." Teloh leans against the glass beside me. I nearly jump to my feet, and only my pride keeps me from bolting. "You entered the Sundo in your sister's name, so even if you win, you cannot rule—she is the one bound to the contract. You will be found out sooner or later. Why have you come?"

Heads turn away, and conversations dim around us. The air feels just a hint cooler beside him, as if I've walked into a different room, though I sit under the summer sun surrounded by hundreds of people. I scan the crowd for Arisa, but I don't see her.

"First you tell me to get away from you, and now you let me in." I do not know how to address him. I am sure that he is not Arisa's favorite Guardian just for his looks. Even knowing this, I can't help myself. "What do you wish now? Shall you order me to fly?"

"Should you not, instead, be begging me not to turn you in? I would be doing you a favor." He mimics Reshar's voice.

"Give me one good reason to beg." I am suddenly conscious of the kris tucked into his sash. I am certain that he would be able to throw me out of the Sundo if he willed it. An inappropriate laugh escapes my lips when I imagine myself slung over his shoulder like a sack of rice.

He raises a brow, and I catch another trace of maybe-amusement. I turn to stare at him and attempt to hold his gaze. His eyes don't seem to fit the rest of him. They are blue-black, like the sky just after the sun has set. They could contain stars. They could swallow you. My skin crawls, and I look away.

"The Baylan have arrested my mother," I say aloud. What I don't say is that I don't care about winning the Sundo, only finding her.

His expression barely shifts, but it feels a shade softer, if you could call a rock soft.

"You really don't remember me?" Teloh asks after a long pause.

He can't be asking about a past life, because his anger seems too raw, and if I ever admitted to my visions, I bet that he would dismiss me as some silly lovestruck farm girl. I am neither of those things.

"Unless I have terrorized you in your dreams, I cannot see how I have offended you. You must have me mistaken for someone else, because I have not set foot in Bato-Ko since I was a baby."

He laughs. It is a glorious sound, and I hate myself for thinking it. But the wheels in my mind turn. Perhaps if Teloh has mistaken me for someone else, the Archivist might have, too. Who is this impostor that he raved about? I shiver and pray my mother has nothing to do with it.

"My apologies, Kuran Jal." He stands and extends a hand, but I do not take it. I pick myself up off the dirt and stick my hands into the folds of my malong.

"I do not recommend staying, but if you must, do not call attention to yourself until the end. Stay quiet. Do not show off with magic. Keep your doors locked at night. Let these spoiled children weed themselves out with their ambition." He pauses to stare at my neck, and I realize that my traitor scarf has unwound itself again. "And keep your marks hidden. Some would kill you just for those."

The lack of judgment in his tone surprises me. And then he smiles. This time the smile is wide and real, as if we have been friends forever, and I am dizzied by it. Is this how people feel around Kuran? At least she does not flutter from mood to mood from one moment to the next. Teloh seems as changeable as the Tigangi weather.

And though I cannot ignore what my instincts warn me about him, the advice seems sound.

Stay quiet. That, I am good at. I knot my silk scarf and wait for the competition to begin.

CHAPTER EIGHT

Shards of reflected light fracture the courtyard, announcing noon with searing brightness. The Seven Datus of Tigang step out the doors of the fortress.

Space opens around the Seven as they pass. Once, our Datus were the rulers of our islands, what foreigners might call kings or queens, but now we have one Datu for each magical sect of Baylan. Every Datu is the foremost expert in the magic associated with their patron Diwata. It can take decades to rise so far, and most never do.

The Datus are the true powers that govern our country, and though they may listen to the Astar's advice, the Astar's position is ceremonial, and they are not obligated to obey her. While the Raja or Reyna is the public face of Tigang's government, sits on public councils, oversees ceremonies, and dines with foreign emissaries, everyone knows that our ruler is the Datus' puppet.

The air shimmers around them like a mirage on a hot day, but no heat follows. The chill mountain wind answers instead, stirring the stray hairs at the nape of my neck.

I recognize only one amongst the seven most powerful people in Tigang—Reshar, who greeted me so kindly at the gate. Even standing, the tattooed Datu seems to slouch.

How could Teloh reprimand him the way he did? Teloh looks like he's barely older than me. He's neither a Datu nor the Astar. There are many Guardians with red sashes. Nothing about him marks him as extraordinary. Everything about him is a puzzle, and I am missing the pieces. I can't figure it out, and it frustrates me.

Reshar's voice carries across the courtyard despite its softness.

"You brave souls must know that win or lose, sacrifice awaits you. We choose a new ruler every ten years to share the burden of power amongst our people. The ruler of Tigang is a channel for the power of the holy Diwata, and servant to our nation. Your life will not be your own if you win. If you have come for glory, this is not where you belong." He yawns and doesn't even bother to fix the loose tie on his robe. The opening in the front reveals more tattoos down the sides of his torso.

"Our ruler is our greatest weapon and shield. It is a sacrifice to rule. You will be the physical conduit for the power of the Diwata. You must give up years of your life for our people's sake, but though you will be assured a short life, you can use it to make a difference, as the Ash Raja once did." The Seven bow their heads, and we all follow suit.

Another of the Seven sweeps her hands toward the iron gates. "Some of you will not exit these gates alive. Those that do will not leave here unbroken. You will be marked so that your mind will be scoured of everything that happens within these walls, but magic is unpredictable, and this spell may take pieces of your mind along with it. You risk your life and who you are.

"But the one that wins has a chance at something more. Riches and influence—yes, this part is true, but you will also have the chance to make a difference. To create history. Will you stay, or will you leave?"

There is nervous chatter as a handful of candidates make their excuses. The rest of us gather into clusters around the Seven. Each holds a bowl of black ink and a pen with a needle-sharp tip. A Datu scrawls a small mark onto the fleshy mound of palm between the base of a boy's thumb and wrist. His cry of pain is followed by tense laughter, as a few specks of blood mingle with the ink to seal the orasyon.

I wait for my turn and pace back and forth in a tiny circle. I do not see Kuran banging at the gates, and I don't know what to feel about it. Part of me wishes that she might shrug off the sleeping spell and come running to stop me. Instead, I get as far from the gates as I can, so that I cannot change my mind.

I back up into Reshar and freeze. His lips curl into something between a sneer and a smile. "Kuran Jal."

I hate that he remembers me.

"Datu Reshar." I incline my head slightly, though it galls me to do so. I keep my expression flat and start to turn away, but he catches my sleeve.

"Since you are so keen to be here, let me make it so." His eyes burn straight through me.

The candidates nearby look my way, some confused, some curious. His grip is tight, but I am strong from carrying buckets of water and hauling bolts of fabric. My first reaction is to whip my arm away, and he shakes visibly, his temper threatening to boil over.

"Do not touch me," I say and plunge my hands to my side. I resist the urge to ball them. He is nothing, just another cruel person, and those are common enough in the world. "It is not my fault that you were caught demanding bribes, po." I add the honorific to rub in the salt.

Several boys snicker, but the laughter dies abruptly.

"Here, child. Let me." A woman's crisp voice rings behind me, and it sends my skin crawling with its familiarity. Arisa. I know a meddler when I meet one. As usual, the Astar wears her sun comb in her hair and jewelry on all her fingers. Teloh looms behind, a silent shadow that refuses to meet my eyes.

I bow my head until it is nearly level with my waist. I dare not move or speak in her presence.

In the corner of my eyes, Reshar turns away and grabs the wrist of a plump, short-haired girl who winces at his rough treatment.

Arisa holds out her palm and waits for my hand. She has no pen or bowl of ink, but her thumb and forefinger are stained blue. I take a breath, smile, and pretend that at least I have chosen this.

But my smile falters when she pulls a thin scalpel from her wide sleeve. She drags me forward into a bow, with my palm up. Then she cuts me. The pain is searing and prolonged. I writhe, biting my tongue to stop from screaming. My blood drips onto the pavement, and the smell of iron tints the air.

"Arisa, that's enough." Teloh's voice breaks her attention and sends my heart racing.

She shoves me back up to standing, and my stomach roils, reacting violently as the magic begins to take hold, as if my body wants to force the magic back out through my mouth. She glares at the Guardian like a petulant child unused to being chastised.

I feel the binding magic spread up my arm and neck, toward my brain like hot liquid. It waits there, dormant, like a trap ready to be sprung the moment I leave through the fortress gates, ready to erase my mind of the Sundo. It's a complication to my plan, but there's always a way around every spell. I am exactly where I need to be. I will find my mother. There is no going back now.

I decide that Reshar's ordinary pettiness would have been welcome over Arisa's, but it's too late.

"A gift of blood begins the Sundo." Arisa turns to the crowd, not once looking me in the eyes or asking my name. Instead, she tosses a roll of gauze at me like a treat for a dog, and I fumble for it as she walks away. Teloh hesitates a moment, then turns after her.

Everyone's eyes turn to me. There will be no staying out of sight now.

I stare at the blood on my palm, half relieved, half repulsed, and try to regain control of my body. The dry heaves continue, and I double over, spit dribbling down my chin.

"Let me see your hand." Before I can say no, the short-haired girl Reshar marked takes the gauze from my hands and winds it carefully around my palm without touching my bare skin. I am grateful, because both my arms shake too much.

I steady myself and mumble a "Thank you."

"Virian," she says and extends her hand, but I don't take it. I offer an awkward smile instead. The mark on Virian's left palm is askew, but Reshar did not draw more than one bead of blood. His precision surprises me.

"I'm Kuran." The name falls dead from my lips, and I worry that she can see through the lie. The girl is shorter than me but not by much. She looks barely eighteen and of mostly Rythian ancestry, judging by the olive tone of her skin and her light brown eyes. Her short black hair bobs around her chin and sweeps across her face in a long fringe. The hairstyle unfortunately calls attention to her nose instead of her eyes, and it is crooked, as though it's been broken once.

"I don't know anyone here," Virian admits. All she's brought with her is the worn traveling sack slung over her shoulder. Rythians are horse people. They roam the plains to the northwest of Tigang, and they travel to different grazing sites each season. It isn't unusual to find Rythians traveling through our country to do business, but they rarely stay in one place long. Virian hardly has an accent, and I wonder how long she's been here.

"Me neither."

"My cousin is a Baylan. He warned me that the judging begins the moment you sign your name at the gate," she says.

I cross my arms. "And how do they choose?"

It feels like there are too many bodies stuffed into this courtyard, but I also know this is too few. Centuries ago, the gates would open only for an hour, and every family would send an heir to do them honor.

"Each Datu scores a test and makes a recommendation, but the Astar always has the final say."

I fight the impulse to laugh. I've already made an enemy of Reshar, I do not trust Arisa, and I am at the mercy of Teloh's whims. Today he laughed and kept my secret, but tomorrow?

"I thought the Astar's position was ceremonial," I say.

"Officially, she has no authority—but you just met Arisa. Even the Datus bow and scrape around her." She shudders.

I could not imagine Arisa being impartial. My hopes fray around the edges, but I hold them close. I don't care about winning. I must only stay long enough to find my mother and get out. I need to stay focused.

The Seven line up in the middle of the courtyard when the inking is done. This time, they set a large box on top of a table, and when they open the wooden lid, the glare of gold burns our eyes, reflecting the sun's glory.

"Change your mind now, and one gold hoop is yours. Take one and leave with our blessings."

I stare at the finger-thick circle of gleaming metal. One gold hoop would be enough to buy food for a few months. One hoop would not help Kuran forever, but it would mean a great deal. Kuran would be angry about the spell, but she would forgive me if I came back.

I don't know what's going on, but I feel something strange, oddly lighter than normal, and like my thoughts refuse to line up in order.

You're here to save your mother! I blink to tear my eyes away from the gold. *Remember!*

At least a dozen candidates step up to receive a ring and leave through the iron gates. The courtyard breathes a little.

"Who is she?" I point to the woman holding the box. This Datu's voice is all honey and warm blankets. She wears a peaceful face beneath shoulder-length waves of unbound hair. Every bit of her clothing is spotlessly white, and a gold sun disk the size of a fist hangs from her neck. I watch her warily. The sun disk is similar to the design that Omu's cultists wear, but the Baylan have always denounced them in public.

"Datu Kalena, head of the Interpreters sect," she says. The Interpreters sect is dedicated to Omu's teachings. They are responsible for writing Tigang's laws and running our court system. They are not to be trifled with.

"Rumor is, she is the nearest thing to Reyna right now," Virian squeaks with unexpected glee, and I wonder how she knows all of this.

"My grandmother is Tigangi," she says as though I am thinking aloud. I see it now, in the flatness of her nose and the shape of her eyes.

"Change your mind now, and twenty gold rings are yours," Kalena says, calling us back to attention. Her voice is soft, but I no longer trust it.

My eyes water as I stare at the box, but I cannot look away. Twenty rings would be enough to buy a new cart and leave Halna behind forever. Kuran and I could buy a modest home. We would eat well for months. The dream is so real that I can almost taste oranges on my tongue and smell jasmine growing half a continent away, in Turium, where no one cares about my marks. My stomach does a flip as I shake myself free of the vision. Magic? I blink and smell it faintly.

I've heard that a strong Interpreter can compel you to do anything. I don't disbelieve it now.

Several candidates push forward and take rings, but there are still over two hundred of us left. I rip my eyes from the box and try to signal Virian, but her eyes are fixed on the box as if it is the only thing that exists in the world.

I turn my eyes to watch a flame-haired candidate leave, but my neck doesn't follow. The girl's sleeves are patched, and her hair hangs limp around her shoulders. She clutches the box in white-knuckled fists, ready to fight anyone who might dare take the gold from her. There is a lifetime of hope in her hands, enough money to change her family's fate. I bite my lip and draw blood. The pain loosens the spell's grip, and I am able to turn my head enough to see.

The girl steps through the iron gate and stumbles when she reaches the other side. The rings tumble away, and the color leaches from them. She wails, either for her loss or because she is lost.

Is this what magic does to you?

Tears blur my vision as the spell whips my head back toward the center of the courtyard.

A single box the size of a bound book is brought forward. Kalena says nothing when it is placed in her hands, but she gently lifts the carved lid hinged with silver. I squint. Inside the box is a diamond the size of an egg, nestled in a bed of rubies, sapphires, and emeralds. This time, her brows knit together with a trace of worry, and the crowd pulses forward, tightening around us. I have never been so close to such a treasure. I step forward and feel Virian move with me, entranced. It calls gently, and I refuse the dreams that begin to form, to take me away from here. I cannot give in.

There is enough wealth in this box to buy a small village and lord over it. I shake my head, and it feels as if I am wading through mud. I step forward despite myself. I think of the poor girl who left here broken for nothing and punished for her poverty. I pinch my hands to ground myself in the pain. None of this feels right.

The diamonds and emeralds flicker, there and gone, as if conjured only by my mind. Virian swallows and turns away. Desire is painted open-mouthed on her face, though she tries to hide it.

"This is the last offer. Only one of you may leave with this box." Kalena gently closes the lid and sets the silver box on the ground. There is disappointment on her face as she steps back. "You will have to sort out who among you wants it most."

The doors of the fortress slam shut behind the Seven, and we are trapped in the courtyard, caught in the magic's spell. The crowd churns, too close, too cramped. My heart leaps into my throat when the gates slam shut. There is nowhere to run.

This will be a bloodbath.

CHAPTER NINE

The crowd surges in two directions, and Virian crashes into me. I spot a little alcove with a door set into the wall of the fortress and tug her toward it. She nearly slips out of my grasp with a scream. If she falls, she'll be trampled, so I pull with all my strength, practically carrying her up the three stairs toward the door. My back hits the wood with a loud thump. I ignore the shouting behind us to fumble frantically with the latch. It rattles in my hands, but the door does not budge.

Hells, will my luck ever change?

Two bodies bounce off our backs and shove our faces flat to the wood. I knock my head so hard that my chin bleeds. The door stops me from falling, but the churn of people kicks dust into my eyes. For a moment, my vision blurs, and all I hear are the screams of candidates either joining the fight or trying to get away. Bones crunch. Dust flies. This is a nightmare. I flatten myself against the door, sick to my stomach, and Virian huddles at my side, trembling.

When my eyes rinse clear of tears, I watch powerless as a lanky boy topples over and does not resurface. Beyond him, several dozen bodies roil like wild beasts fighting over the last scraps of meat. I don't know where to look. Everywhere, there are people moving, taller than me, smaller than me, and I struggle to keep my hands wrapped in the fabric of my sleeves as a boy reaches for the door, seeking shelter, but the crowd sweeps him away before I can pull him toward us.

I try to wrench myself away from the door, but my shoulder slams against the glass of the wall as someone knocks into me and scrambles away. The fabric of my sleeve is torn, and the gauze on my hand is soaked through with blood. Beside me, Virian huddles as small as she can, with her hands over her ears and her eyes closed.

"He's got a knife!"

The shout echoes in the courtyard, repeated by many mouths, gathering volume, and at its peak, it dies out. Swathes of black silk slice through the crowd like sharks coming up from under the waves.

Guardians, I realize. They bark orders and herd us into groups like sheep. Healers drag the injured into the fortress, while the Guardians cull the fighters from the herd and toss them out the gates like garbage.

Virian trembles beside me. "Why did they wait so long? Why didn't they stop it?" she asks, but I cannot answer. My voice is stuck in my throat.

We are forced into a thin line behind a woman clad in a plain brown tunic and tapis cloth with no explanation.

"Welcome to the glass fortress. I will take you to your rooms." She does not offer a smile. She glances down at my malong. It drags against the dirt, and I hastily refold the sloppy waist so that my ankles are visible. The sight of my worn slippers elicits a sniff and the turn of her head. I look away, flushed in the cheeks, and follow as she leads all of us through the main doors of the fortress. The doors loom dark and tall, carved from solid ironwood, depicting scenes from history: a volcano erupting, boats making their way across the ocean, the construction of the fortress.

I don't have time to look long, and I hurry after the others.

We pass through an empty throne room filled with thin, watery light. At the far end wait two high-backed seats: One for our ruler in front, and one for the Astar slightly behind. The room is as wide as the archives are long, but unlike the comforting leather-and-glue smell of books, this room smells like molding cloth and old wax polish; the windows probably haven't been opened in years. Banners that herald each of the first families cascade along arches in its high ceilings, and I spot the Jal name in the corner, nowhere near a place of prominence. We do not linger long enough for it to taunt me.

We make our way into wide, airy corridors that narrow into passages so thin that the wind whistles through them like a flute.

The next place we are led, the walls are smooth stone and braced with the wooden bones of ancient trees, bleached by the sun and time. Thick white pillars weave lace like patterns into the distance, as they repeat, mirroring one another. It is dizzying. It is like walking through a giant's rib cage.

The woman stops at a simple door and pushes it open. Inside are shelves full of linens that she hands out to each candidate in the line and instructs everyone to claim a nearby room. We're last.

"Here." The woman shoves bedsheets into our hands and leaves us standing at the end of a long corridor marked with a red silk flag. The walls already echo with the sounds of conversation, and the scrape of wooden furniture pushed around. The candidates in front of us melt into the rooms one by one. Virian and I pass room upon room, four beds a piece. Most of them are full. How are there still so many of us left?

"May we?" Virian pokes her head into one room with only two occupied beds.

"No space here." A young man wearing a fine silken tunic, shuts the door in our faces.

It seems that the other candidates have also been judging

us since we entered the gates, and it's not just the Baylan we have to watch out for. Doors slam in our faces, and we reach the end of the corridor.

"This fortress is gigantic. There must be someplace we can sleep," I say.

We trace our steps back to the main hallway and cross it. I try to hide my worry, but Virian's face mirrors mine. Without the red flag, we might not ever know there were people hidden away here. Every corridor looks the same.

The adjacent corridor is barely lit, but we peer through the first entrance to the right and find a small room with four beds shoved against its walls. It does not look hospitable. Light filters in through a single hole cut into its roof, and there are no windows. The wooden bed frames are lined with stiff mattresses and dusty blankets.

"This is as good as any." Virian leaves her slippers beside the door and falls onto one of the beds. I nod. It would be so easy to get lost, and I am in no mood to explore. She sneezes as she rolls to her side and rubs water from her eyes. "At least it's better than the floor."

Such optimism.

I set my slippers beside Virian's and choose a bed against the opposite wall. By the time I've checked the sheets for spiders, Virian is snoring. I wish oblivion might find me as easily, but worry over Kuran sews through me like a sharp needle. Fretting is the only thing keeping me together right now, and it brings me no comfort. I hope that she doesn't hate me.

The bed creaks every time I move, and I unfold my malong to full length and clutch it to my chest beneath stiff blankets. I haven't been apart from my sister for a single night for as long as I can remember. It feels wrong not to talk about our day while we brush out each other's hair. Our mother used to do it, but Kuran stepped in when she left us. It always ended our day and ushered in the night. I pretend I am in my cot, surrounded by thin canvas walls, but I cannot hold on to the illusion for long.

My thoughts drift to Teloh and the curves of his cheeks instead. His name echoes somewhere in a dark corner of my memories, and it rattles at my soul. I scratch my mind to place his name in some story, but I cannot. He makes me feel the same way that spiteful girl Arisa does: as if I should run away and never stop.

The curtain flap of our door twists in the breeze. It is enough to provide some privacy but no safety.

I remember his warning and laugh at my luck, because there is no door to lock.

I must have slept, because my eyes fly open at the sound of footsteps and a loud tapping that's accompanied by a metallic rattle. Virian snores in her bed across the room, unaware that someone is coming down the hallway. I don't know if I should wake her. I remain frozen in place, but I ball my fists so tightly that my knuckles are white.

Why didn't I bring a knife? I curse my lack of planning. I've never used a knife on anything but elderly chickens and wilted vegetables.

A shaggy-haired boy pulls the curtain aside, and I let out a breath. A spray of freckles decorates the middle-brown tone of his cheeks. A plastered cast covers the whole of his left leg, and it sticks out straight. He hugs a wooden crutch under one arm, and strings of bronze amulets peek out from beneath the neck of his tunic. They're the kind of cheap amulets a passing charlatan might sell. They tell me he's probably as superstitious as Manay Halna, but at least he is not a cultist.

I open my hands, aware that the crescents of my nails have

made marks in my palms.

"I'm Dayen," he says. "Do you have a spare bed?"

"Hello," I mumble, still too tense to laugh at myself. "Yes."

My scarf, I remember, and scramble to wind it up. I pray that the shadows hid my marks. I'm so aware of the sudden awkwardness between us that at first I do not notice the silent brown-skirted figure behind him, but Tanu's mouth gapes open like a fish at the sight of me.

I push past Dayen and grab Tanu by the shoulders, careful to ensure I only touch cloth, before he can utter a word.

"What in the Freezing Hells are you doing here, Kuya Tanu?" I ask. I can't seem to stop calling him my brother, even though he's broken my sister's heart. There is too much history between us.

I remember the first time we met. Two of his older brothers dangled a book just overhead. "Give it back!" Tanu yelled, but they just laughed and pulled it out of reach every time he jumped for it. I'd seen those big-shouldered bullies around camp and avoided them. "That's mine!"

"What, this? You think you're better than us because you read so much about religion, brat?" The eldest one, with brown hair, pressed his hands together and mimicked his voice. "Omu says we must never raise our voices. Omu says…"

I crept around the side of our tent and picked up a fist-sized rock. Before I could fling it at the boys, my sister, all of ten years old, barged straight toward them. "Give it back to him, you rotten oafs," she growled.

Kuran held out her hand and waited as though it were her right. Eventually Tanu's brothers left the book into her hands and walked away grumbling. I think Tanu fell in love with her that very moment. I picked up the two-stringed kudyapi he'd dropped when his brothers stole his book and returned it to him. After that, it was the three of us, always. He spent more time with us than his family.

"All initiates to the Baylan are assigned to housekeeping for the first year." He does not look pleased to see me, nor about the housekeeping. "Na—"

"Kuran." I cut him off, and he closes his mouth. He nods so slightly in acknowledgment that I almost miss it. There are so many things I need to ask, but questions swarm inside my skull like bees, and I grab onto the first thing that comes to mind.

"How could you run away from my sister like a coward?" My grip on his shoulders is not gentle, and he winces.

"I'm sorry." He sputters: "I thought, maybe…"

Getting words out of him sometimes feels like milking a rock.

"I love her," he admits. "But to be a Baylan has always been my dream. My parents are comfortable, and they have my brothers to watch over them. I'm old enough now, and this is my chance."

Then he didn't love her more than magic. He didn't love her more than Tigang's shining court and the immortal promises of the Diwata. Though others might praise him for it, to me it means that he didn't love her enough. And what about me? He was always someone I looked up to and thought I could rely on. My sister is not the only one he didn't love enough. I don't loosen my grip.

I step toward him. "Swear to me on your soul and the next life that you do not tell anyone who I am. You owe the Jals at least that much," I hiss into his ear.

He drops to his knees and places his hand on his chest. "I swear it."

I realize too late that Virian is awake and both she and the new boy are watching us through the doorway. Heat climbs up my neck, but Tanu remains as composed as ever. Both Virian and Dayen eye him up and down with obvious appreciation.

"Breakfast is in the great hall," Tanu mumbles, then turns on his heels.

This will be a complication. I don't think Tanu would willingly break his word, but I worry that someone might be able to drag the truth out of him.

CHAPTER TEN

I slip in and out of dreams and memories. I catch Kuran hiding behind our wagon, eating a slice of purple ube cake that she didn't want to share with me. I hear my mother laughing as we dip our toes in the Eastern Ocean for the first time. And Teloh follows me through every dream, as though my mind cannot help but summon him. I glimpse his shadow in the rain, and he is swallowed up in a storm. I glimpse the back of his head in the market, and he disappears in the crowd.

But I catch him under the light of stained glass, as beautifully rendered as a painting. *Around him bubbles a bathing pool, and the door to the baths looks as though it is locked. I dangle my feet into the water and very carefully pull twigs and leaves from his hair. He sighs into my touch as I gently comb out his curls with my fingers.*

"You really don't remember me?" he asks as he stares up into my eyes. His words are soft and pleading instead of angry, and this is how I know I am dreaming. But it feels as real as a memory.

I smell the sulfur of spring-warmed waters behind us. I feel the cold stone floor of the fortress beneath me. I slide my hands through his hair, and he closes his eyes. He turns my palm upward and presses his lips to my tender flesh. I feel aflame, like a glorious comet blazing through the heavens. And I want and want...

I jolt awake hot and flush at the touch. I don't fall asleep again.

I'm still awake when the morning gong is rung, and I follow groggily behind my new roommates.

Dayen can't walk fast, but he talks fast. His eyes drink in everything from the vaulted ceilings to the dust gathered upon the windowsills with reverence. His mouth spouts a pure stream of facts about the fortress and Bato-Ko. He talks about everything but what happened in the courtyard.

I wish I could pretend such enthusiasm, but even Virian walks in silent thought. None of us has spoken about the first test, but the memory of it digs like a splinter. Why didn't the Baylan stop things before anyone got hurt? I thought it was their job to protect us, or at least attempt to, but it didn't look like it at the time. It feels as though something is terribly wrong, but I don't have any idea what it could be. In the end, it doesn't matter. I know what I need to do. The Sundo is simply a distraction I need to get through.

I rewrap my scarf for the third time and check my reflection in the smooth stone of the wall. All my marks remain hidden, but the silk doesn't sit right. Nothing does. I'm not sure if I'm more nervous about the Sundo or being trapped in a room full of people I cannot escape.

"The Healers wrote an orasyon onto my bones, so I should be free of this crutch in a couple of days." Dayen swings around to look at Virian, and then at me. "Why are you here?"

His puppy eyes are large and earnest with not a pebble of guile in them, but he wears multiple amulets for luck and protection. If Dayen knew about my marks, I doubt he would speak to me at all.

I say nothing.

"If I told you that, I'd have to murder you." Virian's lips tighten, and Dayen's eyes flicker to her crooked nose. "I need to win this."

Dayen laughs, utterly missing the change in her mood. "I'm the youngest boy in my family, and the inheritance goes to my five sisters. It was either this or joining the Baylan, and we couldn't afford a magic tutor, so that was out of the question. Even if I end up without memories, it wouldn't be so bad to be fed and cared for for the rest of my days, would it? My village would honor my sacrifice."

Dayen seems far too cheerful about this. Risking your life and having every memory taken away from you doesn't seem worth the price. I still need to find a way around the memory spell, but it's more important for me to learn the layout of the fortress and where the dungeons are located. Now that I've seen a little of this place, it looks like that task may be harder than I imagined. The halls and passages make little sense, and I need to get my bearings.

"I'm more curious about your blue-eyed friend." Virian bumps me with her shoulder, and I stiffen.

"You mean Tanu? His mother is from the country of Brel in the North." I tread carefully.

"That's not what I meant," she says.

I pause before settling on an answer. I don't want to give the truth away, but I don't want to lie to them, either. "He broke my sister's heart."

Virian wrinkles her nose. "What a toad licker!"

Her polite Rythian cursing teases a smile from me.

Dayen's attention is already elsewhere. His whole body is angled toward the food arranged upon a long central table.

"Well, it looks like they're not planning to starve us out," he whispers. There are clay pots of hot soup ready to ladle. Crusty buns wait beside inviting bowls of fresh butter. Spicy sweet sausages and fragrant garlic rice scent the air. My mouth starts to water, and my stomach grumbles uncomfortably loudly.

Dayen grins at me, and I decide he might not be so terrible. "Villagers," Virian teases, but there is no bile in it.

I take a breath to ground myself, because the Sundo has hardly begun. I settle down at an empty table in front of a steaming bowl filled with ginger, rice, and chicken boiled in broth until everything falls apart. I spot golden strands of saffron in my spoon, and I am amazed that the cooks do not use turmeric as a cheap substitute to add color, as my mother did.

One day she would cook a pot of rice, and the next day it would turn into soup, and the next day, that soup would be topped with whatever was cheapest in the market. My mother was always remaking our leftovers into something new. My sister and I often made bets about what strange concoction we would have for supper the next day. My mother grew up with cooks and maids. She never learned any recipes, but she tried her best. I slurp at the soup prepared in the fortress kitchens. It's delicious, but it also is missing something I can't name. Maybe it's just that there's so much food laid out for us that this bowl doesn't feel precious. Maybe I just miss my mother.

I banish the sudden pang of loneliness and attempt to fill the empty space with soup and assess our competition.

The carefree expressions worn in the fortress courtyard don't look as convincing in the morning light. The other candidates laugh too loud, eat with too much gusto, and lean back too lazily. But I catch everyone eyeing everyone, the whispers to friends, and the handshakes. Dayen points out groups among the candidates: first families, minor families, alliances. It's dizzying. It seems like most of those who remain come from the first families. They flaunt their wealth and influence like peacocks. The Jals are a first family, but what use is a first family if you have none of its connections?

"Some families hire private tutors for the Sundo, but those tutors cost more than my life." Even though his belly is full,

Dayen still looks hungry.

It's the first I've heard of such a practice, but Virian simply shrugs. "No one knows what will happen during the competition except the Seven. We've got as good a chance as anyone else. We can get further if we work together?" She looks at us both and opens a pouch at her waist. Inside are scraps of paper, drawing charcoal, and chalk for writing spells. "I know a little magic."

Maybe Reshar was right to try to keep me out, but he also misjudged me. I do not give up so easily, and like Virian, I *need* this.

I nod a little too slowly, but Dayen slaps her hands as if they've been friends forever. I need them, and I want to trust them, but I'm not sure I can.

The bowls and plates are carried away by brown-skirted Baylan initiates, and the Seven Datus return to address us. Kalena speaks first, her smiling face framed by dark waves of hair. Today she wears trousers and a tunic, but just like yesterday, her clothes are spotlessly white, and a sun disk gleams at her throat.

"Congratulations, candidates. You have passed the first test. On behalf of the Interpreters sect, I welcome you. The Interpreters' test is meant to weed out the greedy and weak willed. Our ruler must show strength of character, and you have shown it.

"As Interpreters, we speak to the Diwata themselves and make the laws that keep you safe. We follow the Heavens' guidance to create peace and prosperity in Tigang. The seven sects govern alongside the ruler. All of us are servants of Tigang, doing our best to keep you safe and fed, and your souls free."

I don't trust the warmth in this woman's smile. She speaks too much like a cultist, and if the test was of her design, there is no way I can afford to believe the honey in her voice. But I watch the others lap it up.

"Every morning at dawn, we will gather here. There is no need to prepare or to study, because we have created new tests specifically for this cycle. Each test will challenge your mind, your body, and your soul. Some of you will not survive. Some of you will be hurt. We will try to keep you safe, but magic can be as unpredictable as the Diwata."

That means as unpredictable as a summer storm or as devastating as a plague. I shiver and share a glance with Virian. She nervously scratches at her nose.

"The Datus will grant points based on your character and conduct. We will not tell you your score or where you stand amongst your peers. Failing a test does not mean automatic expulsion, because your overall score is what matters, but it will result in a deduction. Any candidates that fall below a certain score will be removed from the Sundo, but the candidate with the highest score will be crowned the next ruler of Tigang."

Virian clears her throat and raises a hand. "What happens if two candidates have an equal score?"

"Then our beloved Astar will provide us guidance," she replies with a fond smile.

I shudder at the thought of who Arisa might choose.

Kalena spreads out her hands, palms up, like a vision of Omu herself. "You may use any free time as you wish. All unlocked doors in the fortress are yours to open, but please do not wander at night. The fortress is confusing, and I do not want you to go missing." She continues to smile, but I spy cracks in her expression now, as if the flesh of her face is a soft mask that hides porcelain beneath.

But this is good news at last. I will be able to roam the fortress freely. Once I find the dungeons, I'll need to figure out how to get in and out. No doubt they must be guarded.

"Each Datu shall conduct one test, and on the eighth day we shall select the new ruler of Tigang. You shall all be fetched for the second test this afternoon."

Kalena bows politely and leaves, but Guardians block each of the hall's exits. Reshar walks to the head of the room, his shoulders hunched like a vulture. Unlike Kalena, he hasn't changed his clothes at all. He wears the same loosely tied robe he wore yesterday, with his tattoos on display.

"There's one among you that should not be here." He inclines his head, and the Guardians fan out.

I lower my head and shrink into the bench. I finish my breakfast as a Guardian goes right past our table and grabs a youngish-looking boy nearby. My heart thuds quietly.

Virian and I look at each other, heads askance, and the candidates murmur, unsure if we have been dismissed. Reshar stares at us, unmoving.

"This boy's parents did not give him permission to be here. We will return him home to face their punishment." He licks his dry lips absently as the Guardians drag the boy out of the room. Today, it was him. Tomorrow, it might be me.

I swallow and check for extra exits. I note three other doors and a pierced screen that initiates disappear behind with their cleaning supplies in tow.

If this is not a test, I need to go. I need to get word to Kuran, even if she will hate me for it. I need to explain so that she doesn't come for me. But how?

"How young you all are." The din of conversation drops away at the sound of Reshar's voice. "I remember being young once."

"Really? He looks like he was born just as he is, tattoos and all," Virian whispers so loudly that a few of the candidates near us snicker.

I nudge Virian with my elbow. "What sect does he head, and how can I avoid it?"

"He's a Seeker. You can't avoid them. They find you if they want to." She leans close and brushes her fringe out of her eyes.

"My cousin told me that he's the best inquisitor they have in Bato-Ko. He can make anyone confess to anything."

I freeze. The Seekers sect is the smallest in numbers but also the most feared. Their ways are secret: torture, spying, manipulation. It's said a powerful Seeker's magic can find anything, including the truth.

I suspect Reshar's methods are not gentle, but nothing about the Baylan is.

He drones on about the Sundo and the honor of ruling our country, but the lines feel memorized. His sunken eyes scan us all, one by one, so I shift myself out of his line of sight.

"This is a fine time to get to know one another, because you may need help for the tests that come." His teeth flash white like a warning. "And you should know who among you is weak, too. But remember: Physical harm against your fellow candidates will not be tolerated *if caught*."

If caught.

A few candidates smirk to themselves. We need to be careful.

When Reshar departs the hall, conversations rush to fill the space like water from a dam unblocked.

"Oh, Dayen." Virian tugs at my sleeve.

It's hard to miss him. He leans close to a solid young man with filigreed gold hoops in his ears and a long gold chain on his neck. Dayen swallows every word that falls out of the boy's mouth. Ingo. He's from one of the first families, comfortably rich and here for the glory of his house. I curl my lip. Dayen's eyes are open so wide that I worry that Ingo will step right through them and pinch out the lights.

"Maybe we should rescue him," I suggest, testing out our fledgling alliance.

Virian agrees with an exaggerated bob of her head. We make our way over to Ingo's small circle, but I walk a little off to Virian's side and hope this will be over quickly.

Two other boys and a serious-looking girl stand arguing in a circle around Ingo. The girl's gaze reminds me of a hawk, as if she is looking straight into the heart of everyone around her instead of at them. The patterned magenta tapis she wears is fixed in place with a wide, brass-buckled belt, and the weave tells me that she is from a province of Tigang to the north.

"And why would you make a good Raja?" Dayen asks Ingo.

"It is what my family raised me for. I know all the laws, and I know more orasyons than some of the Baylan here." From his lips, the words do not sound like bragging, just statement of fact.

"It is not just law or magic that are important." The girl's accent confirms my guess.

"This debate again, Galaya?" Ingo asks, but the girl, Galaya, looks down at my bandaged palm. I curse that Virian is too short to hide behind. Ingo may not be a braggart, but I've dealt with enough rich sons to know what to expect from him. If you are not equally rich, you are invisible. He startles when he notices us standing so close.

"To open the Sundo is auspicious." Galaya inclines her head in my direction.

I'm not sure if it is auspicious or an ill omen, but I don't correct her. Galaya returns to addressing the circle. "For all our Tigangi pageantry, this country is little more than a speck on a crumbling rock. We do not even grow our own rice. Lucky for now, our gold mines are still rich, but when they run dry? What then?" When she moves, I spy a smaller version of Kalena's sun disk hanging at her neck and take a step away from her. She's a cultist. "We are soft and spoiled. We've forgotten how to worship the sun. We no longer walk the path of Omu's bright vision. We do not look forward, only back. *I* would steer you true." With a wave of her hand, she stalks away.

"I bet Galaya and her cult still triple bolt their doors at nightfall." Someone snickers.

"They do this out of respect, not fear." Ingo silences their teasing, and they close their mouths, but one boy in the circle, with a mouth so narrow his face looks pinched from perpetual sneering, signals us. I do not grin back.

"Guess what I found?" he asks, drawing us close and checking over his shoulder.

Dayen raises an expectant brow and leans forward on his crutch.

"A locked door."

CHAPTER ELEVEN

I follow because I need to see more of the fortress. It would look less suspicious if I didn't go off on my own.

We wander back toward our sleeping quarters and take a left turn away from everything familiar. We stop at a mahogany door. It looms above us, taller than Dayen with his arms extended to the sky. Many of the rooms I've seen in the fortress do not have doors, but those that remain are made of the same polished hardwood carved over with scenes from Arawan. I suspect they are as old as the fortress, and that no one has bothered to replace any that were damaged.

"This is a bad idea. It's against the rules," Virian warns. She nervously tucks her hair behind her ear.

"Scared, broken nose?" Nen, the boy with the pinched mouth, scoffs at us. "What do you think is behind it? The Baylan have to be hiding all kinds of secrets in this fortress."

"Your doom," I mutter under my breath, but he hears it. Nen sticks out his thumb in insult, but I don't bite back. This is folly I want no part of, but Dayen seems far too intrigued.

"Prove to us how brave you are." Nen lifts his chin to Ingo, the chosen one. "That you are worthy and unafraid."

Ingo narrows his eyes and presses an ear to the wood. He taps his ring-clad fingers against it. After a few moments of utter silence, he lets out a long sigh. "This is childish nonsense. I will not throw away my chance for this." Ingo lifts his chin and walks away like a prince, but Dayen hesitates. Nen slaps him on the arm, and another boy presses him forward.

Nen produces two small, flat needles between his fingers and waves his hand. "You don't even have to do the hard part. I've already unlocked it for you."

"Don't," I warn, but Dayen's eyes betray an appetite to forge bonds with these privileged fools. I fight the impulse to drag him away. He should know these rich brats will never see him as one of them, but I could never convince him of it.

"Come on, farm boy. My bet is that you're stronger than you look. You could push it open before anyone sees," Nen says, and Dayen fidgets with the strings of his amulets.

My estimation of Nen drops with every passing minute, a record surpassed only by Reshar. I run a fingertip over the doorframe and inspect its surface. The wood is smooth, but the iron of its bolts is rough under my skin, corroded by the fine salt spray of the sea that enters through a nearby window. I breathe in the scent of lavender and lemon. It's familiar somehow.

"Let's go, Dayen." Virian tugs at his arm, but he's still fixated on the door, brows pressed together. "This isn't part of the competition. Quickly, before someone sees us."

"We're all going to end up either dead or have our minds wiped, because Ingo's going to win this. We might as well have some fun while we're here." Nen shrugs as though he's already lost. Maybe he believes it, but I don't. Not yet, anyway.

Dayen hesitates, but his fingers lift.

"No." Suddenly certain, I shove my shoulder so hard against the door that my joints crack. It flies open with a grunt of effort, revealing a closet full of bedding, towels, and cleaning brushes. Bundles of lavender hang from the shelves to ward off moths, just like in the linen room I saw yesterday.

Nen and his friend fold over, laughing so hard they might

lose their breakfasts. I am so relieved I almost fall into the room.

"You sons of goats! Go swallow rocks and jump into the ocean!" Virian shouts and chases them off.

"What if this wasn't just some childish prank?" I ask Dayen as we walk back to our room. Heavens help me, I am becoming my mother when I'd rather be more like Kuran. My sister would have simply laughed.

Dayen's shoulders droop, and there is a mix of relief and apology on his face. He leans against his crutch, and I turn away, ashamed.

"How did you know it wasn't dangerous?" he asks.

"Even Nen wouldn't risk getting thrown out of the Sundo so soon, unless he's as foolish as he seems." I also watched brown-clad initiates carting our dirty dishes down that hallway, so I guessed it was unlikely to hold treasures.

"Kur—"

I flinch away from Virian as she tries to sweep us both into her arms outside our room. Rythians. They like touching. I take a step aside, and a question flickers over her face, but I don't get a chance to answer it.

"What the Hells? Holy Omu." Dayen grabs his amulets as he steps inside the doorway. Virian gasps, and I push past her and into the room.

A headless rat lies in the middle of the floor, and written in its blood are two words: *Go home.*

"Who would do this?" Dayen asks. Someone took a knife to his spare clothes; Virian's pack lies ripped open; our beds and pillows lie in shreds.

"Any of them," I say quietly. "We need to be better prepared."

I pull open cabinet drawers and find a brush and some ink. Virian and Dayen watch as I attempt to recreate the orasyon of protection I saw on Yirin's fence on the wood of our lintel. I frown at it, and after a moment of consideration, I add a little extra that Kuran taught me. I seal it with spit and hope it is enough to keep us safe.

I make each of them spit and press their thumbs to the wood of the doorframe. "I don't know if the magic will work. I've never tried something like this before."

"It looks decent, but I have another idea." Virian pulls a short hairpin from the braid in her hair and dips it in the ink. "This spell is a family secret." She pulls down the neck of her tunic and shows us a small black tattoo. "Tap the mark three times fast if you are in trouble, and we will know where you are."

Dayen doesn't hesitate. He pulls off his tunic. He's so bony that I wonder if his parents are poor or if everything he eats goes directly into growing.

"Wait." My heart stutters at this impulse decision, but I'd rather they knew. How can I trust them if they can't trust me? I swallow, and my voice comes out all air. "I take my vows seriously, but I have a secret. Tell no one, and I swear by my lives that I am with you until the end, even if you are not with me." I balance on the edge of my ruined bed, scarf in my hand. I avert my eyes, because I've already imagined how this will go, but to my surprise, Virian simply laughs when I unwind my blue scarf. It is a broken sound.

"Do you know how many unwanted children fill the halls of the fortress? Sometimes I think those old superstitions are the only way the Baylan fill their ranks." Her voice is all salt and hard edges. "Just look at Arisa! She has marks, and she doesn't bother to hide them."

But she's the Astar reborn, so she doesn't need to hide them. I frown.

Dayen stares, and I recognize the fear that creeps around the edges of his expression at the sight of my marks. I am disappointed but not surprised. Teloh, Arisa, and Reshar, on the other hand, seem to despise me for utterly unknown reasons, so

I know it's not just my marks. Perhaps I am not easy to like. I rub at my heart and try not to show how much every rejection hurts.

"What do you think the curse does?" He tries to keep his voice light.

I remain still as a statue, wishing I were stone. I try to keep my voice even, but it comes out all wobbly. "I don't really know— only that Manay Halna would blame me for everything that ever displeased her: the rain on one day, or the heat on another, or her babies refusing to nap. My mother never believed it was dangerous."

"A sensible woman," Virian says. "You Tigangi are so superstitious. No one thinks twice of those things in Rythia, and I'm quite sure birthmarks are not catchable like the pox. Blemished skin is the least of your worries." Her expression is the painting of a Demon come to life—twisted lips, broken nose, brows raised, and eyes burning hot. "I am a bigger problem. You will need to beat me to survive the Sundo intact. Remember that, Kuran Jal. That will not be an easy feat." Virian thrusts out her fist. "But by my lives I swear I am with you until the end."

Dayen doesn't look happy. He hesitates a moment longer but reaches out, palm up. "I also swear by my lives. I am with you both."

We seal the deal with spit, and to his credit, he resists pulling his hand away too quickly.

Virian draws a small diagram over Dayen's heart and makes a matching one beneath my collarbone. A brief heat pulses against my skin, like I snuffed out a candle with my fingers and nothing more.

When we are done, our fingers are blue and sticky: Dayen from touching the paint before it's dry, and both Virian and I from working with it.

We hardly know one another, but our fates are twined together now. I rewrap my scarf in awkward silence.

"Hello?"

We all jump at the voice.

When I pull the doorway curtain aside, I catch Tanu shoving a pair of spectacles into a pocket, and a hint of a blush spots his cheeks. So, the boy has some vanity after all, and it almost amuses me to discover something new about him after so long. His blue eyes go wide at the mess in our room. "What happened?"

"Someone's just trying to scare us." I smile and try not to sound worried. He's the only familiar thing in the whole fortress, and I feel guilty for asking more of him, but he's the only one who could ever change my sister's mind. "I wanted to find you because my sister is probably going sick with worry. Can you send word that I'm fine and not to come get me? This is my choice. I hope she can respect that."

"I will." He puts a hand on my shoulder. It's as warm and solid as he always is. "But I came here to summon you for the second test. Go, and I'll clean this up."

I nod. The sooner this is over with, the sooner I can start looking for my mother.

✳ ☽ ✳ ☾ ✳

CHAPTER TWELVE

The head Cultivator, Kormar, hurries a group of ten candidates through the twisting hallways of the fortress. I try to remember the way, but each branching corridor looks the same as the last: all cold stone, dust, and mirrors.

"The Cultivators are charged with ensuring Tigang's fields grow lush and weaving wards into the trees that protect our cities," Kormar explains. They manage agriculture in Tigang, and without them, nothing would grow on our rocky soil. They are vital to our country's survival, and I respect that.

Datu Kormar has an elegance about her, despite her dirt-stained clothing. The asog's face glows a luminous shade of deep, polished walnut. The apron hung with gardening tools could be her armor; the shears and spades, her swords.

We head west, toward the ocean, and the halls brighten as we approach the glass outer wall. She stops at double doors carved with vines, and when she pushes them open, I drink in the moist air. Beyond the door is a rainforest in miniature.

Here, the rock was blasted away, and the glass wall was curved into a gently sloping roof. The room is so immense that its walls are hidden by a dark canopy of plants that would never survive a single winter in Tigang. Birds flash colors as they flee from us and scatter into the dark canopy. Wet leaves lick at my skin as if to taste me as I pass; the trees rustle as though they are whispering to one another.

A boy in a yellow tunic shoves past and pushes me into a cluster of leaves. Virian shoves him back and slings her arm through mine and Dayen's like a bodyguard. "We're going to beat those jerks."

I hunch into myself with a grimace. I'm the last thing the other candidates should be worrying about.

At the center of the indoor rainforest grows a massive balete tree. Its trunks twine together, and vines drip from warded branches, stretching thirstily toward soil that is as black as coffee grounds.

"Astar planted this tree with a seed from Arawan. It was she who taught us immortal magic and founded our seven Baylan sects. We Cultivators tend to this tree, but this magic is not ours to control; it is yours." Kormar points out white papers tucked into its nooks and crannies. "This tree has watched over the fortress since it was built. It has been nourished by the magic of the Baylan within these walls, and it will reveal the questions in your heart. To pass the test, you must answer three questions truthfully. The ruler of Tigang must have a pure soul, and this magic will judge yours."

"I've heard that this balete was a Baylan that Omu cursed for a thousand years." A girl stares at it wide-eyed. Kormar simply shakes her head with a small smile. I cannot tell if she is amused or sad. Either way, it isn't a denial.

I look to Virian, but she stands confidently beside me with her hands on her hips. "Easy." She grins. She gazes at the tree with awe and determination, not fear, but I shift from foot to foot on the soft, sinking dirt. The other candidates seem small and diminished beside it, and even the boy in the yellow tunic hangs back.

Kormar guides us apart and spaces the ten of us around the tree. Something beyond the tree's hulking size is unnerving. The air feels so charged with energy that my fingers and toes prickle with pins and needles.

"You may begin!" Kormar shouts, and startled birds spill out of the tree trunk like a cloud of locusts. I huddle to the earth as wings and claws scratch my back. They disappear into the canopy around us, and when I get up, shaking, none of the other candidates are in sight.

Just birds. Just a tree. I take a deep breath and pluck a paper that's wedged between two branches and unfurl it. At first the paper is blank, but as I glower, a line of words appears in my own handwriting.

What kind of Reyna would you be? it asks. Strangely, I hear the words in Teloh's voice, and I picture the Guardian glaring.

I consider my answer with care. "Fair," I say, and the tree rustles softly. *True*, the paper reveals.

A scream is followed by a thud, and I crane my neck to see what's happening. Vines stretch, and I spot a flash of yellow. The boy who pushed me in the grove shrieks as he's lifted into the balete's branches by his wrists. My body tenses as I eye the branches, but they remain unmoving around me.

"Focus on your test, candidates!" Kormar cuts the boy free, and he hits the ground with a whimper. "There is nothing to worry about," she says, but she braids twigs into patterns of protection when she thinks no one is watching, and glances at the tree nervously. I don't have a good feeling about this, regardless of her reassurances.

I snatch a second paper, and words slowly ghost across its surface. *Why did you come here?* it asks in black ink.

"I want to be Reyna," I whisper. For several breaths, nothing happens, but my question is replaced by a single word: *Liar.*

A root shoots out of the dirt and seizes me by the ankle. Its grip tightens and drags me toward the balete's trunk. I drop the paper and struggle to untangle myself.

"To save my mother!" My stomach hits the ground, and I rake my hands to grasp hold of anything I can, but the roots writhe like snakes and I don't find purchase. What else could it be? I kick at the tree as the soil opens around my legs and roots drag me downward. My knees disappear into a hole, and I scream. The roots wrap tightly around my legs, and the weight of the earth presses down, suffocating my body. Their hold tightens further and drags me deeper. My chin hits the dirt, and I flail my arms as the tree sweeps leaves overhead. It's going to bury me alive. I'm going to die here. Struggling only sinks me faster into the loose earth.

"Because I'm tired of all the hateful people and the dusty roads. I want to prove I'm not as worthless as everyone thinks. Maybe I'm just being selfish, but I want more!"

I cough up dirt as the roots release me and tremble as I dig myself free. The worst part is, although I would deny my selfishness to everyone, including my sister, it's true.

Vines surround me as I climb out of the pit I nearly died in. Bits of torn cloth peek out from between the knots on the balete's trunk. Branches that look too much like arms turned to wood stretch out toward me as if there are people trapped inside, begging for help.

I'm not a pious person, but I start to pray. *Heavenly Omu*, I stutter.

The tree creaks and groans like an old ship, and it leans toward me. A vine rustles and pokes me in the back. Every muscle in my body locks into place. I search nearby, but neither Virian nor Dayen is in my line of sight. Every instinct screams *flee*, but I have only one question left to answer.

I snatch a paper above my head and count breaths to calm myself as I wait. Three breaths, twelve breaths, and finally words spread across the length of paper in dark red, as if written with blood. My mouth dries.

Why do you fear me?

"Who are you?" I whisper. The red letters slide down to the edge of the paper and gather into a bead of red liquid. It drips to the dirt, leaving the paper blank. I wait for another question, but none comes. My skin crawls as I wait for an answer.

Kormar walks in my direction. "Well done…"

But when I move toward her, a noose of vines slips over my head and lifts me to my toes. Those branches that looked so much like arms begin to writhe and reach for me. I can't breathe; I can't think. I wish I was home. I dangle, holding on to the vine, but I'm choking. I gasp for air and desperately try to slip my fingers between the vine and my throat.

The tree snatches everything that moves and plucks fleeing birds from the air. I struggle as the balete drags me toward its center. Kormar screams as the tree pulls another boy upside down by his ankles. He hammers his fists against the snaking vines, but they close over his mouth as the canopy swallows him. A vine whips around Kormar's waist, and it tears her away from me. I can't even scream. I sputter for air and kick my legs, but I can't save her. I can't save anyone.

Kormar twists and hacks at the vine with her shears, but roots reach out from the soil and pin her down. The screams echo against the glass wall, and leaves hiss together.

More vines tangle around my arms and waist. They whip around my ankles, squeeze the air out of my lungs, and my vision begins to slip. I am being drawn upward this time, into the canopy where the other boys met their end. Why is everything doomed to go wrong around me, when I have done nothing wrong? I save my last desperate breaths for the truth.

"I fear that I deserve to be cursed. That everything *is* my fault and there is no one else to blame," I cry.

And then it stops. The vines drop away, and I fall to the ground in a quivering heap. Kormar rushes to my side and pulls me free of the roots knotted around my legs.

I cling to her and dig my nails into her arms as I steady myself, but she does not protest.

"This should not have happened," she says, then looks me up and down. Her eyes are on my neck. I don't know what she's seen, but I shrink from her gaze. "Rest. Have a bath and something to eat. All will be well soon." She gently pries my hand from her arm and dismisses me.

It's me. It's my fault. It's my curse bringing everyone bad luck, I want to say, but I cannot move my mouth to admit it.

CHAPTER THIRTEEN

White plaster pokes through a pile of leaves. I rush over and dig through the shrubbery. "Are you okay?" I drag Dayen upright and pass him his crutch.

He spits dirt from his mouth and gasps for air. "I think I'll be fine. You?"

Virian comes running, whole and unharmed, except for the tangle of leaves in her hair.

"I need some air. I'll meet you back at our room." I stumble away, out of the room of plants, out of sight, before they can question me further.

I brace myself against the solid walls of the glass fortress. Each breath I take feels too shallow and too short. It feels like one of the balete's roots burrowed deep under my skin and is squeezing me tight.

There's also a scratching in my chest, as if something inside has wakened from a long, deep slumber. Something pushes and tugs my heart, as though it wants to pull me apart. Voices scream in my head, but I don't hear words, only one emotion: rage.

We Tigangi believe that the ghosts of our past selves live inside our heart. I've always feared my heart was faulty because it never once leaped at meeting someone or whispered secrets to guide me. I've always believed there was something wrong with my heart, or maybe with me.

But now the ghosts are awake and howling. I stumble down the hallway to escape them, but I can't. Halna's voice echoes the worst of my thoughts: *Selfish, Narra! See what you have done?*

I run through spiraling hallways that are so bright I shield my eyes from the glare. I go up and up—two floors, maybe three. I stop counting. I want to find Inay, but no path I turn seems to lead me any closer to the dungeons. The whole fortress feels like it was built to magnify the glory of the Heavens rather than to make any obvious sense. I'm lost but I don't care. I want the feeling in my chest to stop.

The ocean greets me at the end of a long corridor, and I rush to meet it. The water is stormy and roiling today, the crashing of the waves a roar that matches the turmoil within me. Here, the fortress ends in a sheer cliff that drops into the waves, too high to scale and too slick for any to try. A thin stone rail is the only thing that might keep me from falling, and it slides beneath my outstretched fingers, worn smooth where it was once sharp. I suck in a deep breath to calm myself.

Time falls away. In one eye, I stare into the thrashing deep, and in the other, I see Teloh. *I grasp his hands in a vice, as though I am afraid to let go.*

My fingers are thick and callused, and it is not hunger I see in his eyes but fear. Yet his presence calms me. I am not afraid when he is near. When he is not, I stalk these empty corridors like a restless ghost, forever haunted by a past I cannot change.

"She will come for me. I don't know how much time I have left." *My voice is low and deeper in my throat.* *"If something happens, do not let me come back here. Promise me that you won't let the Baylan keep me."* *This time, Teloh is wearing the black of the Guardians. This vision feels newer than the others. "Omu's plan cannot come to pass. I—"*

"Of course, you would never make things easy for me, but I would know you anywhere, in any form." *He sighs and squeezes*

my hands. When he looks at me, it feels like the whole universe stops spinning. He gently reaches out to cup my cheek in his palm, and I close my eyes so that nothing exists but his gentle caress. "I promise."

The vision releases me, and I lean over the rail to suck in a deep breath. The world keeps spinning around me as the past and present collide. What is happening to me?

I turn around, dizzied, and catch a twitch of movement in the distance.

A lone Guardian walks down the hallway. He walks head down, with his shoulders hunched, as if he carries an invisible stone upon his back. A curved blade dips down from one hand, stained red. He slowly unwinds a dark cloth that obscures all but his eyes. His face is smudged, no…splattered with red.

Now my ghosts growl a warning that rattles my ribs. I do not know how to interpret the feeling, only that I have been here before, seen this before. Somehow all things seem believable in Bato-Ko, where all time loops endlessly.

Teloh's eyes lock onto mine as if they are magnets. He steps over the threshold and onto the windy outcropping. I am frozen as he draws near, close, so close. "Have you really gone through all this trouble just to kill yourself? There are nicer places elsewhere in Tigang."

His words break the spell. I turn again and lean over the railing to avoid his unsettling gaze, and I fiddle with my scarf. "The view is worth it." I pretend lightness, when all my thoughts would drown me. A great wave sends a spray of water over us, and I shiver. "I have traveled the entire coast, and I find this one particularly lovely."

"I'm not going to catch you if you jump or if you trip and fall by accident. And if you meant to bathe, I can show you where the facilities are. This is not the most efficient means to that end." He wipes his sword upon the silk of his sash. The cloth merchant that I am winces at the ill treatment of such fine material.

"A bath actually does sound nice, though you need one more than I."

"Would it be better if I lied and told you I butchered a cow?" He runs a hand through his errant curls. Damn him to the hells, his looks are unfair, and he knows it.

"You do not look remorseful." I glance at his sword. So, he is Arisa's personal assassin. No wonder everyone keeps their distance.

"Why should I be? I'm not here of my own free will, nor do I murder people unless ordered. Not all cages have doors." He trembles slightly, fingers tapping against his trousers, as if it takes all the effort in the world to remain still as he waits for my answer.

He is not what I expect, but how could have I expected this? He is dangerous, but I am cursed. He knows it, yet he does not seem bothered by it. And what I feel when he is around is not as simple as either attraction or fear. I am tempted to pick at the feeling like a scab, even if it hurts.

"Lead on." I ignore my better judgment and the quaking in my heart.

What a pretty pair of monsters we make.

He takes a convoluted route and makes small talk as we go. He explains that the fortress is divided into four palaces, named for each of Tigang's seasons. The Spring Palace was where I ran from, where the greenhouse is located, and Baylan reside. The Summer Palace contains the great hall, the throne room, the kitchens, and it is where all the candidates lodge. The Winter Palace makes up the lower levels of the fortress. Though he doesn't say it, I bet the dungeons are in the Winter Palace, but I haven't yet stumbled on its entrance.

I nod and make silent notes as I fight the warnings that would have me run from him. It takes every effort not to look cowed as we walk through the abandoned Autumn Palace together.

The halls here are leaf-littered and dark, but the sense that I have seen this, or dreamed this, lingers here the strongest, and the ghosts in me continue to scrape and tug in agitation. Their featherlight touches and bumps stir an aching in my heart, but I don't understand their strange language.

Teloh leads me to an unimpressive door, but when he pushes it open, light pours out. Colors stream through a stained glass roof, and they fracture our bodies into firelight and autumn hues.

Unlike the dusty rooms we passed, these baths are spotless. Pipes with hot and cold water wait ready to spill into deep wooden wash buckets. A pool lined with tiles waits in its center. There is no water in it now, but a small splash lingers in its bottom.

"Let me know when you're done so I can have a turn." Teloh walks out before I can ask any questions.

It feels as though I'm intruding in someone else's private space, but I take off my slippers, and the marble is cold beneath my feet. I breathe in the sulfur smell of the spring water. It's real. I have seen this room in my dreams, and I don't understand why.

But I'd be a fool to deny any small pleasure I can take from the fortress, so I fill a bucket, then take the longest bath of my life. I crouch on the floor and pour endless scoops of steaming water over my head with a tabo. I want it to wash the tension from my limbs and the dirt from my clothes, but no matter how hard I scrub, I don't feel clean or in control.

Teloh is waiting, leaning against the opposite wall when I push the door open a crack. Though I spot a wrinkle of impatience on his face, he says nothing. He holds a clean malong between outstretched palms. I try not to flinch when I take the fine cloth from him. I don't buy his innocent expression, because he hasn't brought me a clean tunic to wear with it. My old tunic is still dripping wet.

I close the door, and I sling my damp hair over one shoulder. I knot the cloth over my chest like Kuran would and leave my shoulders bare. It would be unthinkable if I were not alone, and I dare to look boldly at my reflection in a mirror.

I look small and unsure. Virian's spell is a small splotchy design beneath my collarbone, and birthmarks mar the column of my throat in an ugly way. I cannot hold my own stare. I retie my malong over one shoulder and wind my filthy scarf back on. It can't be helped.

I open the door and find Teloh waiting there still. He pushes off the wall and reaches out for me—no, for my scarf. He adjusts the tails of it over the parts of my marks that a tunic usually hides. There's a look in his eyes I can't read, and as the tip of his finger lightly brushes my skin, I prickle all over. I recall every vision I've had of him, and they remain sharper than my mother's face. I should be ashamed, but instead I wish for more. He makes me feel as though my curse doesn't matter; as though *I* matter.

I take a step back, suddenly aware of how close we are standing. I feel the heat of him, even though we aren't touching. Though I still can't meet his eyes, I keep my gaze on his dark, glossy hair, my fingers itching to tuck a few stray curls behind his ears. Somehow, I know he hates his hair in his face. I also know, beyond a doubt, that he is mad at me. I can think of no explanation other than that we have met in lives before this one, and that the visions I've seen are true.

Perhaps this is why my ghosts have rattled to life now, why he is so familiar, but I still don't understand what it means or if it is important.

"Who are you?" I whisper, but Teloh whips up straight as if someone grabbed his kris and stabbed it between his shoulders. His eyes are ice, ready to crack, and they are not fixed on anything I can see. He is a terror like this: blood-flecked, teeth bared.

"Arisa is calling." Her name hits me like a slap in the face. The warning in it brings me back to my senses. "The corridor to the left will lead you to the great hall."

He struggles — Against pain? Against words? — as he walks away from me, still bloody.

I let out a breath. What was I thinking? It is ridiculous, surely, to trifle with Arisa's assassin. The Astar is the one I should be worrying about if I want to make it through the Sundo. No matter how alluring my visions may be, they are the past, and this is now. In this life, Teloh is my enemy.

I find the path back to the great hall, still ruddy in the cheeks. My mother's life is all that matters, and I cannot afford the Guardian's distraction. I risk Arisa's wrath by consorting with him.

I must survive the Sundo long enough to get to my mother. I'm not leaving the fortress without her.

Glass clatters to the floor behind me.

I twist around and frown at the familiar Archivist. "Manong Alen?"

He pushes away from a statue surrounded by shattered wish candles, swaying and stumbling toward me. In one hand, he clutches an orasyon for tracking. A few black strands of hair are glued to the center of the paper. *My* hair? He looks even more frail than when I saw him last.

"Are you well, Manong?" I set my wet clothes onto the floor and reach out to steady him. The small rash I noticed the first day we met in the archives has spread up his neck and balding scalp. "What's going on? Is this about my mother, Shora?"

He opens his mouth, and where his tongue should be is a bloody stump. I choke down my scream, because he slides the sleeve of his tunic up to his elbow. A delicate spell was inked onto his forearm, fingernail scratches cut through it. Rashes weep around the orasyon.

Baylan appear in the hallway and race toward us. *Help*, Alen mouths soundlessly and presses the crumpled tracking spell into my hands. He tears off the hair and swallows it. It *is* my hair, I realize. It's how he found me.

"Please, what is this about?" I grip his shaking shoulders.

He moves his mouth. *Astar.*

Arisa? I frown. "What about Arisa, Manong?"

Find Shora. He points at an orange thread glued to the edge of the paper.

"Manong Alen! There you are…"

I pull away as two Healers and a Guardian surround him, all of whom I do not recognize. "Thank you for keeping an eye on him, child. Poor Manong went wandering. He's very sick. Come on now. Come back with us," a Baylan chides the old man.

"Where are you taking him?" I ask.

"To the infirmary. Our Healers will take good care of him."

He slumps as they drag him off, as though defeated. I wish I could do something, but what? I tuck the orasyon into my malong, grateful that the Baylan did not notice it. He risked himself to get it to me, and I need to find out why.

I return to our freshly cleaned room, certain of only two things: I need every advantage that I can muster to get my mother free, and I must use my wits to stay alive until I am able to. But as I make plans, a nagging thought refuses to let go. Something bigger than the Sundo is happening here, and my mother is at the center of it.

CHAPTER FOURTEEN

I t's not late, but Virian and Dayen snore away, exhausted. I
puzzle over everything that's happened and realize that my
life story is full of holes. This I know: A year after I was born,
my father died, and my mother fled Bato-Ko with us children.
This I do not: Why she left Bato-Ko, what caused a rift with her
mother, what her life was like before I was born, and why she
was arrested.

Whatever she did must have been terrible. Enough to
warrant a possible death sentence almost seventeen years later.
Death is usually reserved for only the worst of criminals, but
my mother is no thief, or we would never have lived with so
little. Nor do I think my mother is a murderer, because she
always punished Kuran for getting into fights. That only leaves
treason. She hates the Baylan—yet again, I don't know why. I
wish I could just talk to her. The questions circle in my head like
goldfish in a bowl.

I roll over in my bed. Everything in the room is clean, but
I still imagine those bloody words on the floor. *Go home*, they
taunt, as if there's anywhere I can call home anymore.

I toss and turn on my new mattress, folding and unfolding
the Archivist's tracking spell. I think that the orange thread is a
piece of my mother's headwrap. From what I know of tracking
spells, you need something that belongs to a person to find

them. Alen found me using hair he yanked off my head, and he swallowed the evidence so that the Guardians would not find out.

This spell feels like a lucky gift that I so badly need, but I don't know if I can risk the corridors of the fortress in the dark. Kalena warned against it, and something in my gut tells me there is truth to the danger.

A quiet knock on the doorframe sends my questions scattering. I stuff the paper under my mattress and draw back the curtain.

"Kuya Tan—"

A white-toothed smile slices the darkness like a knife. "Ahh, Kuran Jal. Come walk with me so we don't wake the others." Arisa's dark brown eyes gleam eerily bright in the moonlight, and the smell of rotting peonies sloughs off her like rain. The Astar carries no lamp and wears a dress so dark that she's nearly invisible. For once, she is without her Guardian, and that scares me. I don't trust Teloh's motives, but I know in my soul that he would not let anyone hurt me.

Run away, my ghosts rustle, and they cluster against my spine in a prickly ball, as though they want to be as far from her as possible.

"I should rest for tomorrow." I keep my hands on the curtain. "It's been an exhausting day, and we're not allowed out of our rooms at night."

"Oh, I insist. I promise this won't take long. I have the final say on the Raja or Reyna, after all. You need not fear the dark when you're with me." She holds out a hand as if I am a friend, but I wrap my arms around myself.

Arisa leads me through unlit corridors and does not slow until we reach an alcove that houses a statue of Omu. The Diwata's face glows with the light of wish candles in colorful glass cups. Her stern eyes stare down upon us in judgment, and they seem to shift in the candlelight. I look away.

"Kneel." Arisa pushes my shoulders down, and my knees crack against the cold stone floor. She stands behind me like a hovering executioner. This close, I choke on the flower-and-rot scent of her power.

"You are one of the girls from the Toso party. I wondered why you looked so familiar when I marked your hand. Was the other girl your sister?"

Freezing Hells. I cough and sputter, but she doesn't seem to care. "No, just a friend."

She doesn't seem to buy my lie. Instead, she bends low to examine my face. Her breath tickles my ears, and I flinch away. I pray that my blue scarf is wound tight.

"Mmm… Kormar has such a soft heart. She asked me to check on you because she was worried after your test. She also told me that the balete stopped when you answered the questions you were given. Tell me what happened in your own words."

My ghosts scrape at the cage of my chest so violently that I wince. *Careful*, they warn.

"We were answering questions when the tree came alive. We nearly died."

"So, you did nothing but answer questions?" The candlelight shifts. Her shadows stretch into a sharp fingered shape. I close my eyes.

"Nothing. A boy… A boy in a yellow tunic was hanging upside down after his first question, but Kormar told us not to worry. I don't know what was supposed to happen."

She paces behind me, and her slippered feet tap rhythmically against the stone floor. "And what was the final question?"

"It asked what I am most afraid of."

She stops and kneels before me. If I didn't know better, her expression might have seemed kind. "And what are you afraid of, Kuran Jal?"

"Myself."

"How curious." She looks me up and down, unimpressed. "Tell no one what happened during the test. We must not alarm the other candidates, but it sounds like this was all an unfortunate accident."

The candles flicker, and Arisa swivels her gaze down the hallway. Her mask of smugness falters for an instant. "Hurry back to your room. Do not dally."

When I turn around, she is gone, and I dare not linger. I leave behind the rotting stench of the Astar's words and magic, but though I counted hallways and turns on the way to the alcove, they do not seem to line up the same way. Pools of moonlight break the contours of my path into jagged mosaics that shift and change. I scurry toward an oasis of candlelight and find immortal Madur's eagle statue where I remember it. The protector of Tigang and patron of Guardians stands with his wings flared, and he grips the hilt of a curved sword with taloned fingers.

But a gust of wind snuffs out every candle in the hallway. In the sudden darkness, every terrifying story told around the cookfire comes back to mind: there are shadows with teeth; there is darkness that walks.

I blunder into another hallway as the wind picks up. It sends my skin prickling and pushes me onward. I turn around, but there are no open windows in sight. A sound like waves crashing against the shore echoes down the corridor and builds until it is as deafening as a rushing waterfall.

I go back the way I came and abandon decorum. I run. The shadows shift and tighten around me, strangling away the moonlight.

The red flag marking the candidates' quarters flickers in weak lamplight ahead. I sprint toward it and back to my room.

Jumping into my bed, I pull my blanket to my chin like a child caught in the grips of some waking nightmare. The red flap of our curtain flutters in and out of the doorway, as if the fortress is alive and breathing.

I wait for the shadows to turn into fangs and claws or for something to burst through the door. Instead, footsteps patter down the hallways. Someone human shouts words too distant for me to understand.

Suddenly, the air fills with so much moisture that breathing feels like swallowing honey. The walls drip with condensation that runs in thin rivulets. A mushroom sprouts in the crack where the doorframe meets the floor.

I'm suffocating.

"Go away!" I gasp. "Please." My voice wheezes out in a whisper, but the shadows outside shift as though they are listening. The magic eases its grip, and I gulp fresh air before crumpling into my mattress. Nearby, Dayen turns over in his creaking bed and Virian simply snores.

One dream fades into another. This time, I am lost in a storm, and all around me the glass walls of Bato-Ko are cracking.

*) * (*

CHAPTER FIFTEEN

My limbs ache as though I've climbed a mountain. Everything feels too hot and too tight: my tunic, my malong, my scarf. I push a crust of sweet bread around my plate, unable to work up an appetite.

"Are you sick?" Dayen asks, pushing his floppy hair to one side. "I know an orasyon that—"

"I'm fine, I think." I flush, embarrassed. Being fussed over is something too new and strange for me to accept.

My mother did not fuss, but she showed her love in other ways. If I was sick, she would bring me soup without a word. Fresh fruit, cut and peeled, would appear at my bedside. She still had to drive our wagon, but she would sing as we traveled to put me at ease. "Rest, baby girl," she would whisper when she thought I was asleep. "I cannot lose you, too." And when I opened my eyes, I'd find her curled up on the floor beside my cot in case I needed anything. Perhaps fussing was not her way, but I never doubted she cared.

Still, Dayen and Virian make me think that if I ever had a home away from Tigang, I might have had a decent life. I might've made friends. I might've been happy. Though Dayen's fear hasn't gone, he seems to be trying, so I resolve to try, too. I offer a weak smile, and the grin he returns is crumb-filled.

Dayen stuffs sweet bread topped with a mountain of salty

carabao cheese into his mouth. "I'm just glad to be alive and whole. So far so good, right?"

I nod. He seems to be leaning less on his crutch today. He's lucky that the fortress Healers are competent, but I still don't believe he should have been allowed to be hurt at all.

"What do you think you scored?" he asks.

Virian makes a face. She's wearing her pouch of scrap paper and writing tools at her hip again, the most sensible of us all. "My cousin told me that Kormar passed everyone who took the test with us, because what happened with the tree made it impossible to judge. We set off some kind of magical trap that brought the tree to life, but whoever set it wasn't Kormar. No one seems to know who made it."

I shiver, because who would create such a thing, and why?

"But you want to know something else?" Virian slides her breakfast plate next to mine and huddles close. "Those two boys who died? Their bodies aren't in the infirmary where they should be kept until the end of the Sundo. A few other candidates are missing. Some people think that Guardians tossed them out last night, because we aren't the only ones who've been targeted with pranks. One of the older girls collapsed this morning. Her roommates think she was poisoned."

I wonder who her cousin amongst the Baylan is, if she can get gossip this quickly. Still, I'm glad she's on my side.

No one else sits at our long table today. We all huddle in fractured groups. Everyone speaks in hushed tones except for Nen, the pinched-mouthed boy. He sits with Ingo, whose gold earrings and chains flash in the light. Nen laughs as if he has no cares in the world. I quickly scan the room and wonder who else Arisa might have interrogated in private.

Senil, the head Archivist, totters into the room. The old man reminds me of a gnarled, leafless tree that clings stubbornly to life. He clasps Arisa's arm to steady himself, and the Astar helps him along, but he seems more irritated than pleased by her attentiveness. I think he would rather use a cane.

Virian's posture goes rigid at the old man's appearance, but as usual, Dayen doesn't notice. I brace for whatever cruelty must surely follow.

"You know, Ingo's great aunt was Reyna once, and his great great grandfather was Raja, too. His family sends an applicant every time they can, and they groom their children for it." Dayen still gazes at the rich boy with something akin to admiration, but Ingo's got a poor taste for friends if Nen is one of them.

"It makes no difference. The Sundo is never the same, or we would have a dynasty instead of a competition," Virian says, but her attention is on the Archivist. The bald old man still has sharp eyes, and he gazes back at her with a frown.

A dozen steps behind, Teloh walks in with his head bowed.

I try not to look at Teloh, but I cannot resist the temptation to glance his way. His eyes are unfocused, his jaw clenched. Something is wrong. I see it in Arisa's feigned concern for Senil. He acts as if her touch is poison, and I worry it might be.

Then I notice the bruises. They are faded, but they peek out from under Teloh's sleeveless tunic, on display for all to see. It has the look of a public shaming, but our dear Astar only smiles smugly to herself. I clench my fists. No matter how much he confuses me, seeing him hurt makes me yearn to comfort him.

The head Archivist pulls free of Arisa, and they hiss at each other in tones too soft to hear before the old man barks for an initiate to help him totter away. For a moment, Arisa's expression is a storm, but when she turns back to us, she's all catlike innocence.

"My apologies, children. Datu Senil is not feeling well today and needs his rest, but the test will proceed as planned. Guardian?" She turns to Teloh, who refuses to meet her gaze. "You are knowledgeable in the histories. Let us conduct the test on behalf of the Archivists sect."

Teloh uncoils like a snake in the sun. He winces as though every simple motion causes him pain, and I'm surprised that he does not murder her with his bare hands. Instead, he inclines his head, a perfect picture of politeness.

"Of course, Arisa." The lack of an honorific feels spiteful, but if this needles Arisa, she doesn't show it. I don't understand their arrangement at all. "Candidates, follow us."

Arisa and Teloh led us through the halls, and though I take note of the twists and turns of gently sloping ramps, the only direction I can truly discern is down. An open doorway leads into what looks like a massive cavern, and as we enter, an unnatural chill prickles at my skin. It looks like the inside of a beehive. Rounded stone alcoves are carved into the cavern's curving walls, and each houses the bones of the dead.

"This is the final resting place of all the Rajas, Reynas, Datus, and Astars of Tigang." Arisa waves her hands around her. "Though their souls have passed on, their remains still hold memories of the past. Today you will each be given a memory spell. You may choose any of our ancestors here. You must meditate and describe the vision shown to you. You will be judged on what lesson you can take from the vision, for the ruler of Tigang is not separate from the history of our country but a continuation of it."

Teloh clears his throat, and his eyes lock on mine. "Choose well, for some of our ancestors died cruel deaths. Do not get trapped in a vision you cannot escape."

It feels like a warning, and I flinch away.

An initiate hands each of us a paper scrawled with an orasyon, and I give one last nod to Virian and Dayen before we go off in separate directions. I look up a wall that recedes into darkness.

I don't know the details of each ruler of Tigang, for we have had many. Fewer yet are the Datus who are known outside of the fortress by anything other than their position. And Astar? I dare not attempt to revive a Diwata's memories. I shiver again and walk briskly around the circular room. I need to do this quickly so that I can track down my mother, but I also know that my choice of the dead matters. Skulls and bones peek out of their alcoves, gone yellowish with time, beside offerings of fruit, flowers, and drinks.

Most tombs climb up the walls, but the oldest are set into the middle of the floor. Unlike the open alcoves in the walls, they are covered with thick slabs of silver-veined marble. I walk past one carved into the shape of an old woman. It is so realistic that in the dim light I almost mistook it for someone asleep on the floor. What arrests me is her expression. Though she is lying peacefully, there's something pained in the furrow of her brow and how tightly her eyes are squeezed shut.

I don't realize I've walked toward her until it's too late. The marble woman's eyes open, and she blinks once, twice. She murmurs something in a low tone that I can barely hear.

It's a spell, I realize as her mouth begins to glow. My head pounds like it is being squeezed in a vice, and I scream.

D arkness shrouds me like a wet blanket. I reach out and touch nothing but air. I take two steps back and find there is no door where there should be a door. The cavern of the dead is gone, and the heel of Holy Omu's constellation shines bright red like a ruby in a dark sky where there should be a roof.

The deck is warm under my bare feet as I slowly rise and fall with the waves, and I listen to the song our people sang on our way across the ocean, in a language so old we Tigangi know it only in our dreams. I touch a finger to my chest and find my ghosts sway to its tune.

A striped sail manifests from the darkness, and when it rustles, it makes a noise like the flapping wings of a great bird. I'm on a boat. I taste brine on my lips, smell the salt air, and hear the gulls crying, though I cannot see them.

It is beautiful magic. Like my visions, this feels like it is something true.

Black ash coats my skin, and charred holes mar the fine fabric of my clothing. Everything on the boat glows red, illuminated by distant flames. I run to the side of my boat, past Kuran. Though she does not look the same, I know it's her with the certainty you can only have in a dream. She winds a rope tight to secure our sail, and I look back at Arawan.

All seven islands are on fire, and the great volcanoes that bore them spew clouds of smoke into the sky. A storm swirls above it all, fanning flames on the wind and forking lightning across our forests. A small fleet of boats races against the wind around us, fleeing the dark shores of our homeland.

And behind me, someone is laughing or crying. I cannot tell which, only that it is a pathetic sound. When I turn to look, there Teloh sits. His arms are bound to the wooden mast, so he cannot wipe the tears streaming down his face.

He turns his dark, grieving eyes to me. "What have you done?" he asks.

And Arawan burns.

CHAPTER SIXTEEN

"Kuran Jal."

I sputter awake and scramble out from under Arisa's looming shadow. I don't know how long I was in that vision or what just happened. Magic trickles off her, peony scented. I gasp and accept a cup of cold water from Arisa. I keep drinking until I am numb inside. Interest brightens Arisa's expression, and her silence worries me.

"How foolish of you to choose the first Astar's tomb." Arisa says with a hint of curiosity in her tone. "What did you see?"

It was not my choice. The ghosts are frantic inside me. I feel as though I'm full of bees. They refuse to settle, and my thoughts scatter with them.

"The archipelago burning," I mumble. I stand, with Teloh's help, and realize that all the candidates are staring at me, too. I avert my eyes and stare at the floor.

But neither my sister nor Teloh were ever part of those stories. I reel, dream drunk. I still smell smoke, and I rub at my ash-stung eyes.

"There is still a test," Teloh says, and his voice is a lash that I flinch away from. This Teloh reminds me of our first introduction at Oshar's party. Callous. Cold. All edges. "Be thankful Arisa pulled you out of that vision."

How strange, then, because I never even used the orasyon

they gave me. Something here is not right. I look down at the marble tomb, only to find a single name: Astar. Not a position but a person: the first who bore the name. I throw my arms around my belly to stop from throwing up. Freezing Hells, I can't stop shaking. I did nothing. It was as if she was calling…waiting.

"Tell me the story of Astar and Chaos, then. Tell me how our homeland burned." Teloh stands very, very still. This unsettles me more than his expression. "And tell us what lesson you can make of it."

This is the second time this tale has been requested. It cannot be coincidence. I scramble to my feet and close my eyes. I still feel the boat lurching beneath my feet. It is an old story, from the days before Tigang existed.

"In the time before, across the darkening sea, our people lived on the jeweled isles of Arawan. We wanted for nothing. So spoiled and soft we were that when Holy Omu begged us to heed her warnings, no one listened but the wise Raja Ressa, who sat troubled in his wooden palace. He listened to the rumblings of the volcanoes that birthed their lands, but even he was not prepared for what was to come.

"The Demon Chaos had been cast onto the earth long before humans ever walked upon it. The Demon grew envious of these lazy people who wanted for naught, and it came to the islands upon a strong wind. The Demon delighted as it stirred the wickedness in our hearts. It brought the typhoon and tore the roofs off our houses. It flooded our crops, so we had nothing to eat. Peace turned to fighting. Each island declared itself a kingdom. Cousins took up arms against their cousins. Friendships turned to suspicion. The Demon's taint spread everywhere, and it gorged on it, pleased."

I glance up and notice Teloh grinding his teeth together under a dark scowl.

"But the wise Raja, blessed by Omu, prayed for a miracle

to reunite his people, and one night, Omu sent a Diwata to aid him: Astar, immortal made mortal, imbued with all the wisdom of the Heavens. Astar drew up the earth and trapped the wicked Demon within a volcano, but so enraged was the Demon that the whole of the island chain shook with its fury. Ash rained down from the sky and destroyed our fields, so that nothing could grow, and our green paradise turned to dust.

"'Take these boats,' Astar commanded. 'Omu wishes us to seek a continent to the East. There I shall build you a home of iron and glass. You wicked people shall learn how to survive on rocks and air. You will learn to hear the Heavens' will. You will grow hard, but your people will thrive, and no Demon will dare threaten you again.' So they sailed away, never to return to the archipelago of Arawan."

I take a breath but wilt under his gaze.

"Very prettily told, but is that truly what you saw?" Teloh asks. He seems to know I am lying.

I stare down at my arms, expecting blisters and blood, but my hands are clean. I swallow. I wish I could bury myself in warm blankets or scour away the magic nightmare.

"It matches the stories I've heard."

Teloh snorts, unimpressed. "So, you still think Astar truly came to save your country?"

"You are asking me to speculate on the motives of the Diwata when I am only human. I thought this was a history test," I snap. I am the dupe for pitying him, for thinking there was something between us, when all I feel now is the knife of his fury. My head still throbs furiously. It feels like there is a crack from my skull to my navel.

Arisa watches the both of us with ravenous eyes. Her favorite gold comb catches the light and the glare blinds me for a moment.

"Humans are capable of terrible things," Teloh says.

I grit my teeth. "If Astar were truly human, then she could not be perfect, but she is dead and gone. What does it matter?" I hover near the line of treason, balanced only by my anger at this dressing down in front of so many eyes. In front of Arisa.

"Tell me, then: What possible lesson could you, of all people, have learned from this?" he growls.

"I..." I stutter. I don't know. The destruction of our homeland seemed so pointless. I could feel Astar grieving as she sailed away. Her heart ached as though it had been torn into shreds and could never be woven back together. She did not want to go on. She did not want to sail the ship, yet she did. It felt as though I was wearing her skin, and I still need to scour it off me. And I have no idea what Teloh was doing in that vision. Why he was tied up like a criminal. Why he looked at Astar with such betrayal.

I bow my head and choose the acceptable answer. "I learned that the will of the Heavens is a mystery but Omu led us true."

He stiffens as though the comment is a slap to the face, but Arisa squeezes my shoulder. Her hand is as cold as her expression when her eyes drift to the scarf at my neck. I pray she did not see the marks peeking out from under my tunic. "You may go, Kuran Jal. Your answer sufficed."

I shudder and hurry away from the cavern of the dead as the others complete their tests.

Finding my mother matters more than ancient history, yet I can't shake the vision from my head. I slip into my room to fetch Manong Alen's tracking spell, but Virian and Dayen catch up to me first. Questions are plastered all over their faces, and I curse myself for not holding my tongue.

"I don't know what just happened," I admit.

Teloh was the one who warned me not to be noticed, and yet he called me out in front of everyone. I wrap my arms around myself. It's as if I stood in the room naked.

"I think that was an argument between Arisa and her pet Guardian." Virian tries to smooth her hair, but it only looks more tangled for her irritated efforts. She tucks it behind an ear with a sigh. "Three senior Archivists disappeared last night. It's why Datu Senil was so upset. What I don't understand is why Arisa is so interested in the competition this year. The Astar is not supposed to participate."

Manong Alen mouths a warning about Arisa in my mind. The memory is still so fresh that I can almost smell the sweet stickiness of the Archivist's breath and see the rashes on his arms. I clamp my mouth shut. These disappearances can't be coincidence. That I was led to the first Astar's tomb can't be coincidence.

I lean against the cold stone wall to steady myself. Is any of this coincidence? I rub at my temples. "What do you know about the Astar?"

"Everyone knows about Arisa. Are you so ill-informed?" Dayen perfectly mimics Reshar's inflection.

"So, inform me." I copy the bored expression on his face, and Virian giggles.

"She's only eighteen, you know." Virian leans back and rubs her crooked nose.

I frown. I assumed she was in her mid-twenties.

"There is always an Astar in the fortress, and Arisa is the latest incarnation. When one dies, the Baylan seek her reincarnation."

I *am* terribly ill-informed. "And how do they know she's really the Astar? We've all been reborn, but none of us remember our past lives." Usually not, anyway. I don't know what to think anymore.

"Memories can sometimes be brought back. You need something from your past life and a little bit of magic to bring recall," she says. "But recall is dangerous. Things are different in each life. A former lover might be a sibling or married to someone else. We would mess up our present life with that knowledge."

"So there is a way." I drum my fingers against my chin.

"Yes, but I'd advise against it. You're bound to find pain and disappointment. I'd rather experience every wonder in the world as though it's the first time," Virian says. Her conviction is admirable. "There are also no guarantees that any attempts to remember the past will even work. Why are you asking?"

"I had a vision about the fortress." I look at them both, and their eyes grow wide. I never had a chance to use the memory spell given at the test, so I pull it out of my pocket and unfold it. "Do you want to try it?"

"Hells yes."

The wind whips hard today, and I fight the gale to peel back the loose hairs that keep blowing into my eyes.

Dayen peers over the edge of the balcony and whistles. "That's a long way down."

"This is where you saw the vision?" Virian inspects every bump on the balcony railing, but there's not much to see but stone, the ocean, and the mountains. Bato-Ko remains hidden behind the bulk of the fortress.

I nod in reply.

"If you know me now, it's possible you knew me then, too." Virian clamps her hands on the stone railing and her forehead scrunches together in concentration. "And what did you see?"

"I was me but not me. I didn't have the same face."

She nods. "Your soul in a different body." She traces her hands along the banister, and Dayen pokes at it as though it's coconut jelly, but nothing happens. "What else?"

I look between them both. I wish I could tell them everything. I feel like a balloon full of secrets, about to pop or be destroyed if I say nothing at all. I decide to chance a little bit of the truth. "Teloh was there. I was holding his hands..."

Dayen raises his eyebrows.

"Don't you dare tease me about it," I mutter and look up at the Heavens, but the clear blue sky offers no answers. "It's not the first time, either. I saw him in the streets before the Sundo and had a memory of us together in Bato-Ko, which is impossible, because I've never lived here. And then there were the baths... I dreamed of them the night I arrived, and I've seen them. They're real."

Virian closes her eyes and takes a breath. She takes my memory spell and copies the orasyon onto the balcony with a piece of drawing charcoal from her waist pouch. The wind sends our clothes billowing and churns the waves into white peaks below.

"Close your eyes and stand in the middle of the orasyon," she says.

I do as instructed, and the spell warms beneath my feet. The ghosts in my chest rustle softly as though tickled. "I don't see anything."

"You need someone more powerful, maybe, or we need a better spell to reach into a past life. That one was simply an aid for recalling memories. I bet Datu Reshar could do it," Virian says, and I shudder. I'd rather be left in mystery than have to deal with him.

Virian practically skips the way back to our rooms, undeterred. "It's possible you were a Baylan in another life. Places and things that have strong emotion attached to them are the most likely to trigger memories," Virian explains. "Most people don't have visions but have a sense that someone is familiar, as though you've been friends before."

None of this makes me feel any better. If Teloh were just an old lover reborn, then he might have felt something warm and asked me to dinner. But if he was just an old lover reborn, then my ghosts would not keep screaming in warning. "And how do you know all this?" I ask.

"I read." Virian sniffs. "Were you raised by wolves?"

"My mother distrusts the Baylan, and it's likely why she's in the dungeons," I add lightly.

Virian's expression goes sly as a monkey's. "So that's why you're here."

I raise my arms. "Yes, and now that you know, I have to kill you."

Dayen laughs and twirls on his crutch to stare at us. It looks like his leg isn't bothering him much anymore. "You know what this means, Kuran?"

I arch a brow, and Virian flops onto her bed with a matching expression.

His grin grows wider. "You're going to have to touch that gorgeous Guardian to see if you have any more visions. Maybe more than once, just to be sure."

I grab the pillow from my bed and toss it at him, and he laughs, lets go of his crutch, and ducks behind Virian, who squeals in protest. I grab another pillow to smack him with it, but Virian screams before I make contact.

I drop the pillow. Something in the case twists and coils, and an arrow-shaped head worms its way out of the fabric. We all back up, huddled together in a corner as a yellow-bellied snake winds its way out onto the floor.

"Garter snake," I breathe. "Not poisonous." My eyes drift to the doorframe. I spit and press my finger to the mark I've painted. "And there's a way of finding out who's responsible."

Virian shoos the creature from the room with a slipper.

Dayen smiles appreciatively at the back of her head, and

he panics when I notice. His hands fly everywhere, begging my silence, but he drops them demurely to his lap when Virian turns around.

I stifle a laugh, but all my mirth disappears when my eyes fall on the withered mushroom at the base of our doorframe. The night's terrors return to grip me. It wasn't a dream. I stare so long that a crease of worry appears on Virian's brow.

"What is it?" she asks.

"Archivists are the recorders of our histories, the record keepers. There are only two reasons for Archivists to go missing. Either they are protecting a secret, or they've discovered a secret someone else wants hidden." I take a deep breath. They might think I'm ridiculous, but I tell them about the shadows in the hallway and the footsteps in the halls, but I say not a word about Arisa's late-night visit.

"Someone's doing some big magic in the fortress. Only one of the Seven can channel that much power." Virian looks thrilled when she should be afraid, and I worry her interest in magic might be enough to get her into trouble but not out of it. "We need to stick together. No more wandering at night, Kuran. I don't want either of you to go missing." Virian bounces on her bed like a child. I can't believe she's already eighteen.

"But what if it's my fault? What if my presence means you are in danger?" I ask.

"The curse again?" Virian stills and frowns at my scarf, but Dayen touches the strings of his amulets. "How can our past lives matter if we are not supposed to remember them? It's just a comfort to know that you will meet the people you love again. That's all there is to it, Kuran. Nothing in our history books or our laws says that those with birthmarks should be punished, or that they are dangerous. The curse is nothing but superstition."

Tanu said the same to me before. But neither Tanu nor Virian knows the questions Astar's balete tree asked me, nor what I saw in the first Astar's vision. I don't know what any of it means, only that everything that happened since I set foot in Bato-Ko feels tied together with invisible threads: Alen, Teloh, my mother. My life is a web of lies, and I'm the fly caught in them.

"Please be careful, Kuran. Someone's trying to scare you into leaving. They think you are a threat." Virian points a finger between my eyes. "So, you better prove them right."

I wait until Virian and Dayen are tucked deep into exhausted sleep before I unfold Alen's orasyon. If I'm being targeted, I can't delay what I came here to do, no matter what I promised my friends. I spit on the spell and an invisible force tugs at my hand as the tracking spell activates.

The halls are emptier tonight and the voices from the adjacent rooms sound hollower. The argument between two candidates echoes loudly.

"You can't leave! Who will help me with magic?"

"You weren't there in the first round at the greenhouse," a boyish voice replies. "This is not worth it!" I flatten myself against the wall as a boy stalks out of a room toting a bag and the shadows swallow him.

Another door slams shut down the hallway and its lock turns noisily into place. I almost feel sorry because everything about this place feels as though it is meant to break us. From the tests, to the competition, to the mindbogglingly senseless corridors. No wonder my mother warned me to stay away.

I cling to patches of moonlight, watch the shadows, and listen for wind, but all I hear are distant voices. Following the gentle tugging of the orasyon's magic, I descend into the belly of the fortress. There's no mark to the transition to the Winter palace, but I can sense it. The stone is smoother here, bleached repeatedly by the wind and rain that comes in through paneless windows. There are grooves in the stairs, from hundreds of years of feet passing, but no one treads here now. Evergreens and holly designs are carved into the walls, along with mountain scenes.

I wind down a tight spiral staircase that goes all the way to the lowest level of the fortress, which has several landings, some of which branch off into other corridors, others of which hold intricately carved doors. Reaching the last landing, I push open the very last one and step out of the shadows. At the end of a wide hallway is yet another vast door, painted in spells that run from floor to ceiling. The air vibrates with so much magic it feels as if lightning might strike at any moment. I've found the dungeons.

"You, child—what are you doing here?"

The Guardians standing at their posts were so still that I did not see them in the shadows.

I don't have an answer, so I turn and run back the way I came. I climb up and up the staircase until my legs burn and I am out of breath and dizzy. I lean against the wall to catch my breath.

And then I hear Reshar's voice from below.

CHAPTER SEVENTEEN

I race to the end of the staircase to flee Reshar, only to be stopped short by a glass door that leads to the rooftop.

Behind it is a grassy courtyard where statues of the seven holiest Diwata cast long shadows beneath a purplish sky. A familiar woman in a pure white dress paces under Omu's stone gaze. Kalena's long hair falls around her shoulders as she bends low, but she does not appear to be praying.

I've heard what the Interpreters do, but I've never seen it. I've only witnessed their proclamations passed out: when to plant, what to sow, what prayers must be offered, what tithes must be given. Here, papers scrawled with orasyons flutter at the base of Omu's statue. Kalena waves her hands as if embroiled in an argument with the Diwata herself. Though the statue's stone lips do not move, a whispering sound fills the air.

Kalena turns her head in my direction.

I fling myself flat against the curving wall, hoping she does not come out to investigate. With Reshar in the stairwell and Kalena on the rooftop, I am trapped.

Reshar's footsteps seem to stop a floor or two below me. I cannot see who he is with, but he is not alone. I whisper pleas to the Diwata that neither he nor his companion continues upward.

"Do not underestimate the old woman," Reshar says. "Nanay Oshar has the support of the families, and she is cunning. Never trust an easy smile."

Oshar? I blink. She's the kind old woman who invited my sister and me to sing for her and sent us home with more food and money than we asked for. I inch toward them to hear better. What does she have to do with anything?

"You are paranoid, Datu Reshar," a woman replies.

"Either way, you are for or against us. Choose, because Arisa is getting bolder. Every day more people go missing in the fortress, and Tigang is vulnerable until we choose a ruler. The cultists are recruiting more to their cause, and Arisa's creature is testing its freedom."

The hairs on the back of my neck lift at the memory of the moonlit hallways. It's true, then. There was something outside my door, so close I might have reached out to touch it, and the only thing between us was a flimsy flap of cloth.

"We should have left it in that cell where it's been rotting." Reshar's voice trembles.

"Let Arisa's hubris be the end of her," the woman replies calmly. "She cannot keep control forever. I am more worried about Omu's cult. Their devotees multiply with every drought, and I have heard them calling for violence…"

A door shuts behind them and cuts off the sound of their conversation.

Creature? I wasn't dreaming. I shudder because I saw nothing—I felt it. Liquid darkness. Something huge and angry that could snuff out my life in an instant.

The buzz of magic crawls up and down my arms like an army of marching ants, and I glance out the door. Magic whips the air around Kalena, but she continues to argue with some unseen being. The feel of it makes me want to tear my skin off.

I hurry down the stairs and emerge onto another level of the fortress. A short passage leads me to a narrow and smooth-walled hallway, stretching in both directions. Everything here is silent. I decide to go left and walk along until I find a door to try, but the lock rattles loudly. Freezing Hells, I'm going to get caught.

Footsteps echo in the hallway as someone comes toward me. I scramble straight back, down the corridor and away, but overshoot the staircase entrance and reach the hallway's end.

In front of me is a door with no handle. I see it two times at once.

In one eye, there is nothing remarkable about the door. It's not as beautiful as the mahogany of the great hall. It is a door of simple polished oak, hinged with brass.

In my other eye, the mahogany is carved with braided patterns. A split runs clear through the center of the wood, and half of it hangs askew, revealing a pool of moonlight and tall windows beyond.

I have not been here. I have been here. *Go on*, my ghosts whisper with a sound like moths' wings beating gently against glass.

Time spins for a moment, and I ground myself, palm to the wood. It is smooth under my fingers, and when I open my eyes, all trace of the broken door is gone. A breeze whispers of the ocean through the crack under the door, but there is no latch or keyhole by which to open it.

I shove my shoulder into the oak, but I bounce off the door with a dull thud.

"What are you doing?"

I jump. Reshar lifts the lid off a lantern. The darkened corridor fills with dancing shadows, and I flinch away from the light.

"You should be in your room. It is not safe to be out after nightfall."

I smell fresh grass upon his tunic, and the air around him shimmers like candle smoke. Like Kalena on the rooftop, he must have done magic just now: the kind that requires blood and sacrifice and shortens your life. Instead of his usual loose robes, he's covered up his tattoos with a tunic and long malong. Strands of gray hair frame his face, where I noticed none before.

"I was lost," I say, aware how feeble the lie sounds in my mouth.

"Come with me," he growls.

I pray to the Heavens that my transgression is not worth dying for, because if he were to shove me off a balcony, my body might never be found.

We pass through empty passages. I glimpse the great hall, but Reshar keeps walking. He leads me into a large, warmly lit room and shoves me in front of his body like a shield.

"I found this child wandering where she should not be, Astar Arisa," he says with the proper courtesy. I do not think he's in the mood for a fight tonight.

Arisa looks up from a desk laden with bottles filled with blue and black ink. Teloh leans his elbows on his knees at the foot of her table, cross-legged on the cold floor. He wears a long-sleeved tunic that covers his arms and hides evidence of his bruises. His expression goes carefully blank at the sight of me.

"Why hello, Kuran Jal," Arisa says. Her voice sends a cold spike down my spine. I've heard many stories about Astar, but none of them painted her as cruel.

Her smile is so empty of warmth that I prefer Reshar's glowering.

I fight the impulse to cower. Reshar must be twice her age, but the Seeker flinches behind me as if he does not want to be here either. *Impostor*, Alen warned me once. It makes me wonder if Arisa is who she claims—the Astar who defeated the Demon, who built the fortress, and founded Tigang from ashes. But I've heard stories that do not call Astar innocent in the destruction of Arawan. This Astar, Arisa, is not the Builder but the Destroyer. The two Astars do not fit together at all.

I hide my clammy hands behind my back.

"Why are you wandering in the halls when you were instructed not to?" She swallows me with her eyes, from my head to my slippered feet and back up again. Her gaze lingers on my scarf. I dare not move, afraid to give away anything at all, including how much she intimidates me.

"I have never been to Bato-Ko before. I wanted to see the ocean." The words are jumbled, whispered, and hasty. "And I lost my way."

Reshar snorts, but Arisa's mouth curves into a wide smile. "I'm sure it was just a mistake, but if you wish to stay in the competition, you must prove your loyalty to Tigang." *To me*, the unspoken words say. She sets down her pen and folds her hands together. "Promise to do as I say, child, and I will keep you safe."

Could she be more condescending? I squirm, but Reshar holds me tight.

"Shall I have someone escort you home?" she asks.

Heat races up my neck. I *need* to stay. I still need to get to my mother.

"No, Astar Arisa." I bow my head. "I promise." The words taste sour in my mouth.

She nods. "Then all is well between us, but I cannot let you leave without punishment for breaking our rules."

She turns to Teloh, who is busy carving a divot into the stone of the floor with the tip of his knife and avoiding us both. Strands of his hair have come loose and cut across his fine features.

"Teloh, my pet, why does this child upset you? Your line of questioning during the test was...unusual." She purses her lips. They are plump and petulant. She has the look of someone who has always known power.

The assassin refuses to look up, but tension lingers in the set of his shoulders. "Do you remember the party at the Toso house? She was one of the entertainers. That version of Astar and Chaos is appalling."

I bristle because that was no fault of ours. Oshar asked for it specifically.

"You say this about all the stories. That can't be all!"

"The singer was pretty, but she had the gall to try and foist this one on me."

Now I'm the one burning. How could I have ever wasted a moment of thought on him? I fume in silence. Before the Sundo, I thought I had nothing left to lose. How naive I was. Bato-Ko could strip away even my pride.

"Oh, Teloh, how little you know of village girls." Arisa brays with laughter, unable to contain herself. "Break a finger, then take her to the healers. That should suffice."

She moves back into her chair, and before I can protest, Teloh is in front of me. There is a flicker of hesitation in his eyes. I don't even register the moment my left index finger slides out of place until I look down and find it bent at a strange angle. Then the pain hits me all at once, and every curse I know spills from my lips. I rue the day I ever laid eyes on him and ever thought that there was more to him than cruelty.

Teloh drags me out of the room and resists my attempts to shrug him away. He only releases me when not a soul remains around us.

"I'm sorry," he says quietly. The sullen mask is gone. His face is now awash with contrition and guilt, his eyes dark and pained. "I did not want to do that."

"Sorry?!" I spit. I am not okay. My hand continues to throb, but I bite back any screams. I refuse to let him see me struggle.

"The finger is dislocated, not broken. I will set it, wrap it, and you must be careful with it for a few weeks. You should not go to the Healers, because I'm not sure who's loyal to Ari—"

"Enough of this." The pain isn't the reason I am furious. "I don't understand you, Teloh. One moment you are all polite concern, and the next you treat me as if I disgust you." My voice shakes. "You don't even know me."

He lifts his hands so I can see that there are no weapons in his sleeves, and he turns so that I see he only wears the ceremonial kris tucked into his belt. "You're right. I owe you answers, but first let me fix your finger. Please, Narra."

At my name, the anger deflates. He hasn't told Arisa the truth, though he could have if he truly hated me. The only other people who might tell me the truth are locked away in the dungeons, and I am tired of secrets.

"Fine," I mumble and follow.

CHAPTER EIGHTEEN

I sit on an infirmary cot while Teloh hunches before me, and tapes my index finger to my middle finger. He unwraps the old gauze around my palm to check it. The mark that Arisa carved is scabbed over in places and weeping in others. I let him brush my skin lightly with his thumb as he checks it over. *Let him be cursed*, I think defiantly.

Healers hurry past our door. They look in and then rush away at one glimpse of the assassin. They seem so nervous around Teloh that I wonder what other terrible things Arisa has made him do.

"There is no infection, but the spell was poorly done. I'm not sure it's even complete." He gently rewraps fresh gauze over my palm, careful to make sure it is secure. I grunt in reply.

"Come, let me show you a place I go to be alone." He extends his hands to help me off the infirmary bed, but I stick mine into the folds of my malong. My heart tells me that he is tame, but my head laughs at the notion. A wolf is still a wolf.

I go with my head and hope that I don't regret it.

We pass through the Autumn Palace and pause at a familiar set of doors. I realize that this was where he was headed the day he stumbled upon me, blood-splattered and exhausted. His face relaxes when he passes over the threshold.

The greenhouse feels different in the dark: warm, like a cozy blanket on a cold night. I follow closely and watch for creeping vines, but the trees remain asleep.

We follow a narrow stream lined with pebbles, past towering banana trees bent over with fruits and delicate orchids clinging to fallen logs, past ponds teeming with gold carp toward the edge of the forest. Teloh touches the trunks as if they are old friends as we walk. He seems alive now, alert, in a way his disinterested persona around Arisa would never suggest. This is a different Teloh. I have a feeling that I could spend a lifetime and not know every version of him.

A half-remembered dream bubbles to the surface unwanted. I imagine him curled beside me, asleep, eyes closed, curls unruly, his arm around my waist. I am grateful that the dim light hides the flush in my cheeks. I begin to wonder if forgetting our past lives together is a blessing or a curse.

"You said you would give me answers." I walk up to the glass wall that separates the fortress from the ocean. I try to glimpse the water through the rippled glass, but the moonlight refracts wildly, revealing nothing.

Teloh leans so close that I can smell the coconut oil in his hair. He is an assault to my senses, and I take a small step back.

As if he hears my thoughts, he slides down to the floor to give me space.

I crouch nearby so that I can look him in the eyes to judge if he lies to me, but my eyes follow the curve of his nose down to the tired lines of his expression. He doesn't sleep much, I think, and I make note of the small changes in his demeanor. His shoulders are relaxed, his breathing slow, and I catch the beginnings of a smile. He sticks a hand in his pocket and reveals a palm full of seeds.

"Watch," he says and pours them into my hand. "Stay still."

A small bird darts out of the shadows and alights on my hand. It is yellow-bellied and has orange spots on its wings. It is so delicate that I'm afraid I might crush it.

"Ask me anything you want, and I swear I will answer you, if you answer my questions in return," he says.

"Another test?" I ask, and he grins so wickedly that his smile might be the end of me.

Traitor, I tell my heart's furious beating, and I fumble for a question.

"How old are you?" I begin.

"Eighteen." His lips drag upward as if it is a private joke. I'm not sure if he is lying.

"Is the rumor about the balete true? Was a Baylan truly cursed by Omu and turned into a tree?"

My skin prickles at the sound of his chuckle. "No, but it is a good way to keep them obedient." It's a relief to know that no human magic is that powerful.

I let out a breath. The moonlight highlights the curve of his cheeks and the line of his jaw. And I thought Tanu was beautiful? I can't stop drinking in Teloh's face.

"Do you really think Kuran is pretty?" I blurt and curse inwardly. I say such vapid things when I'm nervous.

"Yes, but most people would." He seems too amused by this line of questioning for my liking, and I wonder what happened to my brain. Why does he unsettle me so? This might not be a test, but it is a game I am likely to lose.

There's something wild about his eyes, but intimately familiar, too. What do I know about him? *Everything*, my heart says, and a picture comes to me of us huddled together on a lonely beach. *Nothing*, my head says as I watch the assassin recline in the greenhouse.

"You are not so tall, and there is no softness about you. Your mouth is crooked," he says, but his tone holds admiration. "You are a swift-moving current that alters everything around you. You are interesting, Narra Jal." His voice is decisive, and my pulse surges at the compliment.

"You knew me from the first moment you saw me, but I am no one. How is this possible?"

"You could never be no one." He looks away, and it feels as if he's ripped the bandages from my skin. "We knew each other in another life. Yes, I recognized you, but I had forgotten what effect you have on me. It makes it harder to hate you."

The memory of Arawan burning shudders back to life. I picture him then, soot-stained and struggling to free himself of the rope I bound him with. His dark eyes burned with seething anger. I see the same defiance in him now, and I know that the vision I saw in the tombs was true.

"It's unfair to judge me on something I don't remember. All my life, I've been shunned, when my only crime is daring to exist."

They are pretty but empty words. They feel rehearsed, because they are my mother's and not my own. I remain a monster in my own mind, no matter what my family might say. Every side glance, every friendship rejected, felt like a slap I deserved.

"I'm sorry," he says, and curse him, he sounds as if he means it. He makes me dizzy, but he makes it all worse, too: the guilt, the loneliness, the confusion. "If returning to Bato-Ko has not brought back your memories, they may never come back. Or perhaps you do not want to remember." He is still for a few moments. "Maybe to be reborn is a gift and forgetting is a mercy."

"Would you forget if you could?" My eyes slide to the sleeves of his tunic, and I wince at his hidden bruises.

"It doesn't matter what I want." He shrugs and cuts off that line of questioning.

I take a breath. "What do you know about the Archivist Manong Alen?"

"I heard he was arrested for treason, but I only do as Arisa commands. She explains nothing to me." Another shrug of his shoulders.

"Do you know why Shora Jal was arrested?"

"Not for certain," he says. "Her mother, Yirin Jal, turned her over to us, and this caused quite a scandal, but I am not privy to the Interpreters' courts."

Yirin did this? I blink in shock. To think that I wrote to her for help and entrusted Kuran's care to her. I truly believed that she might care about her only blood relatives, but I was wrong. My mother was right to despise the woman. I fume, vowing to spit on her name and pray to the Diwata Madur for justice. May she be cursed in this life and the next.

"Do you think my mother will be executed?" I ask.

"Few people are pardoned," he says softly. "You Tigangi have become as hard as your land."

We sit together in the silence for a time. The seeds are gone from my hand, yet I keep it outstretched. Tiredness peeks through the careful stitching of Teloh's smiles. I wonder why he stays—if he was just another unwanted child turned over to the Baylan, or if he simply has nowhere else to go.

He clears his throat. "It's my turn for questions, Narra Jal."

I remember our game and nod, though my heart is not playful.

"Tell me about your life and the world beyond Bato-Ko. Perhaps I know who you were, but I don't know who you are." There's a hungriness to the request that I don't expect, a longing for more than the fates that bind us here.

"I am a cloth merchant," I say. "I've twice crossed the continent with my mother and my sister. Inay was young when she had Kuran. I never knew my father, but I know they were deliriously in love. She never talks about him, but there's this look she gets in her eyes sometimes when she sees things that remind her of him." I think I understand what she was feeling now. When I think of my family, it fills my heart to brimming, and then I remember they are not here and I feel alone once again. "I don't think I've ever heard her tell a joke. She rarely laughs. It's been the three of us for as long as I remember, and it hasn't always been easy."

We loved each other, but we would fight like wet cats. I was never an easy child. There were so many times I raged at my mother. I wanted to see the world, to make friends, to experience every joy and pain, but she was always afraid I might be taken away from her. She held me so tight.

But there were good moments, too. I tell him about the caravan, and the time that I wrote an orasyon that turned Kuran bald, as vengeance for stolen cake. About the wardrobe of red clothes Manay Halna wears to keep bad luck away, and how the desert smells at night when the flowers bloom.

His laughter is halting, as if he hasn't used it in too long, and his questions spin my words into a weaving of stories.

The hours pass, and I don't even realize it.

"You better rest. I hear you have a healing test next." He seems reluctant to stand, and I fumble with my footing. There are still so many questions I wish I could ask, but I don't know how much I can trust him, or what he wants from me.

I find one last question. "Who gave you those bruises?"

"You know the answer. Arisa enjoys being cruel, but I heal quickly." He pushes back his sleeves and reveals smooth skin free of purpling. "But you might not. Promise me you will be careful. No one can know that we've spoken."

I realize how close he is sitting to me. How our knees have drifted to touch each other. Moonlight kisses his cheeks but not his eyes. It doesn't matter, because they stare so intently that it feels like he can see into my soul. And I stare back, mesmerized.

In the darkness, the promise is an easy thing. I could swear on all my lives never to give him up to Arisa, even if he did not ask. He lets out a breath, and the tension in his limbs falls away, as if he's let go of a great weight, but it is replaced by something tenuous and new.

He takes my hand in his warm palms and helps me stand. He doesn't let go, and I don't want him to. We walk in silence to the greenhouse door, and he turns to look at me one last time. His eyes fall on my lips, but he steps away and gently untangles our fingers.

"Goodnight, Narra," he whispers.

And for some reason, I no longer feel tired. I wish he would say my name again, but he's already walking away.

I don't know if I've asked all the right questions or all the wrong ones. I don't know if I have lost my chance to ask more. A hundred new questions spring up in my head, a forest seeded and blooming.

It's early morning by the time I return to our room. Virian grabs me as I pass through the curtain, and I nearly topple over her. "We were so worried! Don't you dare go wandering at night again!"

Dayen blinks sleepily but lurches to his feet, forgetting his crutch. Tanu is there, too, and he rushes to my side.

"What happened to your hand?" Tanu's blue eyes go wide. Behind him sits a pile of fresh clothes and a familiar folded green-and-gold cloth. It's my best malong. He must have gone to see my sister just as I asked. My heart catches in my throat.

"Reshar caught me sneaking around and took me to Arisa. She had me punished," I say.

"N— Kuran, you can't go off like that. I promised your sister I'd look out for you," he says.

I bite my lip. "She was mad, wasn't she?"

"Very angry at the both of us." He does not repeat the curses that were sure to accompany Kuran's wrath. He thrusts the malong toward me. "She wanted you to have this. She said that if you're so keen to throw away your life, you might as well die looking good."

I snort and choke back my tears. Of course she would say such a thing, but I can't bear to take it. It's a reminder of my life before the fortress, of my family, and so far my attempts to help both Kuran and my mother have come to nothing. I need to warn her about Yirin. I need to ask her what she knows about my mother's past. I need...her. My mother is the glue that always kept our family together, but Kuran is my heart, my best friend in the world. I miss her so much.

Tanu sets the malong back on the foot of my bed with the rest of the clothing he's set out for me. The tunics and trousers look borrowed from some Baylan's dusty closet. Serviceable and well-made but not very colorful.

"She asked me to pull you out, but you are marked. I explained to her that there would be..." He pauses. "Complications."

That's a mild way to put losing your memories. I touch the wrapping on my hand. My skin still feels so tender that I may be scarred forever. If my mind were broken, who would I cry out for, and who would come? I banish the thoughts because they lead to nothing good.

"I don't need watching." I glower instead.

"You need to know magic to survive, and you never paid attention when I tried to teach you. To get hurt, all you need to do is choose the wrong door."

I grimace at his choice of words. An omen or another coincidence?

I mumble a warning for him to send to my sister about our grandmother. He nods, and I sigh as he departs.

Virian inspects my taped fingers. "What is this, just a

bandage?" She wrinkles her nose. "I'm no expert in healing, but I know a thing or two that might numb the pain and bring down the swelling."

She picks a writing charcoal from her pouch and draws an orasyon on my bandage while Dayen flaunts a collection he's started. It's a small arsenal of dull dinner knives, bottles of paint, papers, rolls of cloth, brushes, and a small dead bush in a pot. I raise an eyebrow.

"It's a warning system, just in case," Dayen says. "Wear the flowers, and they'll bloom in the presence of big magic."

"And I thought the flower was a gift for me." Virian sighs dramatically. She wears a dried bloom in her hair. He looks chastened by her words but also pleased. He presents one to me as well, but I notice how careful he is to avoid touching my skin. For all his friendliness, I can still sense the fear he hides for Virian's sake.

I weave a flower into a tangle of hair and thank him anyway. "That is a very smart idea," I say, and he blushes. His cast came off while I was gone, and he's walking well without his crutch. The farm boy is taller than I guessed, a giant in comparison to the rest of us, but still all elbows and knees.

"There were Baylan searching the hallways last night. I don't know what's happening," Virian says. "More of us have gone missing. I asked my cousin about it, and even he's worried. He asked me to keep an eye out. I don't believe they've gone home."

"I don't, either." I shiver. They're not supposed to. Not one of the candidates is supposed to leave the fortress either alive or dead until the Sundo is complete. There is something very wrong going on this year, and I would bet it has something to do with either Reshar or Arisa. Reshar exposed his true self the moment he demanded a bribe. He didn't have to turn me over to Arisa, and yet he did, when he was the one sneaking around at night doing magic. And Arisa? I think that power is all she cares about.

I look at our measly defense system and hope we will never need any of these things. "I did find out one thing last night. There's the Healing test this morning. Rumor has it."

Dayen sighs, and Virian echoes it. "If it requires magic, then it's a good thing your left hand was ruined, not your right."

I grimace again, though the pain has subsided. My mouth dries.

"I'm left-handed." What an easy mark I've been, so easily lulled by a fine smile.

Teloh knew.

Here I thought I'd finally found someone who could see past my curse. Who did not willfully ignore it, but who understood what it was like to be forsaken.

I stare at my hand. The spell of laughter in the moonlight dissolves. Even if what the assassin told me is true, even if there is some fate that ties us together from life to life, he still wants me to fail the Sundo. Little does he know, I hardly care about winning, only surviving long enough to do what I came here to do.

I know where my mother is being kept; now I need a way past the guards. A schedule, perhaps, or another way in.

Enough. Be still, I tell the ghosts of my past lives and collapse onto my cold bed. For once, they listen.

CHAPTER NINETEEN

"Look there." I bite my lip when I meet Nen's glare. There's no denying that he snuck into our room. The pinched-mouthed boy hunches at a table in silence. The skin of his forehead gleams smooth and shiny where his eyebrows should be. Kuran would be so proud of me. I remember the first time she used that orasyon on Halna.

Dayen howls so loudly that Virian elbows him hard in the side. He keeps grinning, though. "Hells, of course it was Nen with the snake. No wonder he's had his head down all morning." Dayen slaps his thighs, still shaking.

"I like your style." Virian inclines her head. I make a flourished bow. It's a petty victory, but it's the first I've won since the Sundo began. It's a feeling I could get used to.

Nen returns to staring down at his empty plate. He doesn't answer the cajoles of his friends, and it looks like he would crawl into the floor if he could.

I wait for the day's announcement, tapping my fingers against the table as plates are cleared away.

I steady my breathing to focus on getting through this test. None of the others went too well, but I survived. Now, though, my wrapped-up hand might put me at a disadvantage.

Arisa swishes into the great hall. Any jubilance in my mood evaporates. As always, she wears her sun comb, but today she's swathed in oversize purple robes that make her look so much like a child playing at foreign king.

Behind her sways Teloh. He has that spring in his step again. He almost dances as he moves, but his eyes are devoid of lightness. Once, this expression might have made me think him fearsome, but I know him a fraction better now. It's not joy but restlessness, like his skin is too tight and uncomfortable. He must not like what Arisa has planned.

I follow Teloh's gaze across the room and do a quick count. Yesterday, there were more than a hundred candidates. Today, we are half the number, but no one speaks about it. He meets my eyes silently, and I turn my head.

I don't need the distraction of him now, especially when I know he doesn't want me to be here.

Reshar's perpetual scowl is etched deeper than usual today. He slouches near enough that I can smell palm wine on his breath, though it's still early. I doubt he's slept, because he's wearing the same blue tunic from last night. It's still odd to see him so covered up.

Kalena stands perfectly still, as unreadable as a statue of Omu, betraying nothing but calm assurance and the pleasantness of a warm summer day. I have met many Reshars in my life. It's white-robed Kalena who worries me.

And Arisa? The Astar is everything my mother warned me about; the worst of Tigang's creations.

Arisa's lips peel back when she sees me, and I straighten my shoulders, suddenly aware that I'm hunched over and my arms are crossed. She doesn't hide her pleasure at the sight of my bandaged fingers. She's all smiles today. I want her attention as much as a mouse wants a snake's notice, but I can do nothing about it.

"Dearest candidates. You know that the Sundo is dangerous, yet you stay because you are brave and honorable," she says.

"The Seven will judge who is worthy to rule. Trust that the Sundo will reveal your true merits. You must respect your fellow candidates, because the ruler of Tigang must be both diplomatic and fair."

Arisa is the furthest thing from diplomatic that I can imagine. Reshar scoffs, echoing my thoughts.

"Nen Massa, please step forward."

Nen keeps his head bowed as he stands. I tear my eyes from him, ashamed, though I was not the one who gave him away.

"You played a poor prank on one of your fellow candidates. No harm was done, so you shall not be expelled, but you must be awarded an equally fitting penalty." Arisa cocks her head to the left. "Reshar," she purrs.

Of course Arisa is more concerned with punishing us than the candidates who have gone missing. Virian shakes with indignation, but I follow Reshar's movements. I wonder if he's behind the missing candidates and if this is all a plot to whittle the candidates down to only those he finds worthy. I wouldn't put it past him. I am definitely not on that short list, and I need to be careful.

The Seeker strolls up to Nen and makes lazy circles around him. Reshar's face remains plastered with boredom. He whispers suggestions until one makes Nen flinch. The Seeker snorts, leaves the room, and returns pushing a wooden box into the middle of the floor. Arisa's expression brightens.

"Get in, child." She grips his shoulder so tightly that he winces. The box does not even come to his knees, and I'm not sure he'll fit inside. Reshar grunts his impatience when Nen does not move.

Nen's expression reminds me of a time Kuran woke up to a toad on her face. I can still remember how loud she screamed. Nen, on the other hand, looks too petrified to open his mouth.

"Your punishment will be one hour in the box," Arisa says,

practically singing. Her tone is sticky sweet. A trap. She winks at me as though she is doing me a favor when I want nothing at all from her.

"Astar Arisa, I am sorry. Expel me if you will, but do not make me get in there." Nen falls to his knees, but Arisa keeps her firm grip on his shoulder and drags him to his feet.

"You must be made an example of."

Two Guardians appear at the nod of her head. They wrestle Nen into a ball and slam the lid shut. Arisa turns the lock herself.

No one moves or speaks. Dust motes trail around us, bathed in sunshine, like flakes of snow slowly falling through the air. The minutes pass, and only Nen's screams break the silence. The box shifts across the floor as Nen struggles. His skull cracks against the lid of the box, but it is reinforced with iron bands.

Virian's vacant expression tells me her mind has taken refuge elsewhere. Dayen's guilt turns his head away, while the chosen one, Ingo, stares on impassively. He's already a Raja in his golden chains and earrings, his judgment made.

I stand there shaking. The scene is all too familiar. Once, a washerwoman caught me taking a swim in a river and dragged me soaking wet into the middle of town. Villagers tossed garbage and cursed me as I passed. I know what it's like to be humiliated in front of everyone and have my pride crushed into dust. I know that it doesn't take feet and fists to break someone, because my mother didn't always get to me first.

"Astar, please." I push past two other girls. I cannot stand to witness his suffering, even if I despise him. "I was Nen's target. It was just a childish prank that caused no harm. Let me not be the cause of his pain."

"He was the cause of his own misery, don't you think?" Arisa's lips draw thin, but I cannot accept the twisted gift she's presented me.

Reshar's eyes finally perk a little in interest.

I drop to my knees and press my forehead to the marble in supplication.

Nen yells for air and pleads to be let out. He swears obedience upon his life and all his future lives. His voice is pitched high and desperate. His nails scraping desperately against wood make the sound of fabric tearing but wetter. I want to cover my ears and make it stop.

"Would you assume his punishment for him?" Arisa asks, barely concealing her temper.

"Yes." I traveled stuffed in a cart with two other people for most of my life. What's another wooden box?

Reshar unlocks the box before Arisa can protest, and Nen jackrabbits away wild-eyed. He recoils when someone tries to comfort him and vanishes from the great hall without a word of thanks. But I never expected anything from him.

I fold into the box and grimace. It smells of old puke and Nen's sweat. There is blood in the fresh scratches carved by Nen's nails and dried flakes in ruts carved by those punished before him.

I curl up on my side with my knees pressed to my chin, and I am grateful that I am small. One hour. It's just one hour. The lid slams shut.

I glimpse a little light through a crack in the wood. There's not enough to see by, but I suck at the air greedily and try to occupy myself with guessing at the sounds outside. Gradually, the sounds of the candidates fade away and are replaced by the rhythm of a broom sweeping across the floor and the staccato of dishes stacked in baskets. And then a familiar voice begins to sing.

The muscles in my jaw unclench. Tanu's voice carries in the open hall. I didn't see him at breakfast, but he promised my sister that he would look out for me, and he never breaks his promises.

I lean my head against the wood. He was always there for us. Once, when I was twelve, I vomited all over his shoes after eating leftovers that had gone rancid. Neither my mother nor my sister could afford the time away from our stall, so Tanu sat with me and read his books on the histories of Tigang aloud. He emptied out the buckets at my bedside and held my hair back whenever I hurled. He didn't once complain. He always had so much patience.

Whenever he was apart from Kuran for too long, my sister would get wound up like a spring, and her temper would get shorter. She was always happier when he was around. But maybe we never bothered to ask Tanu what he wanted; we just assumed he wanted the same, because we couldn't imagine anything more.

I know Tanu's song by heart, and I imagine my sister singing along. It's a song of our people crossing the ocean, following the stars to a new home. Tanu would sing it for me when I was little and taught it to Kuran in exchange for a kiss. I close my eyes and see striped sails unfurled in the wind, my sister standing beside me as we sail into the unknown with no assurance of another shore.

It's too late to turn back. The realization hits me like a runaway cart, suddenly real. There will never be any more peaceful days walking dusty roads with my mother and my sister. But win or lose, live or drown, there is only forward.

The bones in my shoulders click uncomfortably as I unfurl myself. Tanu's voice coaxed me through the dark until my hour was done, but he's nowhere to be seen when I emerge.

The great hall stands empty. None of the usual staff are anywhere: the dusters, the sweepers, the floor polishers.

The test must have begun without me. I search the room for

any clue to direct me but find none. Instead, I spot two figures lying on the floor, side by side like discarded dolls. One tall and gangly, one short and plump. I sprint across the room. My scarf nearly unwinds, and I tie it back up as I run.

"Virian!" I pull her into my arms. Her face is pale, and sweat trickles down her crooked nose. Her lips are cracked and faded to an inhuman shade of white.

Could this be the test? But Virian and Dayen would need to be taking the test, not dying. This looks too much like sabotage, like someone wants us gone.

She grips my tunic with shaking hands. "Poison," she whispers. Beside her, Dayen kneads at his stomach as if there's something moving inside. A pool of sour liquid soils the floor nearby, but he's already hacking up clear spit, and it tells me that everything that could have come out has already come out. Oh no.

"I'll find help," I say and try the main doors, but they are bolted from the outside.

"Someone, please!" I scream and bang it with my fists, but the mahogany muffles any sound beyond. No one replies to my shouts, even though my voice grows hoarse from it. Whomever locked us in meant for us to stay in. They meant for us to die. My mind skips the whos and whys because I don't have time for them.

I run to the pierced screen that hides the service entrance used by the fortress staff, but a metal gate blocks the opening, secured with a thick chain.

I kick at the gate, but the chain holds. I catch a flash of brown in the distance, and I scream until my throat is raw. I even scream for Teloh. I know someone's listening, but no one would dare defy the Baylan's orders. I jam a hair pin into the lock, but it does not release. The hinges on the gate look strong enough to keep in an elephant.

A girl in brown peeks around the corner. She wears her hair in a scarf like the kitchen staff, but she looks barely ten years old.

"Please," I plead, and she scurries over, looking over her shoulder. Hells, I hope she won't be punished for helping me.

She tugs at the gate ineffectually. "I don't have a key."

"Can we force it?" I pull while she pushes, but the gate remains lodged in place. If Teloh hadn't dislocated my fingers, I might have been able to pick the lock. I curse him under my breath, and slam my wrists against the metal bars in frustration.

"Wait," she squeaks and disappears down the hall. I have no choice but to sit and do nothing, even though time is running out.

Arisa or Reshar? Poison reeks of Reshar. The cruelty of it is too refined for Arisa. I'm sure she would prefer blunt objects and broken bones. If she wanted someone dead, she would send Teloh or put a knife in them herself, because she would want them to know it. Reshar, I conclude.

The initiate slides back down the hall toward me. No key jingles from her hand, and my desperation grows.

"I stole this from the infirmary." She thrusts a paper into my hands. It's covered in a complicated orasyon decorated with overlapping circles and triangles like some mathematical theorem. "It's only for one person," she says and runs away.

Omu above. I would scream if my throat weren't already raw. I race back to my friends. How could I choose between them?

Dayen's eyes flutter open and closed, but his lips move as his body convulses. He clutches his amulets with white knuckles and opens his eyes when I approach, and they are cloudy white like Virian's lips. His tongue is black. This is no poison that I have heard of.

"I'm afraid," he whispers.

"Me too," I say.

I check Virian. She gasps for breath like a fish trapped on land but remains upright. Her hands are limp, and there is puke on her tunic, because no matter how fierce her expression, she couldn't even turn her head away.

"I can't save you both," I say.

"Heal Dayen," Virian says. "He doesn't deserve this."

Dayen turns and groans so that his head is curled over Virian's and hers nestles in the crook of his neck. The floppy mess of his hair falls into his eyes. "I have no chance at winning; don't waste the spell on me."

"There must be a way," I say. Dayen does not deserve to die this way, even if he has no chance at ruling Tigang. And Virian, oh, she is a flame, and if I had a choice, I would want her to.

My vision blurs, and I wonder if I ingested poison, too, but I taste the salt in my mouth and realize it's only tears.

"Here." Virian lifts a palm, and I see a coin in her hand. It's a silver Rythian coin, stamped with a horse head on one side and the motto "*Until the Ends of the Earth*" upon the other.

I run my fingers over the marks. The horse for Dayen and the motto for Virian, I decide and toss the coin to the sky with a prayer. When it lands, the horse stares back at me.

There must be another way. I tear at my hair.

"Hurry," Virian says. Dayen is hacking again, and each cough sounds like it could be the last.

"Kuran," Virian whispers, and I only realize a moment later that she is speaking to me.

I close my eyes and press the crumpled orasyon to the closest body, but my fingers brush cold skin. When I open my eyes, Dayen is folded over and Virian has stopped breathing. I was too late.

CHAPTER TWENTY

I'm still sobbing when Datu Payan, the head Healer, presses his hand against my shoulder. He bends over my friends. One after another, they gasp, then sputter. Their eyes fly open, and color returns as if a frost melted. This really was a test?

What the Freezing Hells? I wipe tears and snot from my face. How dare the Baylan play with our emotions like this! With every passing day, I feel more and more certain that whatever crime my mother committed must have been justified. These are not tests but torture. My shoulders heave, and I scream aloud in frustration.

Payan looks away, apologetic. "I am sorry that you needed to believe that death was close at hand. When we are done here, eat and rest. You will feel better shortly." Everything about him appears guileless. His voice is soft and soothing, and his wide-set eyes assert innocence. If I ran to him raving that the moon was a dragon's egg, I wonder if he might agree just to soothe me and I would find my convictions firm. I wish I could trust him, but I don't.

Worse yet, I hate myself for not acting quickly. If this were real, my friends would be dead, and it would be my fault. I don't know who I am more mad at: Payan, the Sundo, or myself.

Virian shifts and sighs. Her head still rests in the crook of Dayen's neck, and his chin still nestles upon her hair. When she looks up at him and he looks back, I see something different in the exchange.

"The ruler of Tigang must make difficult decisions," he says. "We had to know how you might react in the face of death. You may think we Healers only fix broken bones and maladies, but never forget that if Tigang goes to war, we spend the breaths of our lives to save all the people that we can. Though we have had peace for centuries, we must also be ready in times of war. Peace does not last forever."

His words ring like a distant warning, but I am too much of a mess to focus. Virian and Dayen are alive, I remind myself, but it doesn't ease my guilt. I worry that if I close my eyes I might open them and a different reality might take us all.

"Today we tested your ability to think quickly under pressure and how well you could cooperate with others."

My anger switches into anxiety. I know we are not automatically disqualified from the Sundo for failing a test, but I don't know how low or high my score must be now. I can't afford to be disqualified. I still haven't figured out a way to get my mother out of the dungeons.

"Virian Saniran, you failed this test. You three were given a single orasyon to save someone. You could have copied it out and saved the both of you. Do you not always carry writing implements and paper?" Payan's eyes drift to the pouch on her waist.

Virian sits up straight and stutters. "But I could hardly move! How could I have copied it out?"

"You could have given your tools to Kuran Jal." Payan shakes his head and turns to Dayen. "Dayen Kam, you chose to sacrifice your chance at winning for someone you thought more worthy. Noble, but you did not think of a solution that would save you both, either. Lives are precious, and we must do what we can to save as many as we can."

My heart pounds, because only one judgment must come next, and I already know the outcome.

"Kuran Jal, your indecision condemned both your friends to death."

I make a shallow bow. I should have acted faster and kept my head. I deserve their scorn, not forgiveness.

"You have all failed this test, but none of you are disqualified, so your fate is not yet decided. But to succeed, you must do spectacularly from now on," he warns. "Remember, sometimes there is no right choice, but you must make one anyway," he says in a gentle tone before dismissing us.

When he is away, I throw my arms around both Virian and Dayen. "I'm so sorry," I say over and over and crush them tightly against me. "I thought Reshar was going to disappear us..."

"Kuran." Virian pushes me back with a gasp. "You're heavier than you look. And why on earth would Reshar do that?"

Because he's mean, difficult, selfish, and clearly up to something secret. I don't have proof, only a feeling.

"At least now we know she likes us both equally," Dayen teases but quickly disentangles himself from my arms, even though I did not touch his skin. "I'm starving."

"First of all, we stink. Second of all, Reshar is a crusty old goat, but I don't think he's evil," Virian says.

"What if he has something to do with the missing candidates?" I ask.

"Do you have any evidence?" Virian asks, and I shake my head no.

"Are you both hungry?" Dayen interrupts us.

"You're always starving, Dayen." Virian wrinkles her nose.

I don't know how they can make light when they might have just died. But I was the one that watched it happen, and I don't know if I could ever watch something like that again. I might be tempted to leave the Sundo first. I shake my head and walk back the thought because I cannot afford to fail.

"First of all, let's grab some food." I stand slowly. "Second of all, there's a place I know…"

It's not my fault, I tell myself, but my heart refuses to agree.

Virian tugs my hand and spins me around to face her. Her posture reminds me of Omu's statue, ready to command or pass judgment.

"Next time, you better choose," she says. "We don't always get to keep it all." Her expression softens, and I wonder what she's already lost and what's brought her here, but she turns into herself and the quiet.

I lead my friends into the Autumn Palace with fresh towels and new clothes draped over our arms. I want to make amends, but I also want to soak away every ache in my body, wash away the guilt stained onto my soul—or at least try.

When Virian steps into the baths, she whistles with delight, and the sound bounces happily in its recesses, multiplying. Soft light tints us all an otherworldly shade, and I half wonder if we've already died and are ghosts.

Dayen turns the tap on the large basin and hoots in victory when hot, milky spring water hisses into the empty pool.

I dip my toe in, but there's a knock at the door. My heart leaps ahead of me.

I stick my head out to find Teloh standing outside the entrance, hands in his pockets. He wants me gone, but I'm too tired to be angry. I step outside the baths and leave the door a little ajar.

I realize now why his gaze is so unsettling. It's not his eyes' strange blue-black color but how intently he stares, as if nothing else in the world exists but me.

So, I stare at his feet.

My mother always told me that you can't control what you feel but you can control what you do about it. I'm not in control now, and I don't know if I want to be. I don't understand what my heart keeps trying to tell me, only that everything is a jumbled mess that gets worse when he's around, because he makes me want to hope for something more.

"Were we lovers or enemies in our past lives?" My voice sounds flatter and calmer than I expect because I already know the answer.

I brace for him to tell me why I am so repulsive, that I deserve to be cursed, that I could never be worthy of ruling Tigang—something I don't even truly desire. I want him to give me a reason to despise him and end the torture of his presence. I lift my eyes upward, afraid to move or make it worse.

"Nothing so simple as either." For a moment, the mess of emotions I feel is mirrored on his face, but the ghosts in my chest remain strangely silent. "At first, I was afraid that you might remember. Now, I am afraid that you are in danger. If something were to happen to you, I could not forgive myself." He looks up at the ceiling, his jaw clenched tight. "The others were given a different Healing test. I thought the poison was real, too, but I couldn't do anything."

I curse him to the Freezing Hells, heart thudding. I still want to hate him. This is not the answer I was looking for.

"I don't understand anything anymore," I say.

"It's called change, Narra." He smiles, and how it warms me, so free and full of life in that instant that it could power a thousand spells. But I am no hero. I am afraid of everything, including myself.

It would take one heartbeat to close the gap between us, and yet, it feels an impossible distance.

"Kuran!" Virian's sudden appearance makes me jump. She

holds a towel primly around her chest. "And *you*. What are you doing here? Has Arisa actually let you off her leash?"

"I have no quarrel with you candidates," Teloh says, and his stance shifts, ready to move.

"Well then the water's ready, and it's glorious." Virian tuts and glides back through the door as elegantly as if she wore a gown. Not for the first time, I wonder about her life before the Sundo.

"Are you coming?" she shouts, and I hear her splash into the pool with a shout.

It takes me a moment to realize that she's inviting the both of us.

Teloh raises an eyebrow, and to my surprise, he removes his boots and walks into the baths ahead of me. He slides into the pool, clothes and all, hardly making a ripple. I watch them there, waiting for me.

Nothing can stay the same forever.

I suck in a breath and follow, unsure where this path goes. It feels like driving a cart up a mountain road on a moonless night, and any bump in the road might send us careening over the edge.

The boys turn their backs so that I can leave my towel at the tiled edge and slip into the pool. It is as glorious as I dreamed. I close my eyes as hot water laps against my skin. I almost purr, and Virian is humming as she smiles up at the ceiling. I catch her slip her hand under the surface to meet Dayen's.

Teloh sees the gesture, and our eyes meet for a moment. It's as tentative as a handshake, and I am the one who looks away.

None of us talk, but this moment is ours, thoughts to ourselves, in the amber light.

Teloh drips in his clothes, back turned, as he waits for us to get changed. It feels like I've started a truce between us. I boldly trace his jaw with my eyes when I'm clothed. I wonder if his skin feels how I think it will; if it is rough, or if it is soft; if to touch it might awaken the sleeping thing inside me.

"No one can curse me more than I have already been cursed," Teloh says, watching my hands balled at my sides. I hesitate when he takes my right hand and turns over my wrist, but he gently uncurls my fingers one by one, so that my palm is bathed in light. When I do not protest, he lifts it to his lips, and my skin burns where his lips touch me, as if I am on fire.

All I can hear is my heart in my ears—he's kissed me like this before in my dreams. It's a gesture as old as Arawan. I forget the pain of my dislocated finger and my scars. My lives crash together. Past and present dance in a circle that leaves me dizzy in the center of it all.

"Whatever I did in my past life to hurt you, I'm sorry." I struggle for my mouth to make sense, but I know that I've erred once the words escape my lips. His expression closes as he gently pulls away. I touched upon a scar that is still healing or might never heal.

"Do not say that unless you know what you're sorry for." There is danger in his tone, and he is gone before I can say another word. And I don't hate him; I hate myself.

Dayen is staring open mouthed, with big eyes. Virian is covering her mouth to stop from giggling. I wish this was as simple as the flirtation it looks like. I let out a long sigh.

"Well, now." Dayen slaps me on the back and whistles. "You have good taste, Kuran."

"So, you like them dangerous?" I ask. "He's Arisa's personal assassin."

Dayen chokes on a cough and his cheeks turn embarrassingly red, but Virian chews her lip thoughtfully.

"Can we trust him, Kuran?" she asks.

"No," I say.

I dare not imagine how Arisa might use him against us.

CHAPTER TWENTY-ONE

I shouldn't be here, but my nannies haven't caught me yet. I stare into the dark pit in the middle of the room. I tossed chocolate into it, but either the bottom is too far away or my friend that lives in the bottom of the pit caught it. The rest of the space is empty, which I think is a shame, but my friend always breaks all the toys I bring it. Everyone fears this place, but I have never. I know I am safe here. No one else in the entire fortress understands me half as well as my friend.

"Are you awake? Are you there? Did you get my present?" I ask.

A raincloud puffs out of the center of the pit like a smoke ring. It spins overhead and sends a sprinkling shower into my face. My favorite is the fog. If I tell a good story, sometimes I get a rainbow. It always likes the most outlandish ones.

"Do you have a name?" I ask and wait for the darkness to answer, but morning comes first. I sit up in my bed and try to wake my limbs, but the dream clings to me like another vision. I scrub at my eyes and steady myself.

Every dream leaves me more confused than before, but the Sundo is real, and every morning in Bato-Ko seems to bring another horror.

After breakfast announcements, my first instinct is to bolt for the doors, but Virian blocks the way. Kalena's latest announcement has Virian hovering like a hummingbird, floating here and there so quickly that I would lose track of her if she wasn't dragging me along after her. Midsummer is Holy Omu's feast, and everyone, including the Sundo, must stop for it. There is to be a party.

Another cursed party. Voices pitch loud around us in the great hall, ringing with an excitement I don't share. Virian replies to everyone in rapid fire, making plans, throwing out suggestions. I pretend not to notice that the other candidates greet only Virian as we pass.

I suppress a groan as Virian tugs the limp strands of my hair and mulls over what to do with it. I shrug at her suggestions. If Kuran were here, she could at least smooth the way, charming everyone so all I need to do is smile and nod politely. It frustrates me that I'm going to be forced to waste another few hours of my short life not knowing what to do with my hands, not knowing what to say, not knowing where to stand, and pretending to enjoy it, while my mother rots in the dungeons beneath the palace.

Hells, if this is another test in disguise, then I am doomed.

"So I was talking with Nen earlier…" Dayen walks over to us and interrupts the spiral of my thoughts. I scowl, because Nen still hasn't thanked me for taking his punishment.

"You really aren't choosy about your friends," I snap, and I regret it at once. I catch the subtle twitch in his fingers, as if he's resisted the urge to flinch away from me.

"I was asking about Arisa's marks," he says quietly and takes a step back. "Did you know that in the southern provinces, birthmarks are considered a sign of power?"

"They also think most of us are not pure-blooded or pious enough, no better than dirt to them," I say. He doesn't deserve the dredges of my ill temper, but I can't help myself. I am all spines today, and I don't know why something as simple as a party has fouled my mood this much. Maybe it's the dreams and restless nights. Maybe it's because Midsummer is Kuran's favorite holiday. Midsummer was always a time for family instead of work. Our mother always would cook us a meal of Tigangi food, no matter where we were on the continent or how rare the ingredients. We would keep our stall packed away, and we would watch the sun rise and set with mugs of hot coffee or chocolate.

Dayen pretends to stare at his toes and fidgets with his amulets. I understand what he's trying to say. He wants to make sense of me, but a lifetime of fearmongering cannot be erased in a few days. I am not making things easier between us. I wish I knew how to, but I don't.

I still need to find a way to get past the guards in the dungeons, but Virian and Dayen have been watching me closely. Since the Healing test, I haven't managed to sneak away.

"You gossip more than my aunties, Dayen." Virian sighs. "You know all the first families are invited to the fortress for Midsummer?"

I'm grateful for the change of subject, even though it reminds me of what I have lost. No one will be coming to meet me. Kuran is alone because I am here.

"My parents are coming. They'll be proud I haven't been disqualified yet," Dayen says, lifting up his head, suddenly as eager as a puppy, but I notice how he still keeps Virian between us.

I miss arguing with Kuran. I miss my mother's steady presence. I even miss Tanu's books. I miss my old life. I wish I were with my sister running through the streets with a pocket full of good-luck money, chasing down cups of iced milk with red beans.

Instead, I'm trapped inside this hulking fortress, and it was all my choice. Not for the first time, I wonder if I made the right decision. Perhaps, I'd have had better chances trying to win over the Elders who will decide my mother's fate, but it's too late to go back now.

I still can't erase the memory of my friends lying dead on a marble floor, even though they are still here beside me. I can't erase the feeling of Teloh's warm lips against my palm, even when it's folly to think of him. I don't know what to feel anymore. My emotions are like muddy water, mixed up and impossible to see through, even though I'm drowning in them.

"You look as if someone just died." Virian tosses her head. "But this is just a party."

Just. To her, it's not another unnecessary cruelty piled on top of the necessary ones.

"There will be food, and Heavens know you're all bones and you need it." Virian catches me before I slip away. Her eyes are as big as a cat's. "Arisa and the Baylan will be busy blessing the city, and that means we can have some fun."

I doubt our ideas of fun are the same.

"Please, Kuran?" She bats her lashes and smiles, as if this would make her more pleased than anything else in the world. It's the happiest I've seen her. The happiest I've seen any of them, and they might need this party in a way that I do not. Guilt seeps in through the cracks cut by Virian's smile. Who am I to deny them this?

A party will not kill me, I tell myself.

"Fine," I sigh and surrender to her.

I don't recognize this part of the fortress, so I pay attention and add it to my mental map. At the end of a wide corridor lit with huge, patterned lamps stands a giant wooden door reinforced with steel bands. Three wheels the size of my head turn three thick metal bolts that lock the door in place, but the door stands ajar, just wide enough for us to slip through.

"Are you sure we're allowed to be here?" I hesitate.

"The Baylan are allowed to borrow from the treasury. Did you ever notice that they're always dripping in gems? They just have to return whatever they take." Virian slides through the crack before I can protest, so I follow. "We're not Baylan, but I asked my cousin if we could borrow something because most of our clothes were destroyed. I can use his name." She taps a logbook outside the door. Names are signed in and out beside lists of items.

I follow her inside, and Virian presents the room with a wide sweep of her hands.

The hinge on my jaw is loose. The room is lined with all manner of containers full of colorful rings and bracelets that reflect the light like polished mirrors. Everything is meticulously organized. There are rows upon rows of bracelets, and an entire wall is hung with necklaces. I have never seen so many hairpins in my life, made from every stone imaginable, semi-precious to precious. Kuran would have been in the clouds and flown from one sparkly thing to another like a magpie. My mother would have rolled her eyes and given us a lecture about valuing material goods, but she grew up with every advantage when we did not. I think she struggled with our life more than we did, because it was all we ever knew.

"We should meet here if one of us is in trouble. We can lock it from the inside," I grunt. My voice grates in my throat, as out of place as I feel in this room, and Virian makes an exasperated sound.

"Really? You're thinking about that now?" She rolls her eyes and strides over to a large adjacent room stuffed full of precious cloth from every corner of the continent.

I reach out and touch a sleeve of linen embroidered with

so many golden threads that the fabric feels as thick as armor. I cannot help the thrill at the feeling of cloth under my hands. It feels illicit, like something stolen, even though Manay Halna is nowhere nearby to scream that I am ruining the fabric. I might be tainting it with my touch, but I don't care. Bolts of fabric are how I've measured the cost of everything in my life, and I've never had a chance to admire it for myself.

"You." Virian looks me up and down. "Need a little color about you. Let's make everyone remember us tonight." She tosses me a yellow gown and shoves me in front of a large mirror.

"And you should wear blue. It will bring out the gold flecks in your eyes," I say.

I press my hands together and practice another smile alongside her as we stare at our reflections. When we stand side by side, we look small and young and more afraid than I expected.

"Do you ever miss your old life?" I ask.

"It doesn't matter. There's nothing for me to go back to." Virian swallows and shakes her head to compose herself, but I glimpse a moment of Virian raw. The girl behind the bluster, who huddled against the wall of the fortress the first day of the Sundo. I wonder how her nose was broken and what she fled to come here, but I know she is not ready to tell me.

"I forget that we have only been here days, not lifetimes," I say. And I wonder if Virian and I have ever met before, too. If everything is destined to repeat, and we are all tangled together with invisible threads.

"Bato-Ko does have that effect. So, let's make this one last as long as we can." She smiles so brightly that I am dazzled.

Soon we are draped in jewels. Virian's laughter is clear and infectious. It fills the treasury as we try on clothes and baubles. I can't help but laugh with her. She teases a tiny bit of happiness from the tight clutches of my heart. For a little while, I forget the competition, and I start to think that my discomfort might be worth the price of Virian's laughter.

But my mirth draws short as we step into the hall. Virian strides confidently ahead of me and my heart aches, because win or lose, we can never remain friends.

CHAPTER TWENTY-TWO

It's only midmorning, but the throne room is crammed so full that I can't extend an arm without touching someone. Virian hacks a path through the gaggle and tugs Dayen behind her. I follow in their wake, hands fisted so tightly that my knuckles are white. We're dressed in finery, but the dead flowers we wear in our hair remind me that things are not as they seem.

They're smiling, but Manay Halna's familiar reprimands echo in my mind. I shouldn't be here. The high neck of my gown covers my marks but leaves my shoulders, arms, and lower back bare. I might as well be coated in poison. I keep my arms tight to my sides and hurry after them.

Virian chose to honor her Rythian heritage by selecting a stiff sky blue gown covered head to toe in complicated silver embroidery. She looks radiant. Happy.

The crowd ripples around us, but Dayen doesn't notice anyone but Virian. The only difference today is that he ran a comb through his hair, but the grin he wears is so wide that it transforms him. He keeps looking down to check that Virian's hand is still twined with his. I think he'd let her drag him through the Three Hells and still smile.

I am envious of them both, because I wish that some lightness would stick to my heart; that happiness didn't come in pinpricks and dribbles.

I rub at the nape of my neck. My heavy hair is knotted so tightly into a bun at the base of my neck that it tilts my chin upward and tugs my eyes open. I wish it might pull my lips into a semblance of a smile, but it threatens a headache instead.

"You look like you're at a funeral." Virian shakes her head and throws back her shoulders to demonstrate the composure I wish I had.

"I don't enjoy people looking at me."

"Then how the Hells will you endure all of Tigang and the continent watching your every move?" Virian teases.

She's right. The ruler of Tigang entertains foreign diplomats and presides over festivals year-round. Then there are the councils to facilitate, and the parades... The ruler is meant to be the public emblem of our country.

"You would be good at it," I say. I'm right, too.

Virian sighs and turns me around to face the masses. "You still need to try."

There is a sea of jeweled bodies before me. I remain frozen in place. The dress I wear is so tight that I am afraid if I breathe too deeply the stitches might come apart. It looks like all of Bato-Ko is in the throne room, and I am a glowing yellow target waiting for an arrow to strike me down.

The yellow will brighten your complexion, she said. *It will be fun*, she said. I remain unconvinced. If I were Virian, I might turn both into truth, but I'm not.

"Nay, Tay!" Dayen's hand lifts into the air, and I steal away before I'm forced to make pleasantries with his parents.

I find a bubble of space around a table carved from ice. Metal cups wait atop the table, full to the brim with shaved ice as fine as snow, dripping with sweet cream and jellied toppings. The cool air and the pooling water keep guests away, but soaked slippers and soggy toes are a price I'm willing to bear.

"Cloth merchant?"

I'm not the only one the cold table attracted. I recognize the voice and turn around, red-faced.

Oshar pulls away from her wife, Sayarala. The Turinese woman is dressed in a gown of cream pineapple cloth that coordinates with Oshar's new shirt and trousers. A golden falcon dangles against the russet skin of Sayarala's throat, marking her as Turinese royalty. I swallow. I had been too distracted to notice it at Oshar's party. I wilt under the directness of her gaze as she scrutinizes me now.

"A moment, my love," Oshar murmurs to her before turning to me. "Your sister performed so beautifully that it felt as if I was there in Arawan. I'm sorry that I never had a chance to thank you properly."

The thought of my sister is almost too much to bear, and I nod, barely managing a smile. Kuran would have thought this party was Heavenly, and I could have endured it if she was here. She would make a formidable Reyna.

I grab a cup of ice and cream instead of asking Oshar for a blessing, but she doesn't chide me for it.

Oshar leans forward to whisper. "These parties are such a chore, but at least there are sweets. What was your name again, child? I'm so forgetful these days. You must excuse me."

I don't believe her for a moment. Though she says this party is a bore, her eyes seem to drink in every detail, and though she asks my name, I doubt she's forgotten. Who is this Oshar Toso, who has even Reshar worried? I curse my mother for leaving me so unprepared for Bato-Ko.

"Kuran, Nanay Oshar," I lie. I know that I am caught when she blinks, but she keeps her thoughts close and does not mention it.

"Good luck to you, child. Though I would not wish the winning on you, I pray that you stay safe." She turns over her palm, and I recognize a faded mark on the mound of her hand.

"You were a candidate?" I sputter.

Oshar hides her mouth behind a hand, and I realize my error. I drop to my knees and press my forehead to the floor because I'm not sure what else to do. "Evergreen Reyna."

"Please don't kneel, child." She waves her hands, embarrassed. "I was ruler a very long time ago, child. Now I am only Nanay Oshar." Only. She says it like a joke, knowing full well that she is more than simple.

"I saw the last Reyna. How are you still so…"

"Vibrant?" She laughs. "The ruler of Tigang is a conduit for the power of the Diwata. Channeling that power will erode your life and age you quickly." She pitches her voice low, for only me to hear. "So you resist. Do not believe everything anyone tells you—not even the lips of Omu herself. Keep your head clear and decide for yourself."

This is what the Baylan are looking for: someone they can control, someone who asks few questions. My stomach roils. Of course that is what Arisa would want, and if I deny her, she will kill me.

"Use your wits to solve your problems instead of power." Oshar pats my shoulder, and I flinch from her touch.

"Is everything all right, dear?" she asks.

I do not know if I can trust this woman, but I've sensed no guile in her, only a sharp intelligence. No one else might know what truly happens during the Sundo, but she survived with her mind intact. I glance around us, but everyone is drinking deeply or huddled together in conversation. I risk at least one truth. "Candidates and Baylan are going missing, and I don't think it is part of the tests. I suspect someone here in the fortress cannot be trusted."

I think of Reshar and his sneers. Between him and Arisa, I don't know who I trust less.

Oshar pulls my head close to hers. "I have heard rumors.

Tigang has enemies, and it makes sense for them to threaten us now. If I hear something more, I will find a way to get word to you. Send for me if you need help or tell your sister to come to me."

"Beloved," Sayarala warns. Guests approach, all smiles and fluttering lashes for Oshar.

"I wish you well, candidate. Remember the uncomfortable stories. Those will serve you well here," Oshar says and meets these newcomers with open arms.

Why does it always come back to stories? I ponder with a frown. Teloh's dismissal of my telling of Astar and Chaos still makes me burn with shame. I don't know why that particular tale would make a difference now, and I don't know what he wanted to hear.

I cannot afford to be weak if I'm to survive the rest of the Sundo long enough to break my mother out, so I fill my belly. I inhale sweet sticky rice buried inside little bundles of leaves and fried rolls stuffed with garlicky meat. I taste sweet steamed yellow cakes and freshly grilled fish. I keep my hands busy and make excuses for not speaking to people with a full mouth.

I lose my appetite when I glimpse Teloh in the crowd.

As always, he's dressed simply in the black of the Guardians. A kampilan sword sways at his side, and his ceremonial kris is tucked at his waist, but many eyes drift to him. Maybe it's his manner that draws their eyes, the way he never seems to care what anyone else thinks.

I wish I could walk around with the same assurance.

A space clears around him as if he wears spiny armor like a blowfish, and though he keeps his eyes to the floor, he's headed straight for me. I feel that tightness in my chest again and remember his lips upon my palm. My first instinct is to run and avoid facing the confused mess of my feelings, but I'm trapped between tables of food and the crowd.

I stand my ground, though I am a river stone nestled in a jewelry box. I'm acutely aware of the bareness of my shoulders and the red finger marks where I've scratched at the itching high collar of my dress. The dress hides my birthmarks, but I feel naked without my scarf.

Teloh stops and looks up, startled, as though he hadn't been paying attention until now. His eyes go first to my neck before flickering up to my face. I wring my hands, unsure what to do with them.

"I…" Teloh pauses a moment. "You look so uncomfortable."

At least he didn't say *terrible*.

"You wanted something?" I don't sound nearly as confident as I wish I did, but he swallows as if unsure what to say.

Who would we be if we met on the road or on the fields? He, some rich man's son; me, a poor merchant. He would not speak to me, nor I to him. We would pass by each other and never cross paths again. It's a useless thought, but I cannot help trying to place him in some concocted history. Nothing fits. In none of my daytime imaginings can I picture the two of us together, with a past or with a future. Only nightmares and uncomfortable visions bring him to mind, and I don't know what it means about him. Or about me.

"How do you keep finding me?" I ask, frustrated that he hasn't moved far enough away to offer relief to my flagging heart.

"You're not easy to miss." He smiles that sly smile of his, and my feigned confidence evaporates. Whatever unbalanced him a moment ago, he has found his footing again. "I have a talent, you see. I can sense change, and it's all around you, like a perfume, like a hurricane." There's something in his expression that I do not recognize, so full of meaning that I cannot pick it apart. "It's why Arisa keeps me close. I'm good at finding troublemakers."

My expression sours, and I curse how terribly I manage to

hide my feelings. "So you're watching me for her."

"No." He slides into the space beside me, and at once he's too close. I can smell him. He is all green things growing and dark soil beneath. His shoulder is nearly touching mine, and to feel his uniform against my bare skin is too much for me. "You are a dangerous distraction," he says.

I've already used up all my patience in politely cutting conversation with strangers, so I glare at him. "Then which one of us will be destroyed this time? If we were enemies in another life, how could you stop it from happening again?"

He does not remove his eyes from mine, though I badly need a reprieve from the intensity of his gaze. My neck is too hot, and my ears burn.

"Perhaps we must try something different, then." He narrows his eyes in challenge. "Kiss me."

I blank immediately, looking at his mouth. Why does he have such lovely lips? They're as full of expression as his eyes. I curse my traitorous brain. I've stopped breathing; I force an inhalation. "What?!"

He waits, and I wonder if it's always been that way between us, like a pile of kindling ready to catch fire. But Arisa... Thoughts of her go scattering, unformed.

I ball my hands, unable to calm my racing heart. This is a dare, not an invitation, but I don't think I could live with myself if I refused it. My brow is still furrowed when we crash together. It is two hard skulls meeting, and it hurts as though I've hit my head against a rock, entirely missing the mark, but before I can recover, he pulls me toward him. His warm hands press against a triangle of bare skin at the small of my back, and this time I fall into his lips. I forget the room, the crowd, and the Sundo. Even my name is a distant memory. It feels like I've plunged overboard into a storming ocean. He fills all my senses, and I do not know if I would rather seek the relief of shore or give in and drown.

"Oh…" is the only sound that escapes my lips. When I open my eyes, his are closed still, and his hands have slid into my hair. I can feel his breath on my face, still so close. His heart pulses under the tips of my fingers, where they've slid to his chest. Every inch of me burns hot, from my belly to my toes, and I don't know what to do or what to say.

A space has opened around us now, and even Oshar peers in our direction. But I am not thinking about anyone else. I don't think I am thinking at all. Everything in my head feels upside down and shaken too hard. I'm glad Arisa is out in the city blessing babies, or houses, or something. I swallow.

"So." He grins, mirroring my surprise, and I hate how much I enjoy the shape of his lips. I touch my fingers to my mouth to see if the kiss was a memory or a hallucination, but I can still taste the salt of his tongue, and my nose is full of the musk of him. It feels like something I've been waiting for—always.

Every part of me is warm and awake, as if some of his breath has given me life. If this goes any further, it will not be a choice between him or me: we will both be destroyed.

But Teloh's expression closes, and his hand inches toward the hilt of his sword. I follow where his gaze has gone, only to find Tanu arranging plates on a table behind us.

"You know Tanu?" I ask, still reeling. I fight to calm my racing heart.

Teloh shakes his head, as if to clear his, too. "He reminds me of someone I once knew." He frowns, and for once he looks his age, not so certain, just barely more than a boy. "About as dull as a wooden spoon, too."

"He's not so bad," I say.

"So you can be swayed by blue eyes and shoulders like an ox?" Teloh quirks his lips.

I roll my eyes. I am curious about this new puzzle but am

more curious about the shape of Teloh's lips, and as I recall the taste of him, my cheeks flush again.

"But that is not important. I wish I had just come for a kiss, but I didn't." His eyes drift to my mouth, and heat spreads all the way down to my toes. "I came to warn you."

This is the Teloh I am familiar with. Disappointment returns me fully to the present.

His hands slip away, leaving me cold. He is still so near that I can feel his warmth, but I don't trust myself with him, with how different the world looks when he is near. This must end now, I tell myself. The Sundo is everything. I must stay in the game, or I will lose my mother and my family forever. And if I do not, I will either forget them all or die.

"On Midsummer, the council of elders passes judgment on those awaiting trial in the fortress. Shora Jal will be sentenced this afternoon. Don't say anything. Don't do anything. Please, I beg you."

"And you kissed me instead of telling me first?" I stare at him, incredulous.

"I didn't think I would get a chance to if I did. Please…"

His pleading doesn't reach me. All that consumes my thoughts is that my mother will be sentenced. Suddenly the party, the competition, everyone staring at us, and even Teloh cease to matter. How could I do nothing?

CHAPTER TWENTY-THREE

I can't stand still. I'm the one shaking, and Teloh, who is always moving, seems an impossibly steady thing. I fight against his arms when the doors to the great hall open and the council of first families leaves the party to begin the trials. The departure of our elders makes the room feel like the party has ended, though so many still linger. The doors shutting behind them feels like finality, like the burying of the dead.

I launch myself toward Tanu before Teloh can change my mind or make me question my motives. He lifts his hands to fend me off.

"Tanu, take me through the service hallways."

"Na—" He stops himself, and the pieces click into place in his head. It tells me that he knew about the trials but not about my mother. He takes one look at Teloh, and his eyes widen.

Tanu folds under my glare. "This way."

But I know by the warning in his expression that Teloh is done making scenes, and if he were to run after me there would be no way it would escape notice. Good. I need this chance. Teloh grunts in frustration as he lets us go.

Brown-clad initiates to the Baylan stare as the pair of us pass. I shouldn't be here, but there are no Baylan in the narrow hallway to stop us. I peek through the pierced screen that hides the service entrance to the great hall and stick my nose between the coiling bodies of snakes and sinuous flowers.

Fifty people sit in a semicircle of wooden benches. They all wear black sashes or shawls, with black pearls in bands upon their heads and necks. Each is a representative from one of the first families in Tigang: the iron of Tigang, for whom we are named.

In the center of them all sits my grandmother. No one sits to either side of Yirin, as if she occupies more space than she is wide. She sits stick straight, expressionless, and unbent—no one in the room matters to her. I see my mother in her posture, but I see myself in her cold eyes. It leaves a bad taste in my mouth.

"This will take a while," Tanu whispers, and we crouch on the marble floor together. I tuck my dress awkwardly around my knees, and he huddles beside me in his brown uniform. It is so loose that it's hard to tell how big he is. Maybe that's the point. Perhaps he spent his childhood making music on a traveling stage when all he wanted was anonymity.

He would have been a good brother. The silence is never awkward between us. We are more alike than my sister and me.

And maybe he wanted a different life, too. I'm sorry I judged him so unfairly for leaving Kuran. My betrayal is worse than his. Kuran could find another lover, but I've left her without family. It's the gravest sin any Tigangi could commit. But what else could I do? What will I do? I breathe in and out to steady myself, because I am doing this for us.

Judgments are passed one by one, but we sit there until the light is dim and lamps are lit.

Then my mother enters the room. She does not look at my grandmother, but Yirin's expression betrays anguish that she quickly hides. My mother has the same bearing as Yirin, as if she is one of them and not a captive. I drink in all her features. She looks so much like Kuran, with those big dark brown eyes, wide and thick lips, and wavy hair. It was shorter when I saw her last; it touches her shoulders now. The wrap she wears around her head is a strip of stamped orange batik we cut together off a swathe of fabric before she left.

Kuran looks so much like her, but Kuran smiles all the time. My mother is not smiling today. She looks straight ahead as if nothing is interesting here. I try to sear my mother's face in my memory, but my tears blur the shape of her. I jump to my feet and thread my fingers through the screen, but Tanu clamps his hand onto mine like a vice and pulls me slightly aside. I'm not sure if the gesture is supposed to be a warning or to provide comfort.

"Shora Jal," a Guardian says, "your accusers stand before you."

Senil, the head Archivist, sits hunched forward at the end of a bench. His bald head gleams in the firelight. He is the only Baylan I have seen all day besides Guardians in black. He flips through a sheaf of papers bound with red thread and finds her name. "Shora Jal surrendered a child to the Baylan upon her first name day, but she conspired with her lover, initiate Joven Lete, to steal the child away. What do you say to this?"

I did not know that my father had ever even been inside the glass fortress, let alone an initiate to the Baylan. I tremble and wonder what else my mother has kept from me.

"The child you sought died with her father when his boat overturned in the ocean." Inay's voice is as clear as a bell, and it does not waver. It's the same voice she uses to tell me to stop asking questions. "I looked for both their bodies, but the waters never gave them up. I am guilty of nothing but being a young mother in grief."

What child? I frown. Why has she never told me this story before? I don't know where this is leading, but I don't like it. Tanu's hands tighten on my arm.

"It does not matter what came of it. Your crime is still

treason, Shora Jal. You sought to undermine our government and the very institution of Astar the moment you decided to steal away the child," one of the elders says, and the crowd shouts in agreement.

Yirin stands. My grandmother leans against her wooden cane. The glass eyes of the Diwata carved into its wood glitter in the lamplight, casting judgment upon us all. Her voice fills the room. "Shora, you say that you mourned this child, yet I saw her with my own two eyes, alive and well, only days ago. How is this possible?"

My mother's eyes flicker. "You are mistaken."

I don't dare breathe. Shadows scrape along the floor around us in the firelight. The truth of my birth, my life—everything I thought I knew about my mother and my family is wrong.

"Did your caravan not come to Bato-Ko with two daughters?" Yirin asks. "I have been to the merchants' camp, and I have inquired. There are many witnesses that have seen your daughters together. The resemblance is indisputable."

"You are mistaken," my mother repeats. "I only have one child, and you are keeping me from her."

"What is that daughter's name?" Senil asks. The Archivist's brows are knit together with worry. It's nothing like the anger mirrored on the faces of the two clashing Jals.

"Kuran," Inay says.

Tanu tugs at my arm, and I fight to free myself from his grip.

I notice Oshar in the crowd, because she stands and makes a loud fuss about feeling ill. She walks away, leaning against Sayarala. She knew that there were two of us. She could expose my mother now, but the doors slam behind her.

Curse all the secrets. Why couldn't my mother just have told me? The ghosts in my chest rattle softly, and I recall the taste of salt water in my nose, in my mouth. A half-buried memory, dislodged. I am drowning again. I draw a long breath, surprised to drink in air.

"You would accuse your own blood of conspiracy, Yirin Jal?" Senil asks.

"Shora may be my blood, but she is no longer my daughter. No daughter of mine would defy our sacred laws and traditions."

"Shora Jal, what do you say?"

There is no defeat in my mother's expression. She looks directly at Yirin as she answers the elderly Archivist. "You will condemn me no matter what I say. Do what you will to me."

"What say you?" Senil asks the crowd. I've seen it a dozen times today, and a dozen times, the answer has always been the same.

Hands lift to the air. A few remain hesitant at first, torn between my mother and Yirin, but as always, the judgment is unanimous. "And the sentence?"

"Death." Arisa's voice is soft, but it slices through my neck from behind me as she walks around the screen. She catches her breath. She's run through the service hallways to catch my mother's sentencing, and her cheeks are pink from the exertion. She should not be here, because her duties should have occupied her until daybreak. I freeze, crouched against a corner of the entrance.

A bead of sweat on her brow betrays that she is human after all. "Shora Jal disobeyed an edict given by Omu herself. That is treason. Disobedience must not be tolerated, or Tigang will be torn apart from the inside out." She strides into the hall, red robes rustling. "I feel for you, Shora, for my mother also parted with me as a child. It is your selfishness for which you must be punished, because the glory of Tigang is more important than one woman's sorrow."

I struggle to break free of Tanu's grip, but he holds me tight. I kick him in the shin, but he only winces.

"Shora Jal will be executed with the murderers and all

traitors to Tigang on the last day of the Sundo. There is no need to inform her family. Kuran Jal, you have heard it here," Arisa says.

I freeze when her outstretched finger points to where I stand, still half hidden behind the screen. The eyes of the council follow Arisa's extended hand. My grandmother falters again, and her mouth opens partway, but I balk at my mother's expression. She does not hide her fury at my appearance, though she should fear death instead.

Tanu tugs me away, and Virian appears around the corner. She helps him drag me down the hallway back to our room. My mother will be executed in days, not months. All my hopes have been knocked out of me. I don't know if I should be angry or afraid. Everything is numb.

The truth is a knife to my soul. Kuran was right. I've wasted my time with the Sundo and thrown away my life. If I'd known the truth, I'd never have come to Bato-Ko. I'd never have meddled. I would have been with my sister, as far from this cursed country as we could get.

"I'm so sorry," Virian says, and she's crying, but I am not. The shock of it all is too much.

But why would my mother lie to me?

I unclench my jaw and pull away from them.

Here, I have puzzled and puzzled over my mother's secret. I have wondered why no one would tell me about our family, and why we always stayed away from Bato-Ko. They have all kept the truth from me. *I* am the secret that my mother is willing to die for and that my father died for.

But I will not allow anyone else to die for me.

CHAPTER TWENTY-FOUR

For once, I don't dream. My head hits my pillow as heavy as a stone. I don't remember falling asleep, but my body reels at being roughly woken. My roommates are already on their feet. Virian grips the handle of her hairbrush like a dagger. The Baylan initiate who woke us dodges a slipper Dayen throws at her face, and she grabs at her singed eyebrows, screaming.

"You'll be late for the test, brats!" the initiate hollers as she storms away. "If you want to stay in your room and be sent home tomorrow, you're welcome to it."

My mother will be executed, I remember, and I shiver awake. I slide my palms down my cheeks. I have no idea what time it is. The skylight above still glows with moonlight. It must still be the middle of the night. I need to get to her as soon as I can, tests be damned, but I can't just leave, or I risk being even more exposed.

We stare at one another a few blinks longer, then hastily throw on more clothes and fix Dayen's dried flowers in our hair, just in case. We run to catch up to the eyebrowless initiate. She does not slow for us. She stalks down the hall and damns us all to the Three Freezing Hells.

The great hall is lit with flaming braziers, and Bamal, head of the Makers sect, pairs us up. It feels too soon for another test, but because the party occupied the day, time must be made up for, she explains cheerfully.

Arisa is nowhere to be seen, and Teloh is not present among the Guardians that travel with the Maker. These are small mercies that I grasp tightly. Heavens help me, I can't stop thinking about our kiss, but I want to scream at him, too. I wonder if he feels as tortured as I do: half anger, half hope.

"The Makers are the keepers of spells and magic lore in Tigang. We teach all the Baylan in the country how to create orasyons. On behalf of the Makers, I welcome you." Bamal interrupts my stray thoughts.

She is all crisp efficiency, with traditional beaded necklaces, and hair in a tidy bun. A pair of spectacles perches on her nose. She sends each pair of us off with an initiate and bag of supplies.

I've been paired with Ingo, the chosen one. It's a dubious pairing, and my impression of Ingo has not improved. Three filigreed gold rings glint in each ear—enough for us to eat for months, I think sourly. He still carries himself as if he's already Raja of Tigang, straight-backed and dripping with disdain. At least one of us looks well rested, and it's not me. He grimaces in my direction and then away with a scowl.

I could not care less. My mother will be executed on the last day of the Sundo. That means winning won't serve me; only survival matters. There are only two more tests after this one, and I need to break her out as soon as I can. The disdain of one rich boy will not stop me, and he'd best not get in my way.

Even at the late hour, Baylan are busy pulling screens loaded with pulp out of water baths and drying freshly made papers. Some Baylan grind minerals and plants into inks, while others copy orasyon onto stacks of papers as we walk past their workshops. It looks as if they are stockpiling enough spells for a siege. Bamal passes the Baylan without even a sideways glance.

She guides each pair into a small room. Our room has one table and two chairs at its center. Upon the table waits a stack of papers. Quills, pens, and bottles of paint in different consistencies cover its wooden surface. There is everything we could need to perform a spell.

The Maker turns to address us. "Spells of blood and spit only power the simplest of spells. Magic is life. Spend a breath on magic, and that is one less breath at the end of your life." Even a child knows this. I fight my impatience. I need this test to be over quickly, so I can focus on getting my mother out of here.

"The door will be locked, and your task is to get out of this room. This will test your knowledge of magic as well as your creativity. The ruler of Tigang does not have to be a powerful spell caster, but they must know the basics of magic and how orasyon may be combined. You've each been matched up based on your abilities so that those who are not trained in magic are not left at a disadvantage. There is no time limit," she says.

I perk up. Perhaps this test will be useful. If Ingo knows a spell to open the door, I can use it to unlock my mother's cell. I could ask Tanu, but he's likely to tattle to my sister, and Kuran would stop the Sundo before allowing me to take that kind of risk.

Ingo smirks, but I don't think that the test will be as easy as it sounds. The bag of supplies Bamal provided us is full of leathery dried fruit and cool bottles of water. She does not expect quick results.

She walks out, and the wall seals shut behind her as if there was never an opening to begin with. I wonder if it is illusion, but if it is, the spells must be written on the outside of the wall and not the inside.

I trace where the door should be with the tips of my fingers. I feel the faint outline of it, though I can't see its seams. The beginning of a vision pulses at my temples, but it disappears when Ingo speaks.

"You shouldn't have taken Nen's punishment." He lifts his

chin at me. His tone makes me feel as if I am a naughty child.

"So much for an easy pairing," I mutter beneath my breath.

"Nen would have been sent home anyway. Now he just looks weak," Ingo says.

I wish I didn't have to talk to Ingo at all, but I'm too tired to be anything but blunt. "I doubt anything I did would change anyone's mind about him."

In truth, I'm not sure if it was the right choice, but it is one that I can't change because it's done. All my notions of right and wrong feel thinly stretched of late.

"Let's just get out of here and over this," I grumble.

Ingo raises his chin. "I suppose your village didn't teach you much magic."

"I was born in Bato-Ko. This is my home, and my family has lived here for generations." My voice sounds more certain than I feel.

"Then why has no one ever heard of you?" he asks.

Of course the other candidates have been gossiping, too. I fight my irritation because this is not my fault but my family's. I just shrug. I have no quarrel with Ingo, only dislike for people who are too quick to judge. "My grandmother is Yirin Jal."

His mouth tightens. Now I am curious, because I'm too aware that I know less about my grandmother than he does. It's the same look Manong Alen gave me when we first met in the Archives: cautious.

"Then I apologize for my mistake." He bows, but his words are hollow, and I know nothing has changed between us. I doubt he would have begged pardon if my family was not one of the oldest in Bato-Ko, so I reserve my dislike for him.

I rub my bandaged left hand and frown because my fingers still ache whenever I touch them. They're useless for writing, and I hate that I put us at a disadvantage. Magic requires precision and a faultless memory. I possess neither.

"My writing hand is no use."

His smile is barely more than a grimace. "I've been preparing for this my whole life. I know what to do."

Ingo opens one of the bottles on the table and dips a fine-tipped brush in various paints. He tests them on a paper. Some paints are thin and watery, while others pool and blob. I know too little about magic to guess what difference in paints might have on an orasyon, but he seems to have a preference, and he settles on a solution that looks like ink.

I sink into the chair opposite him. I wish I could ask him what he knows of my grandmother, but that would make me look even less his equal. Family is everything to the Tigangi, more important than gold. Lovers can come and go, but blood is forever, we say. If Ingo knew that my mother was disowned, he'd treat me as less worthy of respect than the floor beneath him.

He paints several orasyon and symbols onto a paper: circles in circles, geometric lines, each perfectly even in width and thickness. He does it with practiced ease, and his recollection is effortless. His fingers are flecked with blue when he's done, but there is a small, pleased curl to the corner of his lips. I still don't like him.

"Where was the door?" he asks. There is no trace of doubt on his face, but I don't share his confidence. Why would they put two people in a room if one person could accomplish the task alone?

He pricks his finger with a sharp needle and uses the dot of blood to adhere the paper to the wall before incanting a word.

We both topple over from the force of the spell, and my ears ring from the noise. I wince as I stand; I'll have bruises on my hips come morning. Ingo's mouth moves, but I can't hear what he is saying until the ringing stops. *I hope it was an apology*, I think smugly. Ashes slide down the wall and onto the floor, but there is not a scratch on it. As I pat myself down, however,

I notice that Dayen's flower, once dead, begins to plump in response to his magic. I hope Ingo doesn't notice the difference.

"I suppose I'll try, too." I pull over a chair, then grab a bottle of ink and a paper. I copy his posture. I run through all the orasyon I know: for light, to ignite a fire, to remove body hair, to find lost possessions, for sleep. My repertoire is crudely limited. I have no idea what might help. I grasp a brush clumsily with my uninjured hand and drip an ugly blob down onto the paper in front of me.

He sighs. "You must be joking. Don't waste the paper." He grabs a fresh sheet. As much as I hate it, I know he's right. I crumple my page in frustration and tilt the chair backward to wait, even if it's the last thing I want to do.

Sweat circles soak Ingo's tunic, and his cheeks are red. If we looked terrible coming into this room, we are all claws and teeth now. Any patience that might have smoothed the way between us is long gone. I need to get out of here.

Our dimming oil lamp flickers and sends long screaming shadows across the walls. The table is covered in drips of paint and smudged with blood. I can't tell which fluids are which in the fractured light. His hands and forearms are thick with dark stains. Even his neck is smeared, where he's rubbed at his gold chains.

I think we've spent all night locked in this room, but it's hard to tell. The food and drink are long gone. Even the air is stale, because only a thread of wind passes through the tiny opening in the ceiling.

"Are you well?" Judging by the health of Dayen's warning flower, I'm worried that he's done what the initiate warned and used too much of his life to do magic. I still don't think we understand the purpose of this test. None of his spells have made more than a mess on the door. But if I'm exhausted, Ingo looks like he's fallen asleep with his eyes open. When I tap at his shoulder, his cheek slides into a pool of paint on the table.

A fresh red line of bumps climbs up his arms, and the rash spreads. I scramble away from him. Alen the Archivist had a rash just like this. Oh Hells. I frantically check over my skin, but I find nothing. Ingo doesn't wake when I kick at his leg with my slippered toes. The test is forfeit without him, but maybe that's the point. The room suddenly feels too cramped.

I frantically slap the wall and yell for help, but I hear nothing when I put my ear to the stone except my blood pounding in my ears. Maybe they can't hear me. Maybe they don't want to hear me. It feels like the Healers test all over again, only this time, I'm certain that Arisa is involved.

CHAPTER TWENTY-FIVE

I jerk Ingo's shoulders harder, but he does not twitch or groan. His chest rises so little that I bend close to his nose, and a faint exhalation tickles the hairs near my ears. His breath smells of molding oranges, just like Alen's. I move the back of my hand close to his forehead but don't dare touch his skin. He feels too hot. Gingerly, I pull up his sleeves and see the rash has already spread upward. Whatever this malady is, it works quickly, and I'm trapped in here with it. Heavens help me, I hope it isn't in the air, or I'm doomed.

I lay Ingo flat on the floor to open his lungs, and I start banging at the wall. "Is anyone out there? Ingo's sick! I need help!" I might not care for him, but I cannot let him die.

But the door doesn't open. Maybe it's not supposed to. Maybe we're being disappeared, like the other candidates and the missing Archivists. And that means no one's coming to help.

I can't afford to fail this test. Panic rises up from my gut. Payan warned I had to do well or I may not score high enough to continue. I rub at my eyes in frustration. My mother is so close. I just need a little longer.

I need to get out of this on my own, because I am my mother's only hope. I take a deep breath and gather my resolve. There's no time to despair.

I stuff all of Ingo's discarded opening spells into my pockets to try later, and I return to the table and grab a small scrap of paper that isn't yet stained. I clumsily grab a brush with my bandaged hand and drip paint all over the table. The orasyon I draw is barely readable, but I press it against the wall and spit on it. The wall does not budge. I can't even begin to know what to do, but I keep trying. The lamp gutters and dies. The orasyon of illumination I drew fizzles out in seconds instead of minutes because the symbol is so badly done. The gauze on my left hand grows sticky with paint, despite my care not to touch it, and my fingers begin to throb, despite the numbing spells that Virian drew on my bandages.

I return to the desk, less steady than before, and try again and again. My hands burn. The pads of my fingers go numb, and my skin crawls as if I'm covered in bug bites. I spot two red dots on my skin that I want to scratch, but I resist.

Ingo does not seem worse than before, but neither is he any better. When I place my paint-stained hands on him, he recoils.

The rashes spread away from the most stained of Ingo's fingers. Poison in the paint? Maybe this was what Manong Alen wanted to warn me about, but I still don't know how any of it is connected to my mother's secret. A wild theory scratches at the edge of my brain, but I don't have time to puzzle it out. I unwind the stained cloth and spit on my fingers to scrub at it. I'm probably only still conscious because of Ingo's foolish confidence.

I reach out and touch the wall to steady myself. *Show me something, please. I don't know what to do,* I beg my ghosts. I slide to my knees and press my head against the cool stone.

This time, a vision doesn't come easily. I fight the pressure in my head and will the vision into clarity. *I stand on the roof of the fortress, in the middle of the green grass. Teloh hunches over as if he's in pain, but I toss a pair of rattan canes to him. He catches them with a snarl. His face is twisted as though in anguish, and he changes his stance to attack.*

"I can't control it," he growls. I make the first move, and his sticks meet mine with a loud clack.

"You can." I switch my double-handed attack, holding nothing back, because I know he is. His moves are clumsy because this is new to him, but he is stronger than I am. We dance together across the roof as we spar. Sometimes he pauses so that I can adjust his technique. I ignore the way my pulse races whenever he lets me touch him. This is not about me.

Today the darkness clings to him more than usual. There are rainclouds in his eyes, and above us a storm is brewing. I can feel the first scattering of rain on my face.

Though I miss the mark, he backs away from me and screams. He falls to the ground and scrapes at his skin so hard that his nails leave bloody welts. All around us, the air goes thick and heavy. "It hurts." He braces his head between his hands. The grass surges up around him, seeds, and falls to the ground. I drop my canes and kneel at his side.

"I'm here," I say, and he turns to me with those eyes full of pain. I reach out and pull him close. The two of us kneel together, knee to knee, forehead to forehead, as flowers bloom and bushes sprout around us. I hear his breathing slow and watch his jaw unclench. The wind dies down over Bato-Ko.

"You're here," he murmurs and leans against me. He whispers something into my ear, but I don't hear the words. I only feel the hollow ache that the memory leaves behind. The vision is already fading. I need more, but no more comes to me. Teloh makes me want to live in a dream. Each vision is never enough, and ever since I've arrived here, it's always him I see.

I punch the wall and scream. Why? Are our stories so tangled up that they can't exist without each other? I don't understand.

"Not helpful!" I throw my fist against the stone again, and a little plaster falls to the floor. The vision wasn't helpful, but this is. The crack is not very visible, but I feel it under the sensitive tips of my fingers and realize there are more. I trail my fingertips across every inch that I can reach, getting to know the stone.

I walk around Ingo. The walls have been carved out of the mountain itself, and natural stone always has flaws. Though it looks unbroken in the dim light, I map small fractures, created from years of tremors, that have been patched over and polished smooth. I reach up on my tiptoes and crouch down to my feet, running my palms and fingers over the wall, hoping to miss nothing.

Nothing is as reliable as it seems, not even the foundation stone beneath my feet or the story of my life.

The deepest flaw is barely visible, but it branches into two like a fork of lightning. It's not much, but it's something.

I smash a wooden chair against the floor and grab a metal pen. I hammer it into the wall with a chair leg like a chisel, and more of the crack becomes visible. I continue hammering until my hands are numb and watch the cracks spider across the wall. Sweat drips down my forehead, and I've sweated through the armpits of my tunic. I'm covered in scratches, and my nails are chipped, but I keep going.

When I have no energy left in my arms, I ram my shoulders against the wall until I am dizzy. I fall over in a heap of rubble as the wall collapses. The surge of energy at my triumph evaporates in an instant.

I've opened a wall not into the hallway but into the next room. Arisa bends low over Galaya's body. The last time I spoke to her, Galaya told me that my blood to begin the Sundo was auspicious. Now, in death, the northern girl grips the small sun disk at her throat like a talisman. The air shimmers around them, and magic shudders off Arisa's shoulders like a rainstorm. The flower I've been wearing in my hair lifts its head higher. I feel it grow plump in the presence of magic, but magic did not kill Galaya. A wooden knife handle sticks out of the girl's back, and blood stains her tunic the same rich red shade as her skirt.

"Tell me again about Ingo," Datu Bamal demands. The Maker squints at me through her spectacles as though I am a piece of parchment. It's clear that her test has gone wrong.

My eyes meet Arisa's, and the Astar hesitates for the first time. She stands nearby, unaccompanied by her Guardian. She looks her age without the fancy clothes and jewelry. All she wears is her favorite gold sun comb and a nightgown. Her blood-flecked hands shake, and she only half listens to Bamal's interrogation.

The space where Galaya's body once lay feels like it is still occupied, even though we don't speak of her. I stare at the spot. There are smudges on the pale stone even though the blood has been wiped away and her body removed. While I have never been fond of the cultists and their unbending views of the world, I have always envied their righteous confidence. I would have bet money on Galaya lasting to the bitter end, just to prove Omu's superiority.

"I've already told you three times, po." I don't know what she wants to hear. "Do you think Ingo's sickness is my fault?"

"Of course it's not. None of you candidates are capable of magic this complicated." Bamal paces back and forth. Arisa says nothing at all.

"Then could the paint be poisoned, Datu Bamal?" I glance nervously at Arisa, but she does not give away any reaction. I can't stop rubbing at my fingers. They're almost raw, but some spots remain, and they itch as though I've brushed against poison oak.

Bamal sighs, and I start to think that this response is an allergic reaction to village girls. I wish I could be angry, but despite her simple clothing, it turns out she's just like Ingo, and Ingo seems as good as dead.

"The same symptoms have been recorded among the Baylan. It begins as a rash and then turns into a sleep from which no one wakes. No poison that I know of could do this, and I have tested our paints for every substance known in the continent. I have been looking for the source for months." Bamal slides her hands across her neck. "And now this." She stares at the empty space on the floor, too.

Arisa lifts her eyes to the hole in the wall. "How did you do this, child?"

The back-to-dried flower behind my ear continues to nod slightly in response to the lingering effect of Arisa's magic. I smell peonies rotting, and it makes me sick to my stomach.

"I found a crack in the wall and chiseled my way out." It's the truth. I ignore the insult.

"There are no cracks in my walls." Arisa's gaze is curious again, but it is more hawk this time than crow. I do not like that she sees me now, when before I was only an inconvenience.

"After three hundred years, how could there not be? It's just stone," I say.

"Because I am Astar the Builder—and I made it," Arisa replies. I think she will chastise me, but she leans toward me as Healers arrive to inspect Ingo. "Remember your promise to me. Tell no one what happened here. If anyone asks, you must tell them that Ingo and Galaya were sent home. I wouldn't want something terrible to happen to your friends," she whispers. Bamal is too preoccupied with the Healers to notice, but the threat is perfectly clear to me. She waves her hand in dismissal. "Ingo will be taken to the infirmary. You need not worry about the boy."

I help the Healers heft Ingo onto a stretcher and palm one of his earrings. I slip it into a fold of my malong before anyone notices. Arisa is lying. I just wish I knew why.

"Datu Bamal?" I ask, and the Maker turns back to look at me. "About the test scoring?"

A sly smile cracks her lips. "Chiseling your way out of the room was unexpected. You've proven your resourcefulness in the face of a challenge. You've passed. Go on, child. Get some rest."

I step out the door and let out a long sigh. I'm about to walk away, but I hear Arisa speak to Bamal. "My assassin has already dispatched three spies that infiltrated the fortress. So far we have kept it secret, but the cultists are planning something..." Arisa's voice quavers. "I thought the girl might be a liability—"

"We are vulnerable until the Sundo is finished," Bamal says. "What of the traitor amongst us? Reshar says he has found nothing. Can Reshar be trusted?"

There is a long pause and no answer. So, this is what Reshar has been looking for, but it doesn't mean he's not responsible for the missing candidates. None of the Baylan have mentioned them aloud.

"What about your creature?" Bamal asks.

Creature? I shiver as I remember shadows creeping through the dark halls of the fortress. It is not safe here. I need to get out soon.

"It will be no more trouble tonight," Arisa says with a finality that I recognize, and I dare not linger.

I throw open the curtain to find Virian immersed in a book while Dayen lounges on his bed, pretending not to steal glances at her.

"You're fine." I let out a breath, and my legs turn to jelly. I fall into my bed. All I want to do is sleep, but I can't. If I close my eyes, I'll see Galaya.

"Of course. I know what I'm doing." Virian tosses the book aside and leans over me. Her long lashes flutter above my face. "What happened?" she asks with concern.

"Ingo and Galaya are in the infirmary." The lie almost sounds believable. I take a breath. "May I check your skin? Humor me, please."

Dayen turns his back, and Virian disrobes. I find no bumps, but her skin is red in places the paint has touched. She quirks her eyebrows askance, more curious than afraid, but I don't have an answer for her yet.

Dayen surprises me by holding out his hands for his turn. He is stronger than he lets on. His muscles are tough and lean, from working on a farm or running away from rotten sisters. But there's a slight tremor in his right hand, and his skin feels hot. There might be the beginnings of a rash. A bump, maybe two, or just moles. I don't know. Maybe he's still just afraid of my curse.

"Dayen, how did you manage to get paint splatters on your neck?" I ask.

He shrugs his shoulders.

"You should clean it off. Both of you wash your hands again. Be careful if you ever handle the paint they make here."

"What's going on, Kuran?" Dayen asks with a frown. He crosses his arms across his body, suddenly shy again. He and Virian exchange glances in a silent conversation I can't read, but I know they're worried about me, when they should be worried about the Sundo.

I shake my head. "None of us are safe. Trust nothing the Baylan say." I fight the urge to tell them more, but I can't put them in danger. "Don't trust the other candidates, either. Arisa might have gotten to them, too."

Dayen and Virian exchange glances. "Did she threaten you?"

I close my eyes. "Please, just be careful."

"Oh, come here, you." Virian pulls Dayen toward her and wipes at his skin with a wet cloth. A sly smile tugging at his lips replaces caution. Virian doesn't reveal much, but the crinkle at the edges of her eyes makes me think she's pleased.

I trace the symbol that Virian drew our second day in the fortress. It's small and useful, and it did not itch like the paint from the test. "But let's keep these, just in case."

I pick at the dirty blue silk of my scarf. It itches, and it smells of Ingo's sweat. Splotches of paint mar its design. Bato-Ko has tainted everything for me, and I wonder just how much more it will demand before nothing is left of Narra Jal.

CHAPTER TWENTY-SIX

I fish under my mattress. The tracking spell remains tucked where I left it. If I remove the orange thread, I'm sure I can use it with Ingo's earring. Once I know he's safe, I'll use his discarded spells to get my mother out, but I feel like I owe him for them. I drop to the ground and check the spot where I hid the earring but come up empty. I take an unsettled breath. Did someone steal it? I almost laugh at my paranoia. After two eyebrow incidents, even the cleaning staff refuses to enter our room. Most likely, it fell into a crack somewhere.

No matter. I can still find out what's happened to Ingo. The Healers assured me he was taken to the infirmary, but I can't stop this nagging feeling that they lied to me.

The barest hint of dawn paints our room a greenish blue, so I hurry through the halls alone. I expect the infirmary to be busy, but I find only two Healers wandering its rooms. The Healers check on patients that look ill the way of normal sickness. They cough and dab their noses with cloths, while others snore away.

I stop a Healer in the hallway. "I'm looking for a boy named Ingo. He had a rash on his arms and was wearing gold earrings. He was brought here last night."

"Sorry, child. You must be mistaken. We didn't admit anyone last night," he says. "I've been here all shift."

I was not wrong. Someone is lying to us, but I cannot decide between Arisa and Reshar. Arisa looked genuinely shocked at Galaya's death. But Reshar is also up to some secret plot, with at least one other person, and somehow Nanay Oshar is opposing them. I wonder if the disappearances have anything to do with this *creature* they mentioned. I shudder and imagine shadows swallowing me whole. I need to get out of here before it's too late.

"Kuran." My sister's name falls flat off Tanu's lips, and my surprise quickly turns to a frown. I am not happy that he followed me here. I am doubly displeased that it's Tanu and not Teloh who bothered to check on me after my mother's sentencing.

"Did you know that it took almost a hundred years to build this fortress?" he blurts out nervously. I roll my eyes to the Heavens and stare at the pale stone roof. It's carved in the diamond pattern of snakeskin for protection. To protect whom? From what? If it's meant to protect everyone inside the fortress, it's done a poor job.

"There was nothing you could do for your mother at the trial. It's not your fault." He steps in front of me to block the way.

Anger knots my stomach, and I lose my words. How patronizing he sounds, and since when has he worn spectacles? He doesn't hide them away this time. Perhaps the appearance of maturity might be important here in the fortress, or perhaps a lifetime of a nose in a book has strained his eyes.

"Did my sister tell you that I was a secret?" I ask.

"No." His mouth flattens into a line. "She knows I would have disapproved of your mother's choice to hide you from the Baylan, even though I understand it."

Self-righteous worm. He might have turned my mother in, just as Yirin did. He might have turned *me* in if I hadn't guilted him into a promise. Yirin would have liked Tanu. Perfect, serious, and obedient, unlike her *selfish* daughter and her *rotten* children.

"Why are you here?" I ask him. "Do you want me to turn myself over to Arisa?"

"No." He blinks those big blue eyes. "I came to fetch you and your friends for the next test, but Virian and Dayen didn't know where you were. I thought you might have needed new gauze for your injuries." He's still ever so rational, but this time he's off the mark. I'm not here for myself.

I crumple my scarf in my hands. Hells, I wish I could break something. I need to move, to breathe again, to scream. To do something rather than wait for my doom. I've hardly had a moment to search for my mother, and I'm running out of time.

"I promised Kuran that I would keep you safe," he says.

I give him one long, hard stare. He knows more about magic and the fortress than I do, and I can use that. He might recognize the wards on the dungeons, or perhaps the guards might let an initiate inside to do some cleaning, or perhaps I can pry some information from him.

Reluctantly, I turn back toward the great hall alongside Tanu.

"Is there somewhere besides the infirmary that the sick might be taken?"

His eyebrows knit together. "I've only been assigned to the living quarters in the Spring Palace, so I don't know. The fortress is so large. I haven't heard of any, but that doesn't mean there aren't private rooms elsewhere."

I check over my shoulders again. No one is near, but I half expect to turn a corner and find Omu herself walking the halls, ready to smite us.

"What about the dungeons?" I ask. "Ingo was taken away. Could he be locked up there if the infirmary are full?"

He looks at me like I've sprouted another head. "Why would they put the sick in the dungeons?"

"Could I get in to check?" I fish for answers, hoping not to arouse his suspicion.

"Only the Datus have a badge for entry. There is no way in or out." He shrugs, and I don't think he puts my plan together. I doubt he thinks I'm capable of such a thing.

But he's helped me more than he knows. I will steal a badge if I must, and that only leaves the Guardians on shift to deal with.

I jump at a loud bang and collide with Tanu. I only breathe again when I confirm that the source of the sound was just a shutter let loose by the wind. Leaves skitter across the floor in loops, mirroring the hallways, making the music of tiny skeletons rattling in boxes. The first time I came here, I thought it beautiful; now I think it is sad and old and crumbling. I don't know what's changed my mind. It's not the Sundo. Perhaps it is me that's changed.

Tanu keeps his opinions to himself. I wonder if he ever thinks about Kuran—if he misses her. I saw the way he looked at her when she wasn't watching. I remember one day when she stumbled and fell and he gently returned her slippers to her feet. He loved her, but maybe love is not enough.

I wish my sister were here instead of Tanu.

We part ways at the entrance to the great hall. It feels too soon for another test, like the waters of time keep spilling through my fingers no matter how hard I try to cup it in my palms. But the Sundo continues, and I need to make an appearance or I'll arouse suspicion from the Datus. Perhaps I can slip away in the chaos that always seems to follow the testing and swipe a badge from the Datu busy administering it. If not…

I decide that the aged Archivist, Datu Senil, might be the easiest to steal from, and the minute I am alone again, I need to sneak away to find their offices.

I ignore the dark looks and whispers about Ingo's disappearance. Even Dayen and Virian stand a little bit apart. I clench my jaw. I will see this through, and I will keep the people I care about safe.

We've all gathered in the great hall under a midday sky as dark as night. Inky clouds pelt rain at the glass walls of the fortress. A long-promised storm whips the ocean into a frenzy so fierce that I'm afraid it might smash through the stone and wash us all away.

The storm reminds me of the vision the glass fortress offered me, and I imagine sparring with Teloh on the rooftop, a blur of forms, as magic surges around him. *I'm here*, I whisper in my heart like a fool. Maybe I only imagine it, but the wind curls softly across my cheek.

We are led in a silent procession down a ramp into the silent center of the fortress. The tunnel burrows so deep into the stone that no natural light ever touches it.

My ghosts grow frantic again as we descend. They bump and flap against my ribs like birds trying to flee their cage, and I fight to keep my feet from turning the other direction. Right now, nothing matters more than this test. Not understanding Arisa's schemes. Not figuring out who I am. I must not be removed from the Sundo now.

A hooded figure waits at the bottom of the ramp, but I recognize Reshar's pursed lips from a distance. His blue-flamed torch shrouds us all with sickly light. He shrinks and grows as the light flickers, like a guardian to the Three Hells: Reshar but not Reshar.

"Holy Omu governs the day, and Hamshar the Seeker blesses the twilight, but we on earth must also tend to the night." Even his voice is different. It scrapes across his teeth like a stone coffin lid sliding out of place.

At the end of the ramp is a single wooden door. Like the doors that open into the fortress, a story is carved into the ironwood, but it is not one that I recognize. Baylan hide their faces from a storm cloud in one image. In the next, a woman marked with a star on her forehead commands the storm into a box and chains it tight. In the last, the same woman sits atop the box, with a crown on her head. She seems to stare right through me. I shiver and huddle into myself.

"And how do we find our way in the darkness?" Reshar asks.

I remember an old refrain from a tune that all Tigangi are taught as children.

By the light of the stars.
By the Raja's commands.
By the iron in our blood.
And what do we seek?
A beginning.

Candidates enter the door one by one, and when it opens, nothing remains but an empty space. When it is my turn, Reshar stops me at the threshold and fixes his hard eyes upon me.

"This is your chance, village girl. Say the word, and I will send you home before the fortress destroys you. Don't waste your life here like I have."

Beyond the threshold is a gaping hole that the light of Reshar's flame does not touch. It could be a trap. The ghosts tumble over in my chest, and my head begins to vibrate like one of Reshar's brass gongs, but I made my choice when I walked through the gate of the fortress. I keep my eyes on the doorway as the wood squeals open. All my futures wait beyond this moment and through it.

"It's too late," I say, though my ghosts refuse to settle. I take two steps, and the door slams shut behind me. All my senses snuff out like a pinched flame.

There is no breeze. There is no sound. There is no light. And as usual, I am alone.

• • •

A mirrored maze winks into place. There is no roof but a dark sky, nothing to see by but moonlight. The walls chill my fingers to the touch, and infinite reflections follow me as I walk. They are my only companions besides the buzz of Reshar's magic. Prodding. Poking. Seeking. But what?

It can't be real. I grab my taped fingers and bite back a scream as I flex my joints. The maze flickers. Gone, then there again, confirming my suspicions. But magic is rarely harmless.

I walk straight into a mirrored wall, and my reflection twists in surprise. It screams soundlessly and points behind me. New corridors appear. A hundred copies of myself shout and wave warnings, but if they have voices, I cannot hear their silent pleas.

I take a right at a junction and trip over a sitting body. A sun-bleached skull rolls out of a moldy wool hood, and its empty eye sockets stare up at the roof.

"I have a riddle for you. What is my true nature?" the skull asks in Teloh's voice. The skeleton howls in laughter, and its bony fingers clamp onto my arms. I frantically pry myself loose and slam bone into a glass wall. My reflection's scream is audible as it shatters.

"I will find you," Arisa whispers over my shoulder. I spin but see nothing except my fractured self, bloody and beaten, begging for help in another pane of glass.

I run until I am dizzied by the winding route, until I can't feel my toes, until everything in me is numb and there is no air left in my lungs. The tremor of Reshar's magic travels through my bones like an earthquake, shaking loose my foundations and sending cracks through my soul.

"Give in." The whispers follow me, growing louder and bolder.

I slam into another wall, and the glass boxes me in. My reflection wavers as I slam at the mirror with my palms. "Who are you?" it asks.

My ghosts threaten to leap out of my throat to the voice of this command, but I swallow them down.

Behind me, another reflection offers up a gleaming kris. "Show me the deepest parts of your soul. What are you hiding?"

The ghosts in my chest scrape with tiny claws. Their howls to be let out feel like bellows of hot air against my chest, but there will be nothing of Narra left if I do. I cannot. I dare not, for I'm afraid of who I might become if I let them take over.

"I don't know." I spin and see myself reflected over and over. "Who are you?" one reflection asks shyly and looks up from under her lashes. "Show yourself!" Another reflection bangs against a mirror with white-knuckled fists and a scowl. "Please?" My copy nervously tugs at the scarf around her neck. "I don't know!" I pound at the glass with my fists and my feet. The glass spiders, then shatters. I tumble into a cold room and taste blood in my mouth.

Reshar sits before me on a hard chair. Bathed in the last dregs of his spell, I see him before, and I see him now, as the forms of his lives overlap. His skin remains a deep, dark brown, but his eyes are not so full of bitterness.

The magic dies away, and all trace of softness vanishes as if it never was. Those tired eyes and familiar sneer return me to the present.

I bend over and spit blood onto the floor. My soul should have been ready to be peeled like an orange, but my fingers remain Narra's, brown from sun, wiry from work, and utterly unremarkable.

"How hard you resist. I must make you show me your soul to judge your worthiness. Sit."

I cross my legs on the cold stone, and he bends over, takes paper painted with a diagram and presses it to my forehead. Heat sears my skin, and ashes dust my nose as the paper dissolves, but nothing changes. My ghosts barely flutter in response.

"This should not be possible." He growls and sits down so we're eye to eye. "I ask you again: Who are you, Kuran Jal?"

Who am I? The truth is, I don't know. Am I Astar? It sounds preposterous, because I could not think of anyone more ordinary than myself. But who is Narra, anyway?

I take a deep breath of air to steady myself. It smells like the flowers blooming at night, of a fresh rainfall—like Teloh. Maybe I'm losing my mind.

"I…"

A scream echoes in the hallway, and it is followed by another. Reshar jumps straight to his feet, and I do, too. What now? I want to tear out my hair in frustration. Maybe I truly am cursed to a life where everything that can possibly go wrong *will* go wrong. "Stay here and lock the door. Only open it for me."

Something soft brushes against my ear, and I shut my mouth. I raise my hands and find that the shriveled flower I wear has grown plump and waxy. My skin prickles all over, and I tremble. It curls against my earlobes as its leaves spread. *Big magic.*

CHAPTER TWENTY-SEVEN

A searing heat stabs me just under my left collarbone. Virian is in trouble. I feel her tapping at her mark and sense that she's running toward the Summer Palace. And then, Hells—Dayen. I feel him tapping in the other direction, but he's close. I dare not linger in my own terror and fail them again. Desperate screams echo through the hallways, but it is too dark to see. The wind howls through the twisting corridors, screaming with a fury that does not seem natural, as if it is hunting something.

I learned my lesson from the Healing test. This time, I choose.

I run for Dayen and pray that Virian can take care of herself a little longer. I pass ruined doors pried apart by vines that push through solid stone floors. Their long tendrils search for anything to grip onto. Roots crack through the stone, and I dodge them as they rush past me through the doorway of the room I had just been sitting in. The space floods with knotted wood.

Dayen crashes into me. His eyes are so wide the whites are visible. "Virian's in trouble."

"The treasury. She will know to meet us there," I say.

We careen back down the hallway and find ourselves in a nightscape. The glass walls are pitch black, as if a great blanket were thrown over the entire fortress. The air grows so thick that it feels like it might rain inside the fortress and we are only moments from being underwater. The rapid fire of hail against stone echoes in the deserted hallways, like thousands of spilled marbles, growing louder.

I can't tell which direction the sound is coming from; it echoes everywhere. The walls distort the sound and amplify it. Sometimes nearer and sometimes farther.

"Faster!" Dayen screams.

The flower tucked in Dayen's tunic pocket stretches out long vines that tangle into his hair. My flower curls around my head and reaches into my ear canal. It tickles as it searches for a way in. I rip at it, but my scarf tears instead. The flower is so tangled in my hair that I might rip my scalp off with it.

I feel another spike of pain beneath my collarbone, and we both gasp at once. She's right up ahead.

"Virian!" He outpaces me. I feel the rapid drumming of Virian's heart as the mark throbs. I race after him, but he is tall and leggy, and I cannot keep up.

Virian crouches in a circle etched with rough diagrams, her hands and arms covered in blue paint. Her hair dangles limp and sweat-drenched. Unlike the precision I expect, the lines of her orasyon are hasty and splattered, made with fingers instead of a brush. It won't hold.

A dark fog creeps slowly along the floor like a many-headed sea creature searching the land. It reaches its long tendrils toward Virian and tests her diagram with long tongues. I fight against the wind that blows leaves into my face and whips my hair straight back. It flings salt spray from an open window into my eyes, and it creeps ever forward, but Dayen's eyes are fixed on Virian.

Where the hulking shadow passes, orchids raise their heads and open; grasses sprout from the floor and the walls. Roots push through the stone.

I shout warning, but my words are lost in the wind. I wave

at the shadow and bite my lip so hard that there is blood. Stone cracks as the fortress shifts around us and a single yellow eye materializes amidst the darkness. It blinks at me.

I'm here! My ghosts scream so loudly that the whole of my body arcs.

And as if it hears, as if it knows what's inside me, the monster pulls around Virian's circle.

I stare into the eye of the shadow, and the ghosts in my chest snarl in response. They scrape at my ribs with claws extended.

Run, you fool!

I race away from Dayen and Virian, and it follows. I slide on the patterned tiles of the fortress, so I kick off my slippers, and the fog swallows them before they ever touch the floor.

I follow the spiral curve of a hallway, thinking that the narrowness of it might slow the beast, but the fog condenses. It folds its tendrils into itself like a squid and grows black scales and lizard eyes. Claws click and scrabble behind me, but I dare not look for long.

I tear down hallways and find myself at a dead end. There is only a single oak door before us, but I recognize it immediately. It's the same door Reshar found me in front of once before.

My ghosts scream warnings, but Tanu calls my name from somewhere behind me. His blue eyes are wide with fear, and his belt is stuffed full of spell papers. Something dark is splashed on his brown tunic, and I cannot tell if it is paint or blood. He cuts right in front of the shadow creature and runs in my direction. Omu above, the beautiful fool is going to make things worse.

The ghosts in my chest falter as the shadows twist toward him.

"Go back!" I shout, but either he does not hear me or he does not want to. *Freezing Hells!* I curse under my breath. Even though his blue eyes are wide open, he doesn't seem to notice the shadows behind him. Does he not see it? Can no one else?

I shove the door open, catch his outstretched arm, and drag him forward.

We push the door shut behind us, but it rattles as the creature slams into it. The stone floor cracks as roots twist through it and pin the door into place—as though to keep out the monster.

Something huge and solid thuds against the door once. And again. The jars on the shelves behind us rattle as we back up into the rear of the room. A tongue of smoke drifts through the cracks under the door.

Tanu throws one spell after another at the smoke, and they sizzle and spark, turning to ash without effect, until his arms are empty and we have our backs to the wall. I look around frantically to see if there's anything we can use, but even the chairs in this old room look like they might splinter if we sat on them. The shelves behind us are filled with books and toys, dusty and useless. We are trapped.

We scramble up onto the creaky old bed, and its springs squeak beneath my bare feet as the smoke tongue reaches straight for my neck. A brush of air traces upward, across the line of my jaw.

Then it falters. The smoke recoils, and the flower in my hair falls to the floor, no more than a shriveled tangle, but my skin burns where the thing touched me. My entire body feels as though lightning pours through my veins. Everything goes still. The wind. The rain. It feels as if even time has stopped. Vines droop to the floor. The shadow retreats, slowly slipping backward and out until it is gone entirely.

But Tanu shakes beside me as the silence stretches on. He slides onto the bed, a huge ball of a boy, as terrified as I am and breathing hard.

"What were you trying to do in the hall there? Die?" My teeth clatter together.

"I wanted to make sure you were out of danger."

There is blood on his tunic, but it's not his. Only scratches mar his skin, and his clothing isn't torn.

"What was that thing?" I whisper.

"Chaos." He holds out his hands to look at them, but they do not stop trembling. "The Demon is real, and someone's let it out."

Chaos. The end of Arawan. I burn at the memory of its touch and hurl my Demon-tainted scarf out the window.

I bury my head in my arms. Virian's mark near my collarbone has settled down. It means Dayen and Virian are dead—or they are safe. "Hells, you just put yourself in more danger coming after me."

Twice now my ghosts led me here. They wanted me to see this place, but I don't understand why. The room doesn't smell like people. It smells like rotting wood and musty fabric. Toys lay scattered beneath high arched windows. There are dolls, puppets, and wooden animals on strings. I stop at these first, too afraid to touch them, because their eyes are precious stones and their clothes are silk. A rich child's things.

The bed tucked into one corner is not large, but the sheets and bedding are all tightly woven cotton and duck feathers, too fine for a child. Perhaps meant for a child who grew up here.

But someone left the window shutters open, and leaves have settled on rain-warped furniture. Upon the crooked shelves gleams a scale model of the fortress. It is a mountain of glass in miniature that lingers in a sliver of light. In the corner sits a precious dark ironwood chest inlaid with mother of pearl. It must have been brought across the ocean with our people as we fled Arawan.

Tanu's eyes are wide. "This is the Builder's room. No wonder the Demon could not enter."

Though I've always known Astar was human, I never imagined what sort of person she might be. Now I see her incarnations sitting on the bed, reading books, and laying on the floor, peering at the sun through cloudy quartz stones. Real.

But this room looks like it was abandoned long before Arisa was born. Perhaps it wasn't to her tastes, and I don't blame her.

"This is a prison." I shudder.

For a long while, we huddle together on the dusty bed, not daring to touch the floor. Astar's dolls leer at us with their mismatched painted eyes, and I shudder.

My skin burns where the Demon touched me, and I wonder if I will ever feel safe again.

CHAPTER TWENTY-EIGHT

I struggle to undo my tangled bun and pick dead leaves from my hair, but my fingers won't stop shaking. I hardly hear a thing Tanu says, because my mind keeps spinning in circles. Everything leads back to Astar: the tug of my ghosts, the visions of Bato-Ko, the abandoned room, the Demon's retreat.

Astar, Astar, Astar... my ghosts chant.

"Silence!" I shout, and Tanu looks at me like I've sprouted two heads. I ignore him and keep walking. Leaves crunch beneath our feet like empty beetle shells and part around our legs. We pass over limp roots and lush ferns that sprouted with the Demon's passing. There are thorns in my feet, but I barely feel them. I wait for the roots to stir back to life and drag me under, but they remain asleep.

Baylan call for one another and search for survivors. Tanu answers their calls and parts from me. I should thank him, but we turn away from each other in awkward silence instead.

Twice now, the Demon came after me and stopped, though I did nothing, and I could do nothing to protect myself. Why am I still alive? Do the Diwata have worse plans for me yet?

I don't know what any of it means, but the longer I stay here, the less likely it feels I'll ever escape any of it. I need to get my mother out now.

Dayen kneels crouched with his back to the treasury

entrance, and Virian—oh, Virian. Dayen cradles her in his arms, trembling. The circle of paint that she drew remains clear of the poppies that have bloomed from the walls and the roof, but Virian's eyes are closed. Her hair has streaks of white in it—she's aged years in minutes.

There's an explosion of paint all over her hands and arms. It runs down her sleeping gown, onto her legs, and bits of broken glass are caught in the folds of her clothing. But she is breathing. She is alive in the same way that Ingo was alive. And this time I won't leave her fate to the Healers.

"She won't wake." Dayen's voice wavers. "Help me clean her up?"

We carry Virian to the Autumn baths, and I'm relieved to find they remain untouched by Chaos. I turn the tap and let the pool fill.

"Fetch me some soap, white vinegar, towels, and some fresh clothes for Virian." I order him away. I don't want him to see that I'm as scared as he is.

He scrambles off, and I jump into the water with my clothes on. I scrub at Virian's stains with a sleeve I've torn off my tunic, and when Dayen returns, I attack the more stubborn spots with soap and vinegar.

Though her cuts must sting, she hardly stirs when I clean her, stuck in that strange deep sleep. I fight back tears and wash her short hair clean. I hum a song that my mother would sing while she brushed my hair, and I blink back tears.

I wish to the Heavens that this is all some part of the test and that I might wake up to find it some illusion, but I pinch thorns from my feet, and they bleed.

"I will not leave her," Dayen says after we've laid her to rest on the tiles, with a rolled-up towel for a pillow. "All of this seemed worth it because of her."

He looks so beaten that, for the first time, I realize that

forgetting what happens during the Sundo might be a blessing.

I put a hand on his shoulder, but when he flinches back and grabs his amulets, I drop my hands to my sides.

"I will find out what I can." I hide my burning shame and don't meet his eyes. I must keep moving. I must keep taking one small futile step after another or I fear I might not move again.

"Virian said she has a cousin here. Did she ever tell you who?"

Her family must care what happens to her. I don't think anyone else can be trusted.

"Datu Senil," Dayen says. I am surprised but relieved, too, because the head Archivist is clearly no friend of Arisa's. There are many questions I'd like to ask the Archivist, but Virian comes first. I need his help in more than one way. Finally, a bit of luck. Perhaps that badge is finally within my reach.

"Keep her here and don't tell anyone. You can't trust the Healers, either. I'm going to find him and ask for his help."

I hope he survived, because if the Seven cannot survive Chaos, neither will Bato-Ko.

"Narra!" Teloh runs down a hallway and skids toward me just outside the baths. The air vibrates around Teloh, and his hands shake in tune to the magic that clings to him. He smells of freshly churned soil and grass wet with morning dew, but everything smells of greenery, and I cannot tell him apart from the fortress. He is so unsteady on his feet that he braces himself against a wall. "Have you been hurt?" he asks before I can ask him the same. "You lost your scarf... Do you need me to find another?"

I touch my neck and decide to leave it bare because there is no time to waste. Who would notice my blemished skin when a Demon is loose?

I shrug. I'm still numb but thawing slowly. I don't know whether to be relieved or cry now that he has found me.

"Where is Datu Senil?" I ask.

"In his office."

"Take me there," I command, and he simply nods.

We walk side by side in silence, past Baylan and brown-clothed initiates too busy with the mess to notice us. I want him here, but I don't want him to see me cry. I don't want him to see me frightened and weak, or to tell me that this is my fault for coming here and bringing bad luck to us all. I don't want to know why Teloh is angry or what he remembers about me. I wish for all the world that I could just relive that kiss one more time, that things were that simple between us—but they're not.

"I need to get you out of the fortress. It's not safe here. Arisa is weeding out every threat to her authority," he whispers.

I chew at my thoughts and work through everything I know. The Archivists record our name on our first birthday, and now they are disappearing. Alen's face at recalling Shora Jal's name was no coincidence. It is an Archivist's duty to remember. He must have found something in our family books, and now he has no tongue. Arisa was not the only child with birthmarks given over to the Baylan, for I was, too. I escaped, but she did not. What if other children were also brought to the fortress? What if the Baylan chose the wrong Astar?

Could Arisa be the impostor Alen raved about? The possibility seems real and frightening because she has true power—I've seen it. And if she is not the Astar, then who is? *Me?* The idea makes me want to laugh.

But I know that who tells the story also decides the hero. I know that stories are sometimes not what they seem, containing truths as slippery as snakes. I know that some stories are not just stories but are meant to tell us what to think. And who is untainted in all the stories about Arawan? Astar.

Astar gave up her immortality. She was human. She played with dolls and wooden dogs with strings for leashes. But if she came back and remembered, she could change the tune of our songs with time. She could make us forget the blood it took to build this shining city. She could play a game so long that her hands were wiped clean.

I recall Teloh's anger and begin to think it is justified. I press my shoulders together and touch my marks. Arisa is capable of all those things, and I am not.

But I could have been.

"I was one of the Astar children, wasn't I?" I ask, though the idea feels too strange to be real. "My mother stole me away from Bato-Ko so that she could keep me, and that is why she was arrested." It is the only answer that makes sense.

His eyes drift to my bare neck. "When one Astar dies, the Archivists go through great trouble to find candidates for the next. All babies with birthmarks that do not fade are surrendered to the fortress," Teloh says. "And even those who are not chosen remain their whole lives."

My birthmarks. I bite my tongue to keep from laughing. They do not mean at all what anyone thinks. Who else but cunning Astar could have started the rumors about the curse of the marks? How else could the Baylan find her? How else could she trick families into giving their children away, but by telling them that disaster might befall those who did not?

To think that all the miseries I've endured were because some petty former immortal wanted to return to her crumbling fortress in her next life. I curse Astar with every breath in my body.

"In your year, there were two."

"Did Arisa pass the test?" I ask.

"Yes, but she was also the only option that the Baylan had left because you were already gone. And you did not want—"

He does not continue, but I cannot let the thought go. Arisa is everything that I think Astar should be, but the Baylan might have molded her into that shape. And me… Astar's lies shaped me into who I am and damned me, too. My birthmarks put me in the middle of Arisa's warpath.

We turn into a wide hallway that Teloh tells me houses the offices of the Seven Datus. It remains strangely untouched. The door to each Datu's room is glass, and I glimpse Arisa's among them, but most are empty.

Only Senil's door glows with inviting lamplight. I do not feel afraid, just heavy. Every bit of the past I uncover feels like a burden when I once thought that knowledge should bring freedom. But I am here for my mother, and I am here for Virian, not to assuage my guilt.

I enter the room without announcing myself, and I think Senil would have jumped in fright if his old bones let him.

"Has Arisa finally sent you to kill me?" He stares at Teloh wide-eyed. Senil holds a dull kris in his hands and keeps the thick walnut of his desk between us. He looks even more fragile today. His hands shake, and his bald head is slick with sweat. I don't think the blade would be enough to stop me, and I am no trained assassin.

"No, Datu Senil." Teloh reaches his hand out for a blessing, and Senil puts aside his knife to oblige him with a sigh. "But if she does, know that I would regret it. I bear you no ill will. The histories must be remembered, or how will we keep from repeating our mistakes?"

Senil slumps into a wooden chair lined with lumpy cushions and traces his hands over his scalp as though lost in thought. I clear my throat. "Datu Senil, I am a friend of your cousin Virian, who is a candidate for the Sundo. The sickness that has been plaguing the Baylan has taken her, too. She has a rash where her skin touched paint and will not wake. I fear there is something wrong with the paint, but Bamal says poison is impossible."

He appraises me with an arched brow as though deciding

something. "I have been investigating this year's Sundo, because there were breaches in protocol even before the candidates were admitted. I argued that the tests the others designed were too extreme, but Arisa insisted."

He signs deeply. "Virian is my cousin's granddaughter, and she is a very new but talented initiate to the Baylan. I asked her to report to me if things were amiss among you, because not even the other Datus know who she is."

I blink at him, slowly letting the knowledge process through my brain. Virian was never competing in the Sundo. She's a spy. It explains how she knows so much magic and how she always seems to know more about the fortress than anyone else. I blow a deep breath through my teeth. It doesn't matter. She may have lied to do her duty, but it doesn't make her any less my friend. She's been taking the same risks and suffering the same consequences along with us.

"Perhaps the sickness is not due to poison, but the paint may still be tampered with. Arisa controls the Demon, so why not this?"

What? I blink. This explains her odd reaction the night she talked to me in the halls. She had to run to contain it before it could do more damage. This time she must not have gotten to it in time, either that or her control is slipping. It's all the more reason to get out of here as soon as we can.

"Arisa's enemies are falling one by one to this strange illness, and that is no coincidence. I have no idea what she has done with the bodies and the missing candidates, nor any proof she's behind it—but I am not the only one who suspects." Senil slumps, tired, in his chair.

Then I am only alive because Arisa thinks I'm harmless and she doesn't know about my marks. I hastily drape my long hair over my shoulder to hide them.

"If it is magic and not poison, the effect could not last

forever," I say. "The ill might recover if they stay away from its source?"

"Perhaps." He nods. "Or with time."

"But why would Arisa do this?" I ask.

He presses his lips together. "Jal, isn't it?"

I should have expected an Archivist to have a long memory. He knows about my mother, I reason, but he cannot know I am the daughter that was supposed to have died—not for certain.

"Yes." I pause.

"Those that remember the previous Astar question Arisa's legitimacy, but most of us are gone. I stubbornly cling on here because I have nowhere else to go." He folds the edge of a paper in his hand and stares at my neck. "But you do. You still have a choice, Jal girl."

It doesn't feel like it. It feels like I've got my back against the wall and I have no knives to fight back, but I'm not ready to give up just yet. I rub at my forehead and think. All I want is my mother, and she helped me escape the glass fortress once before. I know now that it is not impossible. "Is there a way we can leave here undetected?"

Senil stares at Teloh, and he looks away. The assassin is a dark silhouette against an open window and the gray sky. "Of all people, you would know."

I lightly touch the scabs on my left palm. "We need to take Virian, my mother, and the Archivist Manong Alen. He knows what's happening, and he tried to warn me."

Teloh blinks at me. "Now *that* is impossible. The only unwarded route is the ocean wall. It would be hard enough to get one girl out alone, but infinitely harder still with an old woman and an unconscious girl in tow. You realize you're risking their lives? Manong Alen is already dead."

The knowledge startles me, but Teloh's reaction only strengthens my resolve. Maybe he thinks I'm just a little girl who needs protecting, but he's misjudged me. The only way to honor Alen's sacrifice is to save who I can. "It is a risk, but if I do nothing, then they will surely die," I growl.

"You are still so bullheaded!" He tears at his hair. "There are no guarantees, not even for you. Your mother warned you to stay away from Bato-Ko, did she not? She didn't want you mixed up in this world, and here you are, wasting her efforts."

Is that how she saw it? That she should give up her life to keep us safe? I close my eyes and take a deep breath. Everything in the world stopped making sense after she was arrested, but I will not allow my mother to die for me. My mother wanted to protect me, but saving her is my choice. If I do only one good thing with my cursed life, let it be this.

"I am not afraid of heights. I can swim." The walls of the fortress were meant to keep people from getting in, not from getting out. I want nothing to do with Arisa's plans. I just want to keep my family and friends safe. "I will not leave here without them. And if you truly cared about my safety, you should have let Datu Reshar keep me out of the Sundo."

Senil looks away embarrassed, as if this is a lover's quarrel.

Teloh sighs, and his shoulders slump in defeat. He looks so tired. "And now I wish I had!" he says. "I thought you remembered."

I stand up tall. "We all go, or I stay. Help me break my mother out of the dungeons."

Teloh throws up his hands. "Fine, then, but any blood is on your conscience, not mine. You will regret this."

We form a plan between us, so flimsy that if it were a piece of paper I could see through it.

"Here." The Archivist pulls a small bronze amulet from his desk and spits on it. He ties it to my wrist with a bit of red string. "This will let you through the doors of the dungeons unharmed. Destroy it if you are caught, or Arisa will know I am involved."

"Thank you." I press his hand to my forehead before I leave.

"Tomorrow night, be ready at sunset. I will keep the Guardians away from the dungeons." Senil stares at me, long and hard. "Good luck, Jal girl."

Teloh parts from me before I can ask any questions, and I am both disappointed and relieved. The cold, empty stone corridor seems to wind on forever, but I roll back my shoulders and start walking.

CHAPTER TWENTY-NINE

Dayen, Tanu, and I alternate a watch over Virian a few hours at a time. One thing becomes clear: Dayen is coming with me, and there's no way I can stop him. I doubt that my mother will be as willing.

I am so tired after my second shift that I fall asleep sitting on my bed and only jolt awake when a gag slips into my mouth. A rice sack goes over my head before I can see who is responsible. I kick out and strike a leg out of pure instinct, but multiple hands grab hold of my arms, and no matter how hard I struggle, I can't break free. My heart pounds with terror as they drag me away. *This is the end at last* is all that goes through my mind, over and over again.

I recognize Nen's voice in the mob, but there are others with him. Their slippers echo against the marble, and the air goes chilly as we descend deeper into the fortress than I have ever gone.

When the sack is torn off, a cavernous room comes into focus. My hands remain tied behind my back, and two boys whose names I don't know keep a tight grip on my shoulders. The domed roof drips water where a leak has sprung, and wooden scaffolding that looks a century old, circles the room where halfhearted attempts at fixing the cracks in the stone were abandoned. Flickering torchlights spit and hiss against its sharp edges. There is wrongness that lingers in this room that sets my teeth on edge and makes my blood boil.

A dark pit is carved into the center of the room. Waves crash against stone an unknowable distance below, and I taste brine on my tongue. The pit is so deep that light does not touch the bottom, and when I look upon it, the place where the monster touched me flares with heat. This is the Demon's cage. I twist to get free, but I cannot tell them with the gag in my mouth. My vision begins to double. *This is not the time*, I beg the ghosts of my past lives as I fall to my knees, but another vision wrenches me from the present.

Palm fronds sway overhead as the wind whips at the trees and the surf. Shadows converge into a form that looks like a toddler's drawing: an approximation of a human with many heads. Chaos turns to look at me, and shadows split into a smile. The surf crashes, and the wind howls, but I remain untouched, as though I stand in the eye of a storm.

The Demon's voice is like falling water, everywhere and nowhere, not a sound from a mouth attached to a mortal body. "You and I are the same," it whispers as softly as a kiss.

The vision releases me, and I collapse into the present. Why this vision? Why now? I bite down on my gag and scream in frustration. My useless ghosts do not respond.

An eyebrowless Nen stands at the forefront of a ring of candidates that forms a circle around me. And I thought he would be grateful I took his punishment? It's my mother's trial all over again, only I am the one they plan to condemn. I stifle an inappropriate laugh. I have worried over this fate every day of my life before the Sundo. It seems laughable that my end at the hands of ignorant fools has finally found me here.

I break one boy's nose and struggle to get free of the circle, but there are too many of them. They bind my wrists to the scaffolding against the wall, and my taped fingers scream in protest.

"Kuran Jal, the ruler of Tigang must be the best of us." Nen sneers. "And we have decided that you are not fit."

Who is *we*? I narrow my eyes. Not many can hold my gaze, but then I see Dayen. He struggles to break free of two candidates at the rear of the crowd. His mouth is gagged like mine.

Someone removes the cloth stuffed in my mouth so that I can answer to their charges.

"And what reasons have you?" I spit.

"Seran," Nen hisses, and a boy steps forward. Seran has a long face and spiking hair. Blood still drips from his broken nose. "I saw her sneak off with Arisa the other night, and she's friendly with her Guardian. She's spying on us in return for the Astar's favors. You all saw how Nen was singled out for punishment."

"That's absurd," I reply, but Nen lifts his chin and raises a gold earring between his fingers. It's the same earring that I plucked from Ingo's unconscious body after the Makers test. I thought I'd lost it. My stomach drops.

"Dayen found this in your room. What did you do to Ingo?" Nen asks.

How could I even begin to explain it? I also made a promise to Arisa, backed by a threat. I cannot speak about that night without condemning us all. I look over at the boy who betrayed me, and the shame in his expression is a slap to the face. My eyes blur with hot tears, not from shame but anger. I am *so* close; I will not let these children ruin things now.

"Look at her neck!" someone screams. "Look what she was hiding!"

They swarm forward in a blur of faces and curses.

"The truth will put you in danger. Please, believe me!" I shout, but my voice is lost in the commotion, and I have no idea if anyone hears me.

The wooden scaffolding sways behind me, and I scrape my

bindings against it. The whole structure groans, and I grit my teeth as pain blooms.

"Who are you to condemn me? Have you not seen the Astar's marks? Who do you think truly controls Tigang? I can tell you it is not some puppet ruler chosen in some arcane competition. Arisa will be here long after our next ruler is gone, and the next after her!" I scream, but no one is listening. Nen draws a wicked-looking knife. I pull so hard at my bindings that the rotted wood cracks and I break free.

Dayen elbows the boy to his left and ducks under the arm of the other. He rushes to the front of the crowd, toward me, still gagged.

I hop up the scaffolding to get away. A piece of wood snaps under my left foot, and I clutch the scaffolding with white knuckles. The wood shatters against the hard stone below. I reach for another bit of scaffolding as Nen climbs up behind me.

Dayen reaches for Nen to stop him, but he is too tall and too heavy. When he tests his foot against the scaffolds, the entire structure trembles.

But I don't need saving. Nen is so close. I lean down and kick at the scaffolding in his hands. His grip loosens and a cascade of wood pulls away from its moorings so we are dangling partway over the pit. He clings to the wood, and his face drains of blood as he scrambles for a better hold.

I could let him fall. I've known so many Nens, and I have never done anything but cower. I've never done anything but take their hate or run from it. And it's all Astar's fault that I've been called a monster my whole life when I could have been…

Arisa.

My jaw trembles. I watch him flail for a moment longer before I shout for Dayen.

I extend my right hand to Nen. "Take my hand or fall and die."

He wavers, and I know the terrible choice he weighs: to live cursed or to die. I let him choose and relish the fact he does not know there is no teeth to my curse. He reaches for my hand, and I swing him onto the ledge of the pit with Dayen's help.

No one knows what to say. A space clears around me, and I storm away, leaving Nen sprawled on the stone of the floor. I don't look back. I want to be away from this cursed fortress before I am lost forever.

I touch the familiar marks upon my neck. I was so close to letting Nen die. I wanted to watch him fall. I wanted to watch that smug expression shatter. Worst of all, I don't think I would have regretted it.

I huddle my arms around my trembling body. Maybe I deserve to be reviled.

A sweet mung bean pastry in a bakery box stamped with a shop name waits on my bed when I return to my room. A note on the plate reads: *Eat with care. Ask the kitchens for more.* I nibble at it, too tired to care if it's poisoned, and find a message on a roll of rice paper tucked inside.

Baylan and council divided. Arisa cleaning house. You are not who you say you are. Who are you really, Jal girl? - O

Maybe someone I don't want to be.

CHAPTER THIRTY

An hour later, Dayen finds me hunched over a length of rope in the baths. Virian slumbers unmoving nearby, propped up on pillows and covered to her chin with a blanket. She hasn't stirred once since the Demon's attack on the fortress.

I don't look Dayen in the eye, but he folds his elbows and knees in front of me and makes it impossible to ignore him. I would rather hate him; instead, I only feel small and vulnerable. I thought he was my friend.

"I'm so sorry, Kuran. I didn't know Nen would do this. I only showed him the earring because I knew something terrible must have happened to Ingo."

"And you're still not sure about me." I rub my face with the heels of my hands. I cannot bring myself to forgive him, but I know what it's like to regret a decision. "You will make sure Virian is safe. That is how you will make amends."

"I swear it on this life and the ones to come. I trust you. You didn't have to save Nen, but you did, and that means something." He bites his lip, and he looks so young. His hair seems to have grown longer, and I itch to take some scissors to the floppy mess of it. "Still friends?"

There is nothing but hope in his expression, and I'm too tired to cling to any anger. I nod, and he wisely changes the subject. "Do you think it will work?"

The contraption Tanu rigged out of metal clips and rope looks sturdy. I trust his grasp of mechanics. Several puffed-up bladders serve as floats. It should allow Dayen to strap Virian to his back, but Dayen will have to do the climbing and swimming for the both of them.

An exhausting length of rope coils in my lap. I dare not think about how hard it will be to fight the waves and make it to shore, but what other option do we have? We have no backup plan.

I nod and smile for Dayen anyway.

Teloh is all shadows and lips pulled tight. He paces near the walls, unable to stand still. Since we last spoke, it feels as though we've drifted continents apart. His part in our plan ends on a fortress balcony. He's not coming with us. We can't even look at each other to say goodbye.

Every time it seems like he might say something, he closes his mouth. He helps Dayen carry Virian through the Autumn place, and I secure one end of the rope to three of the railing posts of a balcony. Though it should be strong enough to hold an ox, I tie an extra knot to be sure. Teloh tethers Virian to Dayen's back, and she sags there like a sleeping baby.

"I will be back with my mother in an hour, but if I don't make it back, go without me. Get to Oshar Toso. She's a friend."

Dayen's eyes meet mine. "We will wait for you there if we get separated." *If we survive*, he doesn't say. He goes back to fiddling with his buckles and straps. He touches his amulets, and I pray for a miracle but doubt the Diwata are listening.

"Wait," Teloh says. I can't look at him, not without feeling too many things at once, and I dare not turn around.

"Teloh, what happened to the Astar before Arisa?" I ask. "She died young."

"You don't need to know that." His voice catches.

I close my eyes and refold my green-and-gold malong tightly around my waist. If I die today, I'll die wearing something gifted to me with love. There is no turning back now. "I do."

I hear him suck in a breath. "She fell off a balcony."

My stomach lurches. I imagine the wind in my hair, the salt spray in my eyes, and knowing that death awaits as I fall. My ghosts remain silent, and I'm thankful no memories come. It's too late now to pick any option but the sea wall. I can't afford to be afraid.

"Teloh, watch the rope, please. I'll be back soon." I walk away before I lose my nerve, and he doesn't follow, because he knows I must do this alone.

Vines as thick as my legs creep through the light shafts in the ceiling, and grasses sprout from every surface—evidence of the Demon's attack. I scoot past Baylan taking axes to vines as thick as tree trunks, too busy tending to the fortress to notice me, and spiral down the staircase I used once before.

The dungeon doors loom tall at the end of the hallway. They are scratched and worn as though something clawed at its surface. Today, as Senil promised, the guards are nowhere to be seen.

Orasyons carved into the entire wall surrounding the door pulse with magic that feels hot and scratchy. They illuminate as I approach, as though lit with fire from behind, ready to incinerate any trespasser.

There is only one way to find out if Senil can be trusted. I stride forward quickly, gripping Senil's bronze amulet tight. I close my eyes and brace myself for the impact of protection spells, but sparks shimmer and fall harmlessly off an invisible bubble as I cross the threshold. The head Archivist's spell works. By some miracle, I find my way to my mother's cell unscathed.

I pause outside her door, a mess of fear and longing. My mother kept so much from me in the name of protection, but what good did it do? We are both here now. Maybe if she was honest with me, I would have known why Bato-Ko was so dangerous. I might have stayed away.

But I vowed to save her, and I do not regret my choice.

I suck in a breath, and I enter prepared for a fight, but the sight of her nearly reduces me to tears. I stand there shaking like a small child ready to be reprimanded. I've missed her so much, yet I don't dare reach out for fear I am only dreaming. I made it. I found her. And somehow, somehow, I will get her out, and we will leave this horrid, twisted place with its Demons and its tyrants far, far behind us. We will take Kuran and our wagons, and we will get as far from Tigang as we can. I'll be the good girl she always wished I was and keep hidden. I won't ever complain about her cooking again.

She sits on a thin mattress beside a narrow window. She wears the same orange headwrap I last saw her in, tight around her curls. She looks thinner than I remember, and her eyes look sallower, but she is whole. My mother. Finally. It has been too long. My throat feels so tight that words refuse to come out.

Her thin blanket falls to the floor at the sight of me. A range of emotions flashes across her face: despair, terror, relief, and by the Heavens, love. So much love. Our life may have been small, but at least it was ours.

"Oh, Narra, what have you done?" She rushes to my side and wraps me in her arms. Her familiar scent envelops me. I am home. But I refuse to cry. Not now. Not yet.

"We are getting out, Inay," I say. "And we're getting Ate Kuran and leaving Bato-Ko. The guards will not be gone long. We must hurry."

She slides her hands to my shoulders and looks at me, a deadly calm settling over her face. Who is this woman that stands before me?

"It is a mother's duty to worry about her children, not the other way around. If I leave this place, the Baylan will find me. Maybe not now, but in a few years, and if they do not know about you yet, you are safer if I am dead. Find Kuran and leave me." Her voice is unexpectedly gentle. I expected anger or even concern, not resignation. Does she know all I have endured to get here? Does she think I can just walk away and leave her to die? I bristle and stand my ground.

I remember all the times we fought, but none of those seem to matter now. I think we only got along when we were silent, because though we do not look alike, we have the same hard head.

I do not move. "Are you coming?" I say, surprised that my voice doesn't warble or strain.

"You have changed since you've come here, but it's not a bad thing." There is softness at the edges of her expression. It is the same look she wears whenever she thinks about my father when she thinks her daughters are not watching, but I am not ready to let her join my father in the next life.

"You were always running away when you were a child, and when you were two years old, I almost lost you." She takes my hand and folds it in hers. "We were walking through the market in Pulang Ilog when Kuran ran off after a stray cat. It was such an ugly old thing, but your Ate wanted to feed it and take it with us. When I turned around, you were gone." Her hand squeezes me tighter now. "My heart nearly stopped. I grabbed your sister, and we went to every stall looking for you. We crawled under every table and turned over every dirty basket." She looks up at me, and her voice catches. "Do you know where I found you? Sitting on the docks, poking at a dead crab that the birds had torn apart." She drops my hand and wipes her eyes with her sleeves. "You kept trying to fix it and started screaming because it wouldn't move. You didn't understand that there are some things you can't fix." She looks up at me. "Sometimes you just have to go on."

I grind my teeth together. It sounds like she's given up when

I'm here to set her free.

"Inay..." I plunk down on the cold floor in front of her and cross my legs.

"Guardians will throw you in here with me if you do not leave," she says.

We stare at each other, neither yielding. I may be late to meet my friends, but without my mother, this whole ludicrous plan is over for me.

"You are the reason I came to Bato-Ko and the reason I risked my life to get here. I will not give up on you," I say.

Waves hammer against the fortress, and a freezing wind whips through the windows, but I keep myself planted to the stone.

"Very well," she sighs, and I allow myself a moment to hope.

"After your name-day ceremony and first birthday, your father and I took to the sea to flee the Baylan. A young Guardian helped us steal a boat."

"Curls and dark eyes?" I guess.

She frowns but does not ask the question aloud. I am certain Teloh helped my family. Somehow. Impossibly. Perhaps it was another life's version of him, or perhaps he simply lied to me about his age, but it's a puzzle for another time.

The ocean breeze pushes leaves around us in gyres, and they scrape noisily against the stone floors. We make good time, but the balcony is empty.

Though the early-evening sun remains a dull gray smudge in the sky, there is no sign of my friends or the rope that I tied so securely. I race to the railing and fight dizziness as I stare down. Hungry waves lick at the fortress walls, and salt spray whips my face.

"What's wrong?" my mother asks, but I do not have the chance to answer.

My heart quickens as footsteps approach. Something is wrong. Where is Teloh? I fumble to unknot Senil's amulet from my wrist and toss it into the ocean.

I pull my mother close as three familiar figures appear. Reshar stomps toward us. A brass gong sways at his hip. Beside him strides Kormar; the Head Cultivator wears her clipping shears at her waist like a sword and an apologetic expression like armor. Beside them walks Tanu.

I grip my mother's arm tight. Tanu. That blue-eyed betrayer. He looks away from me. I was never good at hiding what I feel, and he can see exactly what I'm thinking. The guilt of it drags his eyes to the stone tiles.

Did Virian and Dayen get away? I dare not open my mouth to give them up if the Baylan don't know they escaped.

"Kuran Jal." Reshar rolls back his shoulders, and the wind whips at his robe, showing off his tattoos. They seem to writhe as though alive. "Of all the fool things... You would have died if you left the glass fortress this way."

Kormar sucks in a breath as a gust of wind blows my hair from my neck. "Her marks."

"That's impossible." He waves his hand to dismiss her, but he pauses a moment too long. "Kuran Jal is too old," he adds, but he doesn't seem certain anymore.

A wave of Guardians floods the space around us, and in the center of them marches Arisa. Her expression is a storm, and her gold sun comb crowns her head. "Kuran Jal. No one leaves this competition without my say-so."

"Astar Arisa," the Cultivator hisses, "look at her marks. Could it be?"

The Astar eyes my birthmarks for the first time. They are so much like hers, yet different. Mine are flat and black, while hers are red like a brand from a flame. A flicker of surprise transforms into a smile that makes me shudder.

A dozen ways to die flood through my mind.

"Of course not." Arisa's expression does not falter. She lifts her chin, and her gold comb glints in the light. "And that is not my concern. My concern is the Sundo. You have broken our rules, Kuran Jal. You dare defy me?"

"You are not Reyna. The Astar is simply a reminder of the past. You have no true authority in Tigang." I look her in the eyes. For all her finery, there is nothing special about her. She is flesh and bone, just like I am. "You're an eighteen-year-old girl drunk on her self-importance."

A slap to the face sends me reeling.

Reshar averts his gaze but rubs at his stubbled chin as though he's calculating sums. Surely, Arisa would not do anything drastic in their presence? But what would Reshar consider drastic? I wilt at the thought.

"Astar Arisa, we must know," Kormar insists. To my surprise, Arisa falters at the asog's soft demand. The Astar looks me up and down as if seeing me complete for the first time. First, I was a tool; now, I am competition.

She snaps her eyes back to mine. "We cannot stop the Sundo to address some wild speculation, but we must deal with this betrayal."

Guardians drag Teloh toward us. His bare feet slide across the stone, and his body hangs limp between them. His hands are bound, and his head is bent. I bite my cheek and taste blood.

At the crook of her finger, a Guardian passes Arisa a rattan cane.

"For escaping your judgment, Shora Jal, ten lashes. For aiding a felon, Kuran Jal, twenty lashes." Arisa twirls the cane in one hand. "For helping these deviants, my pet, another twenty."

Tanu looks at me, unashamed. He must have carefully

weighed his options before turning me over to Arisa. Perhaps he even believes he is saving me now.

To think I called him brother. I want him to feel the weight of his betrayal, and I do not offer him a twitch of consolation or a glimpse of acknowledgment. I vow to think of him no longer. He is dead to me.

My mother trembles beside me, but it is not Arisa who frightens her. She stares at Teloh as if he is on fire.

"My daughter is guilty of nothing but concern for her mother. Let her go, Astar." My mother drops to her knees. "I beg of you. I am resigned to my fate. Let me take the lashes now or execute me. Please spare her."

My mother should not bend for a girl half her age. My cheeks flush with anger, but if I strike Arisa, I might as well beg for my own execution. I must not let my feelings get the better of me.

"No." I swallow. "I was afraid." I drop to my knees beside her and twine my hands through my mother's. Hers are still strong and warm. They are steady. They have always been what I needed as we traveled the world. Maybe we argued and disagreed often, but we loved each other just as fiercely. "I am just a village girl. I should never have entered the Sundo." I press my head to the floor and debase myself. "Let me take my mother's punishment. She was willing to face her death, but I was not. I forced her to come with me."

Silence stretches thin between us, and when I dare lift my head, Arisa grins toothily. I shudder. The prettiness of her expression and the delicate frills of her dress make her cruelty an even sharper weapon.

"Very well. Back to your room, Shora Jal. You will be executed soon anyway." Arisa gestures for the guards to lead my mother to the dungeons, and I exhale.

She is safe for now, but Teloh is still here. I silently will him to raise his head again and look at me, because if he does, I might be able to endure what is to come.

And he does. When Teloh lifts his chin, his left eye is already black, and purple bruises peek out from under the neck of his tunic. I stand there frozen, unable to offer anything more than the comfort of my presence. Our eyes lock. I cling to that thread of connection in his gaze and hope it is enough to keep the both of us steady.

Arisa appraises me for a long while, but when she turns to Teloh, I realize I have erred. "I have changed my mind. Let the assassin take your punishment and Shora's."

"No—" I plead, but Arisa cuts me off with a dagger of a smile.

"And you, Kuran—you must watch, so that you remember that it is you who did this to him."

My own punishment, I would take without question. I would have clung to the nobility in it, but there's no honor in having an already beaten Teloh suffer on my behalf.

"No!" I scream, but Guardians hold me back. Teloh warned me, and yet I still insisted. This is my fault.

When Teloh looks up at me, his eyes are full—not of the anger I deserve, but resignation. My defiance falls to pieces.

✴ ☽ ✴ ☾ ✴

CHAPTER THIRTY-ONE

Guardian grabs my hair and forces my face toward Teloh. The assassin does not scream at first, but his mouth gapes like a fish as he swallows the pain. I count the lashings one by one, wishing for it to end.

Arisa wields the cane like a two-handed sword. She swings it down over Teloh's back again and again. From the steadiness of her hands, I can tell that she's had practice at this. She leaves just enough time between each strike that Teloh winces in anticipation of the next, and when he finally cries out, it is a broken sound like a bird crushed underfoot.

It goes on and on, until I cannot see because my eyes are too full of water and my screams have long since turned into whimpering pleas. I kneel on the ground, unable to control the shaking sobs that rack my body. I have done this to all of them, not just Teloh. I abandoned my sister. I put Dayen and Virian in danger. Worst of all, my mother is still locked away, and my father is still dead. I failed them all. I wish I could take the lashes for Teloh. Instead, I cower and remain untouched.

When it is done, he lays crumpled upon the ground. He wheezes in wet breaths of air, as if his lungs aren't working properly. There is no blood, but for a little red spit that trails from the corner of his mouth. It is the smallest of mercies.

I crawl on my hands and knees, avoiding a puddle of sour

vomit that is mine. Reshar summons Arisa away, but a bright smile plays upon the Astar's lips as she goes. How could anyone but a monster find pleasure in this?

"Teloh," I whisper and lay down on the cold floor beside him. I rest my head near his and touch the hem of his tunic with my knees. The stone sucks all the warmth out of me, and I shiver as I lie there, but I refuse to leave him.

"I made them—go ahead—when discovered—Arisa." Each word is labored, and the sentence stretches out between breaths.

"Maybe they made it," I whisper, but I cannot tell whether he believes it.

I twine my pinky finger with his and watch his eyes flicker open and closed.

"Hush now. It's going to be okay," I lie with my words and my smile. "I'm here."

I stroke his hair, and his breath grows even. He does not fight for consciousness. Fatigue tugs me in and out of dreams that make no sense. I yell Teloh's name into the wind. I cannot see him, but I know he's laughing. I watch him tearing at his skin as though it is on fire, and flowers bloom where his blood drops. But as always, I return to the waking nightmare that is my life.

When he opens his eyes at last, they are clear and dark. That he can sit up at all surprises me, but he tests his limbs and stumbles to his feet with a wince.

"Teloh…"

"Not here," he grunts, and I brace him as we stumble into the greenhouse together. We pass under a canopy of rustling leaves, and when we reach the glass wall, he sinks down to his knees with his hands over his eyes. He inhales the air as if it is food.

"Thank you," I don't know what else there is to say. I always ruin things by opening my mouth.

"Arisa cannot do any lasting damage to me." He relaxes

his shoulders against the cool glass of the fortress to numb his bruises.

I sit on a large rock and stare at my feet. I'm surprised that I can breathe again. Think again. That he is still alive. That I am not dead in the ocean with my friends. But Arisa will come for me the moment no one is watching. I tremble and huddle my knees close.

"Narra." He mumbles my name as if it is a puzzle.

"Why do you stay?" I blurt. "What hold does Arisa have on you that you don't just leave, and that you allow this to be done to you?"

I regret my words immediately. I don't meet his eyes for long, too afraid to see more anger when I wish for something else. Something impossible. A different life. When I breathe in the flower-scented air of the rainforest, the room spins, and I don't know if I want to cry or to scream.

"She promised me little freedoms for my obedience. I suffer her because she is the only one who allows me out of the fortress," he says. "I am a prisoner here." He shrugs as if it is nothing, when it is his life.

"Why didn't they just throw me out of the Sundo?" I scrunch my malong in my hands, but it does nothing to soothe my frustration.

"If Reshar and Kormar were not there, you'd already be dead, but Arisa is cunning. She'd rather keep you close than let you get away from her now. Make no mistake—she will look for ways to be rid of you."

Teloh's hands twitch, but his posture remains relaxed. He rolls his shoulders back with a sigh, and his joints crackle back into place. Arisa is not weak, and Teloh is not as thickly muscled as Tanu. His ribs should be fractured, his skin split and bruised, but he looks whole. I grimace, and he notices.

"You made me promise to take you away from here, and I

kept my promise. Your father joined the Baylan to be close to you, and he died for your freedom. But you came back, and as always, I couldn't deny you, no matter how angry it made me. I fear it's damned us all again." He sighs and rubs at his eyes. "But maybe there is no escaping our fate." He goes still in that way that makes me nervous. "And that means you must know what you are. Somewhere behind those thick walls you've built, you already know all the answers," he says. "And you must remember because Arisa takes no chances. Look at me," he growls because my eyes have returned to the dirt.

The hurt in his expression is so sharp that it is a dagger through my heart, and my ghosts scream so loudly that I cover my ears with my hands.

He loosens the kris from his sash and unsheathes it. The bright steel flashes in the shadows. It seems to glow faintly with a light that reminds me of the moon. He takes it to his hair and slices off a fistful, and between blinks it grows back into place, as if it had never been cut.

The grimace returns to his lips as he bends over to untie his sash. He peels the tunic off his back, and this time I cannot help but stare. The lines of his leanly muscled frame are plainly visible in the shade of the banana trees, and just a little less so are the bruises.

But what he wills me to see is the orasyon that covers his entire torso in a mass of scars. Words are etched over words, which form a lattice of faint white lines, almost like lace. It looks as though someone took a sharp pen full of acid and drew it across his body.

I do not know what the words say, because the language is not one of this world, but the letters slant unmistakably to the left, and they are written in a hand that looks too much like mine.

And I realize that my visions were all warnings. I looked different in each one, but Teloh always remained the same.

The air around me thickens as if it might rain inside the greenhouse. The trees lean toward us, and fat leaves clap together. The stray hairs on my neck begin to prickle as moisture beads on my forehead and trickles down the side of my nose. I recall the vision I had of sparring on the rooftop and watching greenery sprout around us as a storm raged. He wrote no orasyons to summon the rain. There were no spells to grow plants at his feet. Magic simply poured out of him.

"Who did this to you?" I ask. The words rasp out of my throat, barely audible. I still don't want to believe what he is, but there can only be one explanation.

"Astar." His eyes do not leave mine. "Do you remember yet?"

I stare at Chaos in his human-shaped prison.

My ghosts knock loudly at my chest as the wind whips at my hair. The shadows deepen around him. There has always been something between us. We were always like two falling stars doomed to collide the moment we are anywhere near each other.

This is why the Demon stopped in front of my room and did not enter. This is why it followed me away from my friends. This is why it stopped short of taking my life.

I don't know if there is a tempest outside or inside me, threatening to knock down walls, to tear my life apart, but I run.

CHAPTER THIRTY-TWO

Coward. My world is spinning out of control, and I can't stop shaking. My marks burn as if they are on fire. Not even my name feels right. Was there ever a Narra Jal?

I cannot stop thinking about Teloh. Loneliness obscured all reason, and I ignored any good sense. He warned me over and over, but I didn't listen. My chest aches, but I can't tell if it's simply the pain of a heart breaking, or if it's my ghosts clawing their way out. Pain is pain.

I stumble into the kitchens. No one is there but a young boy in brown, so I gamble on the only clue I have left. I rub Oshar's rice-paper note between my fingers.

"Can you order me mung bean pastry from Aling Myla's bakery?" I ask and unroll the message in front of him. I'm desperate for any handhold to keep from drowning, but this feels like patching holes in a dam with a blade of grass. I need all the help I can get. As long as my mother is alive, I will risk anything.

He does not look pleased by the late-night request. "Yes, po. Of course, po. We are here to serve, po." He rolls his eyes. "What other special requests do you have for me today, oh gracious one?"

I grab him by the shoulders and growl. "Search the coast for two people. They might need help."

His expression could curdle milk. "It will take some time to get into the city." He shrugs his shoulders and walks away, taking half my meager hopes with him.

I tug at my hair with a frustrated groan—this is *impossible*. I pick at Astar's story and try to scratch out truths, but the many versions of the truth tangle together. *In the time before…* The words scatter from me, lost upon the wind. All the sense and comfort I used to take in the stories have gone with Teloh.

No, legends will not help me now.

I pass through the great hall at daybreak, only lingering long enough to hear that our next test will take place at midday, before I head for the fortress archives. Perhaps the public archives might be sanitized, but surely the Baylan's private records must be accurate. I need to find a map of the fortress and another way out. If I have to crawl through the sewers, I will.

"Wait!" Tanu runs up behind me.

I clench my fists, and I don't slow for him, but the blue-eyed boy keeps pace with me.

"I gave Kuran my oath to protect you, and I fulfilled that the best way I could," he says as if this excuses his actions. "You would have died if you climbed down the wall. Do you know how cold the water is at the bottom? You would have died of hypothermia before you ever reached the shore—that is, if you could even have survived the waves. Do you see how they smash at the fortress? There are no wards on that side of the fortress because leaving by that route is as good as committing suicide."

I don't give him the satisfaction of a reply. I keep walking, but though I turn a corner he has no trouble keeping up. Heavens damn his long legs. I slam my hands against his chest and push him back.

"You call this protection? You just condemned both Inay and me!"

"I had to tell someone! You would have died trying to escape, but the Baylan are sworn to keep the candidates for the Sundo safe. This was for the best." He is still so righteous and sure of himself.

"Like they kept all the missing candidates safe?" I mock. "You do not get to decide what's best for me." I want no more of his excuses and justifications. I want him gone, so I can find another way to get my mother out of here. It will be almost impossible now, all because of him. But I will not stop while I am alive.

"I looked up the records, because I could not believe that anyone in your family could be capable of such treachery," he says.

I stop short before hitting a wall.

"And?" I glower at him. "What did you find?"

"Your mother was wrong to hide you away, and your father's sacrifice was worth nothing. If you were one of the Astars, you belong here."

I rattle with a fury I didn't know I possessed. "I am glad I was not raised in this cursed fortress. If I were Astar, I would leave here in a heartbeat." I might have even jumped off a balcony. I close my eyes and inhale. *No*. Not that, I frown, *but I could have been pushed*. A shiver runs down my spine.

I think of my worried vision on the fortress balcony, in which a past version of me asked Teloh for help to escape. He kept his promise. Another me knew what was going to happen. I planned for this.

I scratch at my neck and my curse marks, wishing I could scrub them from my skin. But I don't remember more than fragments: In past lives, I knew Teloh. He is the same boy I dreamed of walking through the Lantern Festival with, whom I sparred on the rooftop with and held close, but also the mist and the storm in the pit of Bato-Ko. The only answer that ties everything together is Astar.

"This is your home, Narra."

I would have hated it without the open sky, without my family, locked up in dusty rooms with ancient toys.

"And do you think Arisa will give up her position just like that?" I ask.

I stare at Tanu closely. He has such an earnest face that I am tempted to forgive his betrayal. He looks even less the villain when he wears his spectacles, like today. How gullible. How easy to use. In another life, who could he have been to me?

Tanu is just as frightened as the rest of us. He means well, but I can't forgive him. Not yet.

I gnash my teeth so hard that my jaw aches. If I were Astar, I might be someone with a little power. Not magic, for I would have to relearn that, but respect and authority.

If I am truly the Astar, I might be able to stop this madness and pardon my mother's crime, but everything feels so out of my control that I don't even know if I can save myself.

I turn on my heels, and this time, Tanu doesn't follow.

There are three ways in and out of the fortress: the main gates, the seaside balconies, and through the archives. Three looming mahogany doors separate the public city archives from this private space. The doors do not budge even a fraction when I lean tentatively against them. Behind the wood, Bato-Ko buzzes with life and noise. The city is so close that I smell fish frying and hear hawkers shouting, but I cannot cross into it. Orasyons cascade down the doors from the ceilings to the floor, barring the way as effectively as a stone wall.

I sign and return to my daunting task. It doesn't matter. The fortress archives span half the size of their public counterpart, but there are still rows upon rows of books. Some books are not made of paper but rolls of bamboo threaded through with rope. Some are dusty leather tomes full of stretched skins, procured from other countries.

I flip through random volumes, and their mundanity disappoints me. Tax records. Lists of initiates. A recording of fortress repairs. I sink to the floor and thread my hands through my hair. I open a large volume, hoping for maps, only to stumble upon admissions of initiates to the fortress organized by year.

I scan the roster of new Baylan, and I find a familiar name amongst them: Kalena Rem; born in Santi City, Tigang; twenty years old. She wasn't head interpreter then, but it seems remarkable that she rose through the ranks so quickly. I flip through several years and find a note that surprises me. The youngest Baylan to ever become Datu was Reshar. I look at the dates and realize that he's younger than I guessed, only in his mid-thirties, when he appears much older.

My ghosts nearly leap out of my chest at the sound of slippers against stone. I bite down on my tongue as I press myself into the shadows.

Nen hurries through the shelves. He looks over his shoulders and checks the skylights to judge the time, as if he is late for an appointment. The eyebrowless boy has a knife tucked into his sash, so I guess that his intentions are not noble. He's foolish enough to get himself killed.

I peer at him from behind the stacks. I wait for the city doors to slide open by some miracle. Instead, he checks the ceiling. Plaster and gilding depict the night sky overhead. In the archives beyond the doors, I recall that the roof was decorated with a reversed image of these. Now I see that Omu's constellation on this side looks as though it's reaching out to touch the center of the wall.

Nen stops underneath Omu's constellation, beneath the star called her heel. He taps his foot against a tile in the floor. It slides out of place and reveals a dark hole that he disappears into.

I wait so I don't give myself away, but it is not Nen who emerges from beneath the floor.

Five dark-clad figures, with scarves covering their mouths and steel in their hands, slip out of the hole like bats escaping a cave. I remember that after Galaya died, Bamal whispered that the Baylan were searching for a traitor. I recall Reshar's secret conversation hinting that Tigang is vulnerable to its enemies until a new ruler is chosen.

These assassins wear gold at their necks, and I would bet my pocket money that they are sun disks. They are gone before I can follow, and Nen, that foolish, foolish boy, comes out of the hole and slides the tile back into place.

I've found a traitor amongst us.

✳ ☽ ✳ ☾ ✳

CHAPTER THIRTY-THREE

I slip around the shelves, toward the tile. The heel of Omu's gilded constellation glints dully in the roof above me. Nothing else marks the marble below as anything out of the ordinary, but when I kick it with my toes, it slides out of place with the sound of a spring.

A rickety wooden ladder leans against a dirt wall inside. My mind races through the possibilities. It could be a way out, but it could also be a dead end.

I climb down a few rungs to check. Loose dirt crumbles around my fingers as I brush it. I squint and make out the outline of another ladder—an exit.

My hopes swell, but a flash of metal warns me that I'm not alone. An assassin dressed like a Guardian lunges for me as I scramble back up the ladder with a shriek.

The scarf-clad assassin catches the hem of my skirt, and I squirm for footing. I kick and catch her cheek with the side of my foot. She lets go.

I stomp on the tile to close it, but a gloved hand catches the lip of the stone. The assassin pushes the tile back, and I sprint toward the hallway. How many assassins? One behind me, five ahead, and Nen with a knife.

The assassin jumps free of the tunnel. She bounds forward with long, powerful strides. My shoulder slams into a rickety shelf as I back up, and it nearly topples. I think quick and shove my weight into it again. This time, the old wood groans and topples into the next shelf, where it gets stuck, creating a narrow tunnel.

A metal dart thunks into the wood of the shelf, missing my ear by a few hairs. I scramble out of the way and turn left to lose my pursuer, but the assassin goes the other direction, and I realize my mistake: she knows the layout of the library. A giant pair of double doors, carved from mahogany and banded with steel, is the only way in and out.

One assassin waits at the door for her companions. I recognize her only by the scarf still dangling loose at her neck. They bark words in a northern dialect I can't understand, but they are dressed like Guardians, and the other melts out the door into the turmoil of the glass fortress unseen. Freezing Hells, I need to warn someone.

My pursuer turns around, and two long daggers glint in her hands as she ducks into stacks one aisle over. I drop a thick tome to the floor at the end of my aisle.

I hear the assassin change course and hug an even thicker tome between my two hands. I swing it into her chest as she rounds the corner.

She stumbles forward, but I've only bought myself seconds, not minutes. I glance at the door, and it still looks unguarded, so I run toward it. I hear the sound of metal clanging, as though a fight has broken out. I only pray that real Guardians have discovered the false ones first.

I find one black tunic and red sash fending off two with sashes of blue. Teloh holds a long kampilan in one hand and a short dagger in the other. His face is calm, though one blue-sashed assassin lunges at him from the front and another raises a dagger behind. But the calm does not hold when he sees me.

A body drops in front of Teloh, but there are still two more.

"Narra," he barks and tosses a dagger to me, and I catch it. There's no time to think. I whip his dagger backward, and it finds flesh.

My pursuer drops to the floor, clutching the dagger in her neck. I am too stunned to react. A scream wells in my throat, but it sticks there, unable to escape.

Teloh shrugs off a third assassin like an old coat.

I blink, and Teloh is beside me, swearing. "What are you doing here?"

"I was... Archives." It feels like flower petals are falling from my mouth instead of words.

He swears again.

"You?" I whisper.

"I was following that boy Nen, but I should really just look for you if I'm in the mood for trouble." His expression betrays a very human temper. "How many more?"

"Three," I say.

"Go back to your room and stay there." He races down the hall and whistles for Guardians without a look back.

I shake and steady myself against a wall. What is happening? Would cultists dare threaten Tigang?

I am still pressed against the wall when the library door cracks open again.

Nen creeps out of the archives holding his dagger in front of him like a shield. I should've realized he'd stay behind, the coward. I shoot over, pinning him against the wood with a grunt. He struggles against me, and though there is blood on my face and tunic, it's still my hands that he stares at. He pinches his lips and watches them as if they are weapons.

Superstitious fool. Footsteps echo down the corridor. All I have to do is shout and they'll all know him for a traitor.

"Galaya? Was she with you and the cultist assassins?" I growl.

"Galaya insisted on playing within the rules." He shrinks

away from me. "She was an unfortunate loss, but we will still win. Omu will be here soon, and we will shape Tigang in Omu's perfect image." He smiles with a wide-eyed recklessness I recognize. Nen doesn't wear a sun disk but embodies that cultist haughtiness just the same.

"You fool! That would destroy us!" The Diwata must be regarded equally so that the cosmos remains in balance. Without that balance, war and destruction would plague the world, even beyond our country.

"We want only what Omu wants. When we listen to her words and follow her command, she blesses us! She would never let us suffer. She's promised good harvests, full bellies, and the sun upon our fields! Our country could thrive, if only we listened. If only we submit."

Dangerous words that I pray never come to pass, because if Omu is anything like her followers, only suffering awaits those who refuse her.

"Who else?" The words scrape against my tongue. He cannot be working alone. He is too obvious, too lacking in talent for Reshar or Teloh not to have caught him, and he could not have dug out that tunnel during the Sundo. "Tell me or I will turn you over to Arisa."

He laughs as if I've told a great joke, and I understand it all at once.

Kalena is the word of Omu herself, and though the head Interpreter has never been seen publicly with any cultists, I doubt the same in private. But Arisa has never seemed reverent of anyone. Perhaps Kalena and the cultists promised her respect. Perhaps they promised to let her keep her power.

Arisa is too young to have plotted out such a long game, but I have no such illusions about Kalena. The head Interpreter was an initiate when the previous Astar still lived. *She* could have pushed Astar off a balcony. *She* could have groomed Arisa and helped her pass Astar's test. My mind leaps to the sun comb that Arisa wears, the same symbol around Kalena's neck. A coincidence? I think not.

"Reshar will not be kind in his questioning of you."

"It doesn't matter," he says and lifts his chin toward my marks. "You've already damned me."

Guardians career down the hall toward us, but Nen twists out of my grip.

"I've caught the traitor, here!" he shouts and slices his neck open.

He drops to the floor with a smile on his face.

"No! No." I stumble to my knees in shock. Blood slips through my fingers no matter how hard I try to press at his neck. I stare in horror. The blood won't stop. Nen's breathing slows. Nen was not my friend, but I am no killer. I didn't wish him dead or cursed. Fools! I scream aloud in frustration. Nen wasted his life for nothing, because I am not the danger here. I shake him hard, and his head knocks against the stone floor, but he refuses to wake.

Guardians drag me away from his body, but I hardly notice them. I don't even feel my feet moving. All I see is Nen's smiling face. Even if I wash the blood from my hands, the stain runs all the way to my heart, and it will stick for all my lives to come.

I laugh, as I realize my curse was no fault of the Heavens. I surely damned myself, and I wonder just how ruined I already am.

✳ ☽ ✳ ☾ ✳

CHAPTER THIRTY-FOUR

Reshar paces back and forth like a caged lion. The Seeker's office is sparsely furnished, and where there might be a rug to make it more inviting, there is only bare stone and dark stains. A bottle of palm wine sits half drunk on the table beside a dirty cup. Incense clouds the air as if it's meant to hide the metallic stink of blood and bleach.

My hands are unusually steady, though I sit in the chair before the head Seeker.

"I am not a traitor," I repeat. I remain as still as a stone and ignore the ghosts that laugh away inside of me. They chew up my guilt like taffy and ask for more when I should feel…something. Instead, I am hollow where once I was whole.

"I know that, child. Nen was just another tool of the cultists, and you killed an assassin to save your life. Don't waste your time worrying over it. Omu's sect would love to see us Datus dead and seize control of Tigang in the holy mess to follow, but we are not so easy to kill." He waves his hands as if to swat away a fly, but his dismissal does not feel like a pardon. "And I will, of course, question every single person left in this cursed fortress, but I will run out of time before I weed all their sympathizers out."

He stares out the window at the blank sky. The ocean beneath is flat and gray, like slate, not water. It mirrors my mood.

We are both waiting for a storm to come.

"Are you working with Arisa, too?" I am too numb to mince my words.

Reshar looms over the chair, and the shadows in his dimly lit office make long lines down his face. He does not answer. He leans back against the wall and rubs at the tattoos on his chest as though his heart troubles him.

"I heard you and another woman speaking about Arisa in the hallways," I say. "Whose side are you on?"

"My mother was right. You are one to watch." He sighs and slides into a faded chair beside his desk. "My sister and I did everything together. We even came out of the womb together. It was never my dream to become a Baylan; it was hers. When Riane came to the glass fortress, I followed, and as she rose through the ranks, so did I. Several months ago, she fell into the sleep no one wakes from. Days after she fell ill, she vanished. Arisa stopped every one of my attempts to find answers, but I did discover this." He pulls a wooden box from the drawer, carefully lifts the lid, and bids me to look inside. It holds fragments of a dry cracker that shows traces of paint.

"Someone has discovered a way to grind an orasyon into liquid and has been tampering with the paint. I don't understand the spell's purpose or what has happened to those who have disappeared, but I intend to find out the truth. I will destroy anyone who gets in my way—even you. Do you still accuse me of being a traitor?"

We are more alike than I ever imagined. I almost pity him. Almost.

"The sleep is Arisa's doing. I saw her put down an Archivist in the street," I say.

He snaps to attention and interrogates every detail of my encounters with Alen. He grinds his jaw as though he is chewing tough meat when I tell him how the Archivist's tongue was ripped out and his warnings about Arisa. Reshar's blank eyes drift to my neck as I speak. My hands race to fix my scarf out of habit, but I only touch bare skin. I fold them carefully in my lap and dare not look up at him.

"Why would an Archivist be interested in you, Kuran Jal?" he asks, and I flinch when he reaches for his gong. He sticks an orasyon to its back and spits upon it. "Sit up. I just realized that you haven't completed my test."

He goes straight to work. The vibrations of the gong grate against my ears. The sound washes over me in waves and makes my skull feel like a hollow gourd. "What did you see during the history test? Where did your mind take you?"

"Over the ocean as we fled Arawan." He plucks the words from my head like weeds.

"And what did you hear?"

"The songs of our people as we crossed the ocean."

"And what did you feel?"

Almost drowning. The salt on my skin. Ash on my tongue. "Fear."

"Who are you?" he asks. "We are all reborn for a purpose, and that purpose is woven to our souls like a great chain. Peel back your lives and turn back time. I want to know what led you here, Kuran."

This time, I fall gently into a vision. *The walls of the Demon's prison are only a half-finished dome around me, but the deep pit in its center is already carved with orasyon. It radiates power. Workers chip away at the solid stone of the hill to carve the walls smooth, and their work fills the space with a tapping noise that reminds me of birds flocking. I wipe the sweat and dust from my brow.*

And I turn, because I know Teloh is here before I see him. Ten Guardians flank a miserable creature bound and gagged. He's chained up so tightly that he can hardly move. I start to walk over to them. "Is that truly needed…"

Two Guardians go flying as Teloh flicks them away like gnats. The air in the room begins to churn with clouds, and workers scream as their lanterns blow out. A storm fills the hollow space and batters the stone.

"Get out!" I shout. "Stay near the walls!" The wind pushes me back, but I fight toward him, clinging tightly to my skirts. I can't see a thing, but I don't need eyes to know where he is. Because he's always there, at the center of things. Lightning streaks around me, and I hear the barred doors of the Demon's prison bang open and shut.

"It hurts!" He tears at the hair on his head as though he wants to dig into his skull. "I cannot do this… Give me a knife… Release me!" He twists and snarls. Chains snap off his body, and darkness licks around him like frantic hounds. Wind slams into my gut and knocks me onto my back; then, with a snarl, the Demon launches off the ground and pins me down between his arms. His skin is shredded, and Chaos leaks out around us. I can't see. I can't breathe. I smell the storm in the air, and my hairs raise. Maybe I should be afraid, but I know he will not hurt me. He stares wide-eyed, as though he doesn't understand what he's looking at.

"Teloh…" I call his name. My heart hurts. It's guilt, it's pity, it's wanting, all at once. And when he looks back, I know his heart echoes mine.

He drops back to his knees. The air quiets around us. I gasp for breath. "Lock me up and leave me here." He curls into himself. "Forget about me. I will only destroy you."

"Please don't…" I wipe tears from my eyes, but he simply steps to the edge of the pit and takes one look back at me before jumping in.

"No!" I return to the present with a gasp.

"What did you see?" Reshar sways his head like a snake

assessing a mouse, still rasping at his gong.

"The Demon." Fatigue washes over me in waves, and I struggle to stay awake. "I was helping build its prison, and it attacked…"

Reshar tuts. "That only tells me that you once helped build the fortress. Hundreds of workers labored on this place. And you would not be the only lovesick Baylan infatuated with Teloh over the years. The common people don't know that we've kept the Demon imprisoned here for centuries, but it is not a secret amongst the Baylan."

My cheeks redden. It's true. None of this proves I am Astar, even if Teloh himself believes it. Could he be wrong? My head and heart both hurt.

"I ask you again." He methodically grates at the brass. "Who are you?"

"My name is Narra Jal." The name feels right. It is the name my mother gave me, the name that stuck, the name I know from the only life I remember.

My eyes refuse to focus on the Seeker, and I struggle against the urge to drift into sleep.

"And who is Narra?" he asks. I shudder into half wakefulness.

"I shouldn't be here. I'm a dead girl." It is the truth but not the truth he wants to know. There are too many feelings attached to my mother's lies, and at the thought of her, his spell breaks. "Shora Jal told everyone that I died, but I didn't."

"I have met few people who refused to open their pasts to me." He stares through me as if I am a goal and not a person. "Those that refuse have a greater fear. What sins have you committed in your past lives?"

"I'm only here to save my mother." It doesn't matter who I was.

The ghosts inside me howl with laughter at the thought. Reshar shrugs. "What a fine bit of trouble you've caused, whoever you are. The missing Astar? A bothersome impersonator?"

Both? I cringe.

"Kormar wants to give you Astar's test, but Arisa wishes to delay. Testing may be the only way to keep you and Shora safe from her, but I need time to make arrangements. For now, you will continue as if nothing is amiss, *Kuran Jal*."

He retrieves a plate from his desk with a trace of amusement. A pale, flaky pastry emerges from a wrapping of thin waxed papers. The small, round bun smells sweet, and the first layer crumbles in my hand. "You must be hungry."

I stuff my mouth with broken fragments of pastry and sweet mung beans. A message waits in a curl of rice paper.

Trust Reshar. – O

I frown at him and glean the similarities in their jawlines and the shapes of their eyes. Reshar never smiles, but Oshar, always.

"My mothers send their regards." He inclines his head and pours himself a cup of wine.

I sense the turning of time in my bones. This is not the first time this has happened. The sense is like a name almost recalled, like distant music. Something echoes through my lives.

I wonder how much I've chosen and how much is fated. My family, Teloh, even Reshar. We are tied together by some horrible truth that keeps our destinies spinning together like dancers tied at the wrists.

I shudder and wonder what cruel game is playing out again.

CHAPTER THIRTY-FIVE

I retreat to the baths near our sleeping quarters when I'm
released. I scrub and scrub, until every inch of my skin is
scoured red, my washing bucket is empty, and the dregs are so
cold that I shiver, but I still see blood everywhere and taste it
on my tongue.

"Kuran Jal?" Someone approaches, and I clench my fists,
ready to fight if I must. A brown-skirted initiate peers timidly
through the door. I grimace. The gossip must have already flown
far and sharpened its teeth. I wonder what everyone is saying
about me now.

I let out a long sigh and stand. "Yes. It's time for the next
test?" I'm being watched too closely. Even now, there are
Guardians waiting outside.

She nods. A sigh warbles through my lips because I have
not the strength to scream. Escape is impossible now. I was
informed that the guards have been doubled in the dungeons
and at the gates of the fortress. I have no way of getting my
mother out by myself.

All my hopes hang on Astar. Not all the Datus are on Arisa's
side, so there is still a slim chance to win them over, as long as
I make it through this. I tug on my tunic and roll up my malong.

I follow the initiate up through the fortress to the rooftop
courtyard, and I squint in the brightness. Here, the raw stone of

the fortress hill is underfoot, and a ridge of spiraled glass circles the space like icy towers. I know this place even though I have never set foot here in this life. No flowers bloom around Teloh today. The grass is perfectly trim. The sky is perfectly blue. And no one smiles.

At the center of the valley, candidates cluster beneath towering statues of our seven holiest Diwata. Their stone faces are worn by three hundred unrelenting Tigangi winters, but traces of personality remain.

Omu holds her hands out to bless us, clad in billowing robes that show off her fully human form. Madur the Guardian is frozen mid leap, eagle wings forever in flight. Monkey-headed Minue the Maker strikes a hammer to an anvil, and shy animals peek out from behind Kitha the Healer's deer-spot robes. Carabao-horned Nenlil the Cultivator hauls a basket of rice ready to be planted, while Hamshar the Seeker turns his huge tarsier eyes across the ocean toward home. Last of all, Rea the Archivist cradles books with her sticky fingers and gecko tail.

I walk toward the young people huddled before them. Some look away from my gaze. Some look me up and down anew, unsure what to make of me. One boy spits on the ground as I pass. *Murderer*, I hear them whisper.

Coward, my ghosts add. I drop my gaze to the ground, but the other candidates' stares burn into the back of my head like a brand.

"We Guardians are the hands and feet of Tigang. We keep the peace, and we go to war when Omu orders it. We enforce her rules." Hendan, the head Guardian, strides before us, but he only gazes at me. He wears black from head to toe, broken only by a gold sash that ties a snake-headed kampilan to his waist. Unlike most Guardians, his tunic is embroidered with orasyon for protection in black thread over black silk. "You must be willing to sacrifice everything for Tigang, including the life you led before you entered these walls. You must know your place in Heaven's great vision and surrender to it. The ruler of Tigang must carry out the Heavens' justice. This is the last day of the Sundo! This is your last test! Let us see you put your country above all else."

A ripple of disquiet travels down my spine. His words remind me of too much of what Omu's cult espouses.

"Today, you will carry out the executions of those condemned for murder and treason," he says as Guardians bring out a line of quiet people bound with their wrists behind their backs.

And I see my mother.

I stumble forward. No. This is not how this is supposed to happen. The executions should be done after the Sundo is complete. I am supposed to be tested for Astar first. This is all wrong!

"Where is Datu Reshar?" I demand, but Hendan grabs my arm before I can rush forward, heedless of the consequences. I can't think straight. I scratch at his wrist with my nails.

"Let go of me!" I yell and struggle against him, but he only holds on tighter.

"This is my test, not the Seeker's," Hendan growls.

They force Inay to kneel in front of a chunk of pockmarked volcanic rock. Her neck curves over its edge as if it is a serving platter. Her hands and feet are bound with rope so she cannot run. The ground around her knees is stained dark and wet with blood.

My mother does not raise her head to meet my eyes, and for once my ghosts remain silent with respect.

Hendan thrusts the hilt of his sword into my free hand. The kampilan's hilt is sticky with sweat, and I tremble as I close my hands around it.

"No," I say, but no words could ever match my feeling. "I will not do this."

"This criminal was found guilty of treason. The sentence is death, and you shall be the one to carry out the order. Refuse this and you fail, Kuran Jal."

Who would ask a child to murder their own family? Hendan saved this particular torture just for me. If this is another trick like the Healing test, I must outsmart it, no matter how cruel.

I take a better look at the woman before me. My mother looks real. There is the familiar mole under her left eye and the small scar at the base of her neck. Her gaze is so cloudy that I suspect they must have given her herbs to keep her docile, because the mother I know would never go meekly into death.

"This is an illusion." I drop the sword. I don't care about the test, only my mother.

"If you need to believe that, then you may." Hendan grips my arm so tightly that I bruise. "But you must still carry out the sentence. The ruler of Tigang must deliver our country's justice. You must send your people to war and to their deaths for the greater good. You cannot flinch now. You must be more than Kuran Jal. You must love Tigang above all else. Your family no longer matters."

He drops my arm, and I cup my mother's cheek with my palms. I lift her bleary eyes toward me. Her smile makes a wreck of my sputtering heart. She is as steady as stone, but warm.

No one should be asked to do such a thing. If I could slay my own mother, what other terrible things could I be capable of? This is a test not about justice but about obedience.

Hendan forces my fists around the kampilan again.

"Narra, my love…" My mother's voice is so soft and forgiving, so resigned. "It's all right. I accept my fate."

I crouch beside her and lean against the sword as if it is a cane. She is the reason I have risked everything. I stare at her long brown fingers, surprised to see that they are so much like my own. It was she who always made sure we girls had enough to eat, even if it meant giving up her own supper. It was she who taught me to read and write when no Tigangi school would take me. It was she who always coaxed me out of hiding when the other children taunted me.

She always believed I was worthy of loving.

If I executed my own mother, there would be no point in going on. Not for me. I could not live with myself. Hendan might as well swing the sword on my neck instead of hers.

I adjust my clumsy grip on his sword. It is too long for me, but the blade has a wicked edge. I gather my courage and lift it high. Hendan nods encouragement. I swing it down with a mighty heave.

The sword whistles as it comes down. My hands are unsteady and shaky, but the rope that binds my mother falls away.

"Run!" I scream and pull her to her feet, but she falls limp against my shoulder.

Hendan barks a command, and the candidates begin to move. A spiky-haired boy reaches me first. He knocks my mother out of my arms, and I fall to the earth when he dives for my leg. My cheek slams hard against the dirt. His eyes are wide and desperate as he searches for Hendan's approval, but the head Guardian is watching my mother. She lies prone on the ground behind him.

"Give up already," the boy says. "There's no point in going on. There is no escaping this."

I toss a handful of gravel into his eyes and scramble left.

"Inay!" I shout and try to get around him, but candidates herd me away from my mother's crumpled form. They only give me space because they are too afraid of my curse to touch me.

"Nen should have killed you." He grabs a fist-size rock and lunges for me.

"The traitor killed himself. I had nothing to do with it." I duck a wild swing of his arm, but the boy persists.

"It doesn't matter. Don't you see, cursed girl? Everyone you touch is destroyed. Ingo is gone. Nen is dead. Where are Dayen and Virian? Even Galaya, who only spoke to you once, is missing. Now look—you will destroy us all."

I only see fear in this candidate's eyes, not hate. But fear is dangerous, too. What better way to make my death look like an accident than this? They've fallen right into Arisa's trap. I want to shout, but I don't have enough energy.

"And we will stop you." The boy balls his hands, as though it is his holy duty to fight, and he throws a fist at my eye. I don't dodge in time, and my vision blurs.

Could they? I wonder. Could they end this? That I might be reborn again, only free, seems laughable. The hate and the fear would just begin all over again.

Bone splinters as stone slams into my body, and searing pain tells me that something in my shoulder is broken. Another boy misses my head, but barely, and a trickle of blood slides down my cheek. I do not want to damn him, but neither do I want to die.

Not yet.

Both my heart and my head go deadly silent.

I don't know this place. I watch with detached interest as though I am separate from my flesh. My body springs back as another part of myself takes over. One that I have no conscious control over. One that is all bared teeth and claws.

I block his fist with my forearm, and stone slides down the length, toward my elbow, but I keep moving. A stone smacks against the back of my knee, and I stumble, but it does not slow me for long. My vision narrows to three things: my mother, the bloody rock, and Hendan. I will barrel through the head Guardian if I must. I will sacrifice my limbs to his sword if I must. I swear it.

You have always been stubborn. I hear Teloh in my head,

and his voice grounds me. *There is too much iron in your will.*

Hells, I wish he was here, but he's not. There's no one to save me but myself. Pain explodes all over my body, but I still have the sense to pull the boy toward me by his tunic.

"You can't stop me." I reach for the bare skin at his neck. He screams when I touch him, though all I feel is skin, rubbery and sweat-slick from exertion. May my misfortune be his, too. I spit at him.

"Enough, child. It's over." Hendan's voice cuts between us.

The candidates freeze. I freeze. My mother's cleanly severed head rolls across the dirt and comes to a stop at my feet. My vision blurs.

I blink, once, twice, thrice, and Hendan comes back into focus. My mother is splattered all over his tunic. The expressionless look on his face makes me want to slam my fist into his jaw. The heat of my anger troubles even my ghosts, and their wings flutter as they flee my wrath.

"Out of the way!" Reshar shoves candidates aside and pulls me to my feet. I barely notice him.

I cannot believe it. I keep staring at my mother's face, waiting for an illusion to fade, for it to turn into someone else or something else, but it does not. She's gone.

"Datu Hendan, you should be punished for your inattention. Look how your children were misbehaving," Reshar tuts. His expression is as blank as always, but his breath comes hard. He ran here.

"My mistake, Datu Reshar," the black-clad Guardian says formally to his equal, but there is no apology in his tone. "Sometimes things get out of hand in the heat of the moment."

If I didn't hurt so much, I'd laugh. Hendan is all ice, not heat. His expression barely flickered when he killed my mother.

My body spasms when Reshar picks me up, but I am too spent to fight back. He carries me past Hendan, who ignores us as we leave.

My eyes close and open, in pain and out of pain. My mother's crumpled shape is the only thing that fills my head. This is the price of power? I recall the withered Reyna and her sad eyes. This is the price of peace? I think of Alen without his tongue.

Pent-up rage rattles in my throat, even though my body is too broken to set it free. Tigang can't possibly keep using the bodies of its people as its shield against the world, or we will consume ourselves.

"I'm sorry I was too late to save Shora. But you must live, child." Reshar deposits me roughly on an infirmary cot an eternity later and rolls up his sleeves. His tattoos look like moving serpents in the dim light. "Healing is not my talent, so this will hurt."

My body explodes with pain as the hum of magic fills the air. This time, when my consciousness flees, I welcome the oblivion.

✳ ☽ ✳ ☾ ✳

CHAPTER THIRTY-SIX

Reshar sits in the doorway and scans the hallway like a guard dog. Everything aches, but my limbs lift creakily at my command. My right shoulder does not rotate well, but it does not feel as shattered as it did before. Even the cuts from Arisa's mark on my palm have closed. The symbol is scarred in places and broken by smooth patches of skin in others. My left hand no longer needs bandages. I catch my reflection in the mirror. I am purple where my skin is exposed, and one dark eye puffs over, half closed, but I hardly care. Nothing I do matters anymore. I have failed: My mother is dead. I cut off my thoughts, because if I think of my mother I will fall apart completely.

"Thank you." My voice sounds dull and flat. Reshar never liked me, and I never liked him, but I am glad I am not alone. "Why did you heal me?" I ask. The exertion takes my breath away. Maybe my bones are in order, but I am not.

"I take great pleasure in being the stone in Arisa's slippers. Besides, what is there to be gained from murdering some helpless little girl?" His lips curl.

Still with the insults. Perhaps Reshar is all vinegar instead of sunshine, but he is not my enemy.

I shrug, and the pain makes me decide to lay still for all eternity. Though the worst of my injuries are healed, I am still bruised everywhere. I start to drift to sleep, but my mother's face waits for me there, so I roll over and let the pain keep me from feeling anything else at all.

The Seeker leans back. Even his eyebrows have gone gray now. It is another sacrifice for my unworthy soul. Another sacrifice I did not demand, but I have no control over other people's terrible decisions.

"Arisa's worries are absurd. Perhaps I'm the right age, but that doesn't mean anything at all," I say. My tongue feels loose, and I suspect the bitter herbal tea he made me drink is the culprit.

"Arisa is not one to show restraint, but neither have I known her to be afraid of anyone. Yet, I have seen her look at you with fear." He ponders this quietly behind lidded eyes.

I expected Reshar to be the most skeptical of all, so his pause worries me. "You couldn't find anything in my memories. You said it yourself—my visions don't prove anything," I say.

"That only means I could not access the right ones." He closes his eyes as if to rid himself of me.

I regret having opened my mouth, but I can't seem to close it.

"You don't fear the marks?" I ask.

"Why should I?" He taps his fingers against his sides. "They say your soul belongs to Omu. You belong here."

Those words again. I shiver at the thought of empty rooms and broken doors. Home is warm arms, laughter, and the open sky. Home is my mother and my sister. I fight the sudden storm of emotions and bid my heart to quiet, but I don't manage it. My mother is dead, and I may never see my sister again. She doesn't even know...

"Why did you ask me for a bribe at the start of the Sundo?" I ask instead. I should be trying to win him over and not parading his foibles around, but curiosity has the better of me.

"I knew you could never pay it. I was trying to save your life, child. This competition is a waste of our youth. There are ways to pick a ruler that do not involve suffering."

And to think, I did not take him for anything more than traditional to the bone. Perhaps there's more of his mother in him than it seems.

"Do you still wish I had never come?" I ask.

He is silent a while. "It doesn't matter. We will both be lucky if we survive tomorrow. No one will enter while I am here. Go to sleep," he commands with his usual gruffness, then looks away, thoughts elsewhere.

It might be a dream. I am not sure. I open my eyes and find Teloh sitting on a stool beside my cot, while Reshar leans against the wall, snoring softly. As always, Teloh fills the room, and I cannot look away.

"Narra, I'm sorry I couldn't protect you and your mother." His face contorts in ways I do not like.

"Stop." I cannot bear to delve too deeply into feeling and focus instead on the lines of his face half bathed in moonlight. His skin is as smooth as polished wood, his mouth expressive. His eyes always stare too deeply, as if they are locked onto the truth at the core of me, and my ghosts stir.

"Who asked you to protect us?" I ask, and I reach out to touch his face, despite knowing what he is…no…because I know what he is and that it doesn't matter. He closes his eyes when I trace the line of his jaw and feel the stubble of his cheeks.

"And why did you help my family escape Tigang if you hate Astar? Don't lie to me."

"I took a chance on you, Narra Jal. Sometimes change is like a waiting fire, and it needs just a single spark to catch." He fights to keep his hands still at his sides. "I thought that a life beyond these walls would leave you humbled, but you are just the same.

You still hate yourself."

It sounds not like admonition but regret.

"You gambled on the wrong child," I whisper. "I have no memories; I have no talent, nor facility in magic. I can't even sing. I am afraid all the time." I take a breath, finally. "And I ruin everything and everyone. My mother is dead because of me…"

All the loathing comes spitting out of my mouth with familiar venom, and tears come with it. I lose my fight with myself, and my mother is all that I see.

I recall her smile the first time I picked up a tumpong flute, how my mother clapped at my first wobbly tune. I hear her voice driving our oxen down dusty roads and lulling me to sleep when she could not sit beside me. I smell the jasmine scent of her soap clinging to her skin. I feel her gently combing out the knots in my hair with her soft hands. Memories flood back, and I drown in them. Memories are all that I will ever have of her.

I don't know how long I sob, but Teloh does not leave my side. He keeps his hands upon mine until my breath evens out and I can think clearly again. My heart feels empty, and my body, just a husk of meat.

His shoulders fall, and his expression softens, as much as the angles of his face could allow softness. "It would not be called courage if you were not afraid. Remembering always breaks you. That is the only true curse." He looks up from under his long lashes, and his eyes hold a different sort of dare. "But you do not know yourself, because you don't want to. Perhaps your life was too cozy until now. Perhaps you needed more than a short jaunt with humanity."

I balk at this because nothing about my life feels like it has been easy. Friendless, always the cursed girl, shunned and hidden away. Beaten for no reason but my marks and blamed for every misfortune. And Astar? In some stories, she is a hero, but in others she seems more the villian. I don't know what to make of her.

But it seems he knows me better than I know myself. "No one is born good or evil, Narra. We did not choose our natures, but we can choose what we do. Only you get to decide who you are or who you will be. You are more than anyone says." He stands and turns from me. "And so am I."

I find no other words. I lie still in my cot and breathe in the bleach-scented air. I do not know when I close them, only that when they are open again, my tunic is wet with tears and the dream of Teloh is gone.

CHAPTER THIRTY-SEVEN

Too soon, it is daybreak. I am standing at the ready when Kalena's escort of Guardians marches into the infirmary. I wish I cared, but everything feels numb inside.

A sneer slides onto Reshar's face when he spies the white-robed Interpreter. He folds all the humanity laid bare in the moonlight so neatly away I think I must have imagined it. The snake is back and ready to bite anything that comes near.

Even the Guardians wince at my bruises. They haven't broken me yet, but pride will not save me. All it does is keep me going when judgment awaits at the end of this corridor, and I go over the words I practiced with Reshar.

There's a relief in being caught, to walk freely with my marks on display and to use my true name. I wear my green-and-gold malong boldly, even though it is stained. There are no more reasons for secrets, no reason to bite back my tongue when I want to speak, because Arisa will have my head no matter what I say.

The great hall is still dark when we enter, but torches blaze on one by one. The room floods with the scent of peonies as Arisa enters along with the rest of the Seven Datus.

Reshar picks at his nails and gazes at them lazily. His smile is the opposite of friendly, even though it is all teeth. "So you've finally come to put Arisa on trial for ordering this child beaten?"

"What happened during Datu Hendan's test was unfortunate, and the candidates who harmed Kuran Jal were expelled for breaking our rules. That matter is closed." Kalena touches the sun disk at her throat as though to praise Omu.

Expelled or vanished? Arisa simply looks me up and down, and I stare back. There's a slight redness in her cheeks and a brightness to her eyes that betray her age today. I often forget that she is as young as I am.

"Then why are we here?" I ask. My mother is dead. I want this nightmare over with.

Darkness is not the domain of Holy Omu, and the Seven fidget in the shadows of early dawn. They have not walked the desert at night with a caravan of silk. They have not sat in shadows, telling truths to Chaos in the moonlight. These are treasures that make me feel stronger, despite the brashness of Omu's light.

Astar? I scratch at my chest, but the ghosts of my past lives remain quiet.

"Because you are an impostor." Kalena sighs. Her expression does not reveal even a hint of feeling. "You are not Kuran Jal. You have misrepresented yourself to us, and for this you must be expelled from the Sundo."

"Are you certain?" The surprise in Reshar's voice is almost convincing.

Senil steps forward with a wince. He seems smaller, somehow. "The girl has been accused, but the accusation has not been proven. Bring me the entrance contract." The old Archivist glances uneasily in my direction. I understand that he is only doing his duty, so I don't bear him any ill will. I know what the outcome will be. He flips through admissions contracts until he finds Kuran Jal's name.

I wonder if Reshar still regrets admitting me to the Sundo, and what might have become of me if I had never come back to Bato-Ko. But I made this choice, and I must accept whatever comes of it. I waver at the thought of my failure. Maybe my sister is better off without me. Maybe they all are.

I provide my finger when commanded, and a dab of blood confirms the truth. I am not Kuran Jal.

"Not a match." Senil runs his hands across his bald head. "This girl is not Kuran Jal, but Kuran Jal's blood indeed was signed onto the contract. The contract to enter the Sundo cannot be unmade."

Reshar warned me last night, but the sight of two familiar figures still sends me reeling. Tanu and Kuran walk side by side. My heart leaps to see my sister, but it's tempered by Tanu's second betrayal. Omu curse the boy into eternity. I swear to torment him in the next life and that he won't be rid of me even if he tries.

"They ordered me to fetch Kuran…" How dare Tanu have the gall to look conflicted! He doesn't deserve to. He could have lied and told the Baylan he could not find her, but of course he did not. I pray that he chokes on his guilt.

And Kuran. She was flaming mad at me the last I saw her. I'd rather see her angry than as tentative as this. She looks small and faded in the dim light of the glittering hall. Her expression only steadies at the sight of me.

I run for my sister, and I throw my arms around her. She squeezes me back, and the bells on her ankles jingle. For a brief, glorious moment, any sour blood between us is forgotten, even though it is I who have condemned her.

But I have also condemned myself. Guardians step between us and pull us apart before I yell more than her name.

"This is the real Kuran Jal," Arisa declares. "You, whoever you are, shall be punished accordingly along with Kuran Jal for conspiring together to infiltrate the Sundo."

"Wait!" My voice tears through the room like an arrow. That

I cannot allow. "I may not be the real Kuran Jal, but I am not the only impostor in this room."

Reshar nods encouragement. Arisa twitches.

This is the only way to save us both now. I square my shoulders and take a breath. "Fetch the Jal family records. I am the second daughter of Shora Jal and granddaughter of Yirin Jal. I was given the name Narra at birth and Astar upon my first name day. I was stolen from Bato-Ko by my parents. My father died in our escape, and my mother was executed for this crime. With the holy Diwata as my witness, I challenge Arisa's authority. I am the true Astar. Let me be tested."

"This child is delusional," Arisa sniffs and fixes the golden comb in her hair.

Murmurs. Questions.

"You cannot deny the ritual words." Reshar silences them all and stretches to his full height.

Kalena nods almost imperceptibly, as if she expected this.

Voices pitch higher as the Seven convene, and I pull my sister toward me again. She can't be mad at me when I am hugging her. I know this because I'm the youngest and she's not the only brat. She mutters a protest but doesn't pull away.

"Kuran, our mother is dead," I whisper into her shoulder.

"It's not your fault." She strokes my hair, and for a moment I feel like the two of us are back in our tent and everything will be okay. "She made her own choices, and she knew the risks she was taking. She...was prepared for this."

And neither of them told me. I tear up because they didn't think I could handle the truth. But in the end, their lack of faith in me doesn't matter as long as I can still get my sister out of the mess I've made.

When Kuran pulls away, there are tears in her eyes, but her grip is firm and reassuring.

"Do you believe all of this?" She looks me up and down

with a frown, and I know all she sees is the same me I've always been. "Astar, really?"

"I don't know." It's the truth. To be Astar would mean I would be exempt from the Sundo. I could banish Arisa, but even then, I would have to stay. I could never go back to carts piled high with silk, linen, and cotton. I would never again be free, but my sister would. Do I want to be the Astar? "Maybe," I say.

Senil returns with a book stamped with the Jal name. It is full of people who have turned to dust and have already been reborn. It is full of people I have not met and do not feel any connection to. I have always been a Jal, but my family has never extended beyond my mother and Kuran. Their stories are not mine, and the rest of them, including Yirin, could hang.

He clears his throat. "Yes, here we are. Narra was the name given to Shora Jal's second daughter, changed to Astar upon her first name day. It also says here that she is deceased." He looks up at me with a small nod of encouragement. I imagine he investigated my family when I came to him for help and made his own conclusions. His faith in me is something I do not deserve.

"I ask only for one condition. If I take this test, pass or fail, let my sister go. She had nothing to do with my choice to enter the Sundo. I knocked her out with a spell and stole a vial of her blood."

Where is Teloh? He is the one person who might vouch for me. Only my ghosts murmur softly, and a different kind of pain returns. It feels much like heartbreak, but it does not summon him.

My sister stands tall beside me. She does not avert her gaze. She does not make herself smaller. She is everything I've always wished I could be. I entered in her name, and if I had actually won the Sundo, she would have been Reyna—a good one.

I don't even make a convincing Astar.

I hold out my hand for the perfunctory swab of blood to confirm my identity, and my middle finger is pricked, so I have two bleeding fingers in addition to my purpling bruises. But I keep hold of Kuran's hand like we are still children. She helps me feel calmer and braver than I have any right to be.

The Archivist closes the book. "This girl speaks the truth. This is Narra Jal, the child who was stolen from the fortress before she could be tested for Astar."

Kalena looks displeased when she surveys the room, but Reshar's sneer is practically gleeful.

"Very well. I agree to your condition. Kuran Jal will be released back into the poverty she crawled out of." Arisa gathers up her skirts, so she looks larger than she is. Anger is plainly visible now, and she's too petty to hide it. "Let us put an end to the speculation. Narra Jal, let us see who you truly are."

CHAPTER THIRTY-EIGHT

The Seven take me away from my sister, and an escort of five Guardians keeps watch as I walk. I should be flattered that they think they need steel to keep me in line, but my stomach does a better job. It churns and complains as if it wants to be sick. My mouth is sour, and I smell like I took a bath in bleach.

I try to hold my head up, as I imagine Astar might, but I take only two steps before I trip on a crack in the stone and curse. The Guardians snicker, and even Arisa doesn't bother to hide her amusement. I spend the rest of the long walk glaring at the floor. I need to be Astar right now, but I cannot seem to stop being my awkward self.

The door to Astar's room flies wide open at Arisa's touch, and it falls off its hinges from the force of it. Nothing has changed since the Demon—Teloh's—attack. Even in that form of shadow and darkness, I realize now that he recognized me. I still don't know what to make of it or him. Everything has changed, but nothing has. I should fear him, and yet I don't.

Shattered shelves litter the room, and roots lay in tangles upon the floor, but no one says a word.

With a quick murmured incantation, the window shutters crack open and let a flood of light into the room. The roots of Arisa's hair gleam white in the brightness. Any other evidence of how often she's tasted the Heavens' power must be hidden with black dye.

"Datu Senil, please conduct the tests. You are the keeper of Tigang's knowledge and of our people's history. You knew the previous Astar, did you not?" Arisa asks the Archivist.

Senil's eyebrows knit together as if this pains him. Kalena, Omu's pet, watches us closely. Every movement the Interpreter makes is deliberate, and she only speaks when necessary. I cannot tell what is hidden behind her mask of calm. She chose her benefactor, Omu, well.

"I did know her," the old man says. "But only briefly. I was only a novice then. She and I rarely crossed paths."

"And what do you remember?" Arisa glows. Her face softens for him, as if he is an elderly uncle instead of someone who might stand in her way.

"She was very serious. I don't think she ever laughed in my presence." He meets my gaze, and a tremor of fear runs through me. "I always thought she was quite sad."

Arisa is not sad. Serious, maybe, but I can't imagine her shedding a tear for anyone. She apologizes for nothing. I wish I felt her confidence for just one day of my life: to live without worrying that I might ruin things for everyone, just by existing.

"But an old man's recollections mean nothing. Only the tests are proof," Senil says with sympathy in his eyes. "There are three tests that Astar must pass."

I lift my head and stand as tall as my height allows.

Senil walks to the bookshelf and lifts the model of the glass fortress from the shelf. He sets it gently in the center of the floor. He also fetches a chipped wooden dog and a silk scarf from the ironwood chest. The scarf is stiff with age, but it is painted with yellow flowers that look freshly bloomed.

Arisa's smug look tells me that she knows the answers to the test before the questions have been given.

The Archivist gazes at me long and hard. "For three hundred

years, we have found our true Astar through this test. If you are her, you have nothing to fear."

If this is supposed to reassure me, I do not feel it. My ghosts remain worryingly silent. I throw a smile Arisa's way and pretend confidence.

"One of these items did not belong to Astar. Which one?" Senil sits down on an offered chair with a wince. "Take your time. You may touch them if you like."

This is a test designed for guileless children, not adults. I crouch on the floor and pick up the model fortress. I have touched it once before, and it feels much like the walls that surround me. It was made by the same hand: Astar's.

I stroke the silk of the scarf under my fingers, and it softens under my caress. It's frayed at the edges and stained in places. It is something I would wear, not unlike the scarf I lost, only made with better care and materials. I lift the silk up to my nose and sniff, but if a scent once lingered, the ocean air and old wood floated it away. I detect nothing.

I turn to the wooden dog and chew my lips. The paint is chipped, and layers of paint are visible beneath. Its eye is misshapen, as if it was painted by a child. The wheels squeak when I tug it across the floor. It's ugly, but someone loved it once. No memories flash through me, but I can imagine a tiny Astar, tucked away from the world with every expensive toy available at her request, loving this one best because it was a gift from her parents. How could a baby understand being ripped from her parents? Who came when the Astar cried? Did she miss her family? Homesickness floods through me, but I dare not think of my mother or I will cry. I set the toy carefully back on the floor.

Time seems to stretch as I consider the scarf and the toy. I don't know. No memories come to me, though I hoped they might appear when I needed them. I wonder if everyone has made a mistake about me. I halt, unsure, and think.

The room was locked and dusty the first time I came here. No one had tread its dusty floor in years. I choose reason over my unreliable instincts and curse my ghosts for their uselessness.

"They're all Astar's," I say.

Motes of dust dance in the silence, and no one tells me if my guess was right or wrong. Reshar peels himself from the wall and tightens the belt on his robe.

"I will administer the second test. I will put you in a trance, and you must answer my questions."

He removes a brass gong from his shoulder and hammers it hard. My head tunes itself to the vibration of the metal. Even my toenails buzz. I am a human tuning fork.

"What is your name?"

"Narra Jal."

"What name were you given on your first name day?"

"Astar," I answer. "My mother kept me a secret." I pluck answers from my memories instead of my heart because my ghosts seem to have hidden away in a dark room and locked the door.

"Think back. Do you see darkness? Before you were born, before you were Narra Jal."

An image winks in and out of existence, and all I am left with is a feeling.

"It was warm and dark. I was alone."

"You are safe," Reshar says. His voice makes a soothing contrast to the vibrating metal. "The darkness is only temporary."

I try to focus. *I float in the dark, and the sky brightens around me. A bright moon bathes everything around me in a shade of blue, and a dribble of sweet lychee juice courses down my chin. Sand slides beneath my bare toes, and the cool dampness of the ocean licks around them.* It is a memory, but it flickers just out of reach, like a fish darting through the water.

"What came before the darkness?" he asks. "Who were you

before you were known as Narra Jal?"

There are shadows around me, as close as a lover.

Don't look at it, my ghosts warn. *Don't look.*

"Look back," Reshar commands.

I try to ignore my ghosts, but they squeeze at my heart and make it impossible to breathe. The image dims as I gasp for air.

"I can't." I tremble as a wave of guilt crashes into me, because I don't truly want the answer. Teloh was right. I am at war with myself, and I am bound to lose.

"LOOK."

Reshar's word forces my gaze around as if he's turned my neck with his hands. *The darkness waits as I turn, forming and reforming into a shape that is vaguely human but has no body to contain it.*

"Narra." Reshar shakes me back to the present. "What do you see?"

I sink into another vision. *I drag Teloh's body across the dirt. Blood weeps from the orasyon carved into his skin, but I have no time to stop and bandage it. The sky grows as dark as night as plumes of smoke blot out the sun over our home, Arawan. The earth shakes beneath our feet, and I stumble, but I don't stop. Volcanoes spit black rocks that destroy everything they touch, but the worst is yet to come.*

"Get up," I plead, but Teloh doesn't open his eyes. He's a dead weight, and I'm not even sure he's alive. I wipe tears from eyes that sting with smoke as we pass a woman's body, her head crushed by a black stone. Screams echo through the city as our people flee toward the water, carrying all that they can on their backs. The remnants of a typhoon still swirl above the largest volcano, fanning its flames and crackling with lightning.

An old man drags a cart to me from a nearby home and helps me lift Teloh into it. I sag with relief. "Thank you, po!" I gasp. "You must go to the boats. Everyone must leave. There's no time."

He shakes his head and returns to the steps of his nipa hut. "I am not leaving, child. I was born here, and I will die here. There is nowhere else for me." Water fills my eyes again, but we are short on time, and I cannot force him. I bow my head and shove my awkward load toward the mass of people boarding the boats on the shore. Drums are beaten to warn the other isles as we take to our boats as Omu instructed.

Teloh groans, and his eyes flick open. They are unnaturally blue-black now, when once I could have sworn they were brown. He screams and thrashes so wildly that I bash his head with a coconut I swipe from the ground. He falls limp again, and this time I'm the one who screams. I haul him forward in the cart, sweating and slipping against the soft sand, as the world falls apart around me.

Everything is wrong. And I don't know what is right anymore. My heart breaks and breaks, in one life and the next and the next.

"Who are you?" Reshar asks again, but the image has faded, and now I am only sore and small.

"Astar," I say because he expects it, not because I believe it.

"This proves nothing. She is a storyteller, therefore a liar, and this version of events is in none of our histories." Arisa scoffs. "We are wasting time, Reshar."

For once, I agree with her. I rub water from my eyes. I've sprung a leak like a ship.

"What's the last test?" I ask. I still taste smoke, and I suck in deep breaths of air to clean my lungs.

"Bring *it*."

I turn to the door, and my attention orients itself unconsciously to the body that walks in. Teloh stares at me wide-eyed. His body shakes because Chaos rattles at its cage. He pleads with his eyes because his jaws remain clamped, as though they've been forced shut.

I rush toward him and take his shoulders in my hands. "Teloh." My voice wavers. He flinches away as though my touch pains him, and I drop them to my sides, because I realize he is all bruises beneath his tunic. They hurt him, and I can do nothing. My fingers twitch, and his expression softens.

"Demon, tell us now. Is this girl our Astar?" Kalena asks. None of the other Datus even flinch. They all knew what he was.

His eyes meet mine, and he does not look away. He doesn't have to say anything. I read the regret and the sorrow in them. Teloh fights against some magical compulsion, but his mouth parts slowly. A trace of dark bruises wicks up the line of his jaw. They look like they were made with fists. Arisa glares at him as if her eyes alone might control him, but I do not smell her flower scent. I smell nothing but growing things, green mosses and curled ferns, because he is here, and he feeds my greedy senses.

"No." His voice is barely audible, but it is my doom.

"And who is the true Astar?" Arisa asks.

"You, my—" He rubs at his arms as if his body chafes, and he screams out. Kalena clenches her wrists as she tugs his invisible strings, and he goes still at the force of Omu's magic. "Astar."

"Expel this impostor from the Sundo. She is no one of importance." Arisa waves a hand. She smiles at Teloh as if he is a great dog who has retrieved a bone. Then she grins and leans close to my ear. "I will find you and destroy you. I'll throw your sister in the dungeons for safekeeping."

"You promised to release Kuran!"

"I did not say when." She smirks. Perhaps she believes she is justified and that power is her birthright. And I see what I might have been: corrupted and entitled.

Before Reshar can protest, or perhaps because there is nothing he can do to stop it, rough hands dig into my bruises. I am strong, but unlike Teloh, I am only human.

Guardians drag me into the courtyard, and I look up at the darkening sky. The air is thick with the promise of another storm. Teloh races after me and pulls me free. He crushes me hard against his chest, despite the hurt he's in. For a moment, everything disappears and we are the only two people in the world. No matter who I am and who he is, being with him feels right and true.

His forehead presses against mine as Guardians wield canes against his back. They want to subdue him, not wreck him. He growls and spins me around in his arms, away from them. He does not cry out as his body absorbs the beating. "Arisa will unleash me and destroy Bato-Ko to bring Omu into this world. Get away from here before the Sundo is done — "

But he is only a human in this form. There are too many Guardians. They drive him back, and he tosses one against the gates.

All the Sundo's tests are finished. That means I have only hours left to warn everyone.

"Wait, no!" I shout and kick at the Guardians swarming him like black ants.

Metal flashes in Teloh's hands, but the nearest Guardian grabs me from behind. I kick hard at the Guardian's shins, but I can't break free, and whatever possessed me on the rooftop refuses to come to me now. The Guardian shoves me through the gate. The moment my feet touch the ground in Bato-Ko, the orasyon carved into my hand erupts with pain.

I take another breath because I cannot fight my body's demands. Magic spreads up my arm and threatens to burn every memory away.

I have failed everyone I love.

And I am undone.

CHAPTER THIRTY-NINE

There is a shadow in the shape of a girl. Her head is full of dry leaves and ashes, like an old, choked hearth. She races beneath branches woven into symbols that draw power from the earth, but the trees droop as if they are weary.

Bato-Ko's glass fortress gleams somewhere behind her. Revelers wear tired faces that tell of too much drink, and the air is still peppered with music celebrating Midsummer. When she cuts through the streets, they avert their eyes as if she is something to fear. To her, they are ghosts that fade in and out of focus. She does not even remember who she is, but her sleeve is rolled up, and there is a name scratched onto her skin: *Kuran Jal.*

The name is a hammer in her skull, as heavy as a stone. Something about it feels important.

A market crowds around her, full of merchants setting up tables and wares. They wave her off and push her back. She crashes into a woman selling fruit on a blanket. The woman flinches as she nears her, and she stares at the girl's neck instead of her eyes.

"Do you know this person?" The girl lifts her arm. "Please. I need your help, po."

"Get away from me!" The woman swats her hands away as though she is filthy. "Or I'll call the Guardians!"

The fruit seller pelts the girl with a rotting orange and

screams, but a young asog takes pity on the girl and leads her away. They stop together at a wooden gate, and she checks behind her as if she's afraid she's been followed. "Here, child." The asog shakes her head and hurries away before the girl can thank her.

The name etched upon the weather-beaten wood reads: "Jal."

The girl drifts over the threshold, but no one rushes to greet her. When she enters the main house, its shadows take her in as if she is one of them. She passes from empty room to empty room, kicking up dust in this shell of a home.

Upstairs, the rattan furniture is polished and clean, but green cushions have faded to yellow, and embroidered flowers have turned the color of autumn leaves. The air smells faintly of tobacco and mold. Was this her home?

An old woman appears in the doorway, so still that at first the girl thinks she is having a vision. Her skin looks cured by the sun. All leather. She wears an expensive-looking baro jacket and loose silken trousers.

They stare at each other, and the girl gleans the resemblance between them by the reflection in a mirror.

"Have you come here to kill me?" The old woman brandishes a wicked-looking cleaver.

The girl puzzles it over. How can the old woman ask such a thing if they share blood? For who are the Tigangi without family?

The girl takes two steps toward her and presses the back of the old woman's hand to her forehead for a blessing. "I am lost. I need your help, po."

The cleaver clatters to the floor.

"Oh, child." The old woman's wiry arms encircle the girl, and she wonders if the floor is shaking, but it is only the old woman. She pours her shame into the girl's back and soaks her tunic with hot tears. "I am so sorry. I thought that to turn in Shora was the right thing to do, that righteousness and adherence to the laws would restore the Jal name—but it has broken me instead. The cost is too much, and I cannot bear it."

"If we are still here." The girl kisses the old woman's forehead. "There is still a chance to make things right."

The old woman wipes her eyes and coils her hair back into a neat bun at the base of her neck to compose herself, but she still shakes like a leaf in the wind. The girl is afraid she might blow away.

She shakes her head. "What I have done can never be forgiven, but I will help you. I've wasted too much time agonizing over what I might have done differently."

"Can you help me, po?" the girl asks.

"No," she says. "But I know someone who can."

A stocky old woman with a cloud of white curls and a pineapple-cloth shawl opens a gate. Her lips twist from amusement to surprise when she notices the girl and the tangled mess of scars on her palm.

"Come inside, quickly." The white-haired woman slams the gate shut and shoos a noisy gaggle of grandchildren off her porch. They walk straight past the main building into a shed dug into the rocky Tigangi soil. Tree roots snake in through cracks in the cellar's walls, and its roof is held up by huge chunks of stone. Dangling roots are braided into wards of protection and quiet.

It looks like a refuge built to withstand some great disaster, but the girl fears it might not be enough. Worry chased her clear across the city, but she cannot remember why. She grasps for answers, but none come.

In the middle of the room lined with jarred pickles, baskets of onions, and bottles of rum sits a lanky boy in dire need of a haircut and a short Rythian girl with a nose that looks like it was broken once. The Rythian girl screams at the sight of the girl and squeezes her so tightly that her bruises bloom in pain. Everything aches, but the girl lacks the heart to chide her.

The boy stares at the girl and hesitates as though unsure if he should fear or appease her. The hesitation in his smile makes the girl's heart hurt.

"The palm spell," the Rythian girl says. "She doesn't remember." The other girl's palm is red as though it was scrubbed over many times, and the boy's palm matches hers. A faint blue smudge remains where an orasyon might once have been painted.

"Please, there is something I must tell you." The girl is certain she should know these two, but their names do not come to her. "I need to remember, or we are all in danger."

The two grandmothers examine the girl's scarred palm and argue over it.

"We may be able to restore your memories if we burn away enough of the affected area, but some damage has already been done. I don't know if we can reverse it all," the Rythian girl says.

"If there's even a small chance, I must take it," the girl says.

The Rythian hesitates and scratches at her crooked nose. "I can't."

"You must. I beg you. Something terrible will happen before the Sundo is complete. I need to remember."

Indecision does not seem fitting on the Rythian.

"I trust you." She takes the other girl's hands in hers.

The Rythian's are cool and clammy, as if a fever has taken her recently, but she does not pull away and takes a deep breath. "Someone fetch a torch, cold water, salve for burns…" She rattles off a long list. There is a smudge more conviction to her voice this time. "We will also need blood."

"I will pay the price. I will give up the breaths of my life or anything else you need. Let my last days not go wasted." The first grandmother rolls up her sleeves.

A Turinese woman returns with an unlit torch. The girl shivers, but she does not change her mind.

"This will hurt," the Rythian says with regret.

The girl accepts her fate, but doubts remain. Who will she be if she remembers? There is peacefulness in forgetting, but it feels shallow.

Her hands shake, but the first grandmother twines their fingers together. They are as strong as iron. She stares at their hands, and she sees not only her own, but her mother's, and her grandmother's, and all the family who came before her. She does not feel so alone, because their blood sings in hers, and it sings strong.

"I'm ready," she says and hopes that it is true.

CHAPTER FORTY

Two things I remember: firstly, my name is Narra Jal, and secondly, no magic can completely numb pain. Painted spells circle my forearm, but I scream as blue flames scorch my skin. The sound is muffled by the rag stuffed in my mouth to keep me from biting off my tongue. But it's worth it, because now I remember what I need to tell them: Arisa will destroy Bato-Ko.

Oshar holds my shoulders, but I cannot stop writhing to be free. Her springy white curls brush against my hair.

"You must fetch the council of elders!" I sit up so quickly that my head swims. "Please, Nanay Oshar—everyone must know what Arisa has planned. Our survival depends on it."

Perhaps she thinks I'm delirious, but Oshar promises her aid.

And there is also Virian. That broken-nosed, demanding demon of a girl directs everyone in the room as if she's born to rule. She doesn't flinch, even though the air smells of burning meat. She feeds my grandmother's blood into a bowl lined with a complicated orasyon and chants to keep the torch flame hot. Sayarala, Oshar's wife, holds the torch against my skin with such calm that I suspect she's seen worse before.

My grandmother, Yirin, slumps beside me with a tube in her arm. Her eyes remain half closed, but she does not appear to be in pain. Her hairs turn from gray to white as Virian's spell draws energy from her.

"Enough." Virian declares at last.

Dayen brings me a mirror, and I reach for it with my burned left hand, but it slips out of my fingers and falls to my lap. When I try to grasp the handle, my soot blackened fingers only twitch in response. Dayen shakes his head and holds up the mirror for me instead. A glimpse shows me that Virian's magic faded the last of my old bruises. I can't feel my left hand, but I look almost human again.

Names and faces have return to me. The memories of my life are distorted, as though I glimpse them through a glass full of water. I cannot tell which things are dreams and which are truths. So little of my life as Narra Jal seems believable now.

"That scat-tosser Arisa tried to be dramatic when she began the Sundo. Our marks were done in semi-permanent ink, but yours was carved into your skin. Your orasyon was broken before you ever left the glass fortress, because your skin healed over." A little color returns to Virian's cheeks and she looks more like the girl I remember. "So it didn't activate properly when you passed through the gates. That's the only reason this worked."

"You are a wonder, Virian. Thank you."

She lets out a breath and flashes a small sad smile at me. "I'm sorry you may not be able to use your hand again."

"I am still alive. I am still me." At the reminder, my ghosts flutter with impatience. There is still so much to do.

"Rest now, po." I flash a weak smile at my grandmother.

"Let's go, Yirin, you frustrating old woman." Sayarala and Oshar help her up. "We have clean beds and plenty of grandchildren to bother you while we wait for the council to arrive."

Yirin sighs and lets herself be led away. Only when I'm alone with my friends, can I forget the bloody mess in the room.

"There are some things I need to tell you." I trip over my tongue and push through my thoughts to seek what should be important. I stutter through bits about Astar. I recall the assassins and Nen's betrayal. The entire tale sounds less plausible and more jumbled with each passing sentence.

"What about Teloh?" Virian asks and I don't want to answer. Hearing his name squeezes my heart and makes it hard to breathe.

"He is the Demon Chaos."

They blink at me, and blink some more, unconvinced.

"We need to be ready," I get up reluctantly. "There isn't enough time to evacuate the city. Arisa is helping the cultists and they plan to harness the Demon's power to bring Omu to the earth. Arisa doesn't care that this will flatten the entire city." Who am I to speak to the council? But no one else has seen what I have seen.

I pace back and forth as they look up at me, confused and horrified.

"That's impossible. How can he be the same Demon who destroyed Arawan? He's been here this whole time?" Virian furrows her brows as if this is a puzzle she can't quite put together.

I shake my head because I scarcely believe it either. "Astar brought him across the ocean with her and built a cage for him beneath the fortress. You've been there." I look over to Dayen, who goes pale in the face, and he nods quietly. "The Baylan have hidden him for centuries, and Arisa uses him to do her bidding. He has no choice but to obey her because his body is covered in spells of binding."

"Oh, so you've seen it?" Dayen asks.

My cheeks go hot at the memory that surfaces and I burst out laughing alongside Virian. Dayen grins. I swear, the boy is becoming sly, and perhaps he'll grow into a formidable man if we survive this.

"Yes, it's as nice as you imagine too." I try to recall that night in the greenhouse, but Teloh's face does not fully form in my mind before the image fades. He remains as murky as a half-remembered dream that I desperately want to relive.

Virian jabs Dayen playfully in the shoulder. He laughs along with us before dropping to his knees. He kisses Virian's palm. Virian smiles almost shyly and tucks loose strands of his hair behind his ears. Despite everything that has happened, I am glad that they have found each other and that they found me too.

"How are you both awake? How do you remember?" I ask as Virian applies a thick cream to my skin. I pluck a vision from my mind: Virian unconscious in Dayen's arms and splattered in paint, but I cannot hold it. The image slips and all that remains are the nebulous feelings of guilt and relief. Emotions stick like the smell of fried fish.

"Fishermen pulled us from the ocean and brought us here," Dayen says.

I can't imagine how long Dayen must have swum, or how fast he must have climbed with Virian on his back. I clasp his hand awkwardly with my right and curl my fingers around his. He doesn't flinch this time, instead he smiles, but there is a weight to his expression that I haven't seen before.

"Virian regained consciousness last night," he says. In the span of two days, my friends seem to have aged, but perhaps so have I. Dayen lifts his wrist and shows me skin scrubbed clean.

Virian leans forward. "Our marks never activated because we didn't pass close enough to the gates. The spell only draws on magic in a single burst, like the spark to a firecracker. It's precisely targeted enough not to draw a lot of energy. But the death sleep? Maintaining that for a long time must take an immense amount of power to maintain. No one could sustain that at a distance. My theory is that you must be near its source for it to hold."

The only people that possess that much power are in the fortress, so Virian's recovery makes sense.

I nod and a shudder travels the length of my body.

I want to linger with them and let Virian and Dayen sharpen my memories with their own, but I cannot.

I leave my friends in the bunker and continue pacing, unable to stop or slow down. I practice my words to the council over and over, and hope that some of them might stick in my mind. It feels like trying to catch water with my fingers. All my memories are a jumble and rebel against straight lines.

Convincing the first families is the only way to save the people of Bato-Ko, and I am possibly the worst person to do it. Who would believe a cursed girl? But I have to hope that the truth compels them better than Arisa's lies, because if they do not believe me, they will die.

I am so lost in thought that I nearly jump when Sayarala reappears. Her deep russet skin and silk dress are somehow still spotlessly clean.

"There is a visitor here for you," she says.

I stop biting my lip when Teloh emerges behind her. All my memories of him burst forth with a joyous clarity that fades too soon. He carries no weapons except the kris in his sash. He needs no weapons to destroy me, but my heart still leaps at the sight of him. And I know it has always been like this between us, in all my lives, no matter how much he hated me.

"Shall I have him killed, or may we trust your lover?" Sayarala asks. She could be speaking of the weather instead of murder, and I begin to wonder what she and Oshar are capable of together.

Lover. I'd forgotten how many people saw us together at Midsummer, and my cheeks go hot at the memory. I doubt she would be so cavalier if she knew the truth of what he is.

"May we speak in private?" I ask.

Sayarala disappears with a knowing smile, and Teloh fills up the space where she stood. His eyes sweep over me with concern, and his mouth falls open at the sight of my left hand. It isn't a pretty sight. My skin is covered in rippling burns and blisters, but I feel nothing below the wrist, not even my own fingers.

"Narra?" he asks, and I nod in reply.

He lets out a soft sigh. "I was afraid you would not be yourself."

"It seems I can't stop, even if I try." I attempt a smile, but it falls flat. Here we are together at the end, but it does not feel like the first time we have been at an end together. "How did you get away?"

"Arisa is busy preparing an orasyon to summon Omu, and I don't have long. She will call me back to her." If she gets her way, it means the end to our way of life in Tigang. The end to peace. The Diwata are not meant to walk amongst us, for who upon the earth could stop them?

"Sit. I'm tired." I plant myself on the edge of Oshar's porch, and he crouches on the steps below me. I can see the top of his head, and those unruly curls pulled back test my resolve. I am too shy to run my hands through it and wonder if I'll ever have the chance.

"Your hand," he whispers.

"Virian's idea for restoring my memory." I rub at my left forearm to try and coax some life into it. It doesn't help.

"If this is how she treats her friends, I would not want to be her enemy. But I am relieved she survived." He stares at the ground. "I am sorry, Narra. Kalena forced the words out of my mouth at the testing. I thought that Arisa might spare you if you were no longer a threat, but the first families are causing trouble, and she is cornered. She will unleash the power trapped within me at midday. I've warned the Datus, but it is too late. She's gone into hiding."

Midday is Omu's hour and the height of her power. It would destroy the city and everyone within it.

"Is there anything I can do to stop you?" I ask.

"I cannot stop myself," he says. "I don't think a mortal can."

"You say I am Astar, but I still cannot remember. I have no power and no magic to draw on." I ball my fists and look up at him. "But if I ran away from the city and called your attention my way, could it spare Bato-Ko?"

"My soul would know you anywhere, and I would follow you anywhere. It might work."

It seems such a futile thing to try, but I can't sit back and do nothing.

"Can you die?" I ask.

"Chaos is immortal, Narra. You are not. Why not just hide in safety? Why risk your life when everyone has treated you so ill? Why not just save yourself?" he asks.

"You took me from Bato-Ko because you had hope in me. My mother…" The space she occupied feels so vast and empty that it might swallow me whole, but there is no more time to mourn. I take a breath and smell jasmine. It brings a whisper of memory that fades away. "My father. The Archivist, Manong Alen. My friends. Even Reshar. They had hope in me, too. I can't walk away from this, or I'll be exactly who I feared." I lean against the railing. "And if I die, I will come back again, will I not? It is not the end of things."

He leans back against my knees, solid and warm. "An infant with no faculty for words cannot save your friends or your family. But death is not my worst fear. Arisa wants to rid the world of you forever, because she knows you are the true Astar." His voice cracks, and I resist the urge to put a hand on his shoulder. "There are punishments worse than death." His eyes fall on the tree in the middle of the courtyard.

"That's not possible. There are rules to the universe, and you cannot permanently change one living thing into another." I think of the balete in the fortress, and I shudder at the thought of living thousands of years without a voice, trapped in one spot.

"A human cannot, but Omu can. Arisa plans to bind her in a human body the way you did me, but Omu must never be allowed to walk the earth. All she knows is how to command— not compassion, not love, not kindness, nor any of the things that truly make humanity glorious."

He doesn't have to say it, but I know the only way to stop Arisa is through Teloh. I lift my left hand to his face but feel only a slight pressure under my fingertips instead of the texture of his skin. I have lost enough, and I don't want to lose him, too. He closes his eyes and cups my hand in his as if it is a precious thing. I freeze, thinking that if I move, the moment might fade away like my memories and cease to be sharp, to feel real.

"I wear the first Raja's body. Does it still please you?" he asks.

I should be startled, but I just stare. So this is how Astar smuggled Chaos across the ocean without a trace.

"What happened to the Raja when Astar trapped you there?" It still seems wrong to think of Astar as myself, because she remains a stranger to me.

"He died. There was no room for the both of us, and I felt his soul depart. I would like to believe he was reborn in another body like all humans are."

I wrinkle my nose at the strangeness of touching a dead man, but Teloh feels so warm and alive that it scarcely registers. His breath traces a warm path up my arm and sends shivers up its length, warming me all the way to my toes.

Perhaps after so long amongst humans, the Demon has changed, too.

"The body doesn't matter, but it is not unpleasant," I say.

An open smile greets me, and it looks too much like an invitation. I pull away, suddenly aware of the heat in my cheeks.

"Do you still hate Astar?" How could he not, when she was responsible for his cage?

Teloh lets out a breath, and his eyes drink me in. "For a long time, I did, but the first Astar was bound to Omu's will and could not defy her. Astar built my cage, but she was trapped here with me." He reaches out to touch the marks on my neck and taps them gently. "Every day for centuries, Astar would come sit by my dark well and talk to me, no matter how I raged or cursed her. But even when I was a creature of storm and wind, Astar never feared me. Everything I know of humanity is because of Astar. I've never met anyone so stubborn." He flashes a grin, and I snort.

"I need to remember the past if I am to be of any use," I say. "But I'm afraid of who I might be if I do."

"Not yet. Please give me a few last moments with Narra Jal, and I might be able to bear what comes. I think I like this you best of all."

"And why is that?" His expression makes my breath leave my body.

"Because you know what it means to love, and that makes all the difference."

He takes my right palm, and when he brings it to his lips, my heart aches so much in answer that I am afraid it might never recover. This feeling is worse than the hissing of the ghosts inside me. It is louder than me. It is larger than me.

I close my eyes, and a storm grows inside me when my lips meet his. It might sweep me away in a flood, but I do not fear it. Kissing him feels like flying with the wind in my hair, high above a world that sparkles like emeralds and sapphire. It makes me feel as if neither life nor death matter, only now.

My hands slip down the length of his back, but I freeze when

I trace the scars beneath the untucked hem of his tunic.

"I always knew you would be the end of me. You know the only way we can be free is if you destroy me."

I can't do it. My already splintered heart fractures.

"Don't be afraid, Narra. I would let you destroy me a thousand times and never regret it." His nose drifts down the side of my cheek, and his breath tickles my neck. "Is this what love feels like?"

I falter. The pull of him is like the ground when you've jumped off a cliff. Inevitable. But Arisa pulled the ground out from beneath us, and it cannot be.

"I think you are confusing love and lust," I tease, and he grins wickedly in reply, but I know the truth. I have loved Teloh in life after life, and even if I do not remember my own name, my heart remembers him.

I let go of him too soon. "But how do you destroy something immortal?"

He removes the kris from his belt and unsheathes it. Even in the midday light, the curving blade shines with its own light. "This is what remains of Astar's power. When the Demon's power is spent, use it on this body. I will be vulnerable then." I take it in my shaking hands and tuck it into the waist of my malong. The plan seems too simple: draw away the Demon from Bato-Ko, and if I survive, put a dagger into Teloh's heart. I don't know if I can do either.

"And what will happen to you?"

"Perhaps I will be formless again, as I was before I was bound. Or perhaps I will simply be the storm, forever roaming the earth. I don't know what will happen to me, but no one must ever be allowed to control my power. When Omu first manifests on the earth, she will be as helpless as a newborn. You will have minutes to bind her magic and stop her."

"But how will I know what to do?"

"You are who you are, even if you don't remember it. You will know."

It is impossible. I want to laugh. Even if I could use Astar's powers, our chance of success seems as likely as threading a needle while blindfolded. I take one last look into his eyes and see myself reflected. "Find me," I breathe.

"Always," he says.

"Narra, the council is assembled." Oshar's curt voice creates space between us, and Teloh is on his feet again. I miss the warmth of him already. It feels like winter now that I stand on a wooden porch away from him.

He needs to go, but I grab his hands and tug him toward me once more. I nestle into his chest. I wish I could stay here for hours, days, forever, and forget the world crumbling around us. He gently pries himself from my grasp and presses a soft kiss to my forehead. "Goodbye, Narra." Teloh bows to me and walks out with one fearful backward glance.

I do not say goodbye, too afraid that to admit it aloud might make it true. Denial. It is another Jal trait I am guilty of as much as my mother and my sister. This, I remember without much effort.

✳ ☽ ✳ ☾ ✳

CHAPTER FORTY-ONE

"Nanay Oshar, my sister is being held in the fortress dungeons. Is there any way you can get her out?" I ask.

Oshar turns in the direction of the fortress and shakes her head. "It's likely the safest place for her right now. When this is all over, I will ask Reshar."

I nod, still unsettled, but Oshar is right. I don't want to leave her there, but I doubt Arisa will collapse the fortress around her. What matters now is the people of Bato-Ko.

Oshar's main yard is packed so full with bodies that people lean down from the balconies. I recognize some faces from the Midsummer festival, but I do not know their names, only that these were the same people who condemned my mother. I search the crowd for a friendly face. Instead, I find my grandmother. Yirin sits quietly on a cushioned chair near the center of the space and rests her head against a pillow. Her cheeks are so pallid that I worry we took too much blood. It's strange to pity her more than I hate her.

Arguments flare over late shipments of rice, cheating at cockfights, and squatters on mine claims, but when Oshar raises a hand, they fall quiet.

"Friends, we have news from the fortress. Narra Jal was among those in the Sundo." She waves me forward, and I stand before them in a ruined tunic. My hair remains undone by Teloh's nimble fingers, and the girl reflected in the glass of Oshar's walls seems small and haunted.

"Arisa is an impostor," I say.

One man sneers outright, while another picks at his skirt as though bored out of his mind. One woman shakes her head as though she pities me. "Arisa is not the true Astar, and she has been working with Omu's cult to overthrow our government. They've sent assassins into the fortress to murder our Datus."

"What proof have you?" someone asks. My words fall apart as I stumble to make sense as I fight the cobwebs that cling to my mind. I swallow sour bile on my tongue and breathe in the cold, bitter air.

"I..."

Oshar stands beside me. "I have seen all those who disagree with Arisa go missing or fall ill. My informants have confirmed that cultist assassins were captured but took poison before they could be questioned. You know Arisa as well as I do. That girl is happily running our country in absence of a ruler, and I believe she intends to keep it that way. Without our Datus to keep her in check, I shudder to think of what she might do."

"Half the people in this courtyard would do the same for power," an elder interrupts us.

A gray-haired old man stomps loudly. "Yes, but the cultists have no respect for the first families. Do you think you'd be spared their righteousness? They bow only to Omu. I've heard them speak of a purge!"

"Nonsense..." Two more point fingers and accuse each other of conspiracies. Soon, the room echoes with rhetoric and blame. I try to raise my voice, and no one hears me, but a delicate arm that sports multiple brass bangles lifts into the air. They clink as they cascade toward her elbow, and everyone falls silent again. "If Arisa is not the true Astar, who is?"

This is the question they should have been asking.

"Me." My voice cracks. I push my hair over my shoulder to expose my bare throat, and I brace for the reaction.

Three elders jump to their feet, shouting and pointing. I search through the crowd with pleading eyes, but no one sees me, only my curse. I catch one woman's eye, but she hides her face behind a fan. I feel so small before them.

"A Jal? Did we not condemn one of you? You have criminal blood in your veins."

Yirin opens her eyes, and her expression goes stiff.

"Is this your game, Yirin?"

A screaming match erupts, and my head rings like a banged pot, but I take a breath and scream. "Quiet! Perhaps you do not believe me now, but you will believe it when the Demon Chaos knocks over your houses and flattens the city." The noise in the room dwindles. "You will believe it when the glass walls of the fortress shatter and Bato-Ko is rubble." I glare at them all. "The Demon comes at noon. Hide your families in your cellars or behind thick stone walls; ward your homes, because there is no time to escape. That is *all* I have come to say."

I shove my way through them and out the door. Even though I doubt that they have been convinced, my time is running out.

The wind tugs insistently at my malong as I run through the streets. The air is so charged that it feels like breathing lightning. Between buildings, I catch glimpses of the ocean, and the waves froth violently, whipped by a wind that gathers its force. It throws stray hairs into my eyes and flings salt spray over the cobbles.

The beginning of a maelstrom swirls above the fortress. It's no ordinary storm. Merchants peer up at the sky and roll out canvas awnings to protect their wares from rain. The wiser ones begin to pack up their things and lock up their carts. I shout warnings as I go, and I hope some of them heed me.

The wind builds. It whips dust into my face and tries to push me back toward the fortress. The leaves on the trees around me stand straight up, dragged toward the hungry storm with a great howl. Laundry lines swing, and clothes fall off their pins. Gates bang open and closed.

The clouds press so low that it looks as if the sky wants to flatten the earth, and even though I cannot tell the time by the light, high noon slams into Bato-Ko with the force of a typhoon.

The storm strikes land and smashes me into the dirt. The strength of its winds blows the roofs off around me, and I roll out of the way as tiles smash into the street beside me. I huddle close to the houses on the street, but my malong catches like a sail, and I slam into a tree trunk. I cling to its bark as rain floods the city from above, and I pray that its roots keep me anchored. All around me, the storm swallows people's screams. I glimpse a family running into an underground cellar and hope that they are safe there.

Then the rain stops. An abandoned horse whinnies with high-pitched desperation. I see it trapped, tied to an overturned cart nearby. Laundry that once hung on lines lays scattered across the cobbles. Tongues of shadow and lightning lick down from the clouds, and tree roots shiver beneath the surface of the city like a thousand snakes, thrown into a frenzy by the Demon's magic Arisa unleashed to summon Omu. The cobbled streets buckle as roots push up between the cracks and twist to pursue the shadows. The city is fighting back, I realize in awe. The wards Cultivators long ago wove into the city's trees are working.

But the Demon is looking for me, and I need to move. I unbuckle the cart off the horse and cut its reins with Teloh's kris. Perhaps the bony old mare is too old to fear me, but it does not protest when I climb up onto its back, gripping a sodden tapis I scooped off the dirt. I wave the red cloth overhead like a flag.

"Come get me, Demon!" I scream, and my fingers fumble as I tie my makeshift flag to my shoulders like a cape. The wet cloth slaps at my back as we ride across the city, but it works. The storm builds behind me.

Another set of hooves clatters against stone nearby, but no grunting horse breaths match the sounds the shadow creature makes. When I look back, I glimpse a piece of the Demon made incarnate. The shadow horse wails, and the grating noise sends all my hairs on end. It leaves a lightning trail as it drives toward us. It cuts a path across the city, and everything the lightning touches bursts apart with flame. Wood planks and bricks fly into the air, smash windows, and litter the street behind it. It smashes straight through three houses like a comet and leaves craters where they once stood.

There is no way we can outrun it, but the old mare I ride tries her best. We both scream as tentacles of smoke snake toward us. A long welt of blood drips across the horse's flank where the Demon touched it. I hop off her back and slap at the poor creature's rump. "Go!" I shout and turn to face the shadow creature.

But the ground shifts, and roots tangle its legs. Whips of burning smoke reach out and scorch whatever they touch, and the air fills with the scent of burning green wood. The trees that tangle the Demon horse in their branches burst into flame.

But more Demon horses wail in the distance, heading elsewhere. The Demon's attention is scattering.

I climb onto the rubble that was once a stone wall and scream until my throat is raw. "Here! I'm what you want!" I stare into the storm that swallows half the city in a dark fog. I have never been afraid of the dark.

The land beneath me tremors as though it wants to buck the demon off its back.

"Teloh!" I plead as rubble falls around me. "I'm here."

The force of the storm turns my way. The wind shifts, and I fight to stay upright. *I'm here*, I whisper again, in my heart. The wind pounds into my back, and I run.

In the distance, a giant yellow eye emerges from the ocean like a bobbing seal. This beast sends eight long arms across the beach. Each one surges forward like a tsunami, and I watch in horror as each arm sweeps away all trace of everything it touches: carts, houses, people. The water creature crashes toward the city, drowning everything in its wake, searching for me.

People scream as they get out of its way. They scramble past me, and I help a fallen mother to her feet when she stumbles. The calm eye of the storm remains centered around the fortress, and I pray they will be safe there. "Go to the archives if you can. Quickly. Tell everyone." She nods and tightens the wrap cradling the baby to her back.

Screams echo through the dark streets. Some are human. Some are not. Carts topple, and roofs blow off the houses behind me. And then the hail comes.

Glass and wood shatter as rock-hard hail pelts the city. It draws blood from my skin and drums loudly against wooden rooftops, but I continue toward the edge of the city and lure the water creature through the least populated areas. It creeps forward, never ceasing. I don't have time to catch my breath; my lungs burn with every inhalation. My legs ache, and my feet are blistered. Every movement is pain, and I know I cannot keep running forever. I want to cry, but I don't even have the breath left for it. I feel myself slowing—eventually, it will catch me.

But I have one hope. I scrape my knees as I climb toward the forest that lines the edge of Bato-Ko. The water creature slides away, dissolving into waves, because it cannot follow me up the steep rise, but three-headed mist wolves with manes of fire take its place. They race after me, hunting together in a pack, and gain ground so quickly that I despair.

I stumble over the lip of the rise and into the greenery beneath the trees Astar planted. The wolves howl with the sound of glaciers cracking into the ocean as roots and branches tangle them up. I dart behind a boulder as a wolf leaps for me, and my heart pounds as I race in the opposite direction.

A wolf appears before me, cutting off my escape. Its heads sway as it looks at me. The creature shrieks out a howl so loud I fear my ears are bleeding. It takes a step toward me. A root shoots over my ankle to bind me. I pull free, but another root drags my slipper beneath the loam. Roots surge from the soil and whip around the mist wolf and drag it under. Its cries cut off as it disappears underground. But the trees are greedy and grasp for me, too, as if I am also a creature that does not belong. They wrap my ankle like a snare, and I struggle to break free, but my muscles barely keep me upright. I scream and kick, but they only tighten and pull me toward them. It's the Cultivators' test all over again, only this time there is no Kormar to cut me free.

Roots drag me to my knees, and the soil opens around me, as if the ground itself would bury me alive.

Why do you fear me? the balete tree asked.

Who are you? I asked back. I thought no one replied, but perhaps I simply wasn't listening. The trees rustle around me and pull me close. This is unlike the magic I've seen the Baylan do. It feels like the Demon's magic, wild and with a mind of its own. It is the magic I felt the day I arrived in Bato-Ko. It's the magic that runs deep under the bones of the city: a sort of watchfulness, like someone waiting.

I stop struggling and take a deep breath. My left hand bleeds where my blisters have peeled open. I drink in one last look at Bato-Ko as the trees tighten their hold. Even now, the city gleams defiantly, reflecting what little light it can find under the dark skies. Windows shatter, and trees lose their battle against the strength of the storm, but they slow the Demon's approach. A path of destruction follows the route I took across the city.

"Astar?" I touch my chest. "Is this your doing?"

The earth rumbles in reply, and I fall to my knees. Astar built this city. Astar planted these trees. Perhaps Astar has been trying to tell me something all along. I press my forehead against a patch of earth. It is warm from the sun and as brown as my skin. "Astar," I whisper.

Teloh once told me that the remembering is what always broke me, but he also showed me that this life was different. He saved me from the fortress. I grew up knowing love. How could that not change everything? I run my fingers across the green and gold threads of my malong. I think of my mother, my sister, my grandmother, my friends, and even the father I never knew. I was loved. I am loved. Love is the thread that holds me together and weaves me into a Narra-like shape.

"I am Narra Jal, and I am not afraid of you." The words come out as shaky and tentative as the flame on a wish candle, but there are some things we must do despite fear. "With the Diwata as my witness, I challenge you, Astar. Show me your truths."

Roots snake over my back and grab hold of my ankles. The sky disappears, and with a great rumble, the earth swallows me whole. And I remember what dying felt like.

CHAPTER FORTY-TWO

In the time before

The pressure on my chest left me gasping. Gravity weighted my lungs like mountains, and every tiny movement left me breathless. I'd fallen like a star, flung to the earth by Omu herself. The Heavens were one harsh bright note, but the earth brimmed with hues I had never known and could not name. Even time felt different in Arawan. I could feel it slipping through my fingers like a cold stream.

I wanted this, I reminded myself and tried to sit up. I was not banished but chosen from all of Omu's children and sent here.

Beside me rested the boy who saved me from drowning. He sprawled on the dark earth beside the waterfall, and his warm brown eyes watched mine. His clothes and curly hair clung sodden to his body, and yet I could tell he was beautiful.

"Omu has answered my prayers." He looked at me as though I were a magnificent statue; something to be guarded or worshiped. My heart sank, for if he knew my true purpose, he would curse me instead.

I struggled to my feet, and he helped me up with gentle hands, but he remained on his knees.

"You are the leader of this island, the one called Datu Ressa?" My voice sounded softer and younger than I expected. "Stand, Datu, for I am only a humble servant of the Diwata. Omu has been pleased by your supplications."

If he had reservations, they did not show in his face. His expression betrayed only reverence. Though I saw no desire reflected in his gaze, he was warm and solid at my side. This was more than the Heavens ever offered, and for that alone I was grateful. I was to be his wife, and I thought that perhaps it would not be too unpleasant. Perhaps one day I might even love him, but such things even Omu could not guarantee, and the secrets I kept already felt like a wedge between us.

We passed between rice paddies, and I glimpsed my reflection. I appeared a short young human woman. Clothes that had been woven from threads of starlight sat dull upon my skin, much like the pineapple cloth that I'd seen the humans weave, but the brown face that stared back was familiar. I touched my mouth and my eyes. They were stiff and firm, like the ground beneath me. I remained myself, just... diminished.

We climbed a terraced mountain, past plodding carabao laden with baskets, clustered nipa huts on stilts, and farmers laying rice to dry on packed dirt roads. People turned when we passed and came to greet their young Datu. I delighted, because their curious eyes turned to me, not because I looked different, but because I was a stranger. When he told them what I was, that warmth changed to fear.

I smiled through my teeth, and greeted them kindly, but their wariness remained. They were right to do so, even though Ressa did not worry. I wondered if perhaps he was a little bit the fool, because Omu's favors always came with conditions.

A yapping dog broke free of its tether, and I tumbled over as it jumped up to greet me. To my surprise, small gashes split the skin of my knees and red liquid wept out of them smelling faintly of iron.

How delicate... I thought. What soft flesh I must build Omu's army from.

"Sorry, po!" A child chased the dog away and one helped me

to my feet. They all looked the same to me. She? He? They? I had never paid much attention to humans before. They laughed and poked and prodded.

"But what do the Heavens smell like?"

"And what is your favorite food?"

"Do the Diwata have parties in the sky? My mother once told me that shooting stars—"

I had only opened my mouth to answer when Ressa came along; he shooed them away. The worry on his face was too much.

"It's nothing." I shrugged, already disappointed that my laughing friends were gone. At least the children didn't fear me.

"It is not nothing." He frowned and picked me up to carry me in his arms like a bride, despite my protests.

A large wooden building sat above the edge of the village. Palace would be too gracious a word for the nipa roofed dwelling, but this was the place Omu described would be my new home. It was bright and open, with banig on the floor for seating. Large windows looked over Ina-Ko, the archipelago's largest city. The city was little more than several clusters of villages, but it was the most beautiful of them all. Beyond the city shone the deep emerald of the forest, and the bright sapphire of the ocean. This far below the Heavens, Omu's presence was softened by the land and its shadows. I was still her servant, but I'd never felt so free.

"Welcome home," he set me down gently in his private rooms and went about washing the wound on my knee. Ressa's personal space was piled high with bamboo scrolls. His pulse raced as he carefully bound my little scratch, as if he were afraid I might crack into pieces like a clay dish. I looked at the beautiful young man before me and swallowed.

"Datu Ressa." I took his chin in my hands, and he trembled as he looked up at me. He was younger than I expected of a ruler, no more than eighteen or nineteen in human years. "You still have a choice. You can send me away. You need not accept Omu's bargain."

"I will do whatever Omu wishes of me," he said.

That needle of worry returned and sewed my gut up in knots. I dropped his chin and stepped back. "She demands obedience," I said. "You prayed for knowledge and the power to change the world for the better." But Omu would decide what was best, not he. "If you make your life hers, the power of the Heavens will be yours. I shall teach your people magic and how to hear the Diwata speak. You shall unite the seven islands and rule them all. We shall create my mother's empire together. But…you do not have to do this…"

"My life is hers. Whatever price must be paid, I will pay it. As they lay dying, I promised my parents that I would be the greatest ruler there ever was. I would bring peace to our land." It was the sky he stared into, instead of my eyes, and I realized there would be no reasoning with him. Even if I warned him, he would never change course, because he trusted in Omu's will. He would have his peace, but I feared he didn't understand the cost. "What shall I call you, po?"

My tongue fumbled as I tried to form my immortal name into human shape. "My name is Astar."

CHAPTER FORTY-THREE

In the time before

"Astar! Does Ressa never feed you?" Ketah was even more beautiful than Ressa. Though she was Baylan of the island and equal in power to the Datu, they were nothing alike. Where he was heavy, she was laughter and air. Her smiles came as quickly as raindrops during a monsoon, while his were as rare as pearls.

We walked across the courtyard, a flat piece of tamped earth that overlooked the city. From the vantage point of the palace on the volcano's slope, you could see all seven islands that made up the archipelago, the striped sails of boats gliding across the water, and beaches of white and gold sand. I never tired of the view.

I wiped a drip of santol juice from my mouth as we passed between tables of students dutifully copying the orasyon I taught to them. Word had spread of the Diwata turned mortal, and Baylan came from every island, from villages both large and small, to learn from me. Already they were calling Ressa the Raja, the Datu of Datus, just as Omu proclaimed. Every now and then, something caught on fire, and I smiled. Things were going well.

But the fruit was a bribe Ketah used to stall our navigation lessons, and it worked every time. "You are right; it tastes better with salt." The sensation of a full stomach was pleasant. How hungry must I have been before? I didn't think I would ever tire of the mortal world. There were too many new things to try. I liked everything but pineapple.

"See?" Ketah laughed, and the bells on her ankles jingled merrily in tune.

"Baylan Ketah, should you not address my wife with more formality?" Ressa looked up from a desk where he sat recording the histories of the Diwata. He looked like just another student. He never tired of my stories of Kitha, Minue, Rea, and the others. He was making notes in the margins again, and I could not help but smile at it. His lips tugged up at my expression, and his smile warmed me.

"There is no need, mahal," I said. To call him so made his face relax, and that pleased me, too. There were many kinds of love, I supposed. He cared for me because he believed it was Omu's will. I cared for him, too. He was kind and true, yet my greedy heart grumbled with disappointment there was not more between us. "We are all equals here."

Ketah wagged her brows, and Ressa sighed. She pretended ignorance just to tease him and to test me. Though lessons always went slowly, she was clearly brighter than most. She reminded me of the colorful birds that flitted past the palace, too fast to catch.

But then the screaming started. An old Baylan ran toward me, babbling in tongues. Her eyes were wide with fear as she slammed into me. Too late, I watched the dagger slice across my side. "Astar will destroy us all!" the Baylan screamed. "I have seen it!"

I staggered to my knees, more stunned than hurt. Blood seeped through the silk of my tunic where she cut me. A chill coursed up my body as guards raced toward us and tackled the old woman. Our eyes locked, and she gazed at me with the certainty of truth. I knew then that she'd glimpsed the very same visions Omu had shared with me. "Wait!" I shouted. "Do not harm her!" No one should ever be punished for the truth. I'd kept Omu's visions a secret lest Ressa and Ketah hate me, too.

Ressa threw me over his shoulder as though I was a sack of rice. He raced me back into the palace, and the view I loved so much was swallowed by guards and my tears. "Promise me—do not harm her!" I begged Ressa, for the Baylan was only trying to protect her people.

"But she hurt you!" he growled. Ketah ran inside after us. I winced as they peeled cloth from my wound. The gash was bloody but shallow against my ribs.

"It's nothing." I shoved him back, my eyes still full of tears. "Promise me! You don't understand..."

"I promise." He tore at his hair. "But only if from now on, you stay inside the palace. If you need to go out, guards must accompany you. I almost lost you! I cannot do this without you!"

Ketah ground her teeth together as she paced beside me. "Would it not be better for Astar to go out amongst the people, so they come to know her? Let them see that she is no threat. That she is no Demon in disguise."

They began to shout, but I pushed myself between them. "Don't fight, please. Not over me. Omu's will cannot be denied. What will be will be."

"Holy Astar." Ressa frowned, ever formal. "Has Omu revealed more of her plans to you?"

"Not yet," I lied, even though lying felt like dragging my skirts through the dirt. I could not escape the future Omu had chosen for me, but time was not important to the Diwata. I prayed that Omu might allow me a few human lifetimes, for though I had no power on the earth, I did not miss the Heavens. Since the Demon Chaos had been banished to the earth, nothing ever changed there. Everything had its place, like scrolls in their cubbies.

"What is that bird called?" I changed the subject as Ketah bound my wound. A dark bird with a yellow belly and orange-spotted wings alighted on the windowsill.

Ketah laughed and tossed her long mane of black curls. "Do the Diwata know anything at all?"

Ressa bit his lip at this almost treason but resisted the bait.

"A storm is coming." Ketah sighed. "You better send everyone home early."

Ressa nodded in agreement. Despite her teasing and their frequent arguments, he always did what Ketah asked.

"I've never seen a storm before. At least not from down below..." I squeezed into the window beside her, and she threw her arm around my shoulder.

"Oh, I bet you will love it." She grinned.

Ressa slumbered in our bed. The curve of his back had grown both familiar and welcome, but night after night, I lay awake. There was no darkness in the Heavens, only fire, and though my mortal body urged sleep, thunder growled, and the sky lit up purple with streaks of lightning. The shutters rattled, and the trees rustled as the storm pounded against our shore. Ressa, as always, slept through it all. Not even the thunder made him stir in his sleep.

For weeks, I'd hardly felt the sun on my skin and did not speak to my students directly. I was sick of being caged. Omu only ruled the earth by day, but I did not fear the dark. I tucked a sleeping spell gently beneath Ressa's blanket and climbed out the window.

Clouds whipped across the sky and plunged me into darkness, then light again. The pouring rain was warm as blood. I raced barefoot as lightning forked above the ocean, fracturing

Omu's sky into shards. The air smelled so full and green, as though everything in the world had come alive. Something about the wildness of the storm called to me, and I raced to the water's edge to catch it.

I buried my feet in the white sand, and waves crashed over my knees. Omu could not look into the storm. With the rain pelting me from every direction, I screamed out my frustration. The cut on my ribs had long healed, but I traced the scar, for it reminded me of what would come to pass. I did not want to be what Omu made me to be. I wanted no part in my mother's plans. I wanted a future that I could decide, because the path she'd chosen only led to destruction. I thought that the human world would offer freedom; instead, it only showed me glimpses of what I was missing.

"Why are you sad, Diwata?" The voice was everywhere and nowhere, not a sound from a mouth attached to lungs in a bag of meat. The howls of the wind turned into a light breeze that tickled the tops of the palm trees.

Omu warned that the Demon would seek me out and that I must win its trust.

I had hoped differently, and my heart constricted as my fate drew near. "Show yourself, Demon."

Chaos laughed, and the storm around us ceased as it spun and condensed into a human shape made of clouds and darkness that crackled with lightning. Its many heads merged into one, and it turned to me with black eyes that contained not anger but stars.

"Does your Raja not please you?" it teased, and I snorted as I scrubbed my cheeks.

"What would you know about pleasing a mortal?" I asked, and its laughter fell around me like drops of rain.

"I've wandered the earth for millennia. I have seen what humans do." It shrugged, but I saw the way it watched me.

Fragrant white sampaguita flowers drifted to me on the wind. They settled on my hair and my shoulders. I scooped some into my palm and breathed in the glorious smell of jasmine. "See, you are smiling."

My traitorous heart leaped a little too loudly in its chest. "You know, Omu has not forgotten you."

"I do not fear Omu." The Demon leaned so close that our noses nearly touched.

"You don't understand—"

Its cool hands traced the red marks Omu left upon my neck, and my whole body turned aflame. I stared into its starry eyes and saw eternities, possibilities, futures. "I only fear for you."

"Come back tomorrow and talk to me?" I asked.

Thus began a new ritual: every night, while Ressa slept, I walked to the beach and looked out over the moon-kissed ocean. The Demon would whisper of all the things it had seen in the mortal world, and I listened beneath the coconut palms. Perhaps it knew this was a trap, but neither of us could stay away. I had as many questions as the grains of sand upon the beach, and we would talk until I was drowsy and must return to my home. I longed for the nights and wasted away the days.

There was something about the Demon that called to my soul. When we talked, I forgot about Omu and her shining court. I forgot my mortality. I could imagine more than Omu's narrow vision.

"Is this what love feels like?" I asked him one night when I spoke to him about my husband.

"I think you're confusing love and lust." The Demon's laughter sounded like crab shells crushed under foot, and the shadows split like a smile around me. "Human bodies are so fascinating."

I leaned against a tree. "There is so much to learn and see that sometimes I forget what I was made for."

The Demon remained quiet for a time. The wind sighed through the trees, and waves crashed against the beach. I feared I had erred.

"And who told you what you were made for?" it asked.

"Omu," I said.

"No one can tell you what you are, Astar."

But I did not understand what it meant. How could I be anything other than what I was created to be? I was created for one purpose.

Chaos sensed my confusion and posed a question instead. "I have a riddle for you, then. What is my true nature?"

"That is not a riddle." I chuckled, but my amusement died in my throat. Here, with the Demon, I felt more myself than anywhere in the Heavens or on the earth. Every inch of me felt truly alive for the first time.

A finger of clouds tucked the stray hair behind my ear. "You are not what I expected, Astar." My heart pounded as I leaned into the soft caress and closed my eyes.

"Neither are you, Demon."

CHAPTER FORTY-FOUR

In the time before

I dreamed of the Heavens.

"You have failed me, Astar." Omu's voice echoed in her great hall. "Where is my conquering army? Where is the empire you promised to win me? I know your heart of hearts, my little knife. You have grown too fond of these humans. Humanity has made you soft instead of sharp."

"I need more time, Mother." I bowed low. The light of the Heavens was so bright and hot that I could not hold my head up to look at her.

"You disappoint me. You know that I do not tolerate failure. See what you will make me do…"

She showed me the seven islands burning and her people burning with them.

"They are not ready," I pleaded, though I knew it made me look weak, and Omu did not tolerate weakness. "I have not had time to build enough boats to cross the ocean. I haven't taught them enough magic."

I was not ready, but I also knew that lifetimes might not be enough for me. She was right. I had lost my resolve. I'd been tempted by fruit, flesh, and whispered secrets.

"Please," I begged and pressed my forehead to the floor.

The light softened.

"I will give you one chance to prove your worth." Omu

dictated her conditions and seared them to my heart with burning light.

I woke screaming. It felt as if I was dying again, and the mark of her hand upon my neck seared like a fresh brand. I remembered the feel of Omu's hands as she choked away my immortality and flung my body from the Heavens like a straw doll.

Ressa bolted awake and held my shuddering body until the dream subsided. His soft words quieted my mind, but they did not stop the tears from falling. Sadness, I realized, was just as painful as any blade, but I could control a blade. I could not command my heart.

I wiped ineffectively at my eyes. The tears refused to stop as I explained Omu's will.

At the foot of the bed gleamed a ceremonial kris that was not there when I lay down to sleep. Its blade glowed as if it was forged from liquid moonlight. A gift from Omu to help me do her bidding.

"I can't do what she asks," I told my dear Ressa. He bent his head close to mine, so that my forehead was buried in his neck. "Tell me, Ressa—do you love me?"

I searched his face.

"Of course. I'm thankful every day Omu sent you to me." He bowed.

He often told me he cared, but the words always felt lacking. The Demon told me nothing, and yet there was more meaning in one of its glances. Love, my heart told me, was not the same as duty, but I still cared for Ressa. Neither he nor the Demon deserved what was to come. "I do not want to do this."

"You will tomorrow. Let us not delay," Ressa said. "I have promised my life to Omu, and she has granted all that I prayed for." He tilted his eyes to mine, so trusting and so tame. "I am not afraid."

Then he is a fool, I thought.

. . .

I held the shining kris in my palms and sat upon a white sand beach. Nothing from the Heavens ever survived with the same power once it was cast upon the earth, but I knew that this weapon remained potent enough, because it was forged from the immortality I left behind. It was a piece of myself.

"Astar?" The Demon's voice was as welcome as a breeze in the heat of the day. I closed my eyes, but my heart didn't need eyes to see it. I would know it anywhere. Chaos and the Destroyer went hand in hand, for my mother made me to be the Demon's other half.

"What have you brought me?" it asked, and the shadows split with amusement, but I could not return the smile. I felt like a broken bowl, spidered through with fractures. The blade sang its purpose as it repeated Omu's will. My fist closed around the kris, and my third eye opened. I could see how each droplet of water and each grain of sand upon the beach was made, but also how it came apart like wooden blocks a child might pile into a tower, then topple over.

"I'm sorry," I whispered, and I whipped the dagger around. I pinned the Demon's arm to the trunk of a palm tree. Its immortality was just another puzzle that I could take apart. The shadow in the shape of a human writhed against the bark.

"You will upend all Omu's plans for the mortal realm. You must be stopped." I repeated Omu's words, though my heart shattered with each one. The Demon hissed, and the shadows swirled in and out of solidity as the blade's magic took hold.

I tore my eyes away. Betraying Chaos felt worse than lying or sadness. It felt as if my heart might shrivel up like dried fruit.

"Omu used you to bait me, and you let her?" Chaos screamed. The answer was yes. How could I refuse my maker? "She made me for this."

I called out for Ressa and blinked back my tears. I steadied my shaking hands as he stepped out from behind a boulder, wearing nothing but a bahag. He walked calmly toward the twisting shape of smoke and thunder.

"My life is Omu's. I do this for our people's future." Ressa held my shoulders to steady me while I stood there shaking. He was always so good, so obedient and favored of the Heavens. "You must not falter."

Chaos screamed a gale, and the winds rose as its temper grew hot. "You do not have to do this!" The Demon's growl sounded like a cavern of stone collapsing. "You are free here, Astar!"

But Omu's brand still burned hot on my neck, and it bound me to her will. I could not defy my mother. I wrote an orasyon onto Ressa's body, using the words Omu dictated in my dreams, though every part of me screamed it was wrong. Ressa did not deserve death for his faithfulness. And Chaos? Who would Chaos be without the typhoon and the wildness? Who would Chaos be, caged?

Chaos twisted like a tethered tiger, growling and clawing at the gleaming blade, but the knife only burrowed deeper. Each of Ressa's screams cut a piece of myself away until I was sure there was nothing left of Astar.

Ressa's eyes grew dull, and the Demon screamed one last time. Its fury was a howling typhoon, and all of Arawan's volcanoes shuddered to life in response. A maelstrom swirled above us, whipping up the wind. Then the torrential rains began.

I stared at Ressa's body as Omu's vision became truth. *This is what I was made for*, I tell myself: sent to bind the demon and remove the one obstacle to her dominion over both the Heavens and the Earth. I am, and was ever, Omu's knife made flesh.

I am Astar the Destroyer, and everything I touch turns to ruin.

And this wrecked body before me was the weapon Omu would use to conquer the world. The rains poured down as though they meant to drown us.

The ground rumbled like an angry beast, and creatures of shadow raced upon the winds, destroying whatever they touched. Terraced rice paddies crumbled into mud. Clouds of black smoke billowed into the sky. The palace I so loved slid downhill, and the volcano's mud flows pushed villages toward the sea. I watched as the remnants of my short human life turned into mud and ash.

"Holy Omu." I fell to my knees. "I have done all you asked." I pressed my forehead to the wet sand. There was no more fight in me. "I will build you a palace fitting of your glory and a country that is faithful. Spare the people and let them remember your mercy instead of your wrath. Let sorrow harden them into weapons worthy of you."

The Heavens' golden light broke through the clouds and filled my vision. Omu's laughter bellowed through my ears. "Very well. I will save the boats for last," she said.

So, I hefted Ressa's unconscious form over my shoulders and ran.

I stood upon a small boat and watched Arawan burn. I strapped Ressa's slumbering body to the mast so that he would not tumble overboard. Ketah turned our boat into the wind. We edged to the front of the small fleet we had saved. So few managed to escape, but those that did raced East and into the wind to meet us.

Ketah read the guilt written upon my tear-stained face and grabbed me by the shoulders.

"Astar." Ketah stamped her feet, and the bells jingled. "You have done this, so now you must fix it. You will repay every drop of blood that has been taken from us. You will help us begin again."

"I don't know how to build anything," I whispered.

"Then you will learn." I could find no solace in Ketah's grief, but her words bound me. It was a curse sealed with ash and sacrifice and written upon my soul for all time.

As we lurched East into the unknown, Ressa cried himself into consciousness. His voice was a waterfall roaring into a pool. It was not the voice I expected, but it was still familiar: "What have you done?" Chaos asked.

I destroyed Arawan, my heart answered.

CHAPTER FORTY-FIVE

Now

I turn over in the dark and breathe softly. Somehow, I am still alive, though I cannot see the sky. The searching wind screams through cracks in the earth above me, but I am stuck in the no-time, the some-when. I close my eyes, touch a finger to my chest, and pry my way back into the present.

When I finally open my eyes, roots lay coiled around me like a bird's nest, and I glimpse a sliver of blue sky above the crevasse I've fallen into.

I tap Virian's mark three times, but I do not feel a reply. Perhaps I am too numb. I claw my way up, one crumbling handful of soil at the time.

The light disappears, and dirt tumbles over my head as the earth shifts, but it doesn't swallow me. A hemp rope lands on my shoulder. I fit a bare foot into its loop and grunt as I push myself while someone pulls from above.

I fall onto the ground as ragged and raw as Astar fallen from the Heavens. My right hand is dirty but brown and familiar. My left hand remains bloody and raw but numb to touch. Brilliant blue cracks of sky streak the clouds above, and the air tastes as crisp as winter apples. Bato-Ko glitters in the distance, a valley of green cradled between the spiny mountains and a rocky plateau. I kneel before it. It is so different from everywhere I have traveled in this life, but here I finally feel like I am home.

Dayen helps me to my feet, and his amulets dangle against my cheek. "I'm so sorry, Narra. I was so scared I'd be too late. I tried to follow you, but the earth opened up..." He stutters and stuffs his amulets back into the neck of his tunic. "I've been a terrible friend. I owe you so many apologies. I want to make it right..."

He pulls me into a hug that is so tight I gasp. Of all people, I did not expect him to come, but he is warm and steady and welcome. Tears spill from my eyes as my heart overflows. Perhaps friendships can be mended just like old clothes.

Laughter spills from my body in racking heaves. Dayen asks me if I hit my head on the way down. But my head feels clearer than it has all my life. I have my answers. I know too much about life and death and love to ever be that girl, Astar, again. Omu tried to make me a weapon, but she did not forge me.

Life upon life, Astar's memories drowned me in guilt, but once, not so long ago, a Demon gambled on my heart and set me free. And he was right. My family and my friends changed everything.

I am Narra Jal, I tell the ghosts in my chest.

They snarl one last time and release me.

CHAPTER FORTY-SIX

The storm has dwindled, but a maelstrom still twists above the spires of the glass fortress. Lightning forks into the roof, setting it alight. There might still be time to stop Arisa, so we hurry through the ruined city. Shards of glass dust the streets like snow in the middle of summer, and the ground continues to tremble beneath our feet like a giant snoring beast. Wooden rooftops rest smashed against gates and walls. Neighbors pull each other from the rubble and tear sheets into bandages. The air smells of vinegar, lemons, and iodine. Spells of healing burn like candles. No hands stay idle.

Along the water, parts of the city have washed away completely. Some trees withstood the storm, a little barer now and stripped of clumsy branches and leaves, but the wards shaped by the Cultivators did their duty. The worst of the destruction follows a path to the edge of the city where I ran. Bato-Ko is damaged but not destroyed. I did not fail the city completely.

Oshar's compound lies in pieces. Its buildings lay crushed by balls of hail as big as cabbage heads. Only the shed where Virian and Dayen sheltered remains intact.

A circle of untouched dirt surrounds the shed. Oshar huddles within the circle with her family, and to my surprise, Reshar crouches at her side. Cuts from flying glass make patterns on his face, but they are small and will heal without scars. The resemblance is stronger when they stand together, though the Datu's hair has not yet gone white like his mother's. In another life, I can recall Oshar bouncing her baby boy on her knees with laughter in her eyes. She could charm even a princess from Turium with her humor, but she was always infuriatingly contrary. It is a trait her son shares. Now I am glad for it.

I stop short upon seeing the long shape laid out beneath a blanket topped with my grandmother's cane. Virian kneels on the ground to the side. Her short hair is tangled with leaves.

"I'm so sorry, Narra," she says.

I fall to my knees beside her. I hardly knew my grandmother in this life, but she's been taken away from me already. Virian clasps my shoulder as I lift the blanket. Yirin's strong hands lay folded at her chest, battered and cracked. The undersides of her nails are black with dirt, but around them, the most perfect spells of protection are clawed into the ground. She saved them, even if she didn't agree with them all.

We humans are contradictions, all bad and good at once. We are more than what anyone says.

My heart constricts. Yirin's loyalty was tested when she was forced to choose between her duty and her family. Once, she chose duty, but in the end, she chose her family. I kiss her forehead, and I am glad she cannot see my expression. If she were anything like my mother, she would have scoffed at my softness. "Maybe in the next life I will have a chance to know you," I whisper. I must attend to the living first.

"Where is Arisa?" I ask.

Reshar flinches. "I was halfway here when the storm began. I only know something terrible has happened," he says. "I could not get near the center of the fortress."

"I must go back and stop her."

"Astar?" he asks.

I nod, and a breath escapes his lips. This gives him more assurance than it should. I have no powers. I only remember moments of the past, not things as complicated as orasyons. Arisa was trained since birth in the ways of the Baylan. I have not trained in anything nor studied anything beyond what was required of a cloth merchant. In this life, I am bereft of magic.

Astar the mediocre would not inspire song, but I was never responsible for the stories the Tigangi told about me. With time, the tales took a life of their own, until most were nothing like the truth at all: I am only human.

But Omu's long, slow plan has finally come together, so patiently executed that I have no idea how many cogs and wheels she set in motion. Astar was just one piece and Arisa another, so that she might manifest on the earth and rule like a God.

But only those of the earth have power on the earth. Binding Chaos was a test—a first step. Now, Omu has all the bodies she could ever use to make her own and all the Demon's power to fuel a spell. If she walks the earth, there will be no stopping her, for no power on earth can match hers.

"I need to get past the guards and the Demon." I stand and brush dirt from my malong. I tie my hair in a knot at the base of my neck, ready for work. To lose Teloh would be like losing a part of my soul, but I swear to do what I must, because Omu cannot be allowed to get her way. I touch the kris tucked in my waist, and it hums in response. "I cannot do this alone, but I will not ask you to come. You may not leave the fortress alive. I may not, either."

"If we die, we come back in another life to piss in Arisa's food," Virian says.

I stifle a laugh that feels so inappropriate but necessary.

"Where you go, I go," Dayen says without hesitation.

Oshar takes the slippers off her feet and presses them into

my hands. Then she picks up my grandmother's cane and leans against it. "My family and the city need me right now. I will rally all our families."

Sayarala touches her thumb to the base of her throat in a Turinese blessing. "Good luck, Astar."

I nod. A trusted friend is worth a thousand strangers. At least, I need them to be.

Reshar says nothing, but he walks out the broken gate behind us. We have as much hope as a candle lit on a windy day, but it will have to be enough.

We snake through the debris and back streets slowly because entire uprooted trees litter the street. Chunks of shale roof tiles stick out of walls and fences. We pass a family frantically digging through the rubble of a flattened house, but we can't stay to help. We pass dangerously close to a patrol of Guardians, but they are too busy answering to the angry people who surround them to notice us. The Guardians look just as lost and uncertain as the citizens of Bato-Ko, and there is no sign of the Seven. Worry grants my tired body another burst of speed.

Clouds still churn above the fortress, but the Seven combined could never control Chaos for long. I quaver at the thought of how they teased the power out of Teloh, because he would never give it willingly.

The Demon was once so desperate to escape its cage that it cut off chunks of its own flesh to set its power free. Flowers bloomed where its blood dropped, and storm clouds gathered with each scream, but his flesh grew back as though it had never been broken. He was a feral thing, once.

But that is not the Teloh I met in the greenhouse, nor the one whose lips touched mine. We have both changed. No matter what Omu wills, change is inevitable for those touched by mortality. The earth is our domain, not hers. Not yet.

But the maelstrom is already smaller than it was only minutes ago, and I lead them into a run.

No one watches us pass through the broken gates of the fortress and squeeze carefully through its main entrance. The massive wooden doors hang off their hinges and look ready to fall over. Fissures travel up and down the fortress's glass walls, and sharp chunks of the roof litter the floor of the great hall. I hope my sister is still safe somewhere inside. I want to go to her so badly, but we need to stop Arisa first.

Virian adjusts her small hip bag packed full of papers scribbled with spells, but I catch a wince of pain at the edges of her expression.

"You don't need to come if you hurt too much," I say, but she only grunts in reply.

"If we don't come, there may be no more Tigang to come back to," she says. "I'm fighting for my home. Where will Arisa be?" she asks.

"Follow the bodies." Reshar shrugs. I offer him a small smile of assurance, but he looks away unimpressed.

We see no one in the halls. I'm not sure if anyone still lives or if everyone is hiding. The fortress was not spared from the Demon's assault. Leaves and branches and vines sprout from the stone in various states of blooming, seeding, and fading. All stages of life surround us, just as time feels like it's spiraled around again.

But Astar started this. Now I must end it.

CHAPTER FORTY-SEVEN

The underbrush swallows the sounds of our footsteps, but leaves hiss on their stems and shake warnings in an ever-present wind. Every surface of the fortress is covered in greenery, but it grows thickest the closer to the center of the fortress we clamber. I dare not slow. The Demon is still loose and could still come for me, but I pray that I might get to Arisa first.

I tug a vine out of the way with a grunt, wishing for a machete or even a kitchen knife.

Dayen lifts a hand to help, but he shrieks as his shoulder ignites. I twist around and choke on the sudden smell of oranges, smoke, and burned flesh.

Kalena blocks the hallway like a serene apparition. The dark waves of her hair float in the air as if she is underwater, and her long dress billows in a nonexistent breeze. The head Interpreter's usually placid expression is missing, and she bares her teeth. Splashes of blood decorate the white of her gown, and strands of her hair turn to white as I stare.

"Holy Omu is glorious and her will a marvel." Kalena raises her hands to the Heavens. Her fingers are streaked with ink and blood. One of her fingernails looks like it was ripped off, and yet she does not seem to feel it.

"Whatever she promised you, the cost is too much," I say, but her eyes remain tilted Heavensward, as if she is looking upon

Omu herself.

Reshar wags a finger, and a small smile plays at the edges of his lips. "You must be made accountable, Kalena. You pledged to serve Tigang, not destroy it."

She cackles and reveals an orasyon cupped in her hands. "Omu is displeased with our people, for we forget the old ways. We are all meant to serve her! The numbers of our Baylan diminish every year, for few wish to sacrifice their lives to service. Our government bows to the greed of the old families and is rife with corruption and nepotism. Sometimes it is better to destroy something and begin again. Let the corrupt burn!"

I don't disagree with everything she has said, but summoning Omu is no solution.

The air around her ignites with the heat of the sun as she summons a ball of fire half the width of the corridor.

Reshar rolls his slumped shoulders and looks her dead in the eye. "The only rotten thing here is you."

Kalena screams as she flings a ball of fire at us. I squeal and drag Virian behind a wall. Dayen ducks flat to the floor as the fireball singes through the entire corridor. Leaves and vines turn to fire around us, heating the air like a furnace, but in the middle of it all, Reshar stands his ground, his feet planted apart, with a chalk tablet in his hands.

The fire does not touch him, and he blows chalk dust in her direction. Leaves turn to metal darts that slice into her knees, and the heat falters as she screams. Kalena rallies with pure force that sends the floor buckling beneath us, but Reshar is all precision. He summons a vine that wraps around her neck. She crumples the used spell and plucks another from inside her wide sleeves. Reshar spits at his chalk tablet, and Kalena's spell slips out of her fingers on a gust of wind.

He looks back at me, and his expression is softer this time. "Go, Astar. I will deal with Kalena. Save us if you can."

For an instant, I recall Reshar the boy running through these halls with his twin sister. He was all smiles when the shyness rubbed away. I do not want to leave him, but Virian tugs me down the hall.

Dayen slaps a wet cloth over his shoulder where the fire singed through his tunic. "I'll be fine," he mutters, but neither Virian nor I have time to check. We climb over roots and duck under vines. We race down the hall and into another corridor, and another, until time is a blur. Everything shakes. I do not know how much time we have left or if we've already run out.

"Narra."

My world comes into focus.

Teloh saunters down the hall and dodges vines that reach out to crush him. The vines are not his magic, I realize, but protection Astar wove into the heart of the fortress long ago. His black tunic is shredded, and in places his skin has been torn away to expose sinew and tendon. Other parts of his body look as if they've been puckered and burned by hot metal. If he were human, he could not still be standing, but he lifts his kampilan sword with two shaking hands.

Astar's kris gleams at my waist as though it knows him. It calls softly, begging for me to hold it. It sings a song of unmaking. My fingers twitch. Part of me wishes I had let the thing burn with Arawan.

Teloh drags his eyes from the floor. "They still have a hold over me. I cannot fight Arisa's compulsion when my body is weak." He lifts the tip of his sword off the floor, and it quivers in our direction. "You should run."

Dayen drags me into another hallway. Branches close the way behind the three of us.

"I only slowed him," Virian says. At least she still has her wits about her. I can't say the same about myself.

We scamper down the hallway, but a great root crashes

through the wall and blocks the way. I spin around, looking for
another way out, but the hallway ends in a pile of rubble. I'm
trapped. Teloh strides into the hallway. His arm shakes as his
grip tightens on his sword. "I'm to bring you to her."

"Kur— Astar!" Dayen barrels into Teloh and whacks him
with a solid branch he picked up from the ground. "You're the
only one who can stop Arisa. *Go*." But Teloh spins around and
tries to throw him. Dayen ducks and slips out of the way before
launching himself against the Guardian again. Teloh has a sword,
and he does not.

"Dayen, no!" I shout, and Virian appears a moment behind.
She presses a spell to the wall. Dayen's branch meets Teloh's
sword with a metallic ring, and the blade drops to the floor.

Dayen rolls and grabs the sword off the ground. He yells in
triumph and swings the kampilan like an axe. Teloh jumps out
of the way, but the tip of its blade slashes across his arm. Virian
yelps in triumph, but I only scream. Where Teloh's blood drops,
roots and vines come to life, and they slam her against the wall,
trapping her in a cage.

I grab Dayen's discarded branch and swing it at Teloh's neck,
but he dodges out of the way. Dayen hacks at vines to free Virian
while I distract Teloh. I aim for his knees, but he's too fast for me.
My past selves know these movements, but I have not trained
this body. I swing the stick to draw him away, but I do not have
enough power in my attack. He catches the branch in a hand and
twists me around to grasp me by my hair. I bite at his forearm,
and he yells.

"Narra!" Dayen shouts and slides the kampilan across
the floor to me. I catch the hilt with my right hand and ram it
backward. I feel it hit its mark. Teloh gasps wide-mouthed at
me as blood drips to the ground from his waist and soaks his
loose trousers.

"Go!" Virian commands, and I tear my eyes from Teloh's

bleeding body as she throws a spell that fills the room with smoke.

Wherever I go, he will follow. I just need to be faster. A plan. I had a plan. I run through the fortress's winding corridors, edging ever downward into the Winter Palace. I hear footsteps behind me, and sure enough, Teloh has followed. His wound is still healing, and he stumbles as he goes. It takes everything in me to run from him instead of to him.

A piece of wall topples into the hallway and blocks the corridor so that there is no way back to my friends.

I twist down the hall and lose sight of him, but when I reach the door to the Demon's prison, the gate is locked shut. Three Freezing Hells! I kick at the lock as Teloh approaches, but it doesn't budge. All I can do is hide behind the statue of Madur that stands guard beside the door, with his piercing eagle eyes and sharp claws.

"I know what you're trying to do. You think you'll be safe there from me? That the wards will hold?" he asks.

I hold my breath and go completely still as he approaches. He's thrown off the black silk of his tunic. The hole in his gut is almost completely healed, but blood lingers on his skin. He reaches for the prison gate and pulls it off its hinges as he throws them behind him. He steps into the circular room to find me, but I'm not there.

I slip out from my hiding spot, ram my foot into his back, and shove him into the circle of wards carved onto the floor. I try to free the moonlight blade from my waist, but I forget myself and reach with my left hand. My burned fingers refuse to close around it, and I lose precious seconds. He flips to his feet, and I slip just out of his reach.

The prison is clear of debris, and the spells upon its walls must mute his powers, but Teloh does not slow, and if he catches me, I won't escape again. Even in his human form, I cannot best him hand to hand. Instead, I forget the kris and climb.

I scramble up the scaffolding someone raised to repair the leaking dome. Everything looks even more precarious now. The mortar shifted in the Demon's attack, and the scaffolding looks like it will barely hold together. The circular pit in the center of the room is a black hole beneath me, and I can hear the waves down below, where they've rushed into the cracks in the fortress's foundations. Teloh climbs up behind me and sends the entire wooden frame shaking.

Perhaps I have no immortal magic, but I know what I built. The dark walls of the pit are thick with spells powered by the waves of the ocean. Teloh would be cut off from his power if he fell in.

Teloh's legs smash clumsily through old wooden planks held by rusted nails, but he does not stop. I snake clumsily over the pit and back around. If I lose my grip, my mortal body will not survive the fall.

He jumps to reach for me, and we nearly both go careening over the edge as wooden boards fall into the darkness below. I use my elbows and legs like hooks to cling to the wood with all my strength. The broken skin on my left hand leaves smudges of blood everywhere. I inhale through my nose and try to gather my wits. I know destruction. Sometimes power is unnecessary. Sometimes you only need to find a point of weakness.

There. I kick at a block in the ceiling, cracked by a root that dug through mortar in search of water. A chunk of the ceiling collapses, and part of the scaffolding peels off the dome with it. I cling to the wood for dear life, but Teloh reaches out for me. The two of us twist and fall together. We land tangled together at the edge of the pit. He breaks my fall, but half his body hangs over the rim of the pit, bent at a painful angle. I did this to him.

I drag him over the rim onto flat stone, and he groans in pain that I can do nothing to help with. "I'm sorry. I'm sorry," I whisper over and over. I blink back tears, but I can't stop shaking when I must be steady.

I take my kris and unsheathe the wavy blade with my right hand. When I hold it, I can see the cage of spells I've woven onto his body as clearly as the blueprints to a new machine. It is delicate work, as intricate as lace. But his mortal body and consciousness have twined so tightly together over the centuries that if I get even one word wrong, I fear I will lose him forever.

Teloh cries out as his broken arm straightens itself. "Now, Narra. It's time."

"What about freedom?" I ask, but he doesn't answer. Tears flood down my cheeks. I wish I were stronger. I wish I were better. I wish for many things, but mostly more time.

"Do it." His breath comes out ragged. "Unmake me."

The kris hums a song that answers the tune of my soul. *I am Astar the Destroyer*, it whispers. This is what I was made for. He is right, yet I hesitate.

The blade glows with moonlight and brightens the dim room. It calls back a memory of white sand beaches and waving palm trees. Of secrets whispered in private and mango juice dripping down my neck.

"Does death hurt?" Teloh asks.

"Dying can hurt, but death does not." I wipe the tears from my eyes. "But living is still worth the pain." It is something Omu would be incapable of understanding: how precious each moment is when it could be your last.

"I'm ready, then."

"I love you." The words echo through all the lives they have gone unsaid. Love is a spell more potent than an orasyon because it is something true. It is something no one, not even the Diwata, can compel. He smiles back at me, and he does not need to say the words, for I hear them in my soul.

I take a breath to steady myself. Teloh is broken because I

made him so. I close my eyes and gently touch his forehead. I can see all the cracks and imperfections in the cage that I built. Chaos may be immortal, but this body is flesh, and it is real. I put my hand on his shoulder, and he stills like a tame bird.

"What I have made, I unmake." The words echo like a string plucked on an instrument, for all time and all the universe to hear.

I plunge my knife into his soul, and it does not mark his flesh. I carve away his immortality, and the pieces that fall away dissolve like mist into sunlight. I sweat as I go, for it is painstaking work. If only I had a week or a month to do this gently, I might succeed in saving him, but I fear I only have minutes.

The earth rumbles beneath us, and my hands slip. My unweaving has gone wrong, but I continue, hoping to make up for the mess. I cut his immortality from his body, his power from his form. His limbs grow limp beneath me, and my heart sinks. We both knew this might happen, and yet I did not want to believe it.

"I know the answer to your riddle of your true nature," I whisper. "Teloh..." I stroke his hair as the air begins to still and remember the language of the Heavens. "Does not mean Chaos but Change."

"And what do you think? Does it suit me?" He closes his eyes, and his breathing slows.

"You are what Omu fears most because she cannot stop you. With every breath, the air in our mortal lungs turns over, our bodies grow older, and our minds alter," I say. "For us, change is inevitable."

"But everything essential remains the same." He smiles, and the galaxies in his eyes grow dim.

The ocean settles and laps as gently against the stone as a lullaby. Sunlight pours through the cracks in the dome and fractures the room around me as clouds peel away from the sun.

The Demon is gone.

CHAPTER FORTY-EIGHT

I leave Teloh's body in his prison and swear to the Heavens that I will destroy Arisa. I grip the kris tight and pray I have enough time to stop her. There is no mistaking where she is. I make my way through the fortress to where the plants choke thickest and the air smells of decay. I squeeze through a hole punched in a wall by a tree root and find myself in a large room that was once a workshop. Sunlight floods into a hole blasted straight through eight floors of the fortress, and it illuminates a slumbering army before me.

I gape at the bodies, stunned. There are perhaps several hundred people altogether, standing in neat lines staggered an arm's length apart, ready to be harvested like rice. These must be all the Baylan and candidates from the Sundo who have gone missing. I clench my fists at the audacity to use the Sundo as a sham to harvest bodies. So many lives wasted, and all for one purpose: to find one suitable enough to house Omu.

I push between them, forgetting the aches and pains in my body. The wrongness of it prickles my skin. No matter if Omu ordered this herself, there is no making it right. Humans are not dolls to play with.

I skid to a stop beside a body in the third row. It's Ingo. Rashes spread around a freshly painted orasyon on his forehead. I push past him and stumble across a body lying prone on the floor. This Baylan is dead and already stiff with rigor mortis, but his eyes remain open, and his mouth contorts as if he died screaming. The mark on his head looks like it ignited, and I can still smell his charred flesh. A spell went wrong. A spell I recognize.

My heart thumps loudly, because once I wrote the same one on Teloh's flesh. Someone has attempted a poor imitation. This orasyon for binding a spirit looks incomplete, but there are plenty of bodies here to practice on. Hells… Omu has had her pick of all the talent and all the magic of Tigang to use for her own. I must stop her.

Reshar cries out somewhere above, and I find him balanced on the lip of the floor two levels up. "Riane!" He screams his twin's name.

I rush in the direction of his outstretched arms and spot Arisa. Burned bodies lay discarded on the floor beside her, which tells me of more attempts at binding that have gone wrong, but she has not stopped. A trio of bodies stand before her, and the symbols on their bodies glow with unearthly light. One of the trio resembles Reshar. It's his sister, I realize.

I tackle Arisa, and we land on the ink-stained floor. Flecks of ink stain our clothes, but most of it is dry, and not even our grasping and rolling break the power locked into the spells she's prepared. A ball of fire smashes into the floor near us, and the fringes of my hair ignite.

Kalena appears in what was once the doorway. "It's too late; it's done!" She cackles, drunk on the power she's drawn, even as it bleeds the life out of her.

"You incompetent fool!" Arisa screams at Kalena. "You almost hit me!"

Another fireball flies through the rows of bodies, and they topple like pins. I dive to the floor, and Arisa tumbles with me. Kalena screams as one of Reshar's leaf darts slices through her arm like a needle. Blood soaks the sleeves of her dress. He swings nimbly down one broken level, toward us, but he's still too far.

Arisa's fists collide with my ribs, but her grip is all wrong, and she shrieks because her thumb jams against my bones. She didn't grow up a target like I did. I am all elbows and knees. I kick back hard, but I don't have time for a brawl. I bite her arm, and she releases me with a shriek.

I need to get to the glowing bodies, but Arisa grabs a spell from her workbench. Debris lifts into the air at her command. Glass shards sparkle like diamonds in the sunlight. It's impressive, and it will waste her power, but she sneers at me, uncaring. She lets them loose, and I dive for the legs of the workbench. I topple the spells she's prepared and flip the bench over just as glass and rock pummel into it. My heart nearly jumps out of my chest as a stray shard slices across my cheek. My eyes water. The air is so thick with magic it feels like breathing coffee sludge.

I hear Reshar and Kalena battling. Somewhere, I hear Virian shout. Assassins? Freezing Hells. Four floors up, I glimpse Virian and Dayen holding off attackers, and I pray that they can handle themselves.

The workbench crumples, and I slide backward on my bottom.

"You irritating worm! You think you can beat me? Omu chose me! Not you. *Me!*" Arisa spits and palms another spell. "You are a disappointment to Omu. I will flourish where you did not. I will be as great as the Diwata themselves." A chunk of the floor above us caves in, and we're swallowed by dust.

Bodies lay crushed beneath the marble, but Arisa simply grasps for another spell. They are not people to her, just acceptable losses. But what does she know of loss? I have lost almost everyone I have ever loved. I would not wish that fate on anyone. I unsheathe my kris and slice it toward Arisa. She flinches back, but I am not aiming for her. I run straight for the glowing bodies. Perhaps I am a disappointment, but I will honor those I have lost with every breath in this body.

I ram my blade into the nearest body with no finesse, and all the light in the sky blots out. Dayen screams on a floor above, but I can do nothing for him. With the kris in hand, I can see a long strand of power connecting this body to the Heavens. Power pours through it, filling the body up like a balloon full of water, and I hack at it, severing the strand with swift strikes. I run to the next body as Arisa screeches. I hear her groping in the dark and chanting the last refrains of the orasyon she's scribbling onto the floor. A second line cut and severed. There is no time to do much else, for a true binding is a thing of art that takes time. Two glowing bodies fall to the floor. There is one body left: Riane.

I hack at the raw power descending from the Heavens. It is thicker than the rest, a weaving of power that I saw thread by thread. My third eye burns from the heat of it, and I fear I will go blind. Arisa goes quiet, but all at once, light bursts from every open orifice in the body before me—where the woman's eyes should be, her nostrils, the gaping hole of her mouth—as if it contains the sun within. The light burns through the spell of darkness cast up above as though it is tissue paper. I need to go faster. The fingers on my right hand are clammy with sweat, and I nearly drop the knife. I grip it so hard that the hilt cuts into my palm and use my numb left hand as a brace. I am almost—

A strong hand clamps around my neck, and I lift up off the ground. I can't even scream. I dangle, choking before Riane.

Omu's molten gaze burns tears from my eyes, but I do not fear death, for I have died before. I swing my feet onto her chest and shove her to the floor. A snarl escapes my lips as I try to sever the last thread that connects her to the Heavens, and she screams at the loss of her power. The sound sends debris crumbling down from above, and I cover my head as chunks of stone and glass tumble around us. Omu marches over and picks me up off the ground as though I am weightless, for though she no longer has all the might of the Heavens, she is still stronger than any power on earth. I shake like a rag doll. She needs no orasyon. Omu simply commands.

Leaves and branches sprout from my head. My arms begin to stiffen. Yellow flowers cascade down my back.

The Diwata who must be Madur wobbles to his feet and stands tall beside his consort. The third immortal throws back her shoulders. Though she is not one of the Holy Seven, War needs neither weapons nor armor for me to recognize her. Her posture is enough.

Light and heat radiate off the three as I fight the spell. Omu rips the kris from my hand and tosses it across the room as though it is poisonous.

"Astar, my little knife." Omu smiles at me with her empty mouth and her empty eyes. "You promised me an empire. I have waited all this time, and all you have delivered me is a rock and some disobedient children. But where you have failed, this one has succeeded.

"For your service, dear girl, I will reward you. I have need of you yet." Omu gazes upon Arisa with what passes for fondness, but when she opens her hand, the poor girl screams. Smoke rises from the birthmarks on Arisa's skin, and the smell of burning flesh fills the air as they ignite. "We shall create a new world together," Omu says and does not relinquish her grip. Arisa writhes before her. "But first—"

Arisa stumbles forward against her will, screaming. But the light flickers, and even Omu goes still. A figure comes shambling out of the chaos.

"Omu, Madur, War." Teloh falls to his knees before the three immortals. I can't tear my eyes away, because he should not exist.

Not like this. There is something washed out about him. He's mortal, I realize. His wounds are open and bleeding. His curly hair has come free of its twine. He cradles his arm as though it hurts, and there is something different about his eyes. His voice pierces my heart as surely as a knife. He bends before the Diwata as though to beg for my life, but he lifts his eyes, and before even Omu can blink, he throws the kris to me. I catch it and take two steps into the heat of the sun. I ram my dagger straight into the strands that still connect Omu to the Heavens.

She screams and falls to the floor. Her power flickers, and it feels like plunging into an ice bath. The branches on my head fall to the floor. My limbs loosen into flesh, and I press the blade harder, nearly severing her strands completely, but Omu yanks it out of my sweating hands and crushes the blade into dust with a scream. A tiny hair of power remains, connecting her weakly above. I was so close.

"Our reunion must wait, Kuya Teloh, but you know I am patient." War bows and grabs Arisa's hand.

Light explodes from the center of the room, and I fall backward.

When I open my eyes, the immortal trio and Arisa are gone.

CHAPTER FORTY-NINE

The hand on my shoulder is warm, and I'm afraid to find a ghost stands there instead of a boy. But I can't help myself, because he is the earth and I am a fallen star.

This Teloh bleeds. He leans upon one leg as if the other pains him, and his eyes, once blue-black, have turned an ordinary brown. He looks for all the world like a human.

"How?" I look him up and down again. I watched his power dissolve into the sky, forever lost to me. "I didn't manage to untangle everything... I failed."

He gently plucks blooms and twigs from my hair—all that remains of Omu's spell. Yellow flowers litter his feet. "I...don't understand it, either, but perhaps what remains of me is what even the Heavens cannot strip away: my humanity."

If it is his humanity that remains, he wears it well. I stare unblinking, still afraid he might disappear and that I am only dreaming. I'm surprised to taste salt tears upon my tongue, and I'm not sure if they are from sorrow or joy.

He cocks his head slowly to one side. "So this body still pleases you."

"It's not the time," I mumble and wipe at my wet cheeks.

But his amusement vanishes too soon. A familiar disinterested mask replaces it so quickly that I fear I only imagined it.

Reshar pushes through the doorway, smoke-stained and rumpled. Virian and Dayen drag Kalena between them. She screams words that do not form sentences in any human language. This wild Kalena is all hackles and claws, like a cat backed into a corner.

"What shall we do with her, Holy Astar?" Reshar asks.

"Call me Narra, please." The name fits me like a familiar blanket. A gift from my mother. "Let us keep her close but safe. Throw her in the dungeons. She may know what Omu is planning next."

Reshar purses his lips and searches the room. Some of the Baylan that succumbed to Arisa's paint spell begin to stir. I shake my head and explain what happened.

"Your sister is dead, Datu Reshar," I say.

Reshar doesn't even blink. I do not know if this makes us enemies or friends, but I cannot stomach any more lies. He shoves Kalena out the door. I cannot see his expression, but he is a worry for another day. My family is a more pressing concern. I need to check the dungeons for my sister, and I need Baylan to unlock them for me.

"Narra?" Dayen asks.

I frown and return to the world outside my head.

"The Sundo isn't over yet."

Freezing Hells. The Sundo was the last thing on my mind. I stare at Dayen and Virian wide-eyed. "We still have to pick the new ruler?"

"Appearances are important, and someone must watch over Bato-Ko," Virian says.

As usual, she is right.

"Not me. No, thank you." Dayen takes two steps back and waves his hands in front of his face. "I do not want to worry about poison every time I sit down to eat."

I study Virian. I would choose her if I were given the option, and she knows this.

"I was never here for the Sundo." She sighs. "I want to become a Baylan. Datu Senil wanted someone to watch the proceedings and get to know the candidates. I was supposed to monitor the competition for any strangeness, because he suspected Arisa's plans but had no proof."

"You seemed like you wanted to win!" Dayen stares back with a mix of hurt and confusion, and I know there's a private conversation they need to have.

"I did. Only because there are things I needed to prove to myself."

I run my hands through the hair at the nape of my neck and sigh at the impossible tangle. Some things don't change.

"Well, I guess we'll have to see if anyone is still foolish enough to want the job."

I take stock of everyone assembled in the great hall. The Seven Datus are now four. Senil, the head Archivist, is dead, and Hendan of the Guardians has vanished. Kalena is rotting in the dungeons with rats for company. Omu and her cultists may not have succeeded this time, but they still destroyed so much. I don't know what will happen next.

There is someone else I have been waiting to see since my memories were returned to me, though. "Narra!" Kuran screams as she bursts into the hall beside Reshar. She pushes through the crowd. I forget what I am and run to meet her. I fling my arms around her, and the world feels a little less sideways. The bells on Kuran's ankles tingle merrily. "What happened to your hand?" She gasps at my burns.

I may not be able to use my left hand again, but my blisters have healed. "I'll be fine," I say and squeeze her harder. "I'm just glad you're safe."

"Thankfully, the dungeons have thick walls." She laughs, looking none the worse for wear. Thank the Heavens.

Our reunion is short-lived. A dozen harried candidates line up in the great hall. We are specks of faded color against white marble, just the leavings of those who began the Sundo. I can no longer tell who was rich or who was poor. All of us look changed.

My own face is a mask I don't recognize. What little softness there once was feels as if it's been scoured away.

The candidates eye me with suspicion even when guileless Payan, the head Healer, makes new introductions with his soft voice. So many of them wanted me dead, but I do not hate them enough to will more suffering upon them. I summon the remaining Datus to my side.

"Let us destroy the spells on the gates. Give the candidates a choice to return to their families or to stay and help us rebuild. We cannot afford to surrender these young ones now." To my surprise, they agree. Perhaps we have all lost the taste for sacrifice.

But I must choose someone. Omu will need time to test the limits of her new body, but I have no doubt that she will return. The cultists remain a threat. I must choose well. I look around the room and realize the choice is obvious.

"I completed the tests in Kuran's name, and we have a contract sealed with her blood. Will that suffice?"

The Datus argue, but Reshar tips agreement in my direction. Nothing would prevent us from choosing my sister.

"Kuran?" I bound back to my sister, suddenly awkward again. I remember just how young I am when the brat scowls at me. She's only eighteen months older. "How would you feel about being Reyna of Tigang?"

She raises an eyebrow as she surveys the fortress around us, clearly unimpressed. The bright blue sky is visible through gaping fractures in the glass wall. Vines as thick as tree trunks creep up the walls, and I fear they are the only things holding the fortress together.

"Are you serious?" she asks.

I admit that I am partly being selfish this time and that I want my family close, but I think this might work. Meeting Nanay Oshar showed me that there is a way to survive this—that not all our rulers must suffer horribly. The past and present mix together in ways that make it hard to tell the past lives we've spent together from the present. Once she was Ketah, a fair and just leader, as well as my friend. She would do far better as ruler of Tigang than I ever could. I have had enough of power.

"Fine," Kuran says and bites her lip. I expected protest and am relieved that we are done with arguments. "Because you're stuck here, and traveling the continent without you wouldn't be the same."

Nothing will ever be the same again, but I dare dream that it might not be so bad. After all, you cannot build something new without first taking something else apart.

"You saved me." I bump my sister's shoulder. "In my first life, you were the one who cursed Astar and demanded better of her."

"Well, you know, I have always been the older and wiser one between us." Our straight faces dissolve into giggles that we cannot stop, even though everyone stares.

We are still laughing when a broad-shouldered figure dressed in brown pushes through the milling crowd toward us. Kuran's mirth fades when Tanu rushes into the room and drops to his knees.

"Datu Astar—wife," he says. His blue eyes are wide and distant as if he's caught in one of Reshar's spells. He sees me, but he doesn't see me. The familiarity between us clicks into place, and I marvel that I never noticed it before. We were not so much older in that first life than we are now, but time is a spiral, not a wheel. I am not the same.

Teloh once mentioned that Ressa's soul departed when

Chaos took over his body. Now I know he returned to the cycle of reincarnation like the rest of us. The magic unleashed during Omu's summoning must have woken something in him.

"Ressa, perhaps you meant something to me in another life, but in this one you betrayed my family twice."

Kuran averts her eyes and hides her surprise. This is not what she wanted, nor what I wanted.

His loyalty was Omu's in this life and before. I am afraid it is still Omu's, and I dare not trust him. "Live your life and be free, but do not return here," I say.

He bows and takes one last long look at Kuran before leaving. It disappoints me that he does not question what I asked of him or argue for a better way, but some things take lifetimes to change, and Tanu is one of them. I hope that he can find happiness elsewhere and that he learns to think for himself.

Kuran watches him go and forces a smile when she catches me looking. I had forgotten how few days passed since we came here. I had forgotten how long it takes to heal heartbreak. I give her shoulder a squeeze.

"So, when do all the beautiful foreign rulers start lining up to marry me?" she asks.

"You need a crown first." I sigh.

"Is it full of diamonds?"

"No. It's made of obsidian and steel."

"Why are we Tigangi so fond of symbolism?" She puts her hand to her forehead and feigns despair. "Can I change my mind now?"

I smile. "Would it help to know that you can ask the kitchen for cake whenever you please?"

"Then I'm yours forever." Kuran's mischievous expression is back.

I throw my arms around my sister. Life always offers a little pleasure along with its pains, and even in Bato-Ko it does not rain every day.

✳ ☽ ✳ ☾ ✳

CHAPTER FIFTY

I wipe my brow with a dusty sleeve. There is so much work to be done. Bato-Ko sprawls out raw around us, but we are stitching it back together a scoop of dirt at a time. Baylan shovel and trim broken branches. The city's residents are out in the sunshine as we clean up the city, picking up all its broken pieces. All of us will have calluses now.

Tomorrow, we will bury our mother, and then soon we must crown Kuran. The streets will echo with songs at her coronation. It is necessary more than it is wanted, and already I feel the weight of what must come next. Tigang must change. The Sundo must change.

My mother thought lies would keep me safe; instead, they made me easy prey. Astar thought the stories she told would keep her safe; instead, they became a cage. There can be no more secrets.

"Astar, you must rest," Bamal says. The head Maker's once pristine tunic is smudged at the edges, and her typically neat hair falls into her eyes. One lens on her spectacles is cracked, but she doesn't complain. My clothes are a patchwork disaster, and my trousers are frayed at the edges. I look how I feel. Maybe we all do.

Bamal holds out her hand for the spade that I've used to attack the stump of an upturned tree. I give it one last smack and surrender.

"Yes, Datu." I press the back of her hand to my forehead and ask for her blessing. This makes her red in the cheeks. Perhaps I should act like an Astar if I want people to believe who I am, but the idea of power makes me as uncomfortable as ever.

I pass Dayen tossing broken shingles into an ox-drawn cart. It surprised me that he wanted to stay, but when Virian announced the same, his reasons became obvious. They both take turns keeping an eye on me wherever I go, and despite my protests, they persist.

This time, Dayen doesn't follow when I hobble past, and I briefly dream of melting back into obscurity, but someone comes up behind me.

I turn to face my follower. Teloh's green tunic is drenched in sweat, and his wounds are bound in bandages. He's cut his curly hair shorter, and though his stitches have not yet healed, he doesn't seem to be in pain.

Guilt stabs at my heart. We have not spoken since Arisa's disappearance, even though we have often occupied the same space and breathed the same air. I have watched the anger balled in his fists as he's tested his mortality. It could not be an easy thing, and I'm surprised that he is here.

"Will you walk with me?" he asks.

This surprises me more than his appearance, and I fall into step with nervous silence. We go past the trees to the edge of Bato-Ko, where the rocky plateau begins, and climb over stones toward the cliffs that edge the ocean.

I hear the language of rocks and the trees now. It is as familiar as my own handwriting. The city mirrors my heart. All of Bato-Ko sings of arms outstretched and waiting, of palms held open but cold. Every stone, every leaning house, every nodding flower, asks a question: Is this enough?

Teloh sits on a lip of stone, and I sit down beside him. He

closes his eyes as if to rest, but this is an obvious fiction. There is tension in every part of him, like a branch tied back with a rope, and I read it in the line of his clamped jaw and the hunched set of his shoulders.

I absently reach for a scarf that I no longer wear and drop my hand when I touch the bare skin of my neck instead.

The weight of lifetimes forces my closed lips open, but "I'm sorry" is all I manage.

"I felt death when you cut out my immortality, but what is death but change?" Teloh's lips form that thin, sad smile I have grown accustomed to. "You put me in a cage, but you also showed me what it is to be human. Without you, I would not be here, and I think I like being here. Let there be no more apologies between us."

We sit in silence together. I dare not speak again, afraid to ruin things as I always do, but his gaze turns to me, and I cannot help but meet it.

He rubs a piece of fabric between his fingers as though he's never felt the texture before. His eyes are a warm, human shade of brown now, but though the stars are gone, when he looks at me again, hope shines as tentatively as a candle in a drafty room.

"I don't feel like this body is trying to contain an ocean in a teacup anymore. I'm still figuring out who I am now and who I want to be. I think that I would like to know what it is like to grow old—to see the world under all the different moons and all the different shades of day. I would like to know you, too, Narra Jal. Now, and not who you once were. I would like to build something new: a life that we choose. Would you?"

I think that he would still surprise me if we were reborn a thousand lifetimes together. Forever with him might not feel long enough. I lift my chin, and Bato-Ko shines behind his profile.

This rocky spit of land should not sustain life, yet Bato-Ko is an emerald cupped between a spine of mountains and the ocean.

Somehow, we humans persist. Kuran once told me that rebirth was an opportunity to start anew, but I never believed it possible.

"I have a new story. Do you want to hear it?" I ask. Teloh groans, but he doesn't move away. "In the time after, an awkward girl sat beside a beautiful boy. She told him her name and held out her hand."

He waits a few beats for me to continue. "That's it?"

"We need to write the ending still," I explain.

Teloh raises a skeptical eyebrow. "And how do we know it's done?"

"That's the thing about living; you just keep going. There are no real endings—only moments where it might be nice to pause. We can try all the good ones."

"That might take forever." He frowns. "Lifetimes."

I reach a trembling hand toward him, palm up. It is such a small thing, an almost helpless gesture. "Let us begin, then," I say. "My name is Narra."

He smiles and reaches out to take it.

ACKNOWLEDGMENTS

There was a long road to the publication of this book, and I would have never gotten here without all the support I've gotten along the way.

This book was written on the unceded traditional territories of the xʷməθkʷəy̓əm (Musqueam), S̱ḵwx̱wú7mesh (Squamish), and səlilwətaɬ (Tsleil-Waututh) Nations. This land shaped me into who I am, and I am lucky to live here.

To everyone at Entangled who helped make this the best possible book it could be. To Alexander Te Pohe, your faith in this story changed my life. To Molly Majumder, Stacy Abrams, and Hannah Lindsey for stepping in at the last minute and getting everything back on track so quickly. To Bree Archer, for the beautiful cover. To Riki Cleveland, Curtis Svehlak, Meredith Johnson, Katie Clapsadl, Heather Riccio, and everyone who worked behind the scenes, I'm so happy that my manuscript ended up with you.

To Léonicka Valcius, thank you for believing in my work, your expertise, and always being on the ball. We're just getting started! I look forward to going after all those big dreams together.

To Stephanie Charette, Aliza Greenblatt, Samantha Bagood, Alechia Dow, and Inez Gowsell, thank you for your feedback and wading through these pages when they were still very rough. I learned so much from you.

To Kristan Hoffman, Stephen Watkins, Arley Sorg, John Wiswell, Grace Fong, Kim Tough, Lisa Wong, Inez Gowsell, Tony Strangis, Doug Savage, Loerella and Eric Weitzel, the Viable Paradisers, the 2023Debuts, and the Filipino writing community online, thank you for your company, advice, and encouragement. Some of you read some truly terrible writing, and I salute you.

To Casey Blair, Nicole Lisa, Aliza Greenblatt, Stephanie Charette, Tam MacNeil, Annaka Kalton, Arun Jiwa, Camille Griep, Kevin Riggle, Dawn Bonanno, Debra Jess and Katrina Archer, who showed up with surprise flowers and support when I was going through a difficult time. I'm so lucky that writing brought you into my life. You have my sword forever.

To Jennifer Modglin and Patrick Heagany, for making me fall in love with writing. I wouldn't be a writer if it weren't for you.

To my parents for epic movie nights and leaving me in the library. You fueled a lifelong addiction to stories.

To my brother P.S. Barbosa for listening to all my publishing rants. You probably know more about the publishing industry than you care to.

And to my children. Everything I write is for you.

The Moonlight Blade is an atmospheric, edge-of-your-seat fantasy romance full of thrilling adventure and unforgettable moments. However, the story includes elements that might not be suitable for all readers. Violence, parental death, bullying, and murder are included in the novel. Readers who may be sensitive to these elements, please take note.

*Some shadows protect you...others will kill
you in this dazzling fantasy series from
award-winning author Abigail Owen.*

THE LIAR'S CROWN

Everything about my life is a lie. As a hidden twin princess, born second, I have only one purpose—to sacrifice my life for my sister if death comes for her. I've been living under the guise of a poor, obscure girl of no standing, slipping into the palace and into the role of the true princess when danger is present.

Now the queen is dead and the ageless King Eidolon has sent my sister a gift—an eerily familiar gift—and a proposal to wed. I don't trust him, so I do what I was born to do and secretly take her place on the eve of the coronation. Which is why, when a figure made of shadow kidnaps the new queen, he gets me by mistake.

As I try to escape, all the lies start to unravel. And not just my lies. The Shadowraith who took me has secrets of his own. He struggles to contain the shadows he wields—other faces, identities that threaten my very life.

Winter is at the walls. Darkness is looming. And the only way to save my sister and our dominion is to kill Eidolon...and the Shadowraith who has stolen my heart.

Let's be friends!

🐦 @EntangledTeen

📷 @EntangledTeen

📘 @EntangledTeen

♪ @EntangledTeen

📰 bit.ly/TeenNewsletter

entangled teen

an imprint of Entangled Publishing LLC